Review Comments

"Whitney LeBlanc's, **Bodacious Blues** is an excellent and entertaining coda to his explosive Creole family trilogy. An engrossing saga, vividly told by this loyal Louisiana native and highly respected theatre artist who intimately understands the many shades of truth that the Big Easy holds. Writer LeBlanc presents the reader with a bevy of colorful multiracial characters who will resonate long after you've finished this haunting and deeply personal read. As with his two preceding volumes—**Blues in the Wind** and **Shadows of the Blues**—**Bodacious Blues** and its lead character Les Martel, takes us on a soulful and heartfelt journey. It was hard to put down."

Robert Hooks -
Award winning actor; producer; founder Negro Ensemble Company, The Group Theatre Workshop & The DC Black Repertory Company.

"What an exciting novel. My mother, her father and his mother were born in Waterproof, Louisiana. Late in life I discovered this and went there. This novel reminded me of some of the stories I heard. There is such a rich cultural history in Louisiana I felt like a fly on the wall experiencing

Les's journey. This feels like as bestseller and a film. Kudos to Whitney for a wonderful novel."

Marla Gibbs -
Lead Actress of 227 series. Major supporting actress of The Jeffersons series. Appeared in over 100 films and television productions. Producer, writer and recipient of many awards.

"Talent will out! As exemplified by Whitney J. LeBlanc. Playwright, award winning theatre and television director, designer of beautiful stained glass windows, Whitney has just completed his third historical novel. Last of the trilogy, ***Bodacious Blues*** depicts the trials and tribulations of the townspeople of Estilette Louisiana in their association with its most prominent families, the Fergerson/Broussards. Blues, voodoo and the inborn racism of the area touches everyone's lives in this, Whitney's tense climatic finish to the Fergerson/Broussard family, and those that embrace and those who would destroy them…Great reading!!!!"

H.Wesley Kenney -
Seven time Emmy winning Television Producer – Director, "The Young and the Restless."

"I have known Whitney J. LeBlanc since 1963 and he is without doubt the most creative man I know. A brilliant scenic designer, playwright, director, stained glass artist and now novelist. Whitney never ceases to amaze. With ***BODACIOUS BLUES***, he draws us into the life of Les Martel, aspiring actor and a southern fish trying to swim in northern waters. It's a wonderful and very entertaining story that finds relevance for our present times. Well done my friend!"

Conrad John Schuck -
Television, movie and stage actor.

Acknowledgements

I wish to thank the following people.

My wife, Diane has been a positive force throughout the years of our life together. She has been supportive of every creative endeavor that I have attempted. She has especially encouraged, critiqued and prayed for my success as a writer, and so have my children. For this I am blessed.

My editors Nina Catanese and Beth Skony have guided me word for word through the structure, form, and proof-reading of the manuscript. It was a pleasure working with them.

My son, Michael Whitney LeBlanc, has done me the honor of putting together a movie trailer for the marketing of this book. I am grateful to God that I am so blessed to have been given such a talented extension of my being to pick up the torch and carry the legacy.

I am especially grateful for the time and passion, a gift from a homeboy, who in response to intercession from Dolly Adams, recalled memories of his past and brought forth the Foreword--Ambassador, Mayor and now friend, The Honorable Andrew Young. Thanks to you both with love.

I am thankful for friends, Thomas D. Pawley III, Winona Fletcher, Ted Shine, Aloha and Robert Collins, Robert

Hooks, Marla Gibbs, Wes Kenney, and Conrad John Schuck for giving love, inspiration, research and proof reading assistance during this writing adventure.

And special thanks to Linda Laing for a cover that tells the story in beautiful visual images.

- Whitney J. LeBlanc

*   *   *

This novel is a mixture of fiction and non-fiction. There are some events chronicled that are analogous to experiences that the author lived in Hollywood. In all of these instances the names of the persons involved have been changed.

Also By Whitney J. LeBlanc

<u>**Blues in the Wind**</u>
<u>**Shadows of the Blues**</u>

Contents

Foreword

I grew up in Louisiana. I was born in New Orleans but traveled the state with my father in a mobile dental clinic that drove throughout the state treating patients for free, courtesy of then Governor Huey Long. That's right, state-supplied services for Blacks, Creoles, coloreds and anyone else that needed dental care. So I ate the gumbo, sang the blues—when my parents weren't around, and absorbed the carefree manner of Big Easy living and the folklore and superstitions of my time. The problem is, we all do the same with our own heritage. We live it without thinking and trying to understand. It is what it is.

Then a great writer will dare to tell our stories and illustrate our culture with vivid plot and sensitive characters and suddenly we say, "Oh my god, he's writing about me. How did he know my family? This is my Uncle Johnny, my Aunt Emma and the old lady that used to bring herbs, and potions to my grandmother. This is like my family: educated, with money, position, and respect that nobody ever explained to me."

Whitney LeBlanc, like any great story teller, helps me to know myself, the intrigue surrounding my upbringing, the taboos and mystery in a world where—if I let them tell me, I'm defined more by my hair than my brain--how I was led to breathe in the cult of self-hatred that stifled the hopes and dreams of many of my friends in public school and the false sense of superiority that my Creole Catholic school friends seemed to exude.

But then there is the joy triumphant that laughs at idolatry of privilege and "moons" the provincial by celebrating the blues. "I may be down but down don't bother me." You get "your mojo working" and the sun shines in your heart even in the most hostile environments.

These are the *"Bodacious Blues,"* which LeBlanc celebrates in the life of Les Martel, his main character. A Southern brother taking on the northern University, challenges Hollywood, and comes home again, he serves us a literary gumbo with the delicate flavors of his complex diverse and challenging saga. It's hot, spicy, and rich with the cultural ingredients of the six national flavors which created life on the bayou.

It reads good and leaves a well flavored view of our life and times. It's both history and entertainment.

A job well done.

Read and enjoy.

Andrew Young
The Honorable Andrew Young,
President of Andrew Young Foundation,
A principal lieutenant to Dr. King during
the Civil Rights Movement.
(Former: Congressman, Mayor of
Atlanta, Georgia—United States
Ambassador to the United Nations)

Prologue

Bodacious Blues is the last novel of the Trilogy-Saga about the Fergerson/Broussard family.

Blues in the Wind and Shadows of the Blues are the novels that told previous stories leading to this final sequel.

Bodacious Blues is the story of Phillip Fergerson's grandson coming of age. He is a descendant of the Creole legacy left to him by his grandmother Martha Broussard and his grandfather, Phillip Fergerson. Les Martel is the son of Phillip and Martha's youngest daughter Lillian who is married to Lester Martel Senior. They have two children, Lester Martel Junior and Ann Marie Martel.

This final sequel of the trilogy primarily follows their rites of passage—Les' adventures as he struggles to fulfill his dreams and Ann's development as a physician.

This story picks up at the end of Shadows of the Blues in 1965 and ends in 1985.

* * *

In Blues in the Wind we discovered that Martha Broussard Fergerson was the desire of any man and the

iii

envy of every woman. She maintained the life that she was taught to believe a good Catholic should live. However, she was never able to overcome the loss of wealth stolen from her great great grandfather, by Judge Kenneth Estilette. She could not tolerate the devil's music and she alienated her blues-loving brother, drove her daughter Lala into a hasty marriage, caused daughter Velma to seek the affections of men for money, forced her husband from her bed, and burdened the life of daughter Rosa with the stigma of abortion.

Love between Martha and Phillip had faded and died over the years as he watched his beautiful Creole wife become an evil, vengeful, prejudiced image of her former self. As much as Phillip wanted a divorce, Martha kept him in the marriage, and no longer loved him because he joined the church of the "heathens." Eventually, Phillip became so resentful that he was forced to lurk in the shadows to be with the woman he loved while pretending to be the loving and dutiful husband of a mentally ill wife.

At the time of Martha's commitment to the asylum, her eldest daughter was living in Chicago. Although Velma's expressed feeling of not wanting "to see Mama like that," was an honest reflection of how she felt, she was also reluctant to return to Estilette because of the cloud of shame that had caused her to leave.

Because Lala had inherited her mama's Creole beauty, she was a victim of Martha's hatred for blues music and the *"niggers"* who loved it. Lala never got over the public humiliation of being slapped by her mother in a crowded blues tavern; and she could not forget or forgive the treatment she received from Martha's hand, and never traveled the seventy-five miles to visit her mama in the hospital.

Rosa, the faithful churchgoing image of Martha, made frequent trips to the hospital. Although Martha did not always recognize her, there was the ever-present fear that a word in a conversation would bring back the memory of what had happened with Tante in the back woods cabin. The abortion was their secret and Rosa wanted to keep it so. However, no amount of denial could completely eliminate the shadow of that dreadful truth from Rosa's mind.

Martha's son Bobby was destined to fulfill Phillip's dream of becoming a doctor and making lots of money. But he died from a mysterious illness at the beginning of his residency. Martha's resentment of Bobby's marriage to the dark-skinned Ruth, rather than the white heir to a family fortune, was the main reason she blamed Ruth for her son's death. It was also the temptation of the "accident," which Martha claimed was caused because her rheumatoid legs could not stop the car in time.

John Broussard was Martha's brother. The people who played the Blues called him *"Lightfoot."* Martha hated the nickname and she hated the people she called *"niggers"* who gave him the name. She had contempt for the music, she called *"gut-bucket,"* and she hated the voodoo practices of his wife, Naomi. Even though Martha was his sister, Lightfoot made every excuse not to visit her in the asylum, and the guilt he felt was because she had nursed him back to health when he was crippled by a fall from the church steeple. He was grateful for that, but did not feel it was enough to cause him to ignore the evil of her nature. He was convinced Martha had made the bed to which she found herself confined.

And so it was, with the people who mattered most in the life of Martha Broussard Fergerson, the daughter of Joseph Broussard, Grand daughter of Antoine Broussard Junior, and heir to the fortune of, great great grandfather, Antoine Broussard, Senior.

This story covers the period from 1934 to 1954.

* * *

Shadows of the Blues continues the saga of color, race and religion that plagued the Fergerson/ Broussard families in the first novel. That was the legacy left by the colossal fornications of their forefathers, and so it was destined that these families deal with these conflicts in perpetuity. The bigotry of a racially obsessed society continued to follow. The yoke of skin color continued to influence personal values. The conflicting, tentacular religious beliefs, some imposed by the masters, and some inherited from the motherland, continued to confuse and bewilder. Yes, the sins of their fathers had cast the inescapable shadows in which they must now live.

The story continues from 1954 with Martha's confinement to a mental institution, where in a state of confusion she confessed to her brother, Lightfoot, mistaking him for a priest, the many sins/criminal acts of her life. When this was revealed to Phillip it created a family dilemma. In the meantime Phillip continued his clandestine affair with Alicia Wallace, a professor at Southern University, and his guilt continued to mount because of this adulterous affair while his wife was in the crazy house.

Phillip's younger daughter, Rosa, met and established, at first a business arrangement, then a lover's liaison with a man of questionable character.

Phillip's middle daughter, Lala, the mother of Les and Ann, separated from her alcoholic husband and moved back to the family home. This created a golden opportunity for Phillip to get to know his grandchildren which he embraced with true enjoyment. Both Ann and Les were the apples of his eye, although Les felt that his grandfather liked him best.

Martha felt, because she has confessed her sins, that she had been forgiven and was told by an angel that now she must return home. In actuality this inclination could have very well been the work of the spirits that Naomi had conjured up as a punishment for Martha's sins. However, feeling that she had gotten a call from God, Martha stole away from the hospital and headed home, and in the process she was killed in a bizarre accident. Her funeral was held with all of the pomp and circumstances due a Creole woman of her standing in the community.

Into the picture comes Martha's heretofore unknown half sister, who looked so much like Martha that she was mistaken for a reincarnation. To some, especially Naomi, who regarded the sister's appearance as a curse---and to Phillip who regarded the sister's appearance as the answer to his unfulfilled dream, this created complications for all members of the family.

In a series of strange events, Lightfoot discovered that his wife was having an affair and came very close to killing her. Rosa eloped and married a man of low character who was wanted by the police, against the advice and knowledge of her father, Phillip, who about the same time discovered that his oldest daughter, Vel, was a prostitute. There was nothing Phillip could do about any of the events that he now regarded as the slow destruction of his family.

In the meantime Phillip continued to expose Les to the history of the blues and its place in the life of people of color. Shortly afterwards Les was an unwitting witness to a murder, and became involved in the trial and the conviction of a white sports hero of the community. Because of resentment and racial threats from the guilty person's friends and family, Les was forced to leave town for his safety. Phillip accompanied his grandson to Chicago and reluctantly left him in the care of his prostitute daughter, Velma. When he returned to Estilette he was confronted by the father of the convicted murderer demanding to know the whereabouts of,

"Your grandson who lied about my son." Phillip of course refused to divulge any information and was severely beaten. Weakened by the assault, which revealed other complications, Phillip died within the year.

This story covers the time period from 1954 to 1965..

Chapter 1
Abuse Revisited

In 1965 Les Martel and Caryn Ericksen compared re-search notes from their study of <u>The Rose Tattoo</u>. They wanted to be sure they were in agreement on the style, symbols, and meanings.

"It's about Sarafina's struggle between puritanical constraint and sexual passion," said Caryn.

Les Responded, "And more than anything else that is what fires up daughter Rosa's determination to be with Jack."

"That rose tattoo on the chest of the dead husband is the symbol of unity between flesh and spirit which haunts Sarafina so much she is determined to close the door on sexual desire."

"And this confuses Jack, because he loves Rosa and wants to be with her sexually but at the same time he doesn't want to violate his promise to Sarafina that Rosa remains a virgin." Added Les.

"So now are you ready to play Jack? Caryn asked.

"Yeah. I've been ready. But all of this analytical stuff is hard work. Is it really necessary?"

"This is what Professor Shaffer wants us to do. Don't forget we have to turn in a research paper."

Les took a deep breath and sighed, "Yeah I know, but it takes all of the fun out of acting. Why can't we just learn the lines and play the scene?"

"Do you do remember the line telling what *bacio* means?"

"Kiss, kiss, kiss. How can I forget that?" Les laughed. Then continued, "Now let's have some fun. You know your lines?"

"Lead on, McDuff."

Les arranged a sailor's cap in a snazzy angle on his head and was transformed into the young, adventurous Jack Hunter. He said in the voice of an eighteen-year-old, "It's dark in here."

Caryn fixed her eyes in a romantic stare, ran the tip of her tongue across her lips, wrapped the gypsy shawl tightly around her hips and knotted it in front right below her navel. She swirled her hips as she strolled in the manner of the wild thing that Sarafina called her. Then she responded with the devil-may-care attitude of a fifteen-year-old, "Yes mama's gone out."

Amazement enveloped Les' face as he observed Caryn's total transition into the character. He took a deep breath, relaxed the muscular tension that gripped his stomach, and whispered out in the voice of Jack, "How do you know she's out?"

"The door was locked and all the shutters are closed! Put down those roses."

"Where shall I. . ."

Rosa interrupted, "Somewhere, anywhere! Come here! I want to teach you a little Dago word. The word is bacio."

"What does this word mean?"

2

"This and this and this!" Rosa rained kisses upon Jack's face and ended on his lips. "Just think. A week ago Friday, I didn't know boys existed! Did you know girls existed before the dance?"

They rehearsed the scene over and over again.

This was his first semester in the acting program at Northwestern University, and it was much harder work than he had previously imagined. Before, he would just learn the lines of the character that he was supposed to play and regurgitate them on stage. Now he had to read and study acting styles and motivation. In addition he had to research and analyze the motivation of the playwright, discover the sense of truth of the actor, create an emotional memory and subtext for the character, and in addition become familiar with the works and teachings of the intellectual wise men of the theatre, Stanislavski, Robert Lewis, and Harold Clurman. And all for the purpose of making the audience believe that he was the character that he pretended to be when the lines were spoken. This required concentration, hard work, and many hours of preparation, and rehearsal, and it was not the fun that Les had imagined it would be.

Lester Martel Junior had not only been given his father's name, he had also inherited his father's good looks and the muscular Adonis look-alike body. And like his father he was a no-nonsense, kickass kind of guy. The boy was absolutely fearless and had a mind of his own which caused him to react to most situations in a bullheaded, devil-may-care manner. And this more than anything else worried his grandfather, who remembered how wild Les was growing up–imagining he was Tarzan, swinging from ropes tied to tree tops, and jumping from roof tops into wagons filled with straw, beating up classmates because they refused to apologize for indiscretions to young girls, capturing alligators from the muddy bayou waters and many other audacious adventures. So Phillip, his grandfather, was worried that the boy might be headed for trouble.

When he was only twelve years old, in answer to his grandfather's question, "What are you going to be when you grow up?"

Les answered, "An actor. I like having fun."

His grandfather's response was, "You can't make a living having fun."

Les said, "The people in the movies do."

And his grandfather answered, "Oh that's an illusion, plus the people in the movies are white. You don't see that many colored people in the movies."

Then Les announced, "No, but I'm gonna change that."

Tucked away in back of his mind was the notion that acting and having fun were synonymous; and no appeal from his grandfather, *to be a doctor like your uncle,* was likely to alter his way of thinking. Nor did admonitions like, *don't set out on a path of wickedness; give your life some substance.*

Nevertheless, Phillip continued to plant seeds of innuendo, suggestion, and counsel, hoping that someday, something would take hold and grow. But not one word from Phillip's mouth would change his determination to be an actor.

However, what Phillip knew that Les would have to learn, was that life was not one great party. It was not easy but rather it was a journey in the process of growth from an idealistic young juvenile to self-discovery of one's life as a responsible adult. It was fraught with difficulties—like a Pandora's box filled with snakes—like a pendulum swinging from light to darkness—like discouragement on the heels of great expectations—like the self-confidence of knowing who you are one day, only to discover that you are a stranger to yourself the next—like a rising sun of faith in human-kind, only to discover that darkness of the soul makes belief a bitter pill, but yet able to continue to be who it is you want to be.

Phillip knew that it was a tedious soul searching process and he had prayed and hoped that Les would have the integrity to survive this rite of passage to self-discovery; knowing full well that many did not have the endurance to survive.

The rehearsal for **The Rose Tattoo** had gone longer than anticipated. It was late, but nevertheless, Les and Caryn decided to continue their analysis of character relationships over sandwiches and coffee. However, it was difficult to focus on acting because of Caryn's popularity. It seemed that everyone in the place, male and female alike wanted to engage the lovely, bright eyed, energetic, blond in a conversation. Needless to say they did not get much accomplished and it was well past eleven o'clock when they left the Campus Coffee Shoppe. By the time Les boarded a bus in Evanston, and arrived at the Ashland Avenue address in Chicago, it was an hour later.

He was tired.

The distance between where he lived and the University was only fifteen miles, but this distance created a major problem because most of his time was spent transferring from bus to bus in clogged traffic. He was living with his aunt Vel because Grandpop, Phillip Fergerson wanted him safe from the threats of death from the racists in Estilette.

Les had been the primary eyewitness in a murder trial, and he fearlessly pointed the finger at the accused, who was convicted on his testimony. As a result, the friends and family of the man sentenced to prison vowed revenge, and made threats against his life. In order to insure his safety, Les was secretly moved to Chicago, for which he was grateful, especially after he discovered his safe haven was in the shadow of Northwestern University where he could study acting. That was in February, but now, nine months later the threat of death did not seem as urgent, so thoughts of living away from the safety of family, and closer to the campus occupied most of his traveling time.

As Les walked up the steps and opened the door at 5022 Ashland Avenue, he only wanted sleep. He entered the faded elegance of what was once a fashionable showplace home located on the west side of South State Street, only four blocks from Lake Michigan. This was once where the rich and famous white people lived, but now it was populated by up and coming Negroes. His aunt Vel had purchased this five bedroom mansion a few years after she started teaching in Chicago, and no one in the family could understand why she needed such a large place.

None of this mattered to Les as he breathed in the familiar aroma of cigarette smoke and stale beer on his way to his room at the end of the hall. As he dragged past Vel's room, he heard loud voices. He recognized his aunt's voice. The other voice belonged to a man, and he stopped and listened long enough to figure that something was wrong.

The man's voice yelled, "And I'm tired of your shit."

"What does that mean?" Demanded Vel.

The man said, "When you moved your fucking action to 55th Avenue you said things would be different."

"And I ain't seen yo ass but once in all that time."

"I told you I was out of town on business."

Vel yelled back, "That's a lie. Red at Big John's said you're a regular at Alberta's."

Les could tell by the intensity of the man's voice that he was angry; and he could hear that same hostility echoed in his aunt's voice.

The man charged, "You're just jealous. That why you're asking money."

Vel responded, "Jealous my ass. I'm not giving it away anymore."

"You said you had special feelings for me, so I could keep coming over here."

Vel yelled, "That didn't mean that you'd stop paying."

"Then what did it mean?"

Vel's voice grew softer and more sensual, like flirting, "It was just a convenience so you wouldn't have to go over to Alberta's or anywhere else to get laid. You could get it here for the same old price." And then she added with a sarcastic laugh, "And I thought I was doing you a favor."

"You lying, conniving bitch!"

The sound of a slap against flesh, and a scream from Vel came to his ears. Les broke through the door with such force it hit the adjoining wall. Vel was lying on the floor naked. Blood oozed from her mouth. She pulled the bed sheet across her body and cried out, "Les!"

The man turned in the direction of the doorway with such ferocity his flaccid penis flapped against his thigh spraying piss in its wake. "Who the fuck are you?"

Vel yelled. "Les, stay out of this!"

Without a moment's hesitation, Les grabbed the man and flung him against the open door, and before the man could recover, Les swung a fist against the man's jaw, and knocked him to the floor. He grabbed the man's clothes and flung them into his face, yelling, "Get the hell out." The startled man gathered his clothes against his flabby, nude, body and slid on his butt out of the room into the hallway. He then struggled to his feet, and staggered out of the front door.

Vel pulled the sheet tightly around her body, sat on the edge of the bed and cried. Les sat next to her, put his arm around her shoulder, and asked, "Are you all right?"

Vel nodded and said, "I'm sorry you had to see this."

"What's going on here, Aunt Vel?"

The moment the words came out of his mouth he realized

that he knew the answer to his own question. But for whatever reason, he could not even explain to himself, he didn't want his aunt to know he had heard enough in the hallway to figure out she was a prostitute. He also concluded that Grandpop had no knowledge of this when he left. He knew his grandfather well enough to know he would have never left him there if he had known his eldest daughter, Velma Fergerson, was entertaining men for money.

Vel cupped her hand over her mouth, wiped her eyes with the edge of the sheet and said, "Just a lover's quarrel."

"You're still bleeding." Les took a corner of the sheet and wiped away the flow of blood from her mouth.

Vel whispered, "I'm all right."

"Are you sure?"

"Yeah."

Les looked back toward the door and asked, "Think he'll come back?"

"Not likely. He probably thinks you're my new boyfriend." Vel looked at Les with a dawning awareness of his manhood. She continued, "You're something else, you know that. Your Mama told me about how you manhandled your daddy when he slapped her around."

This was not something Les was proud of. That incident was a spontaneous reaction to the bad behavior of his father, because he had always remembered his grandfather saying, "A man should never hit a woman." And when he saw his father strike his mother he rose to the occasion, and struck back to protect his mom. He regretted having to raise a hand against his father, because things between them were never the same. That was the first and last time he had struck his father. And now again he found it necessary to rescue a woman from abuse, but he was surprised to hear that his mama had told his aunt about what had happened.

Les was silent. He stood, looked down at Vel and said,

8

"I'm going to my room, I'm tired. Good night."

"Good night."

As Les closed the door, Vel's voice stopped him. "Les, don't say anything to your mama about what happened tonight."

He shrugged his shoulders and continued to his room.

* * *

The very next week, after Les had kicked that man out of his aunt's room, his mama called to say that his grandfather had died.

Les was heartbroken.

He couldn't understand why.

When Phillip left Chicago, nine months before, he was as frisky as ever. Yes, he was a little slower than Les remembered when they fished on the bayou, and although Phillip looked a little worn and weary, no doubt from that trial and the death threats, he seemed fine.

Vel and Les boarded the train to Estilette. For most of the way they were silent but every now and then Vel would say something about what she remembered. "Papa gave me my first job as a teacher."

Les asked, "How long did you teach with him?"

"Ohhh, I guess for eight or nine years. Papa's school was the only one I taught in until I left to go to Chicago."

Les always wanted to know the answer to his next question. "Why did you leave and go to Chicago?"

Vel took a deep breath and looked out of the window as the trees flashed by. Many memories crowded her mind, and finally in a soft whisper she said, "Papa never liked the way I dressed, and we always fussed over the way I taught my students, but in spite of all that, I loved him very much."

9

She had tears in her eyes when she talked about how much Phillip liked the pocket watch she gave him. Les had never heard that amount of expressed feelings for anyone, come out of Aunt Vel's mouth. He had always thought of her as a cold unfeeling person, and he remembered the irritated look in her eyes when his sister, Ann Marie, told how Aunt Vel called Aunt Naomi a "Nigger woman." He was only eleven years old then, but that was what he remembered most about his Aunt Vel.

As she dabbed away the tears from her perfectly applied makeup, Les began to realize what a complicated person she was. She was not as pretty as her sisters, but without a doubt the one with the most "piss and vinegar," as his Uncle Johnny was heard to say. And after discovering that she was a lady of the evening, Les agreed with Uncle Johnny's description. Les was not sure how he now felt knowing she was a hooker. She was, after all, his mom's sister. And although he didn't love her any-the-less, he was sure that his mama would disapprove if she knew that Aunt Vel, the school teacher, was also selling pussy. So he had a problem with how much admiration he should really feel.

When they arrived in Estilette, they were met at the train station by Uncle Johnny. He was much quieter than usual and hugged both longer than Les ever remembered him hugging anybody.

When they got to the house the whole family was there. Lala had food on the table and Vel immediately sat down to eat. But before Les took a bite he went to the parlor to see his Grandpop. He was laid out in the same place that his grandma, Martha, was when she died five years earlier. The room was filled with flowers as before, and the overwhelming aroma of a florist's shop had once again permeated the walls. A few people whom Les recognized, but whose names he did not remember, were seated near the coffin. Ann Marie was kneeling next to the coffin and when she saw Les, she ran into his arms crying and sniffling for breaths of air. Les joined his sister's tears with his own and they clung to each other as though their combined grief would bring their grandfather back to life.

Later, after Les and Ann had finished eating, Lala linked their arms and led them to the den. Lala sat in Phillip's chair behind his desk, and they sat opposite on the leather sofa. Lala explained the details of the funeral arrangements, but mostly she wanted to get their agreement to stay in Frilotville because more sleeping space was needed in the main house.

Lala said, "At times like this we have to put our feelings behind and do what we have to for the good of the family." She went on to say, "There'll be a lot of people needing to stay here, your Aunt Elvina from New Orleans, Alicia from Scotlandville and other relatives, some of whom I don't even know, from Texas and the Tache will need a place to stay. We can use both of your rooms, so you and Ann can stay with your Papa until it's over."

Lala had tears in her eyes as she talked, but Les felt there was something that he had to know. His mama and his daddy were not on speaking terms since the divorce, and he wanted to be sure there would be no more fussing or fighting. He asked, "Does Papa know?"

Lala said, "I talked to him yesterday. It's all right with him for you to stay there."

Then Les made up a reason for asking because he didn't want his mama to suspect his real motive. "I haven't been back home since sugar cane harvest three years ago, and I don't want to have another fight with Papa."

"Everything's O.K. There'll be no problems."

Les looked over at Ann for agreement. She stood and said, "Fine. I'll get my things, and we'll drive over."

* * *

The first minutes with his papa were filled with questions--"How is it in Chicago? Have you gotten used to the weather yet? How do you like living with Aunt Vel? How are your studies in education?"

Since Les knew his father did not like the idea of him studying drama, he had told his father that he was studying to be a teacher, which he knew his father would have no problem paying for, but he did feel a bit uneasy about his little white lie.

They hadn't talked this much in three years since Les hit his father in the head with the rolling pin for slapping his mama around. After that, Les had only seen him once when he came back to help out during the sugar cane harvest. Les felt it was his duty to help like he had always done. After all, Lester senior was still his daddy even though he and his mama had separated.

After some small talk, Lester began apologizing to his son. "I'm sorry about everything—hitting your Mama—the fight we had—sorry that you had to leave Estilette like you did. Those goddamn racists need to have their asses kicked. I hear that man is still in jail for attacking your grandfather. . ."

Les stopped him in midsentence, "What do you mean? Who attacked Grandpop?

"Oh, don't you know?"

There was a surprised, embarrassed look in Lester's eyes, and he didn't say anymore. After several moments of silence, Les demanded, "Papa, what happened? Who attacked Grandpop?"

Lester took a deep breath, ran his fingers through his hair, then crossed his muscular arms over his chest. He shook his head and said, "I'm sorry, I thought your mama or Ann would have told you by now."

"Nobody told me anything."

Lester went to the cabinet and poured a glass of bourbon. He was still drinking. This was the reason he and Lala had fussed all the time. Les looked inquiringly at his father. He was a big man; six feet ten inches tall, two hundred sixty pounds with broad shoulders and a strong back. Les thought, *I must have been out of my mind to even think I could fight him, but I did. At the time my only thought was to protect Mama.* Lester sat at the table and pushed the bottle in his son's direction. "You're over eighteen now."

Les shook his head, *no,* and asked, "What happened?"

Lester took a sip and said, "When Phillip returned home from taking you to Chicago, Walter Rubin broke into the house looking for you, and when Phillip refused to tell him where you were, he beat the shit out of him."

Les could feel tears forming in his eyes. Just the thought, but even more, hearing that his grandfather was assaulted for not disclosing his whereabouts, made Les sick to his stomach.

His Papa went on. "Phillip was in the hospital for a week. Maybe that's what caused his death. Walter Rubin beat him up good. Kicked him in the chest and all over his private parts. But Phillip wouldn't say a word about you being in Chicago. Then BookTau just happened by and ran Rubin out of the house, but not before getting shot a couple of times. You know BookTau, he's tough, and he won't be stopped by no gun. Cat Bobineaux arrested Rubin for breaking and entering and attempted murder. I think he's still in jail, although he should be getting out about now."

Les was devastated.

He had to get away. Be alone.

He went to the bayou where he and his grandpop had spent a lot of time. He thought back over every moment that he and Phillip had spent fishing in the shade of the pecan trees. He thought back over everything they talked about--all of everything that Phillip had taught him about the blues, ladies, the rights and the wrongs of life, the hatreds and prejudices that were out there waiting. All of everything came rushing back as if everything was being retold in memory—even the disappointment on Phillip's face when Les told him he was not going to be a doctor but rather he was going to be an actor. He still regretted the pain that he had brought to his grandfather when he told him about his dream. Phillip had been everything to Les--his friend, teacher, advisor, and even surrogate father when Lala and Lester split up. He relived in memory every moment that they had spent together.

He didn't realize how long he had been away until he heard footsteps in the brush.

Lightfoot appeared. "Boy, I thought I'd find you here. Your Mama's having a fit 'cause she don't know where you at."

"I just had to be by myself for a while."

"I know how it is when you lose somebody close. But she's upset because you're not at your Papa's house."

"I just wanted to be alone."

Lightfoot sat down and rested his back against the pecan tree. He said, "I know. But Lala knows those Rubin people still pissed off at you for testifying."

After a few moments of thought, Les asked, "Did that beating from ole man Rubin cause Grandpop's death?"

"Who told you?"

"Papa."

"You not supposed to know that. I guess your Mama forgot to say anything to your Papa. She musta figured y'all wouldn't be talking anyway."

"Did Grandpop die because of that beating?"

"I don't rightly know. But it did seem that Phillip wasn't the same after that."

"Who would know?"

"Boy, leave it alone. Walter Rubin got his comeuppance. He's in jail. Leave it be."

All of that may have been well and good, but Les had to know. It bothered him to think about what his grandpop had gone through. Just the thought of Walter Rubin laying a hand on his grandfather made him want to kick that man's ass.

Chapter 2
Reality of Death

I t was September, 1965 and Estilette had never witnessed a funeral the likes of this.

BookTau, wearing bib overalls and the new red plaid shirt he had bought for the trial, drove the mules, which pulled the wagon, which carried the body of Phillip Fergerson. He had convinced the family that he had to do this because, *'Fessor was ma very best friend on the face of the earth, and this is, the onliest thing I kin do for him for all he's done for me.'* After much thought, and back and forth considerations, Rosa, Vel and Lala agreed, realizing that if not this, there was nothing else more fitting that BookTau could do to pay his final respects.

The family, the mayor, sheriff, city council, board of education, teachers, students, friends and acquaintances followed the wagon in solemn silence from the Fergerson house to Holy Ghost Church. By the time the entourage reached the church, it was filled, except for reserved seating for the family. This was a great irony because those who chose to follow the wagon had to stand or sit in chairs arranged out-side. The naysayers who shook their heads in disapproval at the, *"Disgraceful way the family is bringing the body of the professor to the church,"* had the most comfortable seats in-side. But the weather had cooperated, and it was a pleasantly warm day in September, so being outside was not as bad as it seemed. Speakers had been placed around and although the people could not see who was speaking they were able to hear.

Every one, who was anyone, had something to say. The mayor, the sheriff, family friends and many teachers from both Southern University and the parish schools, all wanted to express how much of a difference Phillip had made in their lives. The most eloquent obituary was delivered by Felton Clark, the president of Southern University, who recalled the days when Phillip was a student and the chauffeur who had driven his father, Dr. Samuel Clark, all over the nation. All in all, it was a very long ceremony, and a fitting tribute to a man who had given so much to so many. The only significant person in Phillip's life who didn't speak was Felix Mack. He was now ninety-six years old and in a wheelchair, but he in-sisted on coming from Opelousas, thirty miles away. *"I have to be there to say goodbye to my friend."* Mack was the man who, in 1936, had inspired Phillip to establish the program of in-service-teacher-training, which was now practiced all over the state.

Members of the family responded in various and curious ways.

Lala, the youngest and the prettiest, who was always thought to be Phillip's favorite, was stoic and dignified. She sat erect and sublime with her son Les on one side, and her daughter Ann Marie on the other. She was at peace with the knowledge that she and her father had had a beautiful and meaningful relationship. She was a teacher and the only one of his daughters whom Phillip let drive his car. She reminded her father of the beauty that he had once seen in her mother's face, and it was a well known fact that, "Phillip loved beautiful Creole women." Tears streamed down Lala's face during the singing of "Amazing Grace."

At that very moment Vel cried out, "Oh Papa you're gone. . .I was blind to all the love you had for me. . .and all I gave you was a hard time. . ." The ladies of the Sodality came across the aisle to quiet her down, but it was not easy for them to contain her passion. She ran toward the coffin screaming, "I'm sorry, I'm sorry. I loved you more than you ever knew." Two of the ladies turned her around and walked her back to her seat, and with wads of Kleenex, dried her tears and literally stuffed her mouth.

Les leaned out and looked toward the end of the pew at all of the commotion and thought, *What an actress. Her guilt can't be affecting her that much. I'm glad Grandpop never knew she was a whore.*

Rosa just swooned and fainted. Friends and relatives made space and stretched her out on the pew. "Give her some air," came from one of the Ladies of the Sodality who was furiously fanning and pushing people aside. After a few moments, Rosa opened her eyes and sat up to witness the remaining ritual. By this time a reading of the 23rd Psalm was in progress. None of the emotional responses from the family had deterred the flow of Phillip's goodbye service.

Naomi silently took it all in. She reached across and squeezed Lightfoot's hand. She thought, *"What a strange family I've gotten myself hooked up with."* She had always admired Phillip because, unlike his wife Martha, he had given her unconditional acceptance. She felt the others were skin-color hypocrites. She promised herself to make a special plea to the voodoo gods so they would guide his spirit safely through the afterlife.

Alicia and Elvina sat together and comforted each other. Both were in love with Phillip. Although, he had made a choice six months before he died, neither was convinced that the decision had come from his heart, nevertheless spoken from his lips. It was well known that Phillip loved Creole women. Elvina was. Alicia was not, but the one he had chosen to spend his final days with. Both of their lives had been left with holes to be filled, and so they sat through the rites wondering how each would carry-on without him.

As the recession left the church, on the way to the graveyard, Lightfoot noticed a truck parked on a side street. When they got inside the limousine, he tapped Naomi's hand and pointed. In a whisper he asked, "Ain't that Walter Rubin?"

She looked and replied, "The very man."

"I thought he was still in jail."

"Musta had an early release."

"That bastard is stalking the boy."

* * *

Phillip Fergerson was laid to rest next to Martha.

Les went back to Chicago with Vel.

In Estilette, things returned to normal. That is, for everyone except Naomi.

Lightfoot asked, "Where are you going in that outfit?"

"To get a job."

"To get a job? You got a job."

"I'm gonna see if I kin do some housework for the Rubins."

Lightfoot shook his head. "I thought you was up to something dressed up in yo maid's outfit."

"That Rubin bastard is up to something, and I'm gonna find out what."

"Now why you wanna do something like that?"

"I had a vision." With that Naomi was out of the door.

If Lightfoot had been watching what Naomi had been doing, he would have known what she was talking about. She had danced an incantation around some of Phillip's personal possessions—his gold watch, the blood stained shirt he was wearing during the Rubin beating, his hog-butchering boots, his favorite book, *The History of The Negro People,* by Carter G. Woodson, and his fishing pole, and she prayed that his spirit would have a safe and joyful journey through the afterlife, but her ritual was repeatedly interrupted by clashes of thunder and lightening. This was a bad sign. She tried very hard to discover the source of the interference. She danced harder. She chanted longer. She tranced herself deeper. Finally, the foggy mist began to lift slowly and she was able to perceive a face. The face was that of Walter Rubin. It was now clear--this interference had to be done away with so that Phillip's journey would be safe.

* * *

It wasn't difficult. Even thought they were not of the upper social class and were not from old money, the Rubins had always wanted to have a maid. So when the opportunity presented itself, they recognized the deal, and jumped at the chance. Sally Rubin, a pleasant looking, over sized woman, worked full time as a receptionist for the Estilette Seed and Feed. Since Karl, her son, was serving time in prison, she saw the opportunity to make extra money by renting his room. Cooking, cleaning and taking care of the added chores of a rental in the house, were now more than she could handle. She needed help.

Naomi presented herself as a recent arrival to Estilette, who was in need of day work, which she would be happy to do for the lowest weekly rate. The Rubins jumped at the deal. Now Naomi was inside where she could listen to conversations, overhear phone calls and gauge the comings and goings of Walter Rubin. This was easy because of the prevailing low esteem and attitude that was held about "Nigras" by the Rubins, and Naomi played to the hilt, every stereotypical concept that this family held. She was lazy, slow, dumb-witted and ignorant. And this masquerade enabled her to discover that Walter Rubin was out to. . . . "*get back at that Martel boy for putting my son in prison. He was here for the funeral of his grandfather, who finally died from that beating I gave him.*" When Naomi overheard this phone conversation with an unidentified friend, she knew, without a doubt why she was getting interference in her rites. The voodoo gods had revealed his villainy. She had to do something.

She said to Lightfoot, "It's time to bring that bastard to justice."

"What are you planning to do?"

"Just wait and see."

Chapter 3
Judging a Book by its Color

A week after the funeral, when Les got back to school, Caryn told him their scene had been rescheduled for the following Saturday workshop. He was looking forward to this first chance to show off his acting ability to university peers, whom he was told, were the toughest audience one could have. Les and Caryn picked up their rehearsals and polished their scene to perfection. They were ready.

The auditorium was packed. The critique of the scene immediately before was lively and tough but it was also fair and honest. This was the type of critique that Les looked forward to and needed.

A slight shiver ran through his body when he heard, "*The Rose Tattoo*" called out. Yes, he was nervous, with a slight case of stage fright, but he knew that this was good because the increase flow of adrenalin would take his performance up a notch. After a few minutes into the scene, Les began to relax and could feel his character come alive, and he could also feel that quiet listening expectation from the audience.

Then just a moment before the kissing scene, the word "Cut" came from the back of the auditorium. Les turned into stone. He couldn't move. He didn't know what to do. He looked at Caryn. She dropped her head. Les turned in the direction of the voice and said, "Doctor Shaffer we have not finished the scene." His response was, "Cut. Next scene." There was nothing left for Les to say or do but leave the stage.

Caryn found Les in the parking lot. He was crushed. He was num. He was lost. He couldn't figure out why what had happened, had happened. Caryn put her arms around his waist and cried. She reached up and ran her thumb along each side of his nose and wiped away the tears.

She said, "I'm sorry. I didn't believe he would do it."

Les responded, "What are you talking about?"

Caryn then told the incredible story of what had happened while he was away. After Dr. Shaffer heard about the death that had taken Les away from school, he called her to his office. He had checked the school records and asked Caryn if she knew that Les was colored. She told him, "*Yes, and that does not make a difference to me.*" Dr. Shaffer then told her that it was not acceptable for her to do a love scene with a colored man and recommended that she either get another acting partner, or select another scene that did not require kissing. Caryn did not do either.

She went on, "I didn't think he would go so far as to stop the scene."

Les asked, "Why didn't you tell me this before?"

She said, "It would have only gotten you upset. And I really didn't think that he would do anything, especially since you don't look colored. But I did not realize what a prejudiced bastard he is."

Les and Caryn comforted each other for the rest of the day. Then he went to karate class later and took out his frustration and aggression. He visualized Dr. Shaffer's face in the boards that he was learning to break. His instructor looked at his bloodied knuckles and said, "Your inner direction is wrong. For some reason you are angry and have lost perspective about the use of karate. Think about that."

The instructor was right. Les was directing his energy force to hurt Dr. Shaffer for what he had done. Les recognized that he had made a mistake, especially since his instructor was able to easily detect his misplaced rage.

Basically this was a wake-up call; his grandfather had warned him about people who would deny education because of who he was. Now that it was happening he had to deal with it differently.

For the moment, Les wanted to get away from it all--Dr. Shaffer--the embarrassment--prejudice, all of the things that focused on, what his Grandpop had called, "the sins of our ancestors."

When he got home that evening he was restless and could not sleep. His thoughts kept returning to what had happened earlier that day. It was hard for Les to believe that in Chicago at Northwestern University, in 1965, when the entire nation was making an effort to overcome the evils of segregation, there was still a racist on the faculty. It was the same hate and prejudice that had driven him out of Estilette. There was no escape, no running away place. He wished he was back with people he knew--people he could trust and feel safe with, people who believed that everyone should be able to get along. He thought of his Grandpop. He thought of his Uncle Johnny. He thought of the blues.

He found himself on a bus headed to *Big John's Blues Club.* His Uncle Johnny had told him to look up a bluesman from Louisiana named Buddy Guy who was now in Chicago. Whether he was at this club or not, did not matter. Les needed to hear the blues and get closer to home.

As chance would have it, Buddy Guy was there. It was

24

his last night before leaving on a tour to England. Les settled in, had a beer and listened. Buddy played slow blues, the kind that makes you feel like your troubles are everybody's troubles--the kind that brings everything and everyone closer. He just sat there and let the rhythms carry him to another place—one of peace and contentment, joy and the happiness of being alive. He stayed until the last set and then Les did something that he had not planned to do. He went up to the stage, introduced himself and told Buddy Guy he was from Estilette and asked if he knew, his uncle, John Broussard.

Buddy said, "I sure do know Lightfoot. How's ma niggar doing?"

They talked about Lightfoot, the blues, and Phillip's death, which Les was surprised to hear that Buddy had heard about through the small world network of people-talking-back-home. Buddy was curious about why Les was in Chicago--all the while continuing to pack up his music equipment, and when the crating was completed, Les felt better. It felt good to be back in touch with memories of home. However, that feeling lasted for only a brief moment because the ghost was still there—that word, "niggar," *the word that Grandpop did not like to hear*. Les understood that Buddy had used it as a friendly connection, but the sting was still there. Now, in the last few hours, he had come full circle from the racial put-down that the word held for Dr. Shaffer, to the love that it held for Buddy Guy. Les was still pissed off, but there was not too much he could do about it, but then and there, he promised himself that he was never going to take any more shit from prejudiced people.

* * *

Les began to think seriously about whether he should be an actor. As long as he could remember he had planned and dreamed about being on stage or in the movies. He couldn't forget the day he told this to his grandfather by reciting a poem he had learned. Les could tell he was not too happy about hearing that. Phillip was hoping that he would be a doctor. And although Les loved him, he did not want his grandfather to decide what he should or should not do with his life. However, Les didn't know that being an actor would be like this. If he couldn't play the role of a guy in love with a girl on stage because he was colored, then what hope did he have to play this guy on a movie screen? Although he didn't look colored, the fact that he was seemed to be a problem to some people. As much as Les hated what he had done, Dr. Shaffer had opened his eyes, and it had given him a taste of what to expect from the world beyond collegeland.

The only Negro actors that Les knew were Sidney Poitier, Harry Belafonte, and James Edwards. There were a few less known actors he had seen in movies, like *Gone with the Wind, Island in the Sun, Carmen Jones and Intruder in the Dust.* Although Les would have liked to play roles like Sidney had in *The Defiant Ones,* he really wanted to play romantic leads but Dr. Shaffer had pointed the finger and said, "No. that's not allowed." And even though Shaffer was not able to tell Les was a Negro by looking at him, his prejudice went deeper than skin color.

Les wanted to talk with someone. Someone with whom to share his feeling—to find out how others felt about Negroes and White people playing love scenes on the screen.

He knocked on the door of Caryn Ericksen's apartment. She was very surprised to see him. Although they had rehearsed *The Rose Tattoo* for four weeks, they had never talked about anything other than the scene. Standing in the doorway with lamp light behind creating a halo of her blond hair, Les felt that he was seeing her for the first time. Indeed he was. Before this moment she was only an acting partner, but now she seemed like someone he wanted to know better.

She said, "Why Les, how good to see you. What brings you here?"

Les felt like an intruder, but she was so warm and inviting, he said, "If you're not too busy I'd like to talk."

There was a puzzled look on her face and she said, "Talk? About what?"

Les wanted to turn and run, but he had spent a lot of time trying to find where she lived so he thought to himself, *since I'm here I may as well make the most of it.* He said, "About my career . . . about being an actor. Have you got a few minutes?"

She smiled, stepped back and opened the door wider, and said. "Of course. Come in. I was just having a snack before digging in to study. Would you like a bite to eat and something to drink?"

"If it's not too much trouble."

"Ohhh, you silly. Have a seat."

He sat on a pillow on the floor next to a plate of snacks and a bottle of beer that was on a low table covered with books, newspapers, a vase of fading flowers, and an opened book turned over to mark the page. The title of the book was **The Prophet.** He picked it up.

She was watching and said, "Oh, you know Gibran."

"Who?"

"The author of that book, Kahlil Gibran."

"No."

Les didn't know a thing about the book and had never before heard the name of the author. He felt stupid and ignorant because she made it sound like this was someone that he should know.

He watched as she moved gracefully around her small kitchen cutting slices of cheese and placing crackers on a plate. She was attractive. Now he realized why she was so popular. She had dancing eyes that seemed to seek answers to questions she wanted to ask before they were asked. This was one of the features of her face that he liked when they first began rehearsing together. Her eyes made acting with her easy because they spoke the subtext. The actor's subtext was the first thing that Professor Shaffer had taught them to look for in developing characters. *Find out what the character is thinking but not saying and you will discover the essence of their motivation.* And that made Caryn easy to act with. Her eyes told how she felt even before she said a word. As Les watched her now, he could tell she was happy that he had dropped by.

He blurted out, "Where is your home?"

"Minnesota. I'm Danish, can't you tell that from my name?"

"No. My name is Martel, but you can't tell that I'm Creole from Louisiana.

"Ahhhh, that's what I like about our country, we're a melting pot."

"Like gumbo. That's what my grandfather used to say. We're all mixed up."

She laughed. It was a silly inhalation noise that ended with an exhale, which sounded like a chuckle. She brought the plate and a bottle of beer to the table with a smile and plopped down on the pillow opposite her book. She said, "I knew you were mixed up even before I knew you were Creole."

They both laughed. But Les was not really amused because he didn't know exactly what she meant by that statement. She raised her bottle and said, "To friendship."

Les took a swig from his bottle and repeated, "To friendship." He wanted to know more about this fascinating girl and asked, "Were you born in Denmark?"

She said, "No. My parents are from Copenhagen. I was born in Bemidji."

"Bemidji? Where is that?"

"Northern Minnesota. The birth place of Paul Bunyan."

"Who is Paul Bunyan?"

She said with a twinkle in her eye, "Boy, you don't know anyone—Gibran or Paul Bunyan. I've got to teach you a lot." She went on. "Bemidji is on the Mississippi River not too far from where it begins in Lake Itasca. My parents settled there after they finished med school and then—voila, me."

"Your dad's a doctor."

"Both of my parents are doctors."

"Wow! We've got a lot in common. You were born on one end of the Mississippi and I was born on the other. My uncle was a doctor and my grandfather wanted me to be one also, but I wanted to be an actor, like you."

"There is a lot for us to talk about."

And Les wanted to do just that. Getting to know more about Caryn was exciting and he was glad that he had come. But he realized he had a more urgent mission in mind. He took another swallow of beer and bit into a piece of cheese. He looked into her silvery blue eyes and thought, *God she is beautiful. I hadn't noticed before.* However he put that aside and got on with the purpose of his being there.

"Yesterday after Dr. Shaffer stopped our scene, I've been doing a lot of thinking about whether I should stay in the acting program."

Caryn was quick to respond. "Oh, don't let what he did cause you to change your mind, he's just a prejudiced bastard."

"I know, and that's why I've been thinking about this." Les paused a moment and then continued. "As long as I can remember I've wanted to be an actor. When I was in the seventh grade I played the part of a Kentucky Colonel in a play called *An Old Kentucky Garden*. It wasn't a profound or even an important role, but it started me to thinking, how wonderful it is to create the life of an imaginary person and bring it to life on stage. Then I got to play Jason, and Hamlet and Macbeth and a character named Charles Condomine in Noel Coward's Blithe Spirit, and I felt great. I began to feel that the human condition was the same for all people and their problems were universal. And I wanted to do that. I wanted to create the people and bring to life their situations that spoke to and dealt with the problems that all people have. It didn't make any difference to me whether they were white or black or brown; their human condition was the same."

Les was getting worked up and Caryn could tell he was getting emotional. He stopped and took a deep breath, took a drink from his beer bottle and then continued.

"When I told my grandfather that I wanted to be an actor he was upset. And now that I think about it, I don't think his upset was as much about me not being a doctor, as it was about what he knew that I would face being an actor. He knew what prejudice and bigotry that I would face trying to do what I had dreamed of doing. And the other day Dr. Shaffer showed me what my grandfather knew. So now I'm having second thoughts."

Les stopped. And for a moment Caryn thought she detected a tear in his voice. Then he said, "I'm sorry, but I have to go to the bathroom. He excused himself after she pointed the way.

Les had only been in the toilet a short time when he heard a knock at the door. Then he heard Caryn say in a loud voice, "What do you want?" Then there was silence. A short time later he heard a muffled cry-out and some scraping-like-moving-furniture noise. Les figured that he should cut his business short and get out. He opened the door, and at first didn't see anyone, then he glanced around, and on the floor next to an overturned chair, he saw a person with a ski mask straddling Caryn' body. Her dress was pulled up to her waist and the guy was holding a knife next to her throat with one hand and trying to unzip his pants with the other. Les rushed over and pushed him off. The man rolled over but sprang up immediately pointing the knife at Les. He yelled out, "Keep out of this!" Caryn slid back out of the way while pulling down her dress. Les circled to get a better position and said, "You no-good bastard." The intruder jabbed at Les with the knife. Les spun around and karate-kicked the knife out of the intruder's hand. Then Les grabbed his arm and flipped him over. The man landed on the table crashing the bottles and dishes. He was done. This was the first time that Les had used what he had learned in karate class. It had paid off. Les pulled off the ski mask.

Caryn, who was now standing close by said with surprise, "Jason."

"You know this guy?"

"That's Jason Shaffer."

"Who the hell is he?"

"Dr. Shaffer's son."

Les was shocked. "You mean professor Shaffer, our teacher?"

"Yes. He's been trying to date me for weeks and I've always turned him down. It never occurred to me that he would try something like this."

By this time Jason was recovering from the impact of landing on the table. Les yanked off Jason's belt and bound his hands behind his back. He could see stains of blood seeping through Jason's shirt. Les yelled, "Call the police."

Caryn ran to the phone. Jason twisted his face around and looked at Les with anger in his eyes and said, "Who the fuck are you?"

31

"Her boyfriend, you bully bastard. I hate people like you."

Jason was taken away by the police and charged with attempted rape.

Les stayed around long enough for Caryn to calm down. She looked at him with tears in her eyes and said, "Sorry we got interrupted. You were telling me your second thoughts about being an actor."

Les said, "Another time. Try and get some rest from what you've been through tonight."

Then he headed home. As he transferred from bus to bus, thoughts of the strange events ran through his mind as he tried to make the tie in between the bigoted professor Shaffer and his rapist son. The connection was there somewhere but it didn't come to him right off.

Then he wondered if there was any prophecy in his spontaneous response, *Her boyfriend, you bully bastard.*

Chapter 4
Answers to Tough Questions

By 1966 Naomi, motivated by seeing Walter Rubin's truck parked in the shadows of a side street on the day of Phillip's funeral, and believing that Les was being targeted for retribution, had now been working for the Rubin family over six months and they had grown to ownership and trust of "Our gal Safonia." Her once a week cleaning had developed, little by little, into occasions for conversation with Walter to just about everything—his work on the oil rig—hunting—fishing--the separation of the races, and especially the white niggers who looked down on people with her skin-color-black. Gradually, she had won his confidence and one day she felt the time was right to engage him in talking about his feelings.

"Mr. Rubin, forgive me for bringing it up, but I hear tell that some niggers in this town have caused you some troubles."

Walter was cautious. He had never before discussed his feelings, or anything else, with a colored person. But Safonia was different. She was like a child, and did her cleaning work with no complaint. She usually said what was on her mind and was not too bright about worldly matters, so he was curious to find out what she was talking about.

"Where did you hear that?"

"Around. I was cleaning over at Miz Wyble's, and she ask who else I worked for and I tolt her you. And she said, you was the one who had a son in jail because some niggers had lied.

"Now, sir don't fault me none for bringing dis up, but it seem to me, like you and me have the same problems wid the same peoples."

Walter casually walked over to the cabinet and took out a bottle of Seagram's Whisky and began to fill his pocket flask. He looked back over his shoulder and asked, "What do you mean?"

"Well, it's like dis. I'm black as coal. And them look-like-white-niggers treat us black folk like we was nothin'. It's worst than some white peoples treat us. Now, I don't mean you. You're a fine upstandin' man and you and Miz Sally treats me fine."

Walter was silent. He turned up the flask and took a swig. Naomi rolled her eyes in his direction and continued, "But them white niggers don't have the time-of-day for peoples like me." She paused long enough to wonder what was running through his mind. Maybe this was not a good time. He seemed more interested in drinking, or maybe he was just not a talker. She continued dusting, and finished up her chores for the day.

Later, on her way out, Walter stopped her with a question, "Safonia, do you know anything about a family named Fergerson?"

He had taken the bait, but she did not want to appear too eager or too knowledgeable. She put her hands on her hips, cocked her head to one side and said, "Can't rightly recall that name."

"The old man was some kind of teacher."

He had given her a clue that she could not ignore. She shifted her pocketbook to her other arm and said, "Oh yeah. I knows who you talkin' 'bout. Don't know much, jes that they think they somethin' special." Naomi could feel the blood surge through her body. She had piqued his interest and she had to be careful. She waited for his response.

"They special all right. Special troublemakers."

"Ohhhhh?" Naomi widened her eyes, to encourage him to say more.

He continued. "And they're liars too."

Naomi put her hands on her hips, "What you say, Mr. Rubin!" Walter was not accustomed to this idiomatic-nothing-response used to stimulate further conversation without argument or agreement. But he was comfortable with the thought that these childlike, simple-minded people who don't listen too well, would often ask to have something repeated.

He went on, "Yeah, that Fergerson boy and his big dumb friend told lies about my boy that sent him to prison."

Ohhhh, Lord no!" Naomi had him going now, as she shook her head in sympathy.

Rubin said, "Yeah. But a day of reckoning is coming soon."

Naomi responded impulsively, "Whatcha gonna do, Mr. Rubin?" As soon as the words left her lips, she knew she had made a mistake.

Rubin eyed her with suspicion, and changed the tone of his voice. "Why you want to know that?"

"God knows I don't want to know nothin' . . . I'm jes talking my fool head off. I knows how you must feel 'bout peoples lying 'bout ya. They lies 'bout me too."

"Yeah?"

"Yeah." Naomi felt a little relieved. She continued to guide his suspicion in another direction. She went on, "Yes, sir. They lie 'bout me somethin' awful, say that I'm ignorant and low-class and likes gut-bucket music, and jook-joints and such as that."

Rubin laughed. "Girl, you're something else. What, I haven't figured out yet. But I know one thing, you say what's on your mind, and that's something I like about you."

Naomi thought, *Whew. I'd better leave this alone and get my ass outta here!* She went on. "I likes you too, Mr. Rubin."

At that moment Mrs. Rubin entered the room. "And I'd like it better if you did more work and less talk."

"I finished my work, Miz Sally. I was jes having a word with Mr. Rubin before I left for the day."

"Did you clean the spare room?"

"Yes'um."

"Mopped the bathroom and cleaned the toilets?"

"Yes, ma'am, dusted everything, jus like you told me."

"All right then. You can go."

"Thank you, ma'am."

Naomi made a hasty departure, while impulsive thoughts raced through her mind—*I hate this shit. It's getting scary. I'm getting tired of all this pretending and this has got to come to an end pretty soon. It'll be Thanksgiving soon, and I've got to figure a way to give this bastard his comeuppance, and I do have enough to put a spell on him.*

Over the last six months Naomi had been gathering personal items from Walter—hair from his brush, a pair of drawers with dried shit stains, a piece of toilet paper with blood stains from shaving and dried saliva on a cigarette butt, all of which she could use to make a doll in his image that would carry the curse that she planned. All she needed was a lure to get him to a secret place where she could get rid of his ass.

She made her way on foot to the old house she and Lightfoot had stayed in before the one they lived in now. Whenever she left the Rubin's she headed that way just in case they might be driving around and accidentally see her heading home. Before she had changed out of her maid's uniform, and while she was making a doll likeness of Walter Rubin, a thought, like lightning out of the blue struck her head. Les. He was the lure. All she had to do was to get him and that Rubin bastard together, on a bayou in some out-of-the-way place where she could set a trap and feed his ass to the 'gators.

*　*　*

Les had sworn he would never allow bigotry to cast a shadow in his life again, and his recent encounter with Jason served to show his determination to take a stand against bullies who had no respect for the rights of others.

The suspected cause of Phillip's death never left his mind. The more he thought of the beating of his grandfather by Walter Rubin, the more his anger grew, and the more he felt he must do something to avenge the attack. Les felt a compulsion to find out if his grandfather had actually died as a result of the beating; the more he felt the compulsion, the more it became an obsession. The specter of racial intolerance had thrust its tentacles into the daily thoughts of his mind. Finally he took action.

Les boarded the train to Estilette.

He had only a week off from classes for Thanksgiving and had to make every day count. As soon as he arrived he went directly to Stephen Estilette's office. The secretary's announcement that Les Martel was waiting to see him caused

Stephen to put all other work aside, and Les was ushered in. Stephen stood from his chair and extended his hand.

"Les, it's good to see you. How's school?"

"Fine."

"I assume you're home for thanksgiving."

"Yes, sir."

"How's your Mom?"

"O.K., I guess. I just got in."

Stephen was a little confused and slowly sank into his chair. "Well have a seat. Why did you come here before going home? Is everything all right?"

"Yes, sir. I guess so." After a few seconds of uncomfortable movements—passing his hands over his head and around his face and down around his chest, Les said, "Mr. Estilette, I'm sorry for the intrusion but there is something that I have to know."

"Sure, Les, I'll be only too happy to help with whatever I can. Is there a problem at home?" Stephen could not imagine any other reason that would bring Les to his office.

Les continued to feel uncomfortable. He had never spoken with Mr. Estilette about serious matters before. His only conversations were chit-chats about his daughter, Alex, and trivial stuff like sugar cane harvest, or his theatre performances, but he knew that Stephen was a very good friend of his grandfather's, so he decided to bite the bullet. He looked straight into Stephen's eyes and asked, "What caused Grandpop's death?"

Stephen became apprehensive. He did not know what he should say about Phillip's death or why Les was inquiring. He assumed that Les was still grieving, and he wanted to be as gentle as possible, and he did not know what Les had been told. He did know that no one except himself and Doctor Rossini knew about Phillip's cancer. Maybe Phillip had told the family before he died, but he could not be sure. However, he was sure that he had not informed the family about the cause of Phillip's death at the time he presented his will. Now he had to be careful with his response. He said, "Phillip died like we all have to do, it was his time."

Les was impatient and wanted to get right to the issue. "Mr. Estilette, did that beating from old man Rubin cause Grandpop's death?"

Now Stephen was even more apprehensive and he began stuttering...."I . . . I . . . don't know." Stephen knew the moment the words left his tongue, he had made a mistake. He did know that Phillip would have died of cancer whether or not he had had the beating, and he also knew he had promised Phillip he would keep his secret. So he said, "Maybe you should ask Dr. Rossini because I really can't say what caused his death."

Les countered, "But I thought you were his best friend."

"Yes, I was. But because I don't know why he died does not mean that we were not best friends." Stephen took a deep breath and asked, "Why do you want to know this?"

"My dad told me that he thought Grandpop died because of that beating. I just have to know for sure."

Stephen became worried. He did not know where all of this might lead or how to respond to ease Les's anxiety. He was concerned because he knew about the racial antagonisms between the families, and the threat that had caused Les to leave town. He did not want to say anything that might inflame any feelings that Les may be harboring, so he said, "Why don't you ask Dr. Rossini about the cause of death. I'm sure he could give you more information than I can."

"You think he would talk to me?"

"I think so." Stephen was confident that Dr. Rossini's response would be plausible and would most likely not have any racial implications.

After leaving Stephen's office, Les had walked a few

blocks away and decided to take a rest and assess what he was about. He sat on a bench in front of the courthouse. He remembered that this was the place that his mother, Lala, had told him that his grandfather was beaten for trying to vote. Now again he was beaten, for no good reason, and this added to the urge he felt, that he must talk with Dr. Rossini; after all he was considering drastic action and he had to be right.

He continued to Dr. Rossini's office but it was not as easy to see Dr. Rossini, as it was to see Stephen. After waiting about an hour he was able to talk with Dr. Rossini, and was told, "That beating exacerbated a previous physical condition that your grandfather has suffered, but there is no conclusive evidence that the beating was the cause of Phillip's death. He had cancer."

"Cancer?"

"Yes."

"I didn't know that."

"Phillip didn't want anyone to know. And medical science does not know what causes cancer or how a person gets it. I tried to convince him there was no stain in having cancer, but he didn't want anyone to know he had this dreaded disease. He wanted to spare his family, as he said, "The humiliation of knowing.""

Les thanked the doctor and left. But in the final analysis the real cause didn't matter that much anymore. Les was now more determined than before to make Rubin pay for beating up his sick and dying grandfather.

Lala was happy to have Les home for Thanksgiving, although his arrival was unexpected. Now she finalized the plans she was making for a real Thanksgiving celebration. Ann had just announced her decision to study medicine when she finished high school in June. Lala was delighted because, as she said, "Ever since Bobby died, Papa hoped to have another doctor in the family, and now that the family is together we'll give thanks for this in his honor."

Ann Marie felt good about her decision because it made her Mama happy and she knew it would have brought a smile to her Grandpop's face.

Les was happy because it relieved his lingering feeling of guilt about disappointing his grandfather. "Are you planning to go to Meharry, like Uncle Bobby?" He asked as he began questioning his sister's motives.

"Yes. I've already talked with Aunt Ruth."

"What caused you to make this decision?"

"Well, I knew you didn't want to follow Uncle Bobby, so I thought that I would."

"Ohhhh, you vixen. You really know how to kick a guy in the balls."

Ann laughed and hugged her brother lovingly. "It just happened. That day when I cared for Grandpop after the beating, I liked the feeling of making him comfortable. And the sight of blood didn't make me feel queasy as it does to some people and I actually found myself taking control and making him feel better and that made me feel better too. And that time when Papa was in the hospital. . .

Les held up his hand and said, "You don't have to remind me about that."

Ann laughed again. "I know, Sir Galahad. But just like you found yourself standing up against bad behavior, I found that I liked to help sick people. Aunt Ruth is going to help me prepare to get into med school.

"I know you're going to be one hellava lady doctor."

"And maybe one day you'll fight off the dragons that attack my honor."

"Yeah, that'll be the day. Les kissed his sister as his mind shifted to other thoughts.

"Are you all right?"

"Yeah. Why?"

"You have that far away look in your eyes, which means that something else is on your mind."

There was. Les was intent on avenging his grandfather's beating.

The day before Thanksgiving he rang the bell at the Rubin house. Naomi answered the door. They looked at each other. For several seconds both were speechless. Thoughts and speculations raced furiously through both minds.

Les was confused, *What is she doing here? Maybe I'm at the wrong house.*

Naomi wondered, *Why is he here? He's gonna let them know who I am and that's gonna mess up my plans.*

Naomi said in a loud voice, "Can I help you?" Then she changed to a whisper and said, "Get the hell away from here."

Les responded, "Aunt Naomi, what are you doing here?"

In a soft whisper, "I ain't your Aunt Naomi. My name is Safonia."

A man's voice came from the interior of the house. "Who's at the door, Safonia?"

Naomi turned toward the inside of the house, while waving her hand in a go-away gesture towards Les, "Jes a man, sir. I think he bes lost. He's looking for another address."

Walter Rubin appeared behind Naomi and his face clouded over. He pushed Naomi aside and said, "Boy, you're the nigger I've been looking for." He then headed toward Les.

Les backed away and took up a karate stance. "And you're the son-of-a-bitch who beat my grandfather. I've come to kick your ass."

Naomi cried out, "Lord. . . lord. . . lord." Cupped her hands over her face and pressed her back against the porch wall.

Walter rushed toward Les with his oil-rigger-body-muscles rippling for the fight. They circled each other seeking to gain first advantage. Les spun around and jump-kicked Walter in the face. Walter fell backwards over a porch chair; then Les sprang into action delivering several hand-chop blows to Walter's face and one to his adam's apple. Walter gasped for breath. Les drove three vicious kicks to his stomach. "That's for my grandfather." Then Les turned and ran off the porch. Naomi remained petrified against the wall.

For several seconds Walter laid dead-still on the porch floor. Mrs. Rubin rushed through the front door shouting, "What's all the commotion out here?"

Walter stirred and struggled to get up. Sally yelled, "Girl, help him up and get him into the house!" Naomi was trapped. She did what she was ordered. She helped Walter to the parlor sofa and stood back looking down at his swelling, bloody face. Sally, like a fluttering hen, headed first in one direction, then in another and finally around in circles, shouted instructions—"Do something—Stop the bleeding—Get a cold towel, no a hot towel—Call the police. You heard me Safonia, get moving!"

When Naomi returned with a hot towel, Walter was sitting up and Sally was stuffing tissue into his bleeding mouth. She grabbed the towel from Naomi and put it on his swelling jaw and asked, "Should I call Cat Bobineaux?"

Walter's reply was, "Naw. I'll take care of that nigger myself."

Naomi had heard enough. She had seen enough. It was time for her to get out of there. She said, as meekly as she could," Miz Rubin, if you ain't got no further work for me today, I'll be goin'."

* * *

43

The Thanksgiving celebration was everything other than what Lala had planned and hoped for. The food was in ample supply and delicious, the family was together, but the spirit of thanks for the gifts received was totally lacking. Instead there was discord, disagreements and charges of deception.

Les could not understand why Naomi was, as he put it, "Friendly with the Rubins. When I saw you there I wanted to throw up."

Naomi responded with vinegar in her voice, "I work over there and wuz trying to find out what that man plans to do to your ass for testifying against his son. And you was stupid enough to come over and mess up my plans."

"How was I supposed to know what you were doing there. You hadn't told anybody anything."

Lala listened to Les. She was convinced that she was right for not allowing Les to go to the Montgomery march. She joined the condemnation. "You had no right to go over there and attack that man. You're a hothead, just like your father. You're just gonna get yourself killed."

Naomi rose and threw her napkin on the table, "I've been slaving over there as long as it takes a woman to make a baby just to find out how that bastard was planning to kill your ass."

Lightfoot interrupted, "All you did was to get him pissed off again, and now he's sure to try and kill you . . . he was looking for your ass the day Phillip was buried."

Les looked from one to the other in silence. He was angry. Confused. These were not the responses he expected from his family for avenging his grandfather's beating.

Rosa turned to Les. "Love thy enemies and turn the other cheek. That's the message from Jesus. An eye for an eye is not the way, and I don't think Grandpop, or even Martin Luther King would approve of what you did."

Ann's voice was the only understanding expression he

heard. "Les, I know what you feel for Grandpop and how you want to get back at anyone who'd done him harm, but we don't want you to put yourself in harm's way trying to get justice." Then she burst out in tears and ran away from the table.

The voices finally settled down to silence and only the plate noises remained.

After eating his fill, Lightfoot said, "Les, I'd better get you out of here. Get your things and I'll drop you off so you can catch the train back to Chicago." Lightfoot pointed his finger across the table and continued, "And don't come back here 'till you hear from me that things have cooled down."

Later that night, after getting Les safely on the train, Lightfoot took the mic at the Black Eagle, when Vitalee had finished her warm-up session. He looked out through the smoke filled club at the standing-room-only audience and said, "Ladies and gentlemen, now I know summa y'all must be gentlemens, 'cause you're standing up. Welcome to this Thanksgiving Day gig. We have a special treat for y'all tonight. And as I've done in yesteryear, when I was starting out at Tot's Tavern, now I know summa y'all are old enough to remember them days, and like I done then, I'm gonna be the interlocutor tonight and introduce our main act. Tonight we gonna finger-pop, belly-rub and get down to the music of a man who was born and raised in New Orleans. He's played in clubs all over Louisiana, worked the streets as an entertainer, singer and dancer. He plays the guitar and the piano, has several recording labels and sometimes works outside of music as a professional gambler. He's played in Estilette before, at my Blues Tavern before it burnt down, so put your hands together and welcome Professorrrrrr Lonnnng hair."

The club went wild as Henry Roeland Byrd sat at the piano and started banging out, *How Long Has That Train*

Been Gone. A big wide grin took over Lightfoot's face as his eyes roamed over the bobbing heads of the dancing crowd. Then gradually, the smile on his face slowly faded into a frown. He stared in the direction of the entrance door, trying to get a clear focus through the smoky haze. *"Holy shit."* He almost lost his footing as he hurried off the stage down the steps. He dodged, ducked, and side-stepped a path through the dancing couples, as fast as his limping stride would allow, and made his way into the kitchen. He headed straight to Naomi. "Get yo ass outta here fast. That bastard Rubin is out front looking around."

Early the next morning, from the safety of their bedroom, Lightfoot brought Naomi up to date on what happened after she left. "He stayed around and had a good look for about ten minutes. Somebody musta told him Les had a connection here."

"I bet that was Sheriff Cat. You can't trust none of these white folks."

Lightfoot said, "Well it's getting bad. He's looking to kill that boy, if somebody don't kill him first."

"I wuz trying to put a hex on him, but I think that's gonna take too long."

Lightfoot's eyes widened. "Is that what you wuz doing over there? Girl, you gotta be careful. It's really getting dangerous. You gotta stop working for them people. Yo found out what you wanted to know."

Naomi said thoughtfully, "If I don't show up next week, they're bound to figure out I must have a connection to Les. If I was their cook I'd put glass in his cornbread just like Martha done to that priest."

Lightfoot's eyes lit up. "That's it. Poison the bastard."

"Poison?"

"Yeah. And I know just where to get it. It's impossible to trace. But you got to be careful how you use it."

Naomi knew exactly how to do what Lightfoot was suggesting. Lightfoot did not know she was an expert at getting rid of people who brought complication to her life. She didn't say another word. She turned over in the bed, faced the wall away from Lightfoot, and smiled at the thought of what she was about to do--again.

* * *

When she arrived at work, Sally Rubin was getting ready to leave for her job at the Seed and Feed, and Walter was still in bed. Naomi got instructions, "Don't let him sleep past ten o'clock. He's on a forty-eight hour shift that starts at twelve o'clock, and since that boy attacked him he's been over sleeping."

Yessum. I'll get him up in time, you can count on that."

As soon as she was alone, Naomi found Walter's flask in the cabinet next to the bottle of Seagrams. It was already filled. She carefully drizzled several fingers of cyanide crystals into the whisky and shook it up to thoroughly mix the ingredients.

A voice from the doorway shouted out, "Safonia!"

Naomi almost dropped the flask. She quickly put it back and closed the cabinet. She turned. Walter was standing there tying the sash to his robe. "My wife gone yet?"

"Yes, sir. She jus' left."

He took a step into the room and asked, "What you doing?"

Naomi's heart skipped a beat. She didn't know if he had seen her with the flask or not. She was nervous. Trembling. "Nothin' sir, jus' cleaning like I always does."

"Good. "Cause I'm hungry. My wife left before I got up and didn't fix my breakfast. Stop what you're doing and fix me some eggs and bacon."

"Ohhh yes, sir. Be happy to. It'll be ready before you can say Jack Robinson."

"Who's he?"

"Nobody sir. Jus' a saying."

"You people somethin' else. Make 'em scrambled." He closed the door and went to get dressed.

Naomi was so relieved that she would have fixed him a six course meal if he had asked, even though she was not hired as the cook. And since she was cooking, she thought about putting glass in his eggs, but she smiled at the thought because she had not prepared for that recipe, but even still she could put in a little spit. Moreover, she took consolation in knowing that, like always, he would put his flask into his pocket when he headed off to work.

Chapter 5
Discovering Love

Shortly after Thanksgiving, Les received a letter from his mom. It contained a clipping of a news article from the *Estilette Chronicle* that was so incredible he had to read it out loud to convince himself that it was real.

"On Monday after Thanksgiving a strange event happened on an oil derrick in Jennings Louisiana. One of the workers, an experienced rigger, who has been in the oil business over fifteen years, fell to his death. The foreman on the job said the victim, Walter Rubin, was one of the most capable men on his crew, so he was hard-pressed to understand what happened. Rubin had climbed the fifty foot derrick in order to inspect and correct a problem that was causing a glitch in the drilling process of a new well. According to Guidry, the foreman, 'I looked up and it seemed to me that he had taken care of the problem up there all right. Then all of a sudden it seemed that he lost his grip and fell. I knew he was dead the moment I saw him hit the deck of the wooden platform fifty feet below.' A resident of Estilette for over twenty years,

49

*in recent months Rubin has had more than his share of legal
and personal problems. His son Karl is presently in Angola
charged with the accidental shooting of a friend and is due to
be released in twelve months. His wife of thirty years, Sally
Rubin, is overcome with grief over the plight of her son and
now the loss of her husband. Funeral arrangements will be
announced later this week."*

Lala said in her letter that his Uncle Lightfoot and Aunt
Naomi had come by to bring the article and Naomi told her
that she had put a hex on, "that bastard and it worked."

Les had his doubts about her voodoo, so he shared the
information and the article with Aunt Vel. At first, there was
a solemn look on her face, then she laughed and said, "That
ole black woman is always claiming she can put spells on
people, but I don't believe she has that power and neither
did Mama when she was alive. That woman's been a thorn
in the side of our family ever since she took up with Uncle
Johnny."

Les didn't know the truth of such things, but for many
years he had heard stories of the strange goings-on of people like Marie Laveau and Naomi. But his grandfather used
to say, "You can't really know for certain how the spiritual
powers of the church or voodoo can change the course of
people's lives."

Les had not understood why Naomi had gone to work
for the Rubins, but now he figured she must have been over
there for some private reason; and maybe, just maybe she
did have something to do with Rubin's death. What? How?
He didn't know. But it was all very mysterious. He felt a
little tinge of guilt about the things he had said.

It was getting close to Christmas and Les was looking forward to going home for the break, now that Walter
Rubin was no longer around. He felt safe. Although he had

not talked with his Uncle Lightfoot, he did share his plans with Aunt Vel, and she admitted, "I'm also going home for Christmas to get my share of the money. I've been thinking about doing that since I heard Papa's will, read by Mr. Estilette." Les knew then that this meant she was planning to get cash for her share of the property, and he did not want to be around when she put on the pressure to sell his grandfather's house. So for several days he was undecided about what to do for the holidays.

Meanwhile Caryn had a dilemma of her own. Her parents were planning to go on a cruise to Denmark for the holidays and she would be left to spend the holidays with friends or alone at home in Bemidji. When she said to Les, "Why don't you and I spend the holidays together?" He decided to take her up on the invitation. They had been together a lot during the many weeks after the attempted rape, and their friendship had grown. It now seemed that the comment that Les had made to Jason, "I'm her boyfriend, you bully bastard," was a prophecy coming true. Although they had not been intimate, they had gotten to know each other very well, so spending the holidays together seemed a logical solution to both of their predicaments.

Les called Lala. "Mom I know we've always spent Christmas with the family, but I'd like very much to stay in Chicago this year."

There was a silence from the receiving end of the phone. Then Lala said, "We'll miss you but that's what growing up means, leaving home…"

Les interrupted. "Oh, Mom it's not that. It's just that I met this girl, whom I like a lot, and she asked that I spend the holidays with her family. I'll send my presents in time for the Christmas tree."

"I know son. And I did not mean to imply that not being here would be like leaving home forever. It's just that as my

51

children grow up it takes some getting use to; but I know you have your own lives to lead, and I may as well get use to it."

For a few moments after hanging up the phone, feelings of guilt began to creep slowly into Les' mind. However, they were not long lived because he knew he was trying to avoid an unpleasant scene that he did not want to experience or be a part of, and wished that there had been some way to make his Mom aware of what was headed her way, along with the joy of Christmas. He contented himself with the rationale that whatever Grandpop's daughters decided to do with their inheritance was their decision, and was not his business. So figuring that there might be fussing and fighting, he'd rather spend the time with Caryn.

Caryn's family had a cabin in the woods, where she planned they spend the Christmas holidays, and she thought it best their time there be kept secret. Bemidji was a small town of about ten thousand people, where everybody knew everybody; and the fact that the daughter of the town's only doctors was entertaining a stranger while they were away on a cruise would not be acceptable. Les, of course, followed the travel plan as Caryn had suggested. He had breakfast in the train station after his arrival. He looked around at the fully occupied depot and finally saw her sitting across the room from where he had settled, but he was instructed not to show any signs of recognition or make contact. After breakfast he turned left out of the station door and headed in the direction of the post office where she was waiting in her car. They drove to the cabin in the woods.

The weather was cold. Snow covered everything. The log cabin was stylishly rustic, if that could be considered an accurate description, made so by the medieval tapestries and patch-work quilts that adorned the walls, along with Danish and European inspired works-of-art, and Knick-knacks.

Les meandered back and forth admiring the hangings, and gliding his fingers over sculptures that he concluded were authentic works of art.

Caryn had thought ahead and had picked up from the local deli a delicious smorgasbord for dinner. Sitting at a low table in front of a delightful fire, that Les watched Caryn expertly build in the six foot wide fireplace, they enjoyed beet soup topped with sour cream, roast beef with bacon and sautéed mushroom, sweet and sour cabbage, creamed potatoes, asparagus, smoked salmon, shrimp, rye bread and several glasses of Chateanueuf-du-Pape. Les could tell by the well stocked wine cellar of Caryn's father that he, like his grandfather, was a lover of French wines. Their first night together in the cabin, after dish-washing and coffee with Danish pastries, induced by the romantic sounds of Debussy, ultimately evolved into their first sexual intimacy.

In the morning they rebuilt a fire in the fireplace that burned all day and heated the entire cabin. In spite of the chill outside, it was quite comfortable in the living space and the kitchen, but the same could not be said for the bedroom, where the only warmth needed during the night was provided by the goose-down comforters and quilts.

Caryn made coffee the old Danish way. She brewed coffee along with a poached egg. First she put in the coffee and the water and then dropped in an egg. As the egg cooked it trapped the loose grounds and she poured off the delicious beverage to be enjoyed with Danish rolls and fruit.

Around midday the sun would show itself for a few hours of warmth, and they ventured outside. The only sounds came from the geese flying over the lake and the wind making music through the trees. It was great. They were completely isolated and alone. It was a special winterland paradise. The nearest cabin was a mile away, and they walked through their private Never-Never land, and sat on the boat dock, and enjoyed the rhythm of the wind music, and threw snowballs and built snowmen and made love.

The sunsets were spectacular. They would change from a light pink to a deep reddish salmon color right before their eyes, and they took delight in watching the painted sky slowly fade from twilight into night. Les found himself falling in love. This was the first time in his short life of nineteen years that he had such deep feelings for a female companion. This was not the first time that Les had been with a woman. He did not know, but assumed that this was not the first time for Caryn either. But somehow it felt different for both. He had been intimate with several other acquaintances, mostly from Estilette, but Caryn was the one who came closest to touching that part of him that made him feel complete. He liked the feeling. Being with Caryn so many times, in so few days, was absolutely thrilling. It made him feel that he had finally come into manhood.

They walked arm in arm through the forest of trees and silently through the snow. Finally they came to rest on the rocks surrounding the lake, and enjoyed the rhythmical splashing of the waves. The sun warmed their faces and brought a sense of contentment to the cold that surrounded them.

"A penny for your thoughts." Caryn broke the silence.

Les laughed and hugged her closer. "Do you really want to know?"

"Oh, you silly. If I didn't want to know I would not have asked."

Les responded. "Sitting here, and being with you in this place alone, makes me feel like sitting on the bayou with my grandfather."

Caryn looked at him with amazement in her eyes. "Your grandfather?"

"Yes. Those times were the most special in my memory. My grandfather is gone now and he was the most important person in my life. More than my mother, or my father. And now being with you here, feels the same. It's like you are filling that space in my heart that was left when he left me."

Caryn kissed him on the mouth, long and soft. "Thank you."

"Now you."

"Now me, what?"

Les reached into his pocket and gave Caryn a penny.

She laughed and slapped him on the shoulder, "Ohhhh, you!"

Her laughter gradually faded into silence. Then she said, "I know it may sound like a cliché, but I began falling in love with you while we were rehearsing <u>The Rose Tattoo</u>. It was like Jack and Rosa. Now I know this may sound silly and trivial but all during our scenes together I began to feel a deeper relationship. Something that transcended, went beyond what was going on in rehearsal. I really did not know how to handle it. What to do about it. But it was persistent. It kept me awake at night. And I wanted to know for sure what it was about my feeling for you, whether it was a passing fancy or for real."

"And what is it?"

"I think it's real."

Les said. "Me too. I feel I'm falling in love."

Caryn was an excellent cook and in the evenings they had full course Danish meals by candlelight with wine in front of the fireplace. After dinner Caryn read from the **Prophet** of Gibran along with coffee and dessert, and when she did Les would drink in his new found spirituality like a tasty nectar that replenished his thirsty soul. And just as Almustafa revealed for the city-dwellers the truth of their lives, so did Caryn share with Les the words and feelings that were destined to become guiding beacons of his life.

When you love you should not say, "God is in my heart,"
but rather, "I am in the heart of God."

And think not you can direct the course of love, for love,
if it find you worthy, directs your course.

Love has no other desire but to fulfill itself.

But if you love and must needs have desires, let these by
your desires:

To melt and be like a running brook that sings its melody
to the night.

To know the pain of too much tenderness.

To be wounded by your own understanding of love;

And to bleed willingly and joyfully.

To wake at dawn with a winged heart and give thanks for
another day of loving;

To rest at noon and meditate love's ecstasy;

To return home at eventide with gratitude;

And then to sleep with a prayer for the beloved in your
heart and song of praise upon your lips.

Les would discover, during those evenings of revelation, that a prophet of God was speaking the words of love, friendship, joy, and sorrow that he himself embraced and wanted to emulate. And during all of it, he drank from a river of silence as the words and images entered and surged through his entire body and soul.

Only after the sounds of the words had subsided would he dare to share thoughts and feeling from his own life akin to the passions revealed by the prophet. These were the moments, along with making love to Caryn that Les would always cherish.

They knew not how or why, but the power of the words influenced the physicality of their embraces which became as so many moments of touches, as light as feathers with the feel of lightening, and when their bodies melted into oneness, they felt the act of love consummated with a peace and restfulness that had never before been experienced by either.

One night near the end of their week in paradise, while having dessert, coffee, and Gibran, the sound of a truck came to a stop out front. They had a visitor. Caryn was up like a flash. She rushed Les into the bedroom, while pushing his dinner dishes in after him. She quietly closed the door to the bedroom and answered the knock.

Les could tell by the timbre of the voice that the visitor was a big man.

It was cold in the bedroom, and Les wanted to get under the covers but was afraid that the springs of the bed would squeak and tell of his presence. The more he listened, the more apprehension increased. His imagination ran wild. He could see himself being discovered by this intruder in an isolated cabin in the north woods with a white girl. He hid under the bed. It was colder there. He could feel the wind blowing up through the cracks of the floor boards, and began to shiver from the icy air.

The man did not stop talking. He went on to explain that he had seen the smoke from the chimney and decided to come by and check to see if everything was all right. He knew that Caryn's parents had gone on a cruise and figured she was alone and may need help with something. The man's conversation got more and more suggestive. But under no circumstance did Les think it wise to show himself.

Finally after about a half hour, which seemed like an eternity, Les heard Caryn yell "Buster, You're drunk and if you try to kiss me again, I'm going to tell my Daddy."

The man said, "Don't be like that. You're older now, have a drink and let's have a little fun."

That did it. Les threw caution to the wind and opened the door. Caryn gasped and covered her mouth with both hands when she saw him. The man looked around as he could tell from her gesture that someone else was in the room.

The man turned as he put his bottle of whisky on the table and said, "Well looka there, who do we have here?"

Les said as calmly as he could, "Mister, you're drunk. It's time for you to leave."

The man laughed and said, "Listen, boyo, nobody tells Buster what to do."

Les was pissed and the man was drunk. He was a big man. Like BookTau. But compared to BookTau he was a giant. The laughter of the man incited Les as would a slap-in-the- face challenge a duel. Les should have known better, but he advanced toward the man and punched him in the face as hard as he could. The blow didn't faze the giant one bit. Buster continued laughing. He reached out and grabbed Les by the throat and squeezed while he raised him off the floor and pinned his back against the wall.

Caryn began beating on his body with her fists yelling, "Buster, you know that my father told you if you ever came here again you would go to jail. Now get out, and leave us alone!"

The man swung his left arm around and knocked Caryn to the floor. Les could hardly breathe. The man had a strong grip and he kept Les pinned to the wall with his feet dangling in mid air.

Caryn got up, and continued beating and yelling, "Stop this insanity. You're killing him!"

Les passed out.

Caryn panicked and didn't know what to do. Buster dropped the unconscious Les to the floor and was standing over him looking down. Caryn grabbed an andiron from the rack and hit him as hard as she could, at the base of his skull. He fell backwards knocking over the table along with the lighted candelabra that set fire to the table cloth.

The fire raged and grew rapidly along the table cloth.

Caryn grabbed a throw pillow and began beating the flame but to no avail. The fire ignited the rugs, then ran up the walls to the hanging tapestries and quilts, which were like kindling for the dried logs. In very little time the cabin became a burning inferno. Caryn dragged Les out pulling him by the feet, and left him a distance away from the house next to the garage, and she ran back to get the unconscious Buster. He was too big, too heavy; the fire was really blazing now and the smoke made it difficult for her to breath. She ran out coughing and gasping for breath and collapsed from exhaustion next to Les. By this time the fresh air had brought Les to consciousness and he struggled to get on his feet. He asked, "Where's the man?"

"He's still in there. He was too heavy for me"

"Let's get him out." They headed for the door but the heat was too intense. Their faces burned and it was difficult to see anything though the thick smoke. They backed away and watched the flames consume the cabin.

Caryn said, Let's get away from here."

As they drove off, Les looked back at the burning building. It lit up the dark night. There was no moon. No stars. Just a black night lit by the leaping flames. They had traveled about a mile from the cabin when Caryn pulled off the road and stopped the car. "I can't see to drive anymore. You take over."

Les looked at Caryn and saw tears were streaming from her eyes. He reached over and took her hand and she broke down in hysterical sobbing. Les pulled her close and she buried her head on his shoulder and shook with tears for about five minutes. She dried her eyes with the handkerchief Les had given, and said, "Let's change places and you drive."

Sitting behind the wheel Les took a deep breath. He felt horrible about what had happened, and said, "Maybe if I hadn't punched him."

Caryn said, "Don't go there."

He went on, "I don't know why I do the things I do. Sometimes I can't figure me out. Bullies and bad behavior turn me into to someone I don't even know, and I've just got to strike out and do something. There was something about the way he looked at me and laughed, like he resented I was a Negro."

Caryn said with conviction, "Les. He didn't know. You don't look colored."

"I'd forgotten. I guess I'm so sensitive about being who I am, I feel that it's written on my face and anybody can tell by just looking at me."

"Yeah. You've got to stop that. Anyway he was the one with the problem. This kind of thing has happened before. When I was sixteen he tried to kiss me and my Daddy really had it out with him, and told him to stay away from me. Otherwise he's a nice man, would do anything my Dad asked him to do. Often he'd look after the cabin when they were away for long periods of time and I guess he saw this as another opportunity."

Les said, "Yeah, an opportunity to get into your pants." Les didn't know why he said that but that's what he had concluded from what he had overheard, and it just came out. He tried to apologize.

"That's not what I meant. . ."

"I know what you're thinking, and you may not be far from right. He's tried to kiss me before."

The siren sounds of approaching fire trucks brought them to silence. They watched as two fire engines sped by. The vibration shook the car. Caryn said, "The Andersons must have seen the fire and called it in. "Let's go."

"Where?"

"The train station. You've got to get out of here. I'll drop you off at the post office. Take the train to Grand Rapids and then get on back to Chicago."

"What are you going to do?"

"I'll go home and try and figure out what to tell my dad."

"Are you going to call the police?"

"No." My father will take care of that when he comes back. Buster had a key and came in drunk and he tried to attack me. While he was taking another drink I hit him in the head with the andiron and got out of there and went home. Somehow the fire started after I left."

After hearing Caryn's explanation of the events, Les was silent for the remainder of the trip to the post office.

*   *   *

When Les got back to Chicago, his Aunt Vel was there. She asked, "How was your Christmas?"

"It was all right."

"Just all right? I thought you spent it with your girl friend."

He was still shaken up over what had happened and for a brief moment wanted to share the experience with his aunt, but on second thought decided not. He shrugged his shoulders and said, "She's just a friend from school."

That was all that he planned to say about Caryn and that situation, so he changed the conversation. It was planned that Vel would not be back until after New Years, and he suspected that things did not go well in Estilette.

He asked, "Why are you back so soon?"

Vel was evasive and said, "I got lonesome for the snow. It's too hot down there. I've been here so long I miss the snow at Christmastime.

Les felt that his aunt was lying. Something had happened and he was curious to know what. The next day while Vel was out to do some, of what she had said was, "much needed

61

shopping," Les called his uncle Johnny.

"I know Aunt Vel came home to get the money Grandpop left her. How did things go?"

Lightfoot answered his curiosity. "Man, it was war. And I got dragged in to settle it."

"What happened?"

"Well, it was like this. Vel come on down here wearing her fur coats and fine things and puttin' on the dog. And the very first thing she said after her first day in town was 'Let's divide up Papa's money.' Your Mama told her, 'he didn't leave any money. He left the property to the three of us but there is no money to be divided.' And that's when the shit started."

Thus Les learned from his uncle, the details of what had happened during the holidays.

Two days before Christmas, Vel, Rosa and Lala sat around the kitchen table eating dinner as strains of the Twelve Days of Christmas filtered in from the living room along with the scent of pine from the Christmas tree.

Vel swallowed the sip of beer from her glass and said, "My lawyer said that y'all can't keep the property undivided if I want my share."

Rosa rolled her eyes and tipped her head upwards. "Oh my God!"

Lala asked, "You hired a Lawyer?"

Vel nodded her head.

Lala demanded with an edge in her voice, "Why? Why is it necessary to get a lawyer?" Vel's response was, "I'm way up yonder in Chicago and I have no way of knowing what y'all doing with my property. Rosa is running a business outta here and you're not paying rent, but parking yo butt here till you get married again, and I have no way of knowing that y'all gonna take care of the property the way it should be taken cared of. I own property in Chicago and I know what it takes to keep up the property values. So I'd just as soon get my share now while I know what shape it's in."

When Vel finished her explanation, Lala took up her plate and left the table. Rosa buried her head in her hands as tears began to flow.

Early the next morning, Lala and Rosa went to Stephen and explained the situation. He told them that the lawyer was correct. "Vel does have the right to have her share in cash. If y'all want to keep the property as your homestead, the property has to be assessed and Vel's portion paid. I sure am sorry its come to this. I know Phillip would not like this either."

Neither Lala nor Rosa was too happy to hear this. They left crying and went directly to Lightfoot.

Lala said, "We can't pay out a mortgage." Then she added, "Lester has the money but I can't ask him since we're divorced."

Lightfoot exploded, "Well this is some shit. I can't figure why Vel doing this to y'all. But if it's just the same to y'all you can get the money from me or Elvina to pay her off."

Lala looked at Rosa, who raised her head and wiped her eyes. The thought of asking for money from Uncle Johnny or Aunt Elvina had not occurred to either Lala or Rosa. Both Lightfoot and Elvina were their mother's siblings; however Elvina was the outside daughter of Martha's father, whom they had only known for the last six years. So if a choice had to be made, Lala would choose Lightfoot who had been around for as long as they could remember, and she suspected Rosa felt the same. So she said, "Well, getting it from you will be fine with me."

Rosa smiled, "Yeah, with me too. Thank you for offering."

Lala thought about the arrangement and said, "That would mean you would own the property with us? Right?"

Lightfoot smiled and nodded his head. He remembered

that this was the way it was in the past. He and Martha owned the house and the forty acres of land that they had inherited from their father. When Phillip gave Lightfoot his share of the money so he could buy the tavern, the entire estate went to Martha and Phillip. Now it seemed to Lightfoot that ownership in the property had come back full circle. However, he did not tell them anything about the transaction that had taken place many years earlier. Naomi, however, knew.

Naomi stepped out of the shadows of the hallway, where she had overheard the entire conversation, and said, "And that'll be fine wid me too. Y'all both know that means that we'll hold a mortgage on one-third of the estate."

Rosa was shocked. Her face and eyes expressed her distress. Her voice took on the edge of a razor. "You've been listening?"

"Why sure. You're in my house and I have right to know what goes on here."

Lala came immediately to the rescue. "Oh course you do. We're family and that means a lot to both of us. Rosa is just upset over all of this. We'd both appreciate whatever you and Uncle Johnny do to help us out."

Lightfoot said, "Yeah, that's right we'll help you out. We'll hold the mortgage but y'all don't have to make no monthly payments."

Naomi's mouth tightened but she said nothing about the arrangements that her husband had just decided. All she said was, "Y'all want a cup of coffee? I got some fresh, made jus' before you got here."

Les was happy to hear that Uncle Johnny had helped out but he was not too happy to find out that his Aunt Vel was a money grabber. She had this big house in Chicago and he wondered why she had done what she had done to his mama and Aunt Rosa. As far as he could figure she didn't need the money and should have just left things in Estilette as they were. Based on what he had heard from his Uncle Johnny, he now regarded his Aunt Vel with even less esteem than he had when he found out she was a lady of questionable virtue.

Unknown to Les, at the present time, his Aunt Vel was out doing her "much needed shopping." She entered the Century 21 Real Estate Office on State Street. "Hi Jerry just dropped by to make the down on the 55th Avenue property."

"Good. I was wondering if you were serious about going through with the deal."

Vel smiled, "Well like I always told you, I'd buy when I got my inheritance."

Jerry opened his eyes, pursed his lips and raised his shoulders.

Vel said sarcastically, "Yeah, I know you never believed that I had an inheritance coming when I told you that." She reached into her purse and laid fifty thousand dollars on the desk. "Write it up."

Chapter 6
Growing Pains

When classes resumed after the holidays, Les expected to see Caryn. He did not. He was anxious to know what happened and even more suspicious about why she had not returned to school--or if she had, why was she not in the classes they shared--or why had he not run into her on campus--or even at the Coffee Shoppe where she loved to hang out late in the evenings. She had simply disappeared. Someone else was now living in her apartment. He had no way to make contact, nor did he think he should, even though his recently discovered feelings of closeness were still alive in his heart.

As the weeks grew into months, without seeing her, he began to feel that Caryn had regarded him as only a passing fancy, and he was forced to remember all that had passed between them as a delightful dream of love found that turned into an illusion.

Gradually, a new reality of what could have taken place was now beginning to slowly form in his mind. Small fears that he could possibly be arrested for the part he played in the death of Buster, took over his thoughts. He had no proof that Buster had died in the fire, but there was a strong possibility that he had, so he rationalized the event as an unfortunate accident. By the time he graduated, three years later, all of everything that had happened in that Minnesota cabin was only a dim memory of a horrible nightmare.

Coincidentally, so much more had happened in the intervening years, that it made the event in Minnesota seem immaterial. Martin Luther King was gunned down in Memphis in April of '68. Then Robert Kennedy was killed in June of the same year. And if that was not anguish enough, in August, the Democratic Convention in Chicago turned into civil war between the protestors and police. Les was one of the demonstrators in Grant Park protesting the Vietnam War. He barely missed getting clubbed. The only thing that saved him from getting a cracked skull was his skill in ducking the wild swinging clubs of the police officers who charged the scattering crowds of hecklers.

When he got home later that night, Aunt Vel said, "I was watching on TV and praying that I would not see you get hurt."

His brow wrinkled and he said, "It was very rough out there."

That evening Les went to bed angry, confused, and disappointed.

Angry, because the war was draining the blood, literally and figuratively, of the country's resources, in the forms of bodies lost and financial cost—angry because so much of the hope for a better tomorrow had died along with Martin and Robert.

Confused, because he had not yet figured how these events would affect plans for his career, whether he should continue to follow the path of being an actor or become an active protestor of the war and the other injustices that were sweeping the country.

Disappointed, because the country's leaders were not living up to, in his grandfather's words, "The promises of the democracy we hoped for"—-he was also disappointed because racism seemed to be growing. He could see and feel the same attitudes that had run him out of Estilette expressed everywhere--the same buried hatreds that Mr. BoBo had faced and feared. He could never forget the fact that Mr. BoBo was so intimidated by white people that he allowed himself to die by his own fear, rather than risk the possibility of justice. Les failed to see the proposed integration of the schools becoming a reality, and he remembered his grandfather's prediction, "It's gonna be a bitter pill for the white people of this country to swallow." He realized how wise his grandfather was; and although Phillip's prediction did not make Les feel better, he now realized his grandfather's skepticism coming to life as hatred and bigotry raised their ugly heads.

In 1969, on the heels of these dilemmas, came graduation, and Les expected that his family would attend the occasion. They did. However, Aunt Vel had announced in advance that she would not be present because she would be out of town for a previously planned visit with friends. It was just as well. After the family disaster of a past Christmas, neither of her sisters wanted to see her either. Lala and Rosa had booked a hotel near Evanston along with Ann Marie, and Papa Lester.

Graduation brought another disappointment that Les had not anticipated. His father, Lester, discovered while reading the program that his son was not graduating from the School of Education, but rather from the Department of Theatre Production. He was extremely upset, but contained his anger during the ceremony.

In the restaurant chosen for the celebration dinner, after everyone had ordered and was waiting for the food to be served, Lester said, "Son, I want to know why you lied to me."

There was immediate silence around the table. Lala dropped her head. Ann's eyes widened in surprise and Rosa looked from one to the other in bewilderment.

Les was embarrassed, but knew exactly to what his father was referring. He said, "Papa, I'm sorry but I knew that you would not like the idea of me being an actor."

Lester replied with anger, "You told me you were studying Education to be a teacher like Grandpop."

Les was cornered. He didn't know what to do or say. He shook his head and cast his eyes down to the table and with apology in his voice he said, "I'm sorry, Papa but I knew that you wouldn't pay for me to be an actor."

"You're damn right I wouldn't pay for you to be a sissy. You've pissed me off. I'm sorry I wasted my money, and the time to come here to see you graduate as one of them."

With that Lester got up from the table, took out a roll of money, dropped several bills on the table and said, "Y'all have a nice time. I'm getting the next train back. 'Cause I can't stomach no sissies." With that he headed out. His family was stunned and silent. Ann got up and ran after her father. She stopped him at the door.

"Papa, don't do this."

Lester looked into her eyes with tenderness. "I'm sorry, baby, but your brother lied."

"Papa, he's not like what you think. Les is a real man."

"Then why did he graduate in that damn faggot field? He could do anything else that he wanted to do, and I wouldn't have any problem with that."

Ann understood her father's feelings, but didn't know what else to say, so all that she could say was, "Papa, I know how you feel and all I can say is Les is a good person and is not a sissy."

Lester stood tall, took a deep breath, turned, and looked down at her, and said, "And I know you are a good person too and I love you." He took her into his arms and kissed her. She looked into his eyes, reached up and wiped away a tear, and then he was out of the door. Ann watched him disappear into the crowd, then she turned and headed back to the table.

Les stood as she approached and asked, "What did he say?"

"He has a problem with you being an actor."

"I know, but I'm not like who he thinks."

Ann kissed him and said, "I know that too. You're still my sir Galahad."

The dinner was served and all ate in silence for the next five minutes. Then Lala broke the silence and said, "Les, your father is a good man. He just has his own ideas about what a man should be. Don't let that bother you. You do what you have to do and I will help you as much as I can."

Les said, "Thanks, Mama."

Ann said, "And me too. Be the best damn actor that you can."

Rosa chimed in, "And that's the way I feel too." And she added, "Now that all of this is over, I'd like to visit the stockyards tomorrow."

Ann asked with a mouth full, "The stockyards?"

Rosa said, "Yes, the stockyards."

With a frown on his face, Les asked, "Why do you want to go there?"

"Well, Joshua used to tell me stories about how they started way back in the eighteen hundreds, and how, in addition to meat, they made things like soap, fertilizer, glue, buttons, perfume, and violin strings."

Then Ann said, "So, what's the big deal, Aunt Rosa?"

"I'm just curious. And then Joshua said after the Irish and the Germans workers had troubles with the owners, the coloreds were hired as strikebreakers and that's when the riots between the blacks and the whites took place."

Lala chimed in, "Rosa that was a long time ago."

"I know. But I'd like to see where it all happened. And then Joshua said a rich man from New York named Pullman made a special sleeping car because he liked to sleep on the train when he came to visit the stockyards, and it was because of him that a lot of colored men got jobs as Pullman Car Porters."

Ann and Les laughed. Les said, "O.K. Aunt Rosa, so it's to the stockyards."

Lala said, "It seems that Joshua told you a lot about the stockyards."

"And many other things. And I'm planning to go see him too."

Les looked at Ann and raised his shoulders.

Rosa continued, "He's got three years left on his sentence and I haven't seen him since his trial in 1965, the year Papa died, so I feel I have to."

Lala was compassionate but said with a tinge of impatience, "O.K we'll go with you."

Unknown to the others, the visit appointment to the Cook County jail had been arranged weeks before Rosa arrived in Chicago.

Les, Ann, and Lala were asked to wait in an outer room when Rosa was called in to visit with her husband. They waited patiently for about thirty minutes. When Rosa walked back through the door of the inner room she was crying. Lala immediately went to console her. Rosa was led to a bench where Lala provided an endless supply of tissues from her purse. When Rosa was able to talk, she said, "I'm going to have to get a divorce." Then she broke down and cried some more.

Lala asked, "What happened?"

He became a Muslim. That's what happened."

Ann asked, "A what?"

Rosa repeated, "A Muslim."

Lala questioned," What's that?"

"As far as I can figure out it's a religion for colored people. But it's not new, it's as old as Catholicism, and it comes from Africa and most of the people over there belong to it."

"But I don't understand," said Lala.

"I don't either. He came in the room wearing a little black and white cap on his head, and I asked, "What is that?" and he said, "It's a cap that's worn by my brothers in Muhammad's temple." Rosa continued, "I was so confused that all I could do was cry."

Les remarked, "Ohhh, yeah, the Black Muslims. I've heard of them. They're big here in Chicago. They believe in a religion called Islam."

Then Rosa added, "And Joshua said when he got out, I would have to be a Muslim too." This brought a new deluge of tears. Everyone was silent. Then between sobs she added, "But you know I can't give up being Catholic."

"I know," said Lala.

Rosa continued, "He said Elijah Muhammad would not allow him to have a wife who belonged to the devil's religion."

Ann asked," Who is Elijah Muhammad?"

"I don't know, some nigger who calls himself Allah."

Lala gasped, and with an edge of admonishment in her voice, said "Rosa!"

"I'm sorry. I know, I'm not supposed to use that word but I'm so upset I can't think straight. It was awful! Now I have to get a divorce."

Lala put her arm around Rosa, and then looked around. The three other people in the room were looking at them with various expressions of displeasure. Lala said, "Let's get out of here."

They ended up at a small delicatessen not far away, and Les went to the counter for coffee and sandwiches.

Lala inquired, "Did you tell Joshua you were planning to get a divorce?"

"No, but I will. He just kept talking about his newfound Allah, how he had been with the white devil's religion all his life and now he had seen the true light. He says he's not a Catholic anymore, and that Ishmael, the son of Abraham is his true brother."

"Who is Ishmael?" asked Lala.

"I don't know. I don't know any of that crazy stuff he was talking. I'm so confused."

At that moment Les returned with the food in time to hear her last comment. "I know what you mean. So am I. Aunt Rosa, just forget about Joshua. Grandpop didn't like him anyway."

Rosa looked at him with surprise in her eyes. "Did Papa say anything bad about him to you?"

"No, but I could tell he didn't like him."

Lala tried to comfort her. "Rosa, darling. Let by-gones be by-gone. He was never right for you any way."

Then Les said with conviction, "Just divorce him and be done with it."

Rosa took a deep breath and a sip coffee. Then she reached across and squeezed Les' hand. "I'm sorry if I messed up your graduation. First I wanted to go to the stockyard and then to the jail and both of those places left me with bad memories." Then she smiled and added, "And bad smells."

Les said, "Aunt Rosa, where you wanted to go didn't bother me as much as Papa's leaving early."

Ann said, "Les, don't let what Papa did bother you. You know, he's like that but he loves you, and sooner or later he'll come around and be proud of whatever you do."

Lala said, "That's right. In the meantime, do what you have to do."

Les reflected on how complicated his family was getting to be—all the stuff with Aunt Vel and his Mama and Aunt Rosa, making a fuss over dividing the property, his Uncle Joshua in jail, becoming a Muslim, the talk from Aunt Rosa about divorce, the attitude of his father about his career choice. However, he was grateful that he didn't have the problems that his Aunt Rosa had, but at the same time he was not too happy about the ones he did have. Now he knew he could not expect any more financial help from his father, and he realized that if he kept on doing what he believed in, he would have to take advantage of any and everything that would help finance his path to his career.

Soon after his family left to go back to Estilette, he got a job on the staff of the Chicago PBS station as a director-in-training. At this time the public broadcasting system was a newly organized outgrowth of Educational Television, and some of the PBS stations were giving hands-up-training programs to prepare Negroes for staff positions. Les had seen the flyer announcing the program on a bulletin board in the green room earlier, so he applied. He really wanted to be an actor but he saw this opportunity as a stepping-stone on his career path, plus he needed the money.

*　　*　　*

By September 1969, Les was well into his director-training program at WTTW.

One evening after a long day in the studio, he decided to

go to Big Johns for a night of hearing the blues and relaxation. It was early in the morning when he arrived, and he was enjoying the sounds of the local musicians, when he saw Buddy Guy enter with an entourage from an engagement at Chicago's Auditorium Theatre. He went over and reacquainted himself, reminding Buddy that he was the nephew of Lighfoot from Estilette. Buddy remembered their first meeting that had taken place four years earlier right before he took off for a tour in England. He said, "That was in ..."

Les interrupted and filled in, "1965."

"And you're still here. What you be doing all this time?"

"I was in drama school. But right now I'm studying to be a television director."

Buddy's face lit up and he said, "Ain't this some shit. I know this man who's looking for a colored television director." He turned around and yelled, "Walter, git yo ass over here."

Les was introduced to Walter Burns, a civil rights activist who was in the planning stages of a series of television programs at a newly organized public broadcasting studio in Maryland. He was looking for and needed a director for a special program that he described as, the man quoted "A soap opera that tells the stories of a black family, at the same time illustrating the social, educational and economic dilemmas of their lives and revealing the various local, state and federal services that can be used to solve their problems."

Les could tell by the way this lean-hungry looking man rattled off the memorized description, that he was dedicated to his mission. Les was immediately captured and interested. Nothing like this, to his knowledge, had ever been done before; and he wanted to be a part of it. He could tell from their conversation that Walter was a civil rights activist and knew the ins and outs of political know-how, but he was not quite sure if Walter knew anything about television production. At least he didn't sound like he had much experience in the field, and neither did Les. However, at this time, it was not important.

Walter Burns was a forty-six year old, slim, brown-skin Chicago native, weighing no more than one hundred sixty pounds. His eyes were alive with determination and intensity giving proof to what he believed. He had been an activist in the integration of bars, hotels and restaurants wherever, whenever the call was issued, from Chicago east to Maryland. He had finally settled in Baltimore and formed The Urban Affairs Committee, a political leverage group, for the express purpose of making sure that the programming of this newly formed PBS station was integrated. He had recently followed Buddy Guy's performances from Laurel Maryland, to Monterey, California, to Washington, D.C, and finally to the Auditorium Theatre in Chicago, just to make sure that the blues audiences were integrated as they were supposed to be, and if not he'd have another situation to boycott.

Before the time of this early morning meeting was over, Les had expressed interest in joining Walter's project called ***Our Street*** that was scheduled to be produced at the Maryland Center for Public Broadcasting in Owens Mills, Maryland.

Chapter 7
Into the Breach

hree weeks later Les got a call from Walter Burns.

Walter had gotten Les' credentials from the Department of Theatre at Northwestern, and he had also found out the amount of the stipend that Les was getting at WTTW for his director-in-training program. He made an offer that Les found difficult to turn down. He said, "I want you to be the director of **Our Street,** and I'll match what you're getting at WTTW, plus I'll arrange for an experienced television director to be assigned to the show for six months so you can complete your director-in-training program on the job, after which your salary will be doubled and you'll be on your own as the director of the series."

It sounded too good to be true. It was evidence that Walter knew how to get things done. Les said, "Yes" before he hung up the phone, or had an opportunity to wonder why.

Why had Walter hired him knowing that he had no work experience as a director? Why was he, at twenty-four, given this great opportunity? He had just graduated, and had met

Walter by sheer chance. And there was another aspect of this new adventure that was also a curiosity; a man named Walter had recently left his life and now another with the same name had appeared to fill the void. Maybe there was some prophetic meaning to their meeting; and maybe as Naomi would say, "It was the work of the spirits," or maybe he was just lucky. It was all too confusing for Les to sort out, however he could use the money and if Walter felt he could do the job he would give it a shot. So he gave notice to WTTW, packed his bags and headed for Owens Mill, Maryland.

The early days on the job were not easy. There was no support staff--no production assistant, no stage manager, no property assistant, no costumer. There was no budget for sets, props, costumes, or even a tutor for the twelve-year-old actor cast as the youngest member of the Robinson family.

The casting that was done before Les was brought on board was dismal, to say the least. The person cast to play the father was simply not an actor. He was hypertensive, overweight, short of breath, could not remember lines, had to drive over ninety miles back and forth to the studio and was always late. The actor cast to play the mother was inept, could not remember lines or the blocking and paraphrased every speech, thereby making it impossible for the director to follow the writer's script. The actor chosen to play the daughter was totally wrong for the role, had no talent, did not understand the production process, and was cast because her mother had political clout with Walter. The actor who played the middle son was always late, inattentive, argumentative, undisciplined, and a drug user.

After a couple of rehearsals it was immediately apparent to Les that he would have to recast. He knew there was no way he could get anything accomplished with the actors whom Walter had chosen, so he began a search for a cast of competent actors.

He began attending arts programs in the Baltimore area and one evening he went to a dance program presented by a community group. Voila! There he saw the most sensitive and expressive male dancer that had he had ever seen, including dance programs attended while at Northwestern. He continued his search and attended a production of Steinbeck's *Of Mice and Men*. Again, the same creative artiste, Rashaan E. Howard. Not only could he dance but he was also a sensitive and perceptive actor. When they spoke after the performance, Les discovered he was a student enrolled in the acting program at Towson State College in Baltimore County. Rashaan was open to the idea of auditioning for the television series. Les was delighted. He had discovered the level of talent that he was seeking. After the formality of the audition process, Rashaan said he would consider leaving school to be cast as a full time actor with the series; but he had the problem of convincing his parents that this was the right move for his career. His parents were hoping that Rashaan would be the first of the family to finish college. They lived in an East Baltimore ghetto filled with bars, hustlers and street-corner criminals, and his parents did not want Rashaan to fall into this bottomless pit, and felt his way out was a college degree. All Les could do was to assure them that their son had the talent to go as far as opportunities would allow a television actor. Finally they said yes.

Now that this had been accomplished, Les went to Walter. "I need to recast around Rashaan."

"Why?" What's the problem?"

Les could not believe the question. But he was quick to realize that Walter did not know very much about production.

He said as softly and as convincingly as possible. "Rashaan is a very talented and instinctive actor. He has what cannot be taught. He is a natural. We have to build a new cast around his talent. Not one of the people in the present cast can even begin to approach his God given gifts. If we go with what is here, I can guarantee that, one, Rashaan will soon get disgusted and leave or two, the others cast members will feel so inferior that they will soon begin to create problems that will cost time and money, and we will never be able to accomplish anything positive.

Walter listened quietly. Then he said softly. "Go ahead."
Les began recasting around Rashaan.
A call for new auditions for actors for the new forthcoming series *Our Street* was issued.
Walter had now given Les full prerogative to move the series into full gear, and Les was able to find a competent and talented cast of characters. He also brought on a prolific and profound writer, Tommy Sterling, whose many theatrical plays about black urban life he was familiar with. Tommy immediately began turning out fantastic scripts.
Les had another meeting with Walter. "We need a budget for sets, props, costumes, and a tutor for Tyrone."
"Why? I thought our production budget would cover all of that." Walter said defensively.
Les said decisively, "Walter, listen. What they gave you is only enough to cover the salaries of the major producers and staff. The powers-that–be did not give you enough money for the success of production. We are programmed for failure because they did not provide enough money for the success of the series. They can always say, we gave you a chance and you blew it. As my grandfather use to say, this means they regard you as 'the spook who sits by the door.'"
Walter left the meeting with a new determination. "I'll get back to you."
Within a matter of a few days Walter was able to get the budget revised to adequately cover all production expenses, at a bare minimum, but nevertheless it was a fighting chance,

and Les realized that Walter had pulled off a major miracle.

By the time the drama series was ready to go into the taping of the first episode, Les was ready; but no one else was on his time schedule. The sets were not finished, the facilities of the studio had not been scheduled, a costume designer was not yet on staff, and this was only a few of the many other items that still needed to be implemented, although the budgets had been provided.

Les blew his top.

Walter sat silent and listened.

Les took no prisoners and issued an ultimatum, "Either all of the production needs are completed immediately, or I'm quitting."

Walter promised an answer the next day.

When they met, Walter gave him a program from a Broadway show, *The Man of LaMancha.* The program was folded back to reveal the lyrics of a song.

> *To dream the impossible dream*
> *To fight the unbeatable foe*
> *To bear with unbearable sorrow*
> *To run where the brave dare not go*
>
> *To right the unrightable wrong*
> *To love pure and chaste from afar*
> *To try when your arms are too weary*
> *To reach the unreachable star*
>
> *This is my quest*
> *To follow that star*
> *No matter how hopeless*
> *No matter how far . . .*

Les was pissed. "Walter this is bullshit. I've told you that unless all of these production needs were met, I was quitting, and now you give me a song and dance?"

Les walked out of the meeting. Determined that he had better things to do to prepare for life as an actor rather than getting experience as a director to help his journey. He was resolved that he would give notice the next day.

When Les got to his apartment that evening, he had a letter from Tommy Sterling, who was studying for a doctorate at the University of California in Santa Barbara. He was writing to say that he had just received approval from his department chairman that he would be getting credit towards his PhD in playwriting for the scripts that he was contracted to write for *Our Street*. He also said, "Les, in order to make the process easier, you are free to make whatever changes that are necessary so that the scripts will fit the time requirements of each episode." Les' anger began to cool. If Tommy was looking forward to using the scripts of the series for his dissertation, Les felt he could not disappoint him, plus since Tommy had enough faith to give Les carte blanche to edit his scripts; he could not let him down.

He reread the song, *The Impossible dream*, and realized that Walter had issued a challenge that he could not turn his back on. So the next day, with egg on his face, he said to Walter, "I'm sorry for yesterday. I'll give it a try."

Two months later Les got a memo from Fred Bramwell, the director of The Maryland Center for Public Broadcasting. It said:

"Les Martel,

Our Street has hit the air, and we can see the fruits of your labor. The dramatic direction was obvious throughout as being totally professional and impressive. Many thanks for your help in bringing this important series to the point of birth. We look forward to seeing examples of your talent in the future. Please extend my congratulations and best wishes to the members of the cast on a job well done."

Four years and ninety-five episodes later, the series

ended. With it came another memo from Fred Bramwell...

"I can't watch Our Street draw to a close without paying special tribute to you and Walter for making the whole thing possible. When Walter first told me he wanted to produce a weekly drama, I thought he was out of his mind. When he told me he had found a young producer/director willing to tackle the project, I began to wonder about his sanity. The thing I couldn't know was the incredible sense of commitment you were to bring to the show. It's been a fascinating experience from start to end, watching you two guys force success from impossible beginnings. That such a high level of artistry has developed with the show's growth makes the whole thing all the more incredible. Congratulations on a remarkable achievement. You have nothing but my highest respect and appreciation."

Les was overwhelmed. He knew that his grandfather would be proud to know he had touched the unreachable star. He remembered what he had heard him say many times, "Always do your best. Your best may not be the best, but it is all that God expects of you." Les had done his best and he was now ready to move on with the career of the actor he had dreamed of becoming. He was also finally convinced that his work as a director had helped prepare him for this challenge.

Now he felt he was ready to tackle Hollywood, the mecca of his dreams. He had many experiences as an actor in many different styles and types of roles in college, and in addition he had been involved with ninety-five episodes of a drama series, that had not only given him experience and a resume of work as a director, but had also put him in direct contact with the challenges of the actor in performance. He decided he was ready to move on to the next level of his career.

*　　*　　*

In 1974 Les went home to Estilette for a breath of fresh air before heading for Hollywood. His mama, Lala took him shopping to buy clothes for his new adventure in tinsel-town. As they passed the bookstore, Lala stopped to read the cover of a book in the window display. She said, "I know Mary Thomas, I used to teach her." Lala related an experience about a writing challenge she had given her students, "I'll never forget Mary's story for the assignment I gave to write about the most unforgettable experience of your life. It was very graphic, and I remember thinking at the time that this girl has a way with words." They went in and Lala bought the book, *Accept Me Now.*

Les read the book. It was the autobiography of Mary Thomas growing up in Estilette as the daughter of a share-cropper. The event that Lala remembered from Mary's tenth grade writing class was included in the book. At the time of this related incident of sexual abuse, Mary was eight years old and her fifteen-year-old sister and two younger brothers slept in the same bed. At some point during the night Mary was awaken by the feel of warm pee on her leg, from one of her brothers. She got up, took the top quilt, and went under the bed to continue sleeping. Early the next morning the voice of their papa, yelling through the opened door, that it was time to get into the fields, woke Mary up. She was too tired to heed his orders, so she turned over and went back to sleep. She was later awakened by the voice of her papa talking to her sister.

Mary's description in her book continued:

'"Papa's voice from the door asked, "You still sleep."
My sister answered, "I wuz jus getting up."
"Where the others?"
"In the fields wid mama, I guess."
"Das fine, 'cause I wants to be wid you."
I could see the springs sag down over my head as Papa got into bed.

My sister asked, "Papa, what are you doing?"

"Checkin' your womanhood."

"Why, Papa?"

"Yo little titties just peeking out like cotton buds makes my nature rise, and I wants to make love with you."

"But, Papa I ain't never done nothing like this before. Are you sure it's all right?"

"'Slong you don't tell nobody. Dis be our secret."'

Mary went on to describe, the bouncing bedsprings over her head and her fear that the entire bed would collapse.

My sister cried out, "It's hurting, Papa, I thinks you ought to stop."

And then Papa said, "It'll hurt for a little while then it'll feel good. Jus hold on."'

The remainder of the Mary's autobiography told of her schooling in Estilette, her college days at Northwestern University, her entry into the politics of Chicago, and finally her participation in the campaign for the election of John F. Kennedy. It was a fascinating story and Les was intrigued.

He told his uncle Johnny about what he had read. Lightfoot said, "I remember Mary's mother, Susie Mae Thompson. Her papa used to sharecrop for our papa. That's the girl that yo grandma Martha found bleeding to death after she was kicked by the mule she was unhitching."

Les asked, "When was that, Uncle Johnny?"

"Oh, a long time ago. Let's see." Lightfoot ran his hand through his graying hair and said, "Martha was about fourteen then, so that musta been over sixty-five years ago, and if I remembers correctly, Susie Mae was 'bout ten or so. Her papa was no good and left that chile to unhitch the mule and that baby girl was almost killed."

Les was fascinated by the things that his uncle recalled and was retelling. He also found it interesting that Mary's father and her mother's father were both sharecroppers.

85

He could tell from the contents of the book that Mary had struggled to break the chain of sharecropping that had tied her family to poverty. This was a story about over-coming adversity with success. A true Horatio Alger saga indicated by the title *Accept Me Now*. Les wrote a letter to Mary Thomas praising the book and congratulating her accomplishment.

Les also read another book before heading to Hollywood. *Phillip Fergerson; the man who made a Difference,* written by Alexandrine Estilette, the daughter of Stephen Estilette, that had finally been published in 1970, five years after Phillip's death. He was impressed and proud of the achieve-ments of his grandfather, much of which he was familiar with. He did however discover something that his grandfather had prophesied that he did not know—Ann Marie would be the next doctor in the family. Les had a conflicting attitudinal response to this revelation--agonized jealousy.

As always before, when his grandfather mentioned, sug-gested, or expressed that he follow in the footsteps of his uncle and become a doctor, Les felt a bit guilty that he had broken Phillip's heart by not complying. He knew that he did not have what it took to be a doctor. He didn't like to be around sick or infirmed people. He didn't like the sight of blood. And he got a greater pleasure from the response of silence from an audience, deep in thought, listening to the condensed truth of life from his every word. This he was not able to explain to his grandfather, except by saying, "*I want to be an actor*." Over time and the passing years this guilt turned into sorrow that he could not be what he knew his grandfather wanted him to be.

Now that he had read that his sister, Ann Marie, had been foreseen to fulfill his grandfather's wishes, he felt the green-eyed monster come alive in his mind. She was doing for Phillip what he could not do. This was not a small issue with

Les. He loved his grandfather very much and until now he believed that he was his favorite. With the revelation from the book, he now did not feel that this was necessarily the way it was. He remembered the Thanksgiving celebration, four years earlier, when Ann announced that she was planning to study medicine. And now he reads that his grandfather had announced years before, that this was what she would do. He wanted to know more about how Ann had decided to become a doctor.

Les packed his 1968 Ford Mustang Coup with the new clothes purchased by his mama, along with his other possessions and headed for Hollywood by way of Nashville. He had decided to spend a few days with Ann who was in her freshman year at Meharry Medical College.

Ann was surprised but delighted to see him. He arrived the day before the founder's day celebration of Fisk University, Ann's alma mater, located across the street from Meharry. Ann, eager to show off her handsome brother heading to Hollywood to be an actor, insisted that they attend. The famed Fisk Jubilee Singers were, as usual, on the program, and for the first time in his life Les heard the Negro Spirituals sung by a professional group. He remembered that his grandfather had talked about how the blues had developed from the spirituals and the work songs, and unlike most young people his age, Les liked the feel of history coming alive. He had sincerely enjoyed all that Phillip had exposed him to. And now more than ever he regretted that he had not tried harder to make himself become what his grandfather wanted him to be. And yes, he was also envious and jealous that Ann was able to do what he could not.

In the course of dinner after the performance of the Singers, Les got the opportunity to find out more.

"So where did you get the idea to become a doctor?" Les asked as he took the first sip from his glass of wine.

"Les, we've been over this before. I told you it just came to me while I was taking care of Grandpop."

"Yeah. I remember. But is that really how it happened? Are you sure that Grandpop didn't charm you into being a doctor?"

"What are you talking about? Grandpop never said one word to me about becoming a doctor. You were the one he was trying to convince, and everyone in the family knows that. What is wrong with you?"

It was clear that Ann was a bit peeved about Les questioning her motivation. About this time the waiter arrived with the entree and there was silence. After biting into her baked catfish, Ann said softly, "Are you feeling guilty?"

"Guilty? About what?"

"Not becoming a doctor."

After some moments of indecision about how to respond, Les shook his head and said, "No, that's not it at all. I was just wondering. It seemed that your decision came up out of the blue. I had never heard you say anything about that before."

"Does it make a difference?"

"No."

"Then let it be. How did you like the concert?"

It was clear that Ann wanted a change of subject, which Les welcomed. His feelings of guilt had been put to rest for the moment.

He said, "It was cool. I never heard a group of professionals sing the spirituals before. I really liked, *Go Tell it on the Mountains*, especially the fox who sang the lead."

"Oh, yeah, Marian. She and I had a class together while I was at Fisk. She's very talented and wants to be a professional singer. You know, you're good. You can spot talent."

"Yeah, I know."

Ann slapped him on the hand. "I'm talking about artistic talent and your mind is on something else."

"Yeah, I know." They laughed and enjoyed the moment.

They had a good time together, and Les had eased his mind about his grandfather's influence being switched to Ann when he didn't show interest in becoming a doctor. However, it was the sour grapes fairy tale all over again, and although Les could not admit it to himself, deep down inside he resented that Ann was on a path to accomplishing what he had chosen not to; it was a complicated emotional dilemma for Les, but he was satisfied by fooling himself into thinking that it did not matter anymore.

They drove back to Ann's apartment on Meharry boulevard and after Les had made up his bed on the couch and was preparing for an early morning departure there was a knock on the door. Ann, in her night gown and robe, went to the door and asked, "Who is it?"

The answer came back, "Marvin, open the door."

Ann rolled her eyes at Les, who, in preparing for bed had taken off his shirt and was drinking a glass of water near the kitchen door. Ann whispered in his direction, "I forgot."

She opened the door with apology in her voice. "Marvin, I'm sorry. I forgot. Please forgive me. My brother came to town and I forgot all about our date to go to the movies."

Marvin took a step into the room. His eyes fell on Les standing in the doorway to the kitchen bear-chested with a drink in his hand. His face showed his displeasure.

Ann looked into his eyes and said, "Meet my brother Les. Les, this is Marvin Jefferson."

Les advanced with his hand extended.

Marvin said, "Yeah, I've heard this brother shit before," and he slapped away Les' hand.

Ann was horrified. "Marvin, he is my brother and he just dropped by on his way to Los Angeles and I forgot about our date. I'm sorry."

Marvin said impulsively. "Yeah, I've heard about you

Creole bitches from Louisiana and all the men you have."

As soon Marvin's mouth was emptied of that last word, it was filled again with Les' fist. Marvin fell backwards into the hallway. Les was on him like white on rice and kicked him in the ass as he pushed him down the stairs to the next floor. Les, standing at the top of the stairs said, softly with conviction, "Mind your manners."

By this time Ann was standing next to Les. She looked down as Marvin got up, glared back at the two of them above, pulled down his jacket and straightened his tie, then walked out of the door with resentment and anger.

Ann looked at Les and asked, "Did you have to do that?"

As Les turned and walked into the apartment he said, "Yes. He needed to be taught a lesson."

Early the next morning Les headed to Los Angeles.

Chapter 8

A Plunge into Waywardness

It was 1974, and Les discovered that Los Angeles was vast, and traffic was a nightmare.

He had never seen anything like it before, except on the Demolition Derbies that he had watched on television. He didn't believe anything like that happened in real life, but it seemed that the cars driven on the freeway came close to being like the ones he had seen on the demolition shows. The lane changing was unbelievable and the speed that most cars were traveling was greater than the posted speed of the freeway. And just when he had made up his mind to keep up with the speed of the car in front, he looked up in time to see a chain of red lights glaring down as far as his eyes could see. He jammed on the brakes and slid his Mustang to a stop just before slamming into the car in front.

From then on, the freeway was a start-stop parking lot. He had just crossed into the city limits of Los Angeles.

Hours later when he finally reached Hollywood he was so hungry, he could have eaten the pizza sign with the question,

"Had a piece lately?" He didn't want pizza; he needed something to stick to his ribs. Then Les saw a "Fat Burger" sign and drove into a triangular parking lot at the intersection of LaCienga and San Vincente Boulevard. He went in and sat at the counter along with an assortment of strangely dressed and weird looking characters. Although it was one-thirty in the afternoon, there were customers dressed in tuxedos wearing dark glasses, others in jeans with rhinestones and high heels, some in titty revealing, tight fitting halter tops with bare bellies showing navel jewels, and others in mini-skirts revealing crotch and panty lines. There was a lot to see, and as his eyes traveled over the occupants of the booths and the stools at the counter, his mind's eye asked, with wonderment, *What weirdness has this trip wrought?"*

Just then a tattooed, gum-chewing guy with silver balls implanted in his eyebrows, stopped in front of his counter seat, rolled his eyes and asked, "What'll you have?"

It was hard for Les to look at the guy, or whatever he wanted to be called, without laughing. So he looked past him at the menu on the back wall and said, "I'll take the number two."

"With fries or onion rings?"

"What?" Les asked.

The guy raised his pinky finger and pointed backwards without turning around and said, "In the small print. You've got a choice. Fries or onions rings."

"Fries."

"And to drink?"

Les asked, "What are my choices?" Thinking that this may have also been in the small print that he had not read.

The guy taking the order pursed his lips, put the backs of his hands on his hips and said, "Look, fella, I don't have all day, decide what you want to drink so I can take your order."

Les said impulsively, "Doctor Pepper."

"Doctor who? Well, I assure you he's not here. Look, fella, just tell me what you want to drink. Pepsi or coke."

"Pepsi." Les said getting a little pissed.

"Fine. To go or eat in?"

By this time Les had had it. He was tired. He was hungry. He had had a long stressful trip, and all he wanted was a hamburger. He reached out and grabbed the guy's shirt and pulled his face in close to his and said softly, "Eat in. Got it?" Then he pushed him backward.

The waiter straightened up, flashed his eyes, regained his composure and said," All right. No need to get hostile." Then he walked away, twisting his backside.

A leather wearing man with the spiked collar, sitting next to Les, leaned over and said; "I can tell you're not from here. You gotta be firm with the faggots in this town. It's kick ass time or they'll fuck you over."

Les smiled, nodded, and said, "Thanks."

The burger was good. Well cooked and juicy, loaded with lettuce, tomatoes, pickles, onions, mayonnaise and mustard. It hit the spot and satisfied his empty gnawing stomach. Les wiped away the messy, mixture of catsup and mustard from his face, left a pile of bloody looking napkins on the counter, and went to his car.

Now he could think.

Plan.

Decide.

He had just arrived to chase his dream, and his first task was to find a place to live. He looked at the map and found Hollywood Boulevard. It was the best-known location, from where one could see the big Hollywood sign in the hills overlooking the city. That's where he would begin to look.

After driving around for about an hour, looking for vacancy signs posted on likely places that he felt would be acceptable, he found himself parked on Argyle Street, in front of a large grilled iron gate, through which he could see an inviting pool, surrounded by bikini clad women lounging in the sun. He pushed the button labeled office and was buzzed in.

After filling out several forms and paying a deposit and the first month's rent in cash, he was shown to a one bedroom furnished efficiency on the second floor. The bed was a small double with a firm mattress that was tolerable. The kitchen area, just large enough for one to reach into the refrigerator, take out a dish and put it on the stove without moving a step, was cozy and the entire place was clean and comfortable and looked out over the pool. From the back window he could see the hills above with winding streets covered with lush greenery and eucalyptus trees, along with a clear view of the Hollywood sign. Les had arrived in Mecca.

He put his things away and collapsed, fully clothed, on the bed without turning down the spread. It wasn't long before he was dreaming of his newfound destiny.

Les had discovered a fantastic script with Clark Gable playing a role like Rhett Butler in *Gone with the Wind* who had just acquired a large southern plantation and was looking for a foreman who could manage all of his slaves. And being the benevolent master that he was, he chose a young, strong, overseeer, who was, in reality, his son from a sexual liaison with a woman from the Caribbean. Les was cast in that role. The movie was a hit and Les was nominated for the Academy Award, which he won, and became the first Negro to have that honor.

He didn't know how long he was asleep, but he was awakened from his ecstasy of flashing lights and interviews, by an urgent knock on the door. Les rolled out of the bed and opened the door. There stood one of the ladies he had noticed lounging around the pool when he passed on his way to the apartment. She was still glistening with droplets of water sliding on the surface of the oils that covered her entire body. She was very shapely and the bikini barely covered the parts of her body that he was sure she wanted to be seen. She had attractive blue eyes and a beautifully contoured mouth that seductively moved with every chew of the gum that rolled on her tongue.

She said sexually, "Hi. Just thought I'd welcome you to Shangri-La."

"Shangri-La?"

"Yes. That's the name of this place."

For a moment Les's mind shifted to the mythical city in the book *Lost Horizon,* by James Hilton, which he had read in literature class at Northwestern. In this book, Shangri-La was utopia, a place of peace, a permanent happy land, isolated from the world. He looked out over the young woman's shoulder at the mirage of activity around the pool; the exact antithesis of the word title, shrugged and said, "Oh. I didn't know."

"Well, it may not matter to you. But that's what it's called. It's nice here and if you've read the bible, it's really the land of milk and honey that's told about...know what I mean... honey...by the way what is your name?"

"Les."

"Well, Les, I take it that's short for Lester, but I like Les better. My name is Shiela and I live in the apartment right underneath you, so if there is anything you want, or anything I can do to make your stay comfortable just come on down."

Les didn't know what to say. She had come on so directly he was lost for words. Anyway he was tired from the long drive and just wanted to be left alone. He said, "Nice to know you Shiela. And I'll remember, if there's anything I need, I'll drop by."

"Don't forget. Welcome to Shangri-La."

Les watched her walk away. There was no mistaking the

sexy come hither movement of her back-side, and he was sure that she was in the same profession as his Aunt Vel.

Les closed the door and fell back on the bed to get that much needed rest before he began his search for a job.

* * *

Early the next morning he headed for the Screen Actors Guild office. They had just opened and he went up to the counter and asked for an application for membership.

He was told, "You have to work for a producer that has an agreement with SAG before you are eligible."

"And how do I go about finding this work?

"Your agent will know how to get you auditions with the right producers."

"I don't have an agent."

The girl smiled and said sarcastically, "Well you have to get one, just like everybody else does."

"How do I find one?" was his immediate reply.

"Go the book stall on Hollywood and Vine and get a directory."

Les left the SAG office and picked up a directory.

After browsing through the half-inch thick book filled with agents, agencies, producers and studios, he closed his eyes and randomly opened the directory to the section marked agencies and pointed a finger down to the page. It landed on the firm of Winkey, Blinkey and Nodd.

Les found the address, entered the fifteen storied building on Sunset Boulevard, and told the girl at the desk that he was an actor who had just come to town and needed an agent. She gave him a form to fill out and told him to have a seat, "Someone will see you soon."

After more than an hour later, Les was ushered into an office where he waited for another half-hour. Finally a short chubby man, wearing a diamond earring, a flowered silk shirt hanging loose over a pair of pressed blue jeans, entered and approached with an outstretched hand. Les got up from the couch and shook his hand.

The man said, "Hi. Sorry to have kept you waiting. I was in a meeting. My name is Andy Blinkey, and I'm one of the partners. You can call me A.B., What is your name?"

"Les Martel."

A.B., sat in the upholstered chair facing the couch and Les sank into the former impression he had made on the couch. A.B., silently looked at Les and smiled. Then he said, "Well Les, first of all we'll have to do something about your name. I assume that Les is short for Lester."

Les nodded his head but didn't say a word. Already he didn't like this guy.

"El Tigre. That's what we'll call you."

Les looked at A.B., and repeated slowly. "El Tigre? Then he asked, "What does that mean?"

"The tiger. That's who you are. You seem like a tiger. I can tell."

"So, now I'm El Tigre Martel?" He asked with as much sarcasm as he could without sounding too aggressive.

"No. Just El Tigre. That's all. It's short and strong. And it'll get you work. Trust me. I know. Do you have a resume?"

Les extended the two page listing containing everything that he had acted in from Holy Ghost school to Northwestern University. A.B., silently looked it over while nodding his head. "You did some impressive work at Northwestern. Lots of leads in theatre but nothing in film. We'll have to do something about that. Did you complete the application that Jan, the girl out front, gave you?"

Les extended the information form that he had filled out.

A.B., looked it over and said. "There's a mistake."

"A mistake?"

"Yes. You put down Negro for race."

"That's who I am."

"We'll change that. You'll never get work in this town being colored. Plus you don't look colored." A.B., took a pen out of his shirt pocket and scratched out the entry and spelled aloud as he wrote. "W-H-I-T-E. That's your race now." Then he drew a line through Les' name and said,

"E-L-T-I-G-R-E. That's your name now. I like you. Tell Jan to give you the name and address of our photographer and get some head shots. When that's done I'll send you out on auditions. Any questions?"

Les shook his head, "No." But questions formed in his mind. *Why did I let him lie about my name and my race? I know that Grandpop would not have approved, and I don't like doing this, although I do feel that his strategy might be successful in getting me work as an actor.*

He remembered the situation with Dr. Shaffer, who had such deep prejudice, stopped his performance on stage even though he didn't look colored, so he guessed he should not make an issue about the change of name and race. A*fter all, I came to Hollywood to act and it seems to me that he is setting this up to happen.*

Les exited the Sunset Boulevard address and headed to his apartment. It was about three o'clock, and he figured to relax, take a swim, have some dinner and go to a blues club later in the evening.

He had just changed into his swim trunks when a breeze brought the seductive aroma of jasmine to his nostrils. He did not know what it was about that sweet smell, but ever since he arrived in Los Angeles that particular fragrance seemed to be everywhere, and it was like an aphrodisiac. Even the air that he breathed in this place was urging him to think sex. The musky aroma aroused his libido.

Les opened the door with the intent of heading to the pool. Standing there was Shiela holding a tray covered by large cloth napkins. He was surprised, and realized that he must have missed hearing a knock. She seemed to also be surprised, and starting giggling.

Les said, "Oh, have you been knocking very long?"

"No. I just got here. Looks like you're going for a swim."

"Yes. I thought I'd try out the pool."

She walked right past him into the apartment, and went directly to the nearby table and put down the tray. He realized, as she passed, that the jasmine was her perfume. She was dressed in a colorful sarong that was split up the center revealing her legs as she walked.

Les followed her to the table. She lifted one of the napkins to reveal a plate filled with baby back ribs, cole slaw, potato salad, and grapes. The other napkin stilled covered the mound of whatever was underneath, which he assumed were glasses and a bottle of something to drink.

Les asked, "What's this?"

"Dinner. It's your welcome meal."

"Look,…er…"

She filled in his struggling attempt to remember her name.

"Shiela."

"Yeah. Shiela. Look, Shiela. I had other plans for the evening. It's very nice of you to do this, but…"

Before he could get the rest of his thought out of his mouth, she put a finger on his lips and said, "Don't say another word. I've just changed your plans for the evening." Then she slid her hand from his mouth down the center of his chest and across his left nipple as she moved toward the door, which she closed and stood against with her back while she turned the thumb lock.

Les was not ready for a pick up. He didn't know who she was or what she was about. She was very attractive, and she was wearing the jasmine perfume that turned him on. But there were so many unknowns about her he was uneasy. He felt he had to resist.

He said, "Look here Shiela, we just met yesterday. It's too soon for all of this."

She moved very close to him and said softly, "Oh, ain't you a cautious, wary fella, Les. But you don't have to worry. I'm not going to hurt you. I just brought you dinner because I thought that you might be hungry."

She moved to the table and began dividing up the food onto a second plate that was sitting underneath the one that contained the fixings.

He watched. She went about her chores with precision and expertise; she had not scrimped on anything. There were no paper plates; the dishes were real. The eating utensils were stainless steel not plastic, so he could tell she had put some thought into the planning. After the food was divided on both plates she took off the second napkin revealing two glasses with a bottle of Champagne. She had thought of everything.

As Les was trying to figure out what this was all about, she reached over and gently grabbed the waistband of his swim trunks and pulled him to a chair at the table.

"Have a seat and enjoy your food."

He followed her instructions and sat. She settled into the chair across the table from him, and said the blessings "Good God, good food, let's eat." Then she crossed her legs, and he saw for the first time a tattoo on the inside of her left leg. It was a picture of a man and woman in a sexual position with a caption underneath that read, *Eat drink and be merry*. Although he had seen her in a bikini lounging on a chair at the pool, he had not noticed the tattoo.

She observed his focus of attention on her legs and she asked, "Do you like what you see?"

"That is a nice tattoo."

"Why don't you try your ribs?" Then she reached over to his plate, took a rib, thrust it into his mouth and held it while he bit around the bone and chewed away the meat. Then she slid the bare bone out of his mouth, placed it on the center of her extended tongue, closed her lips over the bone and began to suck on it. She closed her eyes and made sexual sounds of *ohhhhs* and *ahhhhs*.

Les asked, "Is it <u>that</u> good?"

Shiela said, "Here bite into this." She pushed a grape into his mouth and said, "Pretend it's a titty."

After laughing, Les bit into the grape. And they began eating the food and drinking the Champagne, with few words spoken. Les thought it was time to find out who he was dining with, and he asked, "Who are you?"

"A country girl from a small town in Iowa."

"Is that the truth?"

"What do you care if it's the truth or not? All you have to care about is enjoying what you have."

"And what do I have?"

"Me. If you want me."

At this point Les had a problem. She was beautiful. She was desirable. She was sexy. He was horny. His dick was bulging and stretching the fabric of his swim trunks. She reached over and gently traced the profile of his enlarged organ. Les felt he had to resist the temptation, and pushed her hand away.

She repeated, "Like I said, if you want me."

So he said, "And why should I want you?"

Suddenly, Shiela started crying. They were real tears.

Les could not believe what was happening. She had come on as a real professional hooker with all of the pizzazz that he had heard tell about, and just as he was about to cave in to her cunning and sweet talk, she collapsed into remorse.

She asked softly, in short staccato breaths of air, "Why should anyone want me?" She picked up one of the napkins and dried her eyes, and continued. "I'm sorry. I just can't help it."

"What's going on here?" Les knew something was not right, and he wanted to get to the bottom of whatever was happening.

"You must think I'm an awful person, but I'm not. I am really a country girl from Iowa. I came to Hollywood determined to show the people back home that I could make it as an actress. And about three weeks ago I got cast in a film called *The Scarlet Hooker*. After the first week of shooting the director pulled me aside and told me that he liked the way I looked and moved, but he said that I needed to really get into the part, and that I needed to do some research and learn how real prostitutes worked."

"And you're telling me this is your research?"

"Some of it. For a few days I followered the girls on Hollywood boulevard and watched the way they picked up men and did the do. But it didn't seem right for the character that the script called for. I decided to try a more sophisticated and subtle approach. I wanted to make the men I chose want me more than I wanted their money. So I did everything to make myself desirable and attractive, including the tattoo."

Les felt he was now getting some answers to his many questions and he continued to probe. "And how do I fit into all of this?"

"You checked into the Shangri-La and walked past my chair."

Les laughed. "That's all?"

"That was enough. It was really like the script, because

the girl I'm playing finds her johns in the pool areas of the rich resorts and fancy hotels."

"So what went wrong?"

"You asked, "'Why should I want you?'"

Les was now getting more fascinated by the minute and decided to follow wherever his curiosity took him. "And that made you cry?"

Shiela got up from the table and began gathering the plates, glasses and utensils and placing them on the tray. She said, "Look, Les I made a mistake. I'm sorry." At that moment Shiela, seemed to take on a different persona. She took the gum out of her mouth and dropped it on one of the plates; her eyes were mostly downcast and had lost the sexual-come-hither sparkle that was so obvious a few moments before.

"What happened?"

"Your question took me a long ways back."

She picked up the tray and headed toward the door. Les followed. She stopped at the locked door, turned and looked back over her shoulder. "My hands are full. Could you unlock the door please?"

He answered. "No, not until you tell me what happened."

"It's not important."

"But it is to me."

Shiela turned and looked into his eyes. He felt that she was about to cry again. He could see a sincere and honest feeling surging from her blue eyes along with the lingering aroma of jasmine drifting from her body. He reached out and took the tray from her hands and brought it back to the table.

She began crying again. He went over, put his arm around her shoulder, and walked her back to a chair. As she sat, the edge of her sarong fell open, and she pulled it up to cover her thighs. This gesture of modesty was not the behavior of the hooker who had entered his apartment a few minutes earlier.

Les continued probing. "What's the matter?"

"I'm not like that girl who brought this tray, although I did want you to have something to eat." She smiled, then wiped her eyes with the napkin. "You're a very kind man and something about you made me feel stained, especially the way you said, *Why should I want you?* I had heard that question before and all of a sudden I was back home in Ottumwa."

Les made himself comfortable and sat on the floor at her feet. The same way he had sat at the feet of his grandfather when he was about to hear information that he didn't know before. She continued.

"It all started after the homecoming game. I was the first maid to Sandra Miller, the most popular girl in school. All the boys were in love with her, and the word was out that she was free and easy. But I wasn't. I was in love with Brad, the star quarterback of the team and we had been dating for over six months, and we had never done it. But it was common knowledge that most of his teammates dating the other girls had. Well, after the game, which Brad won by throwing four touchdown passes, there was to be the big homecoming dance and celebration, and it was all arranged that I would go with Brad. As was the custom, the winning football was presented to the homecoming queen by the captain of the winning team. So Brad made the presentation to Sandra. I was proud of Brad and I was happy for my friend Sandra because she didn't have a steady boyfriend, and I figured that after she got the game ball, there would be lots of boys who would be proud to have her as a steady. I was standing right next to her when Brad put the ball into her hands. Then he leaned over and kissed her on the mouth, and after the kiss he said, 'You're going to be my date for the dance tonight.' I was shocked because it was all arranged that we were going together, I even had my corsage that he had pinned on before the game. I said, 'But Brad I am supposed to go with you to the dance.' He looked at me and said, 'Why should I want you? You're only a maid, not the queen.' I was never so hurt before in my life. I cried for two weeks and I was ashamed to show my face. I left Ottumwa and came to Hollywood."

Her story had found a soft spot. Les shifted his position from sitting on the floor at her feet, to kneeling between her legs and giving her the kiss that she did not get from Brad.

The intoxication from the aroma of the jasmine and the empathy from her story, induced him to throw caution to the wind and he descended into waywardness. This was the first time that Les had been with a woman who had done it for money. He didn't know exactly how to begin, so he started to make love with a kiss. It was a long, tender, kiss on the lips, the type he figured that she had wanted to get from Brad. When his tongue had awaken Shiela's baser instincts, that had recently been perfected by research into the habits and practices of a street whore, she began to fuck. She bit into his lips, with a pleasure-giving sharpness that was perceived as an aphrodisiac, then his ears, and from there, she bit and sucked from one titty to the other. Then in one skillful movement she stripped away his trunks and thrust his dick into her mouth and continually circled it with her tongue, as was demonstrated earlier with the rib bone. Les realized that he was being fucked, by a professional, not being made love to by a country girl from Ottumwa, Iowa.

When he was awakened by the warm sun of morning, Shiela and her tray were gone.

Chapter 9
Trouble in LaLa Land

The day after his night of waywardness with Sheila, Les answered a call from his agent, A.B. He had arranged for him to attend an open audition, which he said, "Is a cattle call, but it will get your feet wet and give you some experience and exposure to the industry. It's for an untitled film the name of which will be decided later."

Les dressed quickly, for the last minute call, and took off to find the address. After heading in the wrong direction on the Hollywood Freeway, then getting off and taking several wrong turns and streets to get back in the right direction, he arrived late, which was reason enough to conclude that Los Angles was so large, and traffic was so heavy, that he should always leave with plenty of time to spare.

It seemed there were hundreds of people in the line ahead of him and others were milling around in small groups, some talking, some drinking colas, and some sitting quietly on chairs and benches around the large rehearsal hall. He finally got to the registration table and was given a form to fill out and be returned with his headshot and resume. Then he joined other hopefuls sitting around.

After about an hour the name *"El Tigre"* was called several times, and after looking around to see which person would answer to a name like that, he finally realized it was his new name.

He was ushered into a smaller room with five people sitting at a long table filled with stacks, of what he later learned were called *sides,* the scenes used for auditions. The people at the table were sitting behind hand-lettered nameplates that identified *Producer, Producer's Assistant, Studio Rep, Director, and Director's Assistant,* who he recognized as the person who had called him into the room. It all had a feeling of being official and important.

His heart wanted to jump out of his chest and he tried to calm himself, remembering that an adrenalin rush was good for performance. But what he was really feeling was more like fear and he perceived his body trembling. The director's assistant put a *side* in his hand and pointed to a spot in front of, and about ten feet away from the table. Les went to the spot, closed his eyes and took a few deep breaths until the trembling in his legs subsided.

Then he heard an impatient voice say, "Well, are you going to read or not?"

Les opened his eyes and turned back the title page of the *side* and started reading.

"Interior Dining Room Bates house - day." A voice stopped him.

"El Tigre, I'll read that. You read the character Jordan. His speeches are underlined."

Then the Director's Assistant turned and looked back at the director, hunched his shoulders and raised his hands in a gesture as if to say he doesn't know what he's doing.

The Director replied, "Start over."

This time the assistant picked up the description of the scene that Les had read previously and he went on, "Jordan is washing windows, J.B. is talking to him."

J.B. - "Amy is a counselor. She knows what she is doing, and she is giving her time to...

JORDAN - "I didn't ask her to."

J.B. - "But I did."

JORDAN - "Why?"

J.B. - "Because you need to learn to read."

JORDAN - "I reads just fine."

JB- "At a sixth grade level. You're nineteen and you've been out of school since you were sixteen."

JORDAN - "Why the fuck do you care?"

J.B. - "Because...

JORDAN - "Yeah, I know... (Mimicking) 'It makes me feel better.' You know I'd just as well be back in prison as reading and doing all these chores and shit."

J.B. -"Everybody carries their weight around here."

JORDAN - "And it seems like all you do is throw yours around."

J.B. – "Anytime...

JORDAN - "Yeah, I know, anytime I don't like it here I can go back to prison."

J.B.- "You have a negative attitude that makes it tough on anybody who tries to help...and you're doing a lousy job on that window. Do it over."

When Les got to the last page. It didn't seem to Les to be conclusive enough. He asked, "Is this all there is?" The assistant turned to look at the Director, who said, "Give him the next side."

The assistant put some more pages into his hands and Les asked, "What is this scene about?"

The assistant said very impatiently, "Look, just read what's on the side we don't have time to talk or explain."

The Director held up his hand and said, "It's all right, Rickie." Then he turned to Les, and said. "The character J.B. is the director of an alcohol drug abuse treatment facility named Bates House, which is one of the titles of the film that we are presently debating. Well, JB works closely with the prisons by detoxing abusers, and this young guy named Jordan is one of the patients that the prison has assigned to JB for recovery. And to make a long story short, through a series of events, it is discovered that Jordan is JB's illegiment son. Now with that as a back-story, read the next scene with Rickie."

Les said, "Thanks, that helps a lot."

The assistant began reading. "Interior of the meeting room - day. All of the regular patients are present and Frank has just told his story."

AMY - "Any one else needs to vent?" (Jordan stands)

JORDAN- "Hi, my name is Jordan and I'm an alcoholic. In high school I had a real good friend name Jack Daniels. I used to visit with him every day and then I got kicked out of school. After that, all day long I'd hang out with my friends, and then I ran away from home and I got mixed up with some dudes who killed a man and I went to prison. While in prison I was introduced to another friend name Heroin and we got real tight and I'd visit with him 'most every night. And that's been my whole life. (After a pause he continues) I haven't seen my mother for two years. She's very pretty..... a fashion designer and model. I stopped writing to her 'cause..... it was...well, I donno, maybe 'cause I didn't write too good, then when she came out to the prison to see me, I wouldn't go out to see her. One of these days I'm gonna make her proud of me again and then I'll change my name back to what it was before. I feel real bad about the hurt I brought to my mother, and it seem like all she ever got was hurt. She was engaged to marry my daddy but he left before I was born and she never heard from him after that. She would cry every time she told me about him, and all I ever did was to add to her pain."

When Les finished the speech the room was quiet. He felt the same silence he had felt in performance when he knew he had done a good job.

He went to the table, put his side on the stack, and said to the Director, "It's the sins of the father."

The Director asked, "What does that mean?"

Les said, "That should be the title of your film. <u>The Sins of the Father</u>."

No one said a word and Les headed for the door. On the way out he heard the voice of the Director say, "Thanks for the title."

When Les walked through the door leading into the large rehearsal room, he heard the name Caryn Ericksen called. Shivers went through his body and he stopped, petrified.

Then he saw her approach.

Their eyes met.

They embraced and tears flowed.

"Les!"

"Caryn!"

"It's been a long time." Les got in the first words.

"I don't believe it. Here in Hollywood, we meet again."

The Assistant Director was getting impatient, and he yelled out, "You're coming in or not?"

Caryn kissed Les again and said, "Wait for me." Then she disappeared behind the door into the audition room.

*   *   *

They headed to the Melting Pot, a restaurant on Melrose Avenue that Les had passed when he was looking for a place to live. She followed in her car as he struggled, through traffic, trying to find the landmark patio that he had remembered seeing. They finally found parking spaces two blocks away, and settled in looking forward to having a delightful luncheon reunion.

His first words were, "What happened after I left Bemidji?"

Caryn began the most incredible story that Les had ever heard, and she answered all of the questions that he had conjured up about their relationship and the reason she had not returned to school.

"After you left, I went home and waited for my parents to return from their cruise. The day after the fire, a call came on the message machine from the fire department saying that our cabin had burned down. There was no mention of Buster being found so I didn't know what had happened. I was a basket case. There was nothing that I could do but wait for my parents to return. Finally, when they did I told them what had happened. They were horrified and concerned for my well being because I told them the story that Buster had come in and tried to molest me and I had to hit him in the head to defend myself, and the fire started when he fell against the table and knocked over the candles. And I left and came home, believing that he had died in the fire.

The next day Daddy contacted the fire department and found out that there was no body found in the cabin. I didn't know what to say. They looked at me with suspicious eyes and began to question me about what had really happened. What could I tell them? I didn't know what had happened to Buster or what else to say."

Les was as flabbergasted as she was. He asked, "So what happened then?"

My parents tried to find Buster. There was no trace of him anywhere. He had disappeared. There was no evidence of a body being burned in the ashes. There was no trace of his truck outside. Of course the fire had melted the snow so no tracks were left. They contacted the place where he lived and found out that he had left a few days after Christmas and left no forwarding address. It was all very very mysterious and I began to slowly go out of my mind."

Les asked, "What do you think happened?"

"I came to the conclusion that he must have gained consciousness before the fire got to him and he found his way to daddy's wine cellar through the trap door in the kitchen, which he knew about, and waited out the fire. After the firemen left he came out and drove away in his truck. It was dark and the firemen probably didn't even notice the truck parked in the trees."

"Why do you think he didn't come out and tell what he knew had happened?"

"He must have been frightened. He was scared of my father. Buster knew my father had lots of influence in town and Buster knew he could have him put in jail for attacking me. Plus he knew that the fire started because he was drunk and I don't think he wanted my father to know that, so he just left town."

Les asked, "And after you told your parents what had happened and they did not find a body, what did they do then?"

"Oh, it was hell for me. They believed that I had lied and created the Buster story to cover something that I had done to cause the fire, so they would not let me go back to school, until I told them the truth of what had really happened--said it was my punishment. I begin to have nightmares and horrible images of flames consuming Buster's body while he chased me through the woods yelling, 'you're old enough now.' And I couldn't get away from him, I tried to run but my feet kept sinking into the snow, and he got closer and closer. It was terrible. I'd wake up yelling for help and my mother would come into my room and hold me close and reassure me that everything was all right and I was safe at home in my bed. But after several weeks of this they put me under the care of a psychiatrist friend, and I had weekly session for the next two years. When that was over I had to get away, so I came to Hollywood to continue my career."

For the next two hours they filled in the space of the last four years in both of their lives. It was a wonderful reunion and Les was looking forward to rekindling their intimate relationship.

It was time to leave and Les called for the check. When it came he reached for his wallet and found his money was gone. He knew that he had over three hundred dollars left after paying his apartment rent. He realized that Shiela had taken his money along with the tray of dirty dishes, when she left in the morning. He was pissed. Caryn had to pay for the lunch and they said goodbye and he headed back to the Shangri-La to find Shiela and get back his money.

*　　*　　*

He banged on the door of the apartment below his; there was no response. He turned back and surveyed the area around the pool to make sure that he had not missed her sunning herself. She was not there. He banged again. Finally the door was opened by a sleepy sexy looking lady tying the sash of a see-through robe over her panties and bra, "Yeah, what do you want?"

"I'm looking for Shiela."

"She ain't here." Then she started to close the door.

Les put out his hand to stop the door. "Where is she?"

"Look, mister, all I know is. She ain't here. You got business with her, leave your name and number and I'll have her call you."

113

"What's her name?"

"Shiela. Just like you said."

"No, I mean her last name."

"Longstarr. Shiela Longstarr."

"What kind of name is Longstarr?"

"Indian I think. She's Native American. Look mister, what's this all about?"

"She owes me some money."

The lady laughed. "Well, that's a switch-a-rue. Usually you Johns owe her money. Mister whatever you name is, take all of this up with Shiela. I works nights and was trying to catch up on my beauty rest. Now if you don't mind, I'd like to get back to sleep."

"Thanks." And before she closed the door, Les said, "One more thing, where could I find Shiela right now?"

The lady rolled her eyes impatiently and said, "She's working. If this will get rid of you, you might try Hollywood and LaBrea and points west near the Chinese Theatre."

"What's the name of the place she works?"

The lady laughed again. "Mister you don't know nothing. That's the area she works. Now leave me be. Goodbye."

Before she could close the door, he leaned in and planted a kiss on her cheek. "Thanks."

"Yeah, for the freebie." She smiled as she pushed the door close.

Les parked in a restaurant lot on LaBrea near Hollywood boulevard. He looked up and down in both directions. No Shiela. He got out and walked the street heading west as the lady said. Sure enough there was Shiela leaning in the passenger side of a BMW on the curb in front of the Chinese Theatre. She was doing streetwalking solicitations. Whether she was doing research or not, he did not know, and really did not care. He just wanted to get back the three hundred some dollars that she had taken. When the car pulled away she walked to a bench in front of the theatre and took a seat. Les sat down next to her.

"Hi, Shiela. Remember me?"

She seemed baffled at first then recognition dawned. "Oh, yeah the nice man upstairs."

"Yeah the nice trusting man upstairs, from whom you stole money. I want my money back."

"Oh that. I just borrowed some money 'cause I was short and owed my rent, but I plan to pay you back."

Les looked into the innocent eyes that he had seen the night before, when she told her sob story about Brad, and the same jasmine aroma wafted into his nostrils. But he knew that she was a thief. He said with anger in his voice. "I want my money now."

She said, "I have some of it. But I have a debt to pay and I'll give it all back when I come home."

Les took her by the wrist and twisted it hard. "I want my money now, Shiela. Now!"

A man stood in front of him. "Unhand my lady."

Les looked up into a face blocking the setting of the western twilight sun. He was dark skinned with a neatly trimmed beard around the lower part of his face. A half smoked cigarette dangled from the corner of his mouth. Les could tell he was trouble and meant business.

Les released Shiela's wrist and brought his hand to his forehead to shield his eyes from the glare of the sun haloing the man's face. He said as apologetically as he could, "The lady owes me money and she was just going to pay."

The man smiled, took a long drag from the cigarette and removed it from his mouth with a forefinger and his thumb, blew the smoke in Les' direction and said, "Do tell. Where I come from, you owe her money."

Shiela spoke up. "Freddy, he's right. I borrowed three hundred fifty dollars from him last night and planned to pay him back today, after work."

"A likely lie. If you were with him last night, where is my cut?" Then he grabbed her purse, took out a wad of money, and fingered through it. "There's only five bills here and you owe me half, so how you planning to pay all of that?"

Les said from his seat, still looking up and shielding his eyes, "Mister, I'm not trying to get into your business. I just want my money and I'll leave you and Shiela to take care of yours."

The man leaned over, grabbed Les' shirt, brought his face close to his and said, threatingly, "Listen, buddy, my lady don't owe you shit. If you were with her last night you owe her. Got that?"

Les knew that trouble had found him. He pushed the man back, and karate kicked him in the balls. The man fell to the ground grasping his injured genitals with his hands still clutching the money. Les knelt his knee into the man's chest and hand jabbed him in the throat. While he gasped for breath Les took the money out of his hand, counted off his three hundred fifty dollars and threw the rest into Shiela's lap. Then he said. "Don't ever make that mistake again."

Shiela's face was the picture of fear and bewilderment. Les rose, pushed his way through the crowd of onlookers that was beginning to gather, and walked leisurely down the street. About a half block away he turned back to make sure he was not being followed. A couple of the onlookers were helping the pimp to his feet and moving him to the bench next to Shiela. Les kept walking casually towards his car parked at LaBrea.

And all of his troubles had come because he had shown kindness and compassion to a young beautiful girl, with a sweet smell of jasmine. She was a victim of a cruel comment from the man she loved, and he had only tried to comfort her. He realized he had to be careful in this place. There were people here who couldn't be trusted, and it was a long way from Estilette, but then again he had had trouble there also; a different kind but trouble just the same.

Les wondered what his grandfather would say if he had known what trouble he has gotten himself into. He suspected he would have said, something like, *you fight at the drop of a hat.* But he also knew his grandfather didn't know the kind of world he had found out here, that he had to protect himself from people wanting him to change his name and lie about who he was and other people taking advantage of a kindness, and the pimps and whores and liars and deceivers, so he had to fight. But somehow Les figured he had to put all of this together with what Grandpop had taught him and wanted him to be.

And he knew one other thing was very clear; he had to move out of the apartment that he had just rented. That was the end of his brief visit to Shangri-La.

Chapter 10
ReDiscovered Love

L es packed his belongings as soon as he got back to his apartment, and then headed toward the office across from the pool, to get back his unused rent money. Half-way there he stopped. He changed his mind. *Hell no, I'm not gonna do that.* He didn't want the management to know that he was moving out after moving in the day before. He figured they would want a forwarding address, or would even ask questions about why he was leaving, which he had no intentions of telling. *I'll let 'em keep the money.* He was paid up to the end of the month and figured, by that time he would simply put the key in an envelope and send it back with a note saying he did not intend to rent the next month. On top of all that, he suspected that the pimp would be snooping around after Shiela had given him the apartment address. He realized that the Shangri-La was not all it was cracked up to be, and he was in unfriendly territory and had to be careful whom he trusted. He went back, put his things into the car, and headed out to find Caryn's place.

As he drove along he smiled at the thought of how lucky he was to have run into Caryn at the audition. Now he had a place to stay. It was a strange happenstance--almost like a spirit thing, as Naomi would say, even though he didn't believe in voodoo. He was grateful that Caryn understood when he called to tell everything that had happened after leaving the Melting Pot. He didn't plan to stay long, only until he could find another place; or maybe, just maybe they would pick up their relationship from where it was four years earlier.

As reality began to dawn, the smile slowly faded from his face. He had to get a job because the money he brought from home, except for three hundred fifty dollars, was almost used up. And even though his mama had said she would send money when he needed it, he didn't want to put that burden on her for too long.

He finally arrived at the Address on Oxford Avenue near Western and Santa Monica Boulevards. It was a different section of Los Angeles and the working class people walking the streets didn't seem at all like the classy touristy types he had seen walking Hollywood Boulevard. There was little chance that he would happen to bump into the pimp shopping at a super market in this section of this spread-out town. Although Les felt the confidence of being able to take care of himself, the anxiety of the pimp getting revenge was still in back of his mind.

Caryn's apartment was in a newly built complex of twenty-five units, surrounding a central, kidney-shaped pool. Les was becoming convinced that there were lots of pool-people in this town. Caryn met him at the door with an arms-around-the-neck kiss that was more than friendly, and Les felt good about being there. She showed off her one bedroom unit with its large open area living-room/common space, and the adjoining medium-sized well equipped kitchen/eating area, and the open balcony sleeping space, which overlooked and was connected to the living room by a curved stairway. There was plenty of light from skylights and small windows placed high in the walls for security and privacy. It was idyllic and as Caryn explained, paid for by her parents as a gift for all they had put her through in the last four years. She was delighted that he was there. "I don't feel so alone in this town now that you're here."

Les was equally thrilled. "Why don't we celebrate? Let's go out on the town."

"Great idea. What do you want to do?"

"Let's see. Last night I was planning to go to B.B King's Blues Club but I didn't get the chance to find out where it was."

Caryn volunteered, "There's a news-stand on the corner with those free magazines. 'What to do in LA.', I'll run out and get one."

When she reached the door, Les asked, "Where will I sleep?"

"Upstairs with me, silly. Find an empty drawer and put your things away." With that Caryn was out of the door.

Les followed her instructions. As he opened and closed the drawers of the bureau, looking for a space, he noticed an ashtray with a partially burned butt of a cigarette. He had never known that Caryn smoked. He picked it up and discovered that it was not commercially rolled; rather it looked like a joint. He brought it to this nose and, yes it was reefer. Although Les had never smoked a joint before he was aware of the smell. So it seemed Caryn was smoking pot. He continued putting his things away.

Caryn returned with the magazine, and they found the listings of blues concerts for that evening. Next to the ad announcing the attraction at B.B. King's Blues Club, was a listing for Brownie McGhee and Sonny Terry at the Lighthouse in Redondo Beach.

Les said, "Oh, wow. Brownie McGhee. My uncle used to tell me about him."

Caryn looked at him like he was out of his mind.

Les responded, "What?"

"Your uncle?"

Les knew that he had a lot to explain. "Yeah, well, I never told you about my uncle, Lightfoot. His name is John but everybody calls him Lightfoot because he walks with a limp. His right leg is shorter than his left because many years ago he fell from the steeple of the Catholic Church and broke his leg but it never healed right."

"I take it he is a Creole like you?"

"Yeah, he was my grandmother's brother, but they never got on too well, but that's another story for another day, anyway he has a blues club in Estilette and he used to tell me about Brownie McGhee." He said, "'When Brownie was a young boy he had polio and it left one of his legs shorter than the other.'" So he walked with a limp just like my uncle Lightfoot, and he felt because of that they were brothers. And in addition, Sonny Terry plays a harmonica just like my uncle Lightfoot."

Caryn was sitting on the edge of her seat, so to speak, and said, "Well, there's no doubt that's where we should go. Where is it?"

Les looked at the ad and said, "The Lighthouse."

"Do you know where that is?"

"No. It says Redondo Beach but we'll find it."

On the way, as Les navigated and negotiated his way south down freeway 405 to Torrance Boulevard, Caryn was a constant source of questions about her initial exposure to this thing called the blues, which she was beginning to understand was the music that had formed the basis of what she now knew as jazz.

"So how did you get to know so much about the history of the blues and all?"

"I don't know a lot, just what my uncle, grandfather and

Mr. BoBo told me."

"Who's Mr. BoBo?"

"Oh, a remarkable old man. He was old when I met him, black as coal, and as wise as Solomon. He told me everything he knew about the blues people; about Bessie Smith, Ma Rainey, Robert Johnson, Lead Belly, Muddy Waters, and even Elvis Presley."

"Elvis Presley? Did he play the blues too?"

"You ever hear Hound Dog?"

"That's the blues?"

"Well, not exactly. It's rhythm and blues, and he stole it from Big Mama Thornton who recorded it as blues in 1953, but he made it a hit."

Caryn said, "Isn't that something?"

"Yeah, and it connects us to everything."

She was taking a delight in the new image of Les that she was perceiving. She bit her bottom lip and asked. "It seems to me that you love the blues, why so?"

Les never took his eyes off the traffic but Caryn could tell he was thinking and his answer came as if in a trance. He began slowly, "Because it makes me feel whole—it makes me feel clean and dirty at the same time—good and bad—happy and sad—strong and weak—it changes my body rhythm and my mood—it makes my thoughts as clear as light, then again as dark as night---I feel everything that I could be, and have the possibility to be in that one instant, that's why." After a moment of silence, as he changed lanes in the traffic that was slowing down, he continued. "In the blues I can seek the heights of the mountains or the depths of the oceans. Like in Gibran, the blues makes me feel the completeness of me---my entire humaneness."

Caryn continued. "You like being who you are don't you?"

Les took his eyes off the traffic for a moment and focused

on Caryn. "What do you mean?"

"Looking like you do, one would never believe that you think as black as you do."

"Yeah, and that's who I am, and proud of it, except for the me who has become El Tigre."

"What the hell are you talking about?"

"That's another story for another time. We're here."

They got settled into their seats in the popular subterranean venue of blues and jazz on the beach of the Pacific Ocean. While waiting for the next session to begin, they sipped wine and Caryn continued to quiz Les about the blues. "So what are we going to hear?"

"I don't know, but it could be any number of songs they have recorded over the years. Maybe *Brownie's new Blues*, or *Walking my Blues Away,* or the *Sweet Woman Blues*...I donno, but you'll like whatever they do."

"How do you know that?"

"I know you. You have soul. You were the one who introduced me to *The Prophet*. It's all the same. Truth and feeling for what is right--a basic understanding of what connects us as human beings."

Caryn reached over and squeezed his hand. "That's why I love you."

About this time a spotlight picked up the MC. "Good evening ladies and gentlemen. Welcome to the Lighthouse. We apologize for our lack of space, and right at this moment we're trying to get chairs for you people standing in the back."

Les looked around and people were standing against the walls and in every aisle. The place was packed and it had all happened in the space of the half-hour since they had arrived.

The MC continued. "You're in for a treat tonight. You're going to hear the country blues. Not since Lead Belly has the country sound been heard as much as it is when Brownie McGhee and Sonny Terry play. Now I'm not talking the urban blues or the B.B. King sound, I'm talking the early, beginning country blues sound. And both of these musicians were the protégés of Blind Boy Fuller. And like Fuller, Sonny Terry has been blind most of his life. When he was a young boy an accident took away his ability to see, but at the same time his hearing was sharpened and he played the sounds of nature on his harmonica-- the wind rustling in the trees, the calls of the birds, and the sound of the train, and then Blind Boy Fuller took him under his wing as a disciple. So it was like a work of providence that these two would be united by the same musician. Brownie McGhee got Fuller's guitar when he died, and Sonny and Brownie have been together ever since. And although they come from Carolina and Tennessee, these bluesmen are really folk singers, like Lead Belly and Josh White, in the truest traditions of the down home blues. So sit back and enjoy, and oh yeah, keep buying those drinks. Ladies and gentlemen, please welcome the great Sonny Terry and Brownie McGhee."

The thunderous applause led into a standing ovation for Brownie and Sonny as they took the stage and delighted the audience for the next two hours.

In the car on the way back, Les and Caryn sang the lyrics of the songs they had heard in the concert, and this continued until they got home, as they finger popped and danced to the rhythms of the blues around the pool in the complex. When the two people swimming came up for air, they looked at them and thought, *They're either drunk or crazy.*

Les said, "Let's take a dip."

Caryn responded, "No, I'd rather stay with the spirit we're in. I have a Billie Holiday album. Let's put her on and cool out."

"Hey, that's fine with me."

They waved goodbye to the swimmers and headed inside.

The music played softly. Les stretched out on the floor with his head propped up by a beanbag, sipping wine.

Caryn descended the stairs, stark naked, slowly balancing her glass while taking puffs from a joint.

Les was curious. "When did you start smoking that stuff?"

"During the time I was in therapy. I had to do something; I was going out of my mind. I met up with a girlfriend I was with in high school and she brought me into ecstasy. Wanna take a hit?"

"Why not?"

Les took a drag and slowly released the smoke. Then he took another, and they passed the joint back and forth. This went on in silence as Billie's voice floated with the smoke. Les closed his eyes and begin to feel that tingling sensation all over his body. He was suddenly aware of everything--- the silence between Billie's phasing--the cool softness of the wine as it left his mouth and trickled down into his stomach---Caryn's fingers, as they made their way through the buttons on his shirt and caressed his flesh like a thousand flashes of lightning touching his body all at once. He had never before experienced anything like this; he was floating in space with no physical attachment to anything, everything in the room spoke to him, the space, the music, Caryn's aura, his breathing, the smell of jasmine that wafted through the window on the light breeze which felt like a tornado; and he could feel his clothes being ripped from his body, but in reality Caryn was slowly undressing him after saying, "It's no fair for me to be so naked and you're so covered up." Les was on his back, his head still propped on the beanbag and Caryn lay beside him on her stomach, silently perusing his face.

He rolled his head slightly to engage her eyes and said, "What?"

"I was just taking you all in. Your eyes are hazel. I used to think they were brown, but they're not brown, they're copper colored with little flecks of light."

"My Mama has gray eyes."

"That's it. Copper colored with flecks of gray. And your skin is the same color whiteness as mine, except yours has a bronze tinge that brings it alive, like you were born with the tan that most white people pay a fortune to get." She ran her hands through his hair. "Your hair is as soft as silk and just as wavy as a flag in the wind, and as black as the deep holes of space."

"My grandfather always said my Mama's hair was like black gossamer."

Caryn's hand left his hair, and slid down his neck onto his chest. She caressed his nipple, between her thumb and forefinger, and kissed it softly, then her hand continued to explore his body. "Your biceps and your abs are as hard, strong, and firm, as a Michelangelo sculpture."

"I have a body like my papa."

"Did all of this come from being Creole?"

"I donno. What's with you tonight? Is it the pot that's making you so...sexy?"

"It could be. But for the first time I'm really seeing you. You are one handsome sonofa-bitch."

"Now watch your language, don't let the pot and the wine go to your head."

"You're talking too much." Caryn kissed him long, hard, and deep. "There now, that should keep you quiet for a while. Let's just float and enjoy everything around us, especially that jasmine."

Les' mind traveled back to Shiela, but that was not where he wanted to go or be, so he closed his eyes and shut her out, and remained in the here and now with his rediscovered love.

Chapter 11
A Whiff of Hollywood Smoke

Two weeks later Les got a second call from his agent, who asked, "What's going on. You've been in Hollywood less than a month and you have a new phone number?"

Les explained that he had moved to a better apartment and he would be at the new number from now on.

A.B. explained, "This is not for acting. It's for directing. The producer of The *Rhoda Show* saw your resume and was impressed, because he also graduated from Northwestern along with Charlton Heston, so I sent him your tape from *Our Street* and he wants to have an interview."

Les could hardly believe what he was hearing. Although he wasn't interested in working as a director, he wanted to be an actor, but he had experience as a director and this was so flattering that maybe this was the way he should go. He said, "Yeah, well when is this going to happen?"

"I'll have to call back when I find out. I wanted to check with you to see if this was something you'd be interested in." Then Andy went on, "The regular director is Robert Mason, and he's scheduled to direct the movie, *Murder by Death* starring Truman Capote. As of yet the date when he will have to leave the series is not yet set. And there is another situation that I wanted to run by you."

"Yeah, what is that?"

"The star of the show has expressed a desire to have a minority director."

Les was silent. Here it was. The catch 22. Just a few weeks earlier, this brilliant agent had made him change his racial identity because, as he said, "You will not be able to get work as colored." And now he was telling him that there was an opportunity for a minority. Les finally said, "So?"

"So, I'm asking if it is all right to change your race on your resume to colored."

"That's who I am. You were the one who wanted to change it to white."

"O.K., O.K., I hear you. So I'll set it up and call you back."

Les hung up the phone and shook his head. He didn't know if he was ready to deal with these Hollywood twists and turns--which, he would later learn, were called, *blowing smoke up the ass.*

Caryn was standing in the kitchen overhearing the conversation. "Is everything all right?"

"Yeah. I guess so. That was my agent. He has a TV series that he wants me to interview for."

"Oh, that's great. What's the series?"

"*The Rhoda Show.*"

"Rhoda? Are you kidding?"

"Well, nothing's set yet."

"Ohhhh, man, that's a great show. If you could get that you'd have it made. What part are you're going to audition for?'"

"It's for directing."

"Directing? You're shitting me!"

"No. But it's not that simple." Les was not too happy about opening the door of sliding identities. He had just agreed to change his race from white to colored, but he didn't want Caryn to know about all of this, so he didn't explain further. He continued, "There's still a question about when the director is leaving to take another job."

"Well, I sure hope you get it."

That was all that was said about this situation, and he left it like that.

On July 22, 1974, Les got a call to observe *The Rhoda Show* in preparation for finishing out the season in place of Robert Mason, whose departure was scheduled within the next couple of weeks. There were six shows left, and the producer felt they were secure enough to end the season with a new director. Les was elated. It seemed like a sure thing. He met with the producer, who expressed his anticipation that as soon as Les was acquainted with the process of shooting and editing, he would be ready to start.

Les followed Robert Mason around the set and observed everything he did--how he selected shots, marked the script, his editing process, the timing of the episodes to fit the studio requirements--everything necessary to make the *"buy"* of an episode for producer/studio acceptance.

After the first few days of being in this process alone, there appeared another person; Hank Storrie, an actor, recently arrived from the Broadway stage, who wanted to be a director. Through his Jewish connections he had been channeled to *The Rhoda Show's* search for a fill-in director. So now, Les had a competitor who was looking to capture the same prize that Les had been assured was his.

During the days of observation, Les and Hank talked freely and he revealed that he felt that Les was more qualified to fill the spot than he was because, as he said, "You've directed over ninety-five episodes of a continuing drama, and I haven't directed anything. I've just been an actor all of my life, so I'm sure they will select you."

Wrong.

Hank Storrie was chosen over Les to direct the remaining six episodes of *The Rhoda Show*.

Les was a basket case. Caryn did not know what to do to calm him down. She pleaded. Explained.

Rationalized.

Nothing would suffice or satisfy.

Les was convinced that this was discrimination. The selection was intended, or so it was indicated, to go to a minority. He was better qualified with years of television experience, Hank had no experience as a director and was chosen because he was Jewish and it was as simple as that, as far as Les was concerned. He then announced that he intended to go to the Director's Guild with a complaint.

Caryn, asked, "Are you a member of the Guild?"

Les, said, "No, but I would have been if I'd been selected."

Then Caryn said, "So now Storrie is, what is the point? And who is to say he is not considered a minority?"

Les was silenced. There was nothing more to say.

For the next few weeks Les did not go out to any more auditions. He only reported for work as a valet parking attendant, which he was now doing to make money to pay his share of the living expenses.

Les had gotten a whiff of Hollywood smoke. He was filled with despair. He had lost hope. He couldn't understand how this could happen. It was like the disappointments of life that the blues singers told about in their songs. Now it was happening to him. Now he knew first hand the trials and tribulations that they had gone through. He understood the heart ache and pain that brought the blues. But from everything that he knew, and had been taught, the blues could also bring hope and sunrise, but darkness and despair was all he was getting. Yes, there was some blues that spoke sadness and sorrow, but always there was a silver lining, however this did not seem the way it was with the Hollywood blues he was now experiencing. Even Hank himself knew that Les was more qualified for the position. However, it was now clear to Les, that decisions were made differently in Hollywood. First, he had learned how truth could be twisted and changed around, now this--smoke up the ass.

Life was depressing. Both he and Caryn had settled into a routine of looking for work through frequent phone calls and letters. Les had contacted, and continued to call for updates on openings with Reuben Stein, Danny Thomas, Aaron Spelling, Bernie Rothman, Garry Marshall, Don Nicholl and Barbara Schultz--any and everyone who was a producer of a series on which he felt he had a chance of directing or acting in. He was trying his best to keep hope alive. But no such luck.

Then one day he received a call on his message machine from his agent, A.B. "Hi El Tigre, I'm just calling to tell you to mark a date on your calendar for a big shindig at my place. Septermber first. Within the next few days you'll get an invitation but I wanted to give you an advance to save the date. Bye. See you then. Love, AB."

Les thought it was a strange message, particularly the way it ended. But after listening to it again and then erasing it, he thought no more about it. Sure enough the invitation arrived within the next two weeks, the address and all of the details were there. He decided to accept. He was curious and felt that he had nothing to lose. He took Caryn as his date.

They arrived at the Beverly Hills address and it seemed that the entire Hollywood establishment was also there. He gave the keys of his mustang to the valet parking attendant, and he and Caryn approached the entrance of the mansion in front of which was a beautifully draped table manned by a beautifully dressed wannabe, who, as they approached, asked for a name and the invitation, then pinned them with name tags. On each side of the door was a male attendant dressed in a Roman toga, holding a tray of Champagne, a glass of which was presented to each guest. Les was impressed. It seemed he had now been accepted as a Hollywood celebrity. The name card, pinned to his jacket said, "El *Tigre*," and he and Caryn entered the main marbled salon with tables of food and drink lining each wall. They stopped and took a deep breath while taking in the vista of it all.

Caryn asked, "Who the hell is El Tigre?"

"That's me."

"Since when?"

"Since my agent decided that's who I am."

"You're shitting me. You of all people, a proud Creole, would answer to the name of an animal, decided by a great white hunter?"

Les didn't like the implications of Caryn's sarcastic re-mark, which he ignored and said, "Let's get something to eat."

They picked up china plates and piled them full of broiled shrimp, crab, pates of every description, artichokes, smoked salmon, pickled asparagus, roasted beef, smothered lamb, and more side dishes than they could decide on trying. Finding a table on the patio in the pool area, they settled with glasses of wine and enjoyed their feast, along with the cool jazz of the quartet playing in the gazebo that overlooked the lights of the valley below the Beverly Hills.

Hovering over all were male servers, flitting in flowing Roman togas, and carrying trays of drinks and food, to re-place the consumed delicacies of the guests. The bikini clad gorgeous women, diving and swimming in the pool, were a visual pleasure to Les, much to the disgust and consternation of Caryn, who said, "I've looked better in the dark than these bimbos." Nevertheless, it did not deter Les' admiration of the attractive women. And there were also the attractive men, who, swaggered and flitted with hands on their hips, much like the waiter, he remembered from the Fat Burger. Because of their overwhelming numbers and constancy of presence, Les was prompted to remember the comment made by the man sitting next to him at the counter, "You gotta be firm with the fags in this town. Its kick ass time or they'll fuck you over."

Les turned to Caryn and asked, "Do you think those guys are sissies?"

"What?"

Sissies. You know, fairies."

"Oh, you mean mama's boys?"

"Yeah."

"No doubt about it. Look at 'em. They're like women, trying to attract every man they see. Why'd you ask?"

"Just wondering."

Then one of the beautiful boys approached Les, with hands on his hips, fingers flaying in the air and asked, "Are you El Tigre?"

"Yes."

"Follow me."

Les was confused. He looked at Caryn, then back at the boy and asked, "Follow you? For what?"

"Your presence is requested."

"Where."

"Just follow me."

"I'll have to bring my friend."

The beautiful boy shrugged his shoulders and said, "Well, what must be, must be. Come on."

Les and Caryn followed the boy up a long curved

stairway to a mezzanine that encircled the area below, and then to a smaller stairway leading to a room on the third floor, then down a hallway filled with prints from the Roman orgy baths.

The boy stopped at a door, behind which was heard laughter and music, then waved his hand indicating that they should enter.

Inside the room were mostly men, shirts open revealing glistening abs and nipple rings. And there were also several women wearing tightly fitting, sheer blouses that revealed erect nipples, some standing out more than others. All were having a good time finger popping, and hip swaying to the jazz music blasting from speakers mounted in the ceiling.

Caryn and Les stood just inside the door and took in the scene, allowing their eyes to flow with the cloud of smoke-laden, pot-smelling aroma that assailed their nostrils.

Caryn breathed out, "Oh, wow."

Les was too overwhelmed, mesmerized, surprised and confused to say anything. He had never seen anything like it before. Men were kissing men. Women were kissing women. There was a low table, in the middle of the room, around which several people on their knees leaned in to sniff from a twelve inch wide mountain of white power with straws, in front of a right angled couch, which was occupied by mostly men who sat on each side of AB. When his eyes connected with Les, A.B., stood and said, "El Tigre, sit over here."

Les looked at Caryn. She nodded, "Yes," and sauntered off in the direction of the women.

Les squeezed his body into the space between A.B., and a strange looking man with long curls hanging down over his shoulders. When he was settled, A.B., put his arm around Les' shoulder and said out loud, looking left then right at the other guests, "This is El Tigre, my next star. I want you all to mark this moment. He's going to be big. Biiiiig. And I want you all to remember this. He's just been cast in *The Sins of the Father*, his first leading role."

There was applause from the people sitting around, and Caryn turned and her face lit up when she heard the news. Les smiled broadly, impressed by the announcement of his future.

Perhaps this was the silver lining that he had expected from the earlier disappointment, and the entire event could have been easily scripted as The Hollywood Blues.

A.B., sat down next to Les, took a straw from the table, gave it to Les and said, "Enjoy." Then he leaned over and took a nose full of the blow from the table and leaned back and said to Les, "Ambrosia. Now you try."

Les was apprehensive and reluctant. He didn't know how to respond. How would his grandpop want him to respond? It was a different world and everyone was having fun and a good time, like he had always imagined. Now he was on the verge of becoming the actor he wanted to become; his first movie role had just been announced so it was time to celebrate.

Les took the straw and leaned over toward the table. As the tingle of the powder rose into his nasal passage, and he felt the rush, he also felt his shirt being pulled out of his pants, along with the touch of flesh upon flesh as fingers squeezed pass his waist down onto his butt, caressing one of his cheeks and then continuing down into the abyss of his ass.

Les was up like lightening. He ripped the hand out of his pants and turned to face the perpetrator. It was A.B.

Les instinctively brought his full fist against the left jaw of A.B.'s face and shouted out, "Don't ever put your hands on me like that again."

A.B.'s body was thrust backwards into the soft cushions of the couch as blood spewed into the air. Caryn was dumbfounded. The other guests were speechless. There was total silence. Les pulled down his shirt and tucked it back into his trousers.

By this time A.B., had recovered enough to stand up and face Les. He drew the back of his hand across his bleeding mouth, then put his palms on Les' chest and pushed him back, with the admonishment, "You will never work in this town! You nigger bastard, get out of my house!"

His last words were hardly out of his mouth, when Les brought his knee up viciously between A.B.'s legs. As A.B., bent over in agony, Les straightened out his body with a fist to the face. A.B.'s entire head swiveled forty-five degrees to the right as he fell backwards to the couch.

No one in the room made a move.

No one said a word.

Les said softly with meaning, threw clinched teeth, "Don't you ever breathe the word *Nigger* again."

Les and Caryn waited for the car to be brought around. Caryn slipped her arm around Les' waist, leaned in and whispered, "Why?"

"Why, what?"

"Did you hit him?"

"He ran his hands down into my pants. I'm not like that."

Caryn said softly, "Well that was a sudden end to a brief and brilliant career. You are a kickass kind of guy, aren't you?"

"I guess so."

Les thought of his grandfather, and remembered a conversation they had many years earlier when he was a twelve years old altar boy. He remembered the conversation as if it had happened yesterday. They were fishing. It was a beautiful and tranquil day under a clear blue sky speckled by widely separated floating cotton balls of clouds, the only interruption to the constant chirping of the crickets was an every-now-and-then bird twitter from one tree to the next. Les broke the silence.

"Grandpop, I've got a question."

"What is it, Les?"

"Last Sunday after I served Mass with Joseph Martin, we were taking off our cassocks and, he asked me if I wanted to go with him and Father O'Reilly on a picnic."

"On a picnic?"

"Yeah, he said they had fun. They took the wine left over from communion and Father brought a nice lunch and they went to the woods near the Amite River and had fun."

"How did he say they had fun?"

"Joe said that Father prayed that God would bless them and help them to find love, then he said they went swimming. He also said the Father O'Reilly told him it would be more fun if he could bring one of his friends along, so he asked me. Do you think I should go with them?"

Les could still see his grandpop's eyes close and after a few seconds they opened and he said, "I don't ever want to hear that you went with Joseph and Father O'Reilly on a picnic."

Les asked, "Why?"

"Because it is not right for a grown man, who is a priest, to take a young boy or even two young boys on a picnic alone. Something is wrong."

Les was persistent. "What is wrong with having fun with a priest, Grandpop?"

Phillip said, "In the bible it says it is a sin to lie with a man as one lies with a woman."

"Grandpop, what are you talking about?"

"I'm talking about a sin that is being committed. From

137

what you have said that Joe told you, it seems that Father O'Reilly likes young boys as men like women."

"Grandpop, you mean like sissies?"

"Yes, like sissies."

"Well, Grandpop, I don't want to be a sissy."

"And I hope and pray that you won't be."

Caryn broke the silence. "So now what are you going to do?"

Les had no clue. He put his arm around her, held her close and said, "Let's go home and make love."

The car came and they left.

Les and Caryn had sex like he knew a man and a woman should.

He had paid a heavy price--he had no agent, no work as an actor, and no work as a director. He had gotten a whiff of Hollywood Smoke. It smelled like shit.

*   *   *

A week later Les got an envelope from his mama. Her note said, "The enclosed letter came a few weeks back. Mary called and wanted to know if you had received it. I told her you were in Los Angeles and I would forward the letter. She wanted your phone number and I gave it to her."

Les opened the enclosed letter.

"My dear Les,

I want to thank you for the kind words about my book. I have known your family for many years and your mom was one of my favorite teachers. After receiving your letter saying how much you liked my book, I did some research on you. Your studies in theatre at Northwestern, my Alma Mater, are impressive and your work in television is outstanding.

Things have moved rapidly after my book was published

over a year ago. *I have recently completed the first draft of a proposed television series based on my book, <u>Accept Me Now</u>. I am looking to go into production soon and would love to have you as a part of my production team. We will be shooting in Estilette. I will contact you soon to find out your availability.*

> *Sincerely,*
> *Mary Thomas"*

Les was elated. He read the letter over again and again. He showed it to Caryn and filled in all of the details about the novel she had written, her participation in the Kennedy campaign for president, and her personal growth from daughter of a share-cropper to author.

*   *   *

It was not Mary; it was Al Buxton's assistant. Les' relentless letter writing and phone calls had paid off. Al Buxton, vice president of Reuben Stein's Productions, had arranged an appointment for an interview and Les accepted immediately. It was the longest and most intensive interview that he had ever had. It was also the friendliest so Al Buxton certainly did not fit the mold of people whom he had recently met in Hollywood. Buxton had previewed a tape of Les' work on Our Street and seemed genuinely interested in discovering his background, experiences, and objectives. Then finally, Buxton revealed the purpose of the interview; Tandem Production was in the process of looking for a director of the new series, *The Jeffersons*, which was about a Negro family climbing the socio-economic ladder. A minority director was being considered.

Les was overwhelmed to be considered, although he realized he did not look like the Hollywood concept of Negro, but he knew in his heart that, as a director, he had the experience to bring the subtleties of the life lived by segregated people to the series. He gave Al Buxton every assurance that he could live up to the challenge, and he left the interview with the understanding that a final decision would be made within the next few days.

Early the next week, the call came and Al Buxton suggested that he return to the office to hear the decision. Les did. He waited in the anteroom to Buxton's office. The waiting time of almost one hour passed before Buxton reappeared. He sat next to Les and there was much pain on his face. Les knew immediately that the decision was not in his favor.

Buxton said. "It was a tough decision. But it didn't have anything to do with your qualifications. As a matter of fact that is the reason it took so long. In the final analysis, most of the decision makers in the room felt that in spite of your talents, there were too many firsts for this series--the first sitcom dealing with an economically rising colored family, the first sitcom with a mixed marriage, and to add a first-time colored director seemed too much of a risk for the network to expect success. So the majority opinion was to go with an experienced staff director. But most of the decision makers in the room were impressed with your resume and we will keep you in mind for the next opening that comes along."

Les was disappointed. He smelled the Hollywood smoke again, but understood the dilemma faced by the people in charge. He thanked Al Buxton for the consideration, and was given a promise that they would keep in touch.

On the first of August Caryn answered the phone. "It's a call from Mary Thomas."

Les grabbed the phone. "Hello."

"Les Martel?"

"Mary?"

"Yes, Mary Thomas from Estilette. I wrote you a letter.

Didn't your mother tell you I was going to call?"

"Yes, she did. You wrote the book, *Accept Me Now*. But it's been over a year since I wrote about how much I like it."

"Yeah, I know, and a lot has happened since. I wrote and told you that I'd be calling for you to direct the pilot for my television series. Now I'm ready for you. Get your ass down here. I want you to be the director of a pilot for a television series."

"Wow! This is great. When is this going to happen?"

"Production planning is scheduled to begin next week in Baton Rouge at the Bell Monte Inn, and I want you here. Shooting will be in Estilette, and I've made arrangements with Delta Airlines for your ticket, so don't worry about a thing. See you at the end of this week."

Mary filled him in on the details and addresses that he needed when he got to Baton Rouge within the next four days.

After he hung up, Les told Caryn everything that had been discussed. Then he called his sister, Ann, and told her that he was going to be directing a movie in Estilette. She was excited and wanted to know, "How did Mama take the news?"

"I haven't told her yet. I want it to be a surprise. I'll be there in a couple of days."

"Oh this is great. I know Papa will be speechless after the way he carried on about you being in this business," said Ann.

"I can hardly wait to see his face."

As Les hung up the phone his grandfather was in his thoughts and he wondered what he would say now about his being in the movie business.

Caryn watched as Les took out his suitcase and began packing. She was filled with questions that Les should have gotten answers to, but hadn't.

"Les, what's a pilot?"

"Ohhh, I donno. I guess it's the first episode in a series."

"How many episodes are going to be in the series, and which network is it going to be aired on?"

Les looked up after counting his underwear and stacking them next to his socks. "I don't know that either. She didn't say. I guess she'll tell me all of that when I get there."

"Les, are you going to get an agent to negotiate your contract?"

"I don't think that'll be necessary."

"Why?"

Les paused his packing, walked over to Caryn put his arms around her waist and said, "Where I come from a person's word is their bond, and Mary's from my hometown."

Caryn said, "But Les..."

Her words were interrupted by a long kiss. "There now. That's the end of the questions. With all that's happened to me in this town, I'll take anything to get away from Hollywood smoke."

When Les arrived at the airline counter there was no ticket. He demanded that they look again, and call for confirmation at the number that Mary had given for the hotel headquarters. The receptionist at the Bell Monte Inn said that a production operation was in the planning, but it had not yet been established and she knew no one there by the name of Mary Thomas.

Les was confused and frustrated, but he was all packed and ready to go, and standing at the counter of the air terminal, so he said to the clerk, "Look I'll pay for the ticket." He did. He was on his way back home to direct his first film. He could do no less.

As the plane brought him closer to his destination he

reread *Accept Me Now*. It was truly an Abraham Lincoln story told by a colored woman—about her endeavors to get an education against insurmountable odds—about her long-sought struggle for success in the fight for justice.

In reality it was the story of her growing up in the small town of Washington, Louisiana as one of eight children of a sharecropper father who had abused her older sister. Mary had entered into a conspiracy of silence about this with her sister in order to keep peace in the family. In addition to daily work as a farm hand, planting, weeding and picking cotton along with tending other crops of corn and sweet potatoes, there was a dedication to school. Mary walked the four miles both ways in the heat and cold and even the rain because she wanted to get an education. And when she completed elementary school she convinced her parents to let her move to Estilette to live with relatives so she could attend high school, because there was no school in the backwoods community where she lived. She was in her senior year when she experienced the most traumatic event of her life--a cousin who was active in the NAACP voter registration drive was shot dead when he answered a late night knock on the door. The sound of the blast brought Mary to the opened doorway in time to see her cousin's faceless body writhing on the floor.

Filled with pain and bitterness Mary left the south and struggled and worked to get through college at Northwestern University where she was a political activist. After graduating she worked with the campaign for president of John Kennedy. Later the assassinations of Kennedy and King were paralleled in her memory with the murder of her cousin. All of this drove her to tireless efforts in the political arena. In her book she described graphically, the smoke filled rooms, deals, infighting, prejudices and the courage it took to get things done and decisions made.

From a share-cropper's cabin in the backwoods of Louisiana to Washington, DC, this woman had a story to tell and in less than two years since her book was published, Mary had moved with surprising speed to get a movie pilot for a series.

Les was impressed and wanted to help her tell this story. It felt a lot more hopeful than the Hollywood blues he had recently experienced. He reread, and skimmed the book over and over again, and was convinced that it would make a powerful series. He was proud to be a part of this historic event.

He stepped off the plane and was greeted by the hot muggy, clinging, summer night air that he had grown up accustomed to, took a taxi to the Bell Monte Inn and checked in. Yes, just as Mary said, there was a reservation waiting.

Chapter 12
FilmMaking

Early on the morning of August 6, 1975, Les went in search of Mary. She opened the door dressed for the day, and immediately blurted out, "Les," just as if she expected that he would be the person making the early morning drumming on her door.

They embraced and she smothered his face in her bosom. She was a striking woman, taller than he had imagined, so it was necessary for him to look up to her because he was only five feet ten. She had a plain uninteresting face that was transformed into a magnet when she smiled. Her head was wrapped in a colorful tignon. She had beautiful teeth that complimented her light tan completion, and there was something reassuringly magical about her smile. It projected that everything would be all right--the glass was full. And this captivated Les from the very beginning. She spoke rapidly in a high pitched voice and asked too many rhetorical questions, the likes of, "You know what I mean? or Do you understand what I'm talking about?"

He was invited to sit for coffee and Mary began to explain why she had not met him at the airport, which Les had not even expected, but apparently it was important to her that he understood that she had every intention of meeting the scheduled plane she had arranged, which the computer at the airlines was never able to verify. Nevertheless, she told in detail about her attempts to get the airline manifest showing his arrival time, but the information was denied even though she claimed she had made the reservation and had the ticket billed to her account.

Les saw his opening and explained that he had ended up paying for the ticket because there was no record of a pre-paid reservation. And he continued, "Since I've not worked in several weeks, I need reimbursement for the plane fare as soon as possible because I'm broke." And he smiled.

And she smiled back and her response was a favorite phrase that Les would hear often over the next few days, "Your expenses will be paid and you'll have extra money to jingle in your jeans."

She then put a thick manuscript into his hands. "Here's the treatment. It's all ready for the writer."

This was a surprise. Even though Les had not done a film before, he knew there should be at least a first draft shooting script by now, since, as she had indicated earlier, they were scheduled to go into production in a few weeks. However, as he flipped through the pages of the treatment, it seemed thorough and complete, so his concerns tended not to be as urgent.

He said, "Good, we can get right to work."

Her response was, "And that is exactly what we will do."

She made a phone call, and five minutes later there was a knock on the door. She opened it to her chauffeur, Ron Higgins, and Maggie Morgan, her secretary. Both were white and Les was impressed that she had already acquired a staff and was now reversing the history of time by using whites to help tell the story of her rise from the chains of segregation.

They piled into the1975 Cadillac limousine and Mary instructed Ron, "Stop by and pick up our director Harold Henderson."

Les was shocked. It was his understanding that he was the director. With the slam of the door as Ron exited the limo, he asked, "Mary, what's going on here? I thought I was hired as the director."

She reached over and put a kiss on his cheek, smiled and said, "Darling, I thought I had told you that you are now my producer. You'll get more money, know what I mean? I had some problems with the asshole who was the producer. He wanted to take control of the money that I had raised for this project, and we had words so I fired him. Now you're my producer." Then she turned to her secretary, "Isn't that right, Maggie?"

Maggie nodded her head and smiled.

Les didn't know what to say. He didn't feel he had the experience to be the producer but if she believed that he could do the job he would try. Then he remembered the questions that Caryn had asked about a contract before he left Hollywood. He said to Mary "Shouldn't we have a written contract about all of this?"

"You're right, and we will." She looked over at Maggie and said, "Take a note to remind me to draw up a contract for Les."

By this time the door of the limo opened and Harold, the director, entered. He had a strong-no-nonsense gaze on a face framed by a well shaped Afro-bush and looked to be only a few years older than Les. There was not much more for Les to say after the introduction, so he listened to the conversation engaged by Mary and Harold and he learned that this would be Harold's first film as a director.

Les was now very uncomfortable. *Why was she staffing the project with first timers?* He realized that everyone had to begin someplace and he was grateful that Mary had given him a chance as a first-time producer but to put together an inexperienced director and producer to lead the project, meant one of two things, either she had extreme faith in the people she had chosen or she didn't know what the hell she was doing. He chose to believe that she had faith and trusted the talents of the people she had chosen, so he remained glued to his seat rather than jumping out of the limo and running to catch the next plane back to Los Angeles.

Mary shouted out instructions to Ron, "Let's go to the capitol to see Governor Edwin Edwards."

As they headed in that direction she began reciting what she called, a *Talking Paper,* to her secretary. The memos she dictated were concerned with the previous day's scouting locations in Washington, and the anticipated production center to be set up in Estilette. It was in great detail, methodical and to the point. As Les listened, he marveled at her wise use of time because this cut down on meetings and as they drove from place to place, work was being accomplished.

The capital building loomed in the distance and all of a sudden Mary stopped dictating, reached over and tapped Ron on the shoulder and said, "Let's go the Film Commissioner's office first. I want my people to get acquainted with them."

Ron did a right turn at the next corner and headed in a different direction.

From the moment they entered the Commissioner's office and were introduced, Nick Powell endeavored to impress everyone with the experience he gained from other Hollywood movies made in Louisiana, *The Drowning Pool, The Tower, and Hurry Sundown.*

Nick was in his mid fifty's, and even in the heat of August, he wore a short-sleeved shirt and tie. His classic appearance was enhanced by a Van Dyke beard, and he puffed on a pipe, which constantly required re-lighting. He was a take-charge kind of guy, and he loaded them down with books, casting directories, and maps they could use for scouting locations, selecting crews, scheduling film equipment and making teamster contacts for transportation, along with his experienced advice on who to engage as actors, and equipment suppliers.

He seemed helpful but there was something about him that Harold and Les did not like from the start. In a private exchange around the water cooler, they expressed their feelings and speculations about Nick's tendency to take control and make decisions that they felt were not his prerogative. Harold said, "We have to watch this S.O.B." With this meeting of the minds Les was drawn closer to Harold and it seemed they were on the same wave length and had the same opinions, at least in this, their first exchange on matters of the project.

During this entire time Mary was on the phone in Nick's office. When she came out she announced, "It's time to go."

After settling into the limo, Ron turned, looked back at Mary, and asked. "The governor's office?"

"No. Governor Edwards is not able to see us because of other commitments, but I did get a chance to speak with him briefly, and I filled him in on yesterday's truck incident. He's going to get his people to look into it." Then she continued with new instructions to Ron, "Let's head over to Maggie's house for refreshments."

Harold returned to the subject of the incident, and addressed his inquiry to Mary, "I wondered why Nick didn't say a word about what happened. I know you had told him about it because I heard you express your outrage."

Mary responded, "That's why I wanted to see Edwin Edwards, know what I mean?"

Les was curious and he asked, "What's going on? What's this about a truck incident?" The details were related first by one and then another.

The day before, Mary, Harold, and Maggie were returning from scouting locations in Washington, and a large construction truck had attempted to force the limo off the highway.

Mary added, "If it had not been for Ron's skill as an off road racing driver, we would have ended up in the Little Teche Bayou."

Ron added, "I had my eyes on that truck, which had been following us since we pulled away from the traffic light in Washington. He stayed close on my tail for miles and could have passed any time but didn't. I got suspicious and made a note of the license plate, and as we neared the bridge over the bayou I noticed he picked up speed and came along side while we were crossing the bridge. I saw the name, *Cajun Construction,* printed on the side as he side-swiped us. I hit the brakes hard and spun around, and away from the impact, heading in the opposite direction. He kept on going."

Harold continued, "All of this was reported to Nick and he even inspected the damage on the driver's side but he just puffed on his pipe, and said nothing. I don't trust the bastard."

Les listened silently, and wondered what he had gotten himself into. He had an uneasy feeling in his gut.

They relaxed at Maggie's house with lemonade, snacks, and small talk. It was a pleasant respite from the heat, but Les felt the disappointments of his first day as a producer-- not meeting the governor-- the less than impressive meeting with Nick Powell--and news of attempted violence.

After an hour or so, Harold asked if it was possible for Ron to drive him to New Orleans to catch a plane. "I've got a project coming up with the Johnson Publishing Company and there's a production meeting I'd like to attend tomorrow. I'll be back in a couple of days."

Maggie looked at Mary, who was silent at first, but smiled and said, "This is the first I've heard that you have to leave us, know what I mean?"

"Yes. I know. But after I found out that we don't have a shooting script yet, I realized that I could make my meeting in Chicago in order to set up my next project. I doubt if you'll miss me. There's nothing for me to do here until you get a shooting script."

Les shifted his eyes from one to the other, like watching a tennis match. During the exchange Les began to analyze Harold Henderson. All he knew about him was that he was a first time director, and he could only assume that he must have been capable because Mary had chosen him, no doubt in much the same manner that she had chosen Les. Les could tell that Harold was an aggressive type who was a risk taker, lighting his candle at both ends, attempting to nail down one assignment before the other was even started. He wondered if this was a premonition of what to expect from Harold during the course of this film, taking off at the last minute to make a production meeting assignment in Chicago, and if it was, they were destined to have conflicts because Les did not operate in this manner. He could also tell that he and Mary were different managers in this regard and he was relieved that she had not called on him, as the producer, to make this decision.

Mary smiled. "O.K. Go on to Chi town, but get back here by Monday. Bob Peterson, the writer, is coming in tomorrow, and I'll need your key so he can stay in your room until your get back."

There was a silent tension in the air. Les could tell that this concession had not been thought of by Harold. Now he would have to take belongings brought for a four week stay with him for the weekend.

After taking a deep breath, Harold said, "That's a deal. But I have to leave in time to get my things out of my room and make it to New Orleans in time for my flight."

"Fine."

Then Les chimed in. "I'm going to hitch a ride back to the hotel so I can get some rest."

On the way, Ron reached into his coat pocket and passed a newspaper article over the front seat and said, "Read this."

It was an article from the *Estilette Chronicle*. The headline read; *Movie to be Filmed in Washington.* Then it explained that it would be a ninety-minute film for the pilot of a series based on a book written by Mary Thomas of Estilette, who was born and raised in Washington Louisiana. And it went on to state that opposition to the movie had already raised its ugly head. The daughter of the former sheriff in Washington explained that her father had been cast in a most unfavorable light in the book. *"There's nothing but lies about my father and if that's in the movie, I'm going to sue."* The article continued to quote other comments from the various city officials and their feelings, pro and con, about the anticipated film.

Les read the article then passed it to Harold. He finished reading and pushed it back over the seat to Ron, who said, "I think maybe the truck incident had something to do with this article that came out Tuesday, August fifth, the very day that we almost got killed."

There was silence the rest of the way to the hotel.

Harold got his things and he and Ron headed to New Orleans.

Les went to his room, ordered food, and tried to get some

rest between imaginary bizarre thoughts that came and went through his mind.

* * *

Day Two - Thursday

In the morning Mary knocked on the door of Les' room. As soon as the door was opened she started talking. "We've gotta make an early start. Have to move our production center to Estilette so we'll be closer to Washington."

Les smiled, thinking to himself, *this is the chance I've been waiting for.* Now he had to figure out a way to take off from the group to visit his family and make it known that he was the producer of the movie that had been announced in the paper.

During the sixty-five mile trip from Baton Rouge to Estilette, Ron announced that a second attempt to force him off the highway had taken place on his way to the New Orleans airport with Harold. This time it was a dump truck that had tried to side swipe him after following for some distance. Mary shook her head and said, "The governor is going to hear about this too, know what I mean? Did you get a license number?"

"No. It was dark."

"Did he bang into the limo, like the other truck did?"

"No. I swerved and left him in the dust. Harold almost shit in his pants, traveling over ninety miles an hour."

Mary shook her head and said, "You did good. I'll tell all of this to Governor Edwards."

They pulled into the Downtowner Hotel. This newly acquired showplace was the pride of Estillete that Mary had selected for their headquarters. Prior arrangements had been made and they were greeted by Jim Rossini, assistant to the Mayor. It did not take long for Les to discover that the familiar sounding last name was the same as his family's doctor.

Jim's father, Dr. Anthony Rossini, was, for as long as Les could remember, the only doctor who had treated the ills of his family, and for many years had also hired Martha, his grandmother, as a nurse. And then Jim proudly revealed that he still shared drinks with Lightfoot on his many visits to the Black Eagle.

Mary overheard their reclaiming of yesteryear memories and said, "Now you know why I wanted to have you as my producer. Your family's name is special in this town, understand what I'm saying?"

Les was curious when he heard this, and wondered if Mary had a hidden purpose in hiring him as producer. Maybe she had figured she didn't have to pay him because his family had money. Then Les took the opportunity, and asked to speak with her privately. They walked toward the bar as if going to have a drink.

"It's been two days now and I have not been reimbursed my plane fare."

"I know. And I have not forgotten. The bank is still setting up my accounts. The pre-production money is being wired to my bank in Baton Rouge, and as soon as that is completed, you'll have money to jingle in your jeans. In the meantime charge everything to your room bill, and I'll take care of it."

Les said. "Fine I'll continue doing just that. Now, what about our contract?"

"As soon as our production office is set up, I'll have Maggie type it up. You're my right hand and I know you'll take care of my business, know what I mean?"

She smiled her captivating smile, gave him a kiss on the cheek and said, "I've got some business to take care of with the manager of the hotel. You and Jim go ahead and set up everything."

With that said, Jim and Les got down to the business of setting up the production office. Les went over, in exact details, everything that was needed, and interviews for office staff were scheduled and detailed arrangements for an opening press conference to be held at the city library were completed.

It was five o'clock when all was done.

Mary said to Les, "It's time for the film staff to visit your family homestead."

Les had not expected this. He had planned to go home at the end of his workday anyway, but Mary's announcement that all would be included came as a surprise.

The huge limousine filled the entrance drive to the house, and the shrill horn sent the summer sparrows scurrying out of the pecan trees. Lala and Rosa were on the porch with the same urgency as the scattering birds. They looked suspiciously at the huge black monster that had invaded their peace and quiet. Ron got out and opened the door, and when Les stepped onto the ground of his ancestral home he was immediately engulfed by arms of happiness, and his face was bathed with tears from his mama.

Both Rosa and Lala hugged Mary and planted kisses.

Lala said, "Years ago when you wrote that essay about your family, I knew then that you were a writer. And now here you come, bringing my son as the director of your movie."

Les quickly looked at Mary, then to Lala, and said, "Mom, I'm not the director, I'm the producer."

Then Mary added, "Mrs. Martel, I promoted your talented son to producer and he's doing a great job."

Lala was so overwhelmed she gave Mary another big hug and said, "Thank you. Now all of you come on into the house, I'll make some lemonade."

On the way into the house, Lala stopped at the door, turned around to face her impromptu guests and said, "I've

155

changed my mind. We're going to the Black Eagle and I'll treat everyone to dinner."

There were instantaneous ooohs and ahhhs, and from Mary came, "I've always wanted to go to that club but never got the chance."

Lightfoot was taken by surprise but delighted to have the movie people as guests. He ordered a special table set up near the stage because Vitalee was the featured local blues singer for the evening.

It didn't take long for word of, 'the *film people that were in the paper are at the Black Eagle now,*' to get around town.

Naomi was behind the bar when Dora walked in. She spotted her immediately.

"Well, as I live and breathe, Dora Johnson. Girl, where you been?"

Dora extended her arms and Naomi filled the space. "Doing my thin' teaching and moving into my new place. You just have to come over and see it."

Naomi said, "I'd like that. Your boyfriend is back in town and he'll be here soon."

"I know. I heard."

Naomi was shocked. "You heard all ready? My God! In this here town, gossip travels faster than lightenin'. He's only been back a couple of hours and it was not planned in advance that he'd be here tonight."

"Dora said, as she sat on a stool at the bar. "At any rate I thought I'd come over to see him."

Naomi wiped the area of the bar in front of Dora, "You want something to drink?" She watched Dora's eyes widen and take on a sparkle.

Dora smiled and said, "Yes. Gin and tonic."

She reached back and instinctively took the bottle of gin and poured and fixed the drink while she talked. "You have grown to be one beautiful brown-skinned, black woman. With class and culture and smarts. How's the teachin' profession goin'?"

"Oh, it's all right. I'm thinking of studying for my master's degree soon."

"Go girl." Naomi set the drink in front of Dora. "This is on me. Now lemme ask you, how long you and Les been boy and girl friends?"

"Since our freshman year in high school. But it seems we've known each other forever. Our families were close. My father was a teacher in Professor Fergerson's school for many years before he died."

Naomi pursed her lips and tipped her head to one side. "I didn't know that." She leaned in close over the bar, and in the manner of a confidant asked, "Have you and Les…?" Then she jiggled her hand in the air, "ever got it on?"

Dora smiled, took a sip from her glass, and said, "I've always been a good Catholic girl. That's the way my momma raised me."

"Lord have mercy." Naomi continued as she passed her hand over her braids. "Lemme see, if I 'members correctly, the last time you saw Les was that night he kicked the asses of those boys who disrespected you. And that was right over 'dare." Naomi pointed toward the entrance door.

"You're right. And soon after that was the trial, and then he had to leave town so those racist bastards could not find him."

"Chile, that's the last you seen of him?"

Dora nodded her head.

"Well, my dear you got you some work to do. Now you take my advice, and you get that man in bed. Do him up good and make him want some mo'. That's how I got his uncle. Ain't nothing wrong with dat. Dat is if you want him. Do you?"

Dora nodded her head, "yes".

"Now you come on in the dining room and let me get you somethin' to eat. Bring yo drink. And den you take it from dare"

Soon after there was a constant trickle of curiosity-seekers. They took seats at the bar facing the stage so they could observe this strange assortment of characters from Hollywood. Actually, Les was the only one of the group from Hollywood, Mary was from Chicago, Ron and Maggie from Baton Rouge, and the writer Bob Peterson, who had arrived early in the morning, was from Boston, but it did not matter; they all held a fascination for the people of Estilette.

Naomi piled on the food. Lightfoot poured on the drinks.

Les looked around and standing next to his chair was BookTau. He said, "Hi, Les can I be in the movie?"

"BookTau, it's good to see ya. How did you know I was here?"

"It's all over town that you come back to make a movie. Can I be in it?"

"I don't know, BookTau. It's not for me to say. Mary Thomas over there is the one who makes that decision."

BookTau ambled over to her seat in his young-child-sheepish-walk, and addressed her, "Can I be in the movie?"

Mary said, with her infectious smile beaming, "Of course you can. There is a scene in the movie where one of the men picks a hundred pounds of cotton. Think you can do that?"

"I sure do. I done it many times 'fore." Then he spun around a couple of times and headed off towards the bar, laughing and shouting, "I'm gonna be in the movie!"

That was the only incentive that the other curiosity-seekers needed. Immediately, a line formed next to Mary's chair and all requested to be in the movie. Mary directed all of them to Les, who wrote down names and numbers, and gave the promise they would be called when needed. It was a fantastical promise of hope for the bright lights to shine on the lives of these plain-folks of Estilette. Les was proud to be part of their great expectation.

Lightfoot mounted the stage and announced the presence of "the movie people" and dedicated tonight's performance by Vitalee to the success of the movie that, "My nephew is going to produce for our own hometown gal, Mary Thomas." There was thunderous applause. The place was packed. Word had gotten around and it seemed that everyone that Les knew or had seen before was there. It was overwhelming.

Les felt someone take his hand and he looked around. It was Dora. They hugged and kissed. They had not seen each other in the ten years since Les was forced to leave town to save his life. She looked great--like a sexy fashion model--no longer the blossoming bud that Les remembered when they were dating. She whispered, "We've got a lot of catching up to do."

"Yes, we do. Sit right here next to me, and we'll catch up later."

Before Les could take his seat, he felt the familiar strong hands grab his shoulders and turn him around. It was his father, Lester Martel, Senior, greeting his son with a bear-hug that had never before been manifested.

"Son, I'm so proud of you. The whole town is talking about this movie that you going to do. I guess I was wrong about you being in this business."

"Thanks, Papa. Come, I want to introduce you to Mary Thomas who wrote the book."

"I know Mary, she was your mama's student. And I know all her people. She was just a young gal when she left here."

They were reacquainted and Lester took a seat between

Mary and Lala, and the evening wore on with food, drinks, Lightfoot playing guitar and Vitalee singing the blues. The film people let the good times roll. Maggie at first was a little stiff, but then let her hair down and began snapping her fingers and bobbing her head to the blues rhythms. Ron got up and danced with colored girls he had never seen before, and seemed right at home. Bob, the writer got into a deep and serious conversation with Naomi, about local life styles so he could bring a ring of truth to his script. Mary stood up and extended her hand to Lester for a dance and that was only the beginning of the many to follow. Les danced with his mama and Dora and the evening wore on and on.

Finally about one in the morning, Mary said, "Ron is ready to leave, so anyone going back to the Downtowner can jump into the limo. I'm gonna hang around to hear the last of Vitalee and Mr. Martel is going to drop me off. So y'all do what you gotta do. Know what I mean?"

With that the group split up. Dora took Les by the hand and said, "And I'll drop you off after you check out my place."

It was early in the morning when Dora dropped Les off at the hotel, with her protesting that he could have spent the night with her. But Les had early schedules for the next morning so, he said, "I promise to stay over the next time."

*　　*　　*

Day Three - Friday

Ron knocked on the door at seven. A much-too-early-wake-up for a guy who had had only about two hours of sleep after the previous full night's activity.

"Rise and shine, we've got a full day today. We're meeting the city people in Washington."

Les got dressed and stumbled into the limo.

Mary said, as she put the finishing ties on her tignon, "We'll have some breakfast at the Palace Café on the highway."

As they got close to Washington, Mary pointed to a car parked off the highway and said, "They have us under surveillance."

Les looked out to see a blue mustang parked in an otherwise deserted area, and high on telephone pole near the car was a man dressed in everyday clothes, minus the customary telephone-man's tool pouch, talking on a phone tap-in. It was beginning to appear that someone did have their eyes on the movements of the group. On several other occasions Les had noticed that cars with two-way radio antennas would blink their lights as they approached.

Ron would say, "They know we're here."

Les had no idea who "they" were, but he hoped that they were the friendly forces to whom Mary had reported the highway incidents. He was getting a little frightened because he knew they were headed into a hornet's nest of rednecks.

Bob the writer said, "Tell me about this place we're going."

Mary responded, "Washington is the second oldest town in the state."

Then she went on to tell that it was on the bank of Bayou Courtableau, and was settled in the early nineteenth century; that the bayou connected it to the Atchafalaya River that made water transportation a possibility; that it was beautiful, and covered with moss hung trees, azaleas and camellias, and had many historic landmarks. And soon after it was settled, a freed Negro, Antoine Lemel, bought up a great deal of land and many slaves, and later, because of the great number of colored people generated by such a large number of slaves, it was called Niggerville, by the whites.

And she finished up saying, "So now all of these colored

people are forced to live in the rural areas outside of the town in the shadow of redneck domination."

Then Bob observed, "So we're going back to your home, in used-to-be-Niggerville, to tell your story. I like that. It's a stroke of genius."

He echoed the same feelings that were running through Les' mind, although Les did not utter a word. He decided to keep his thoughts to himself until he was more convinced that Mary's imagination was truly the stuff of genius.

While sitting around the table at city hall, the mayor did not mince words, and made his displeasure known. "There's a scene in your book that makes fun of one of our beloved citizens, and we can't have that sorta thing."

Mary responded, "That was a rumor that I heard tell while I was growing up here, but it's not likely to be included in the movie."

"Well, until I'm sure that I can trust what you say about that, I'm gonna do everything in my power to stop this thing. I just want you to know that. Now I'm not gonna waste no more time with this nonsense, so I'll leave you to talk with these councilmen."

The mayor left two members of his city council to continue the meeting. They were in favor of the movie because they welcomed the, "positive effect" it would have on tourism. One said, "We've got some great historic sites around this town. Well, hell it'll bring people here like a gold rush."

The other member of the council looked around and leaned in toward the center of the table, in confidence. "The sheriff is with the mayor against this thing, but I believe we can get them to change their minds. Money talks in this town. But I sure would like to see what the mayor is talking about in your book. Do you think I could see a copy?"

Mary said, "Sure. Les, go to the limo and get a copy."

162

As Les approached the limo, he saw a man trying to see into the tinted windows through cupped hands.

Les spoke to the man, "Can I help you, sir?"

The man turned, "You with these people?"

"Yes, sir."

"Who are you?"

"I'm Les Martel the producer."

"You're the one I want to see. I'm Police Chief Lastraps."

Les' heart skipped a beat. There was no point in pretending that he was not frightened. When a colored man is in redneck territory they are aware that anything can be the cause of an accusation or even worse. Les was careful to end all of his responses with "sir".

"What do you want to see me about, sir?"

"When is Clay coming?"

"Who is that, sir?"

"Clay. Cassius Clay the fighter. I hear he's gonna be in the movie."

"He's not in the book, sir. So he will not be coming."

"That's why I gotta read that book. 'Cause he's not welcome here. He's a militant."

Les was not about to engage the police chief in a debate over whether Cassius Clay aka Muhammad Ali was or was not a militant. Les smiled and said, "It was nice talking to you, sir. But Clay will not be in the movie."

The man said as he walked away, "Be damn sure he's not."

Les opened the door of the limo and reached in for the book, and went back to City Hall.

Mary's face was curious. She asked, "What took you so long?"

"I was talking with the police chief."

One of the men laughed, "Ohhhh Chief Lastraps, he's

against making this movie because that was his uncle that Mary's rumor is about."

Mary presented the book to the councilman and they finished their business, then quickly left Washington.

In the cool of the limo, Bob, made a request, "Now, Mary, tell me about this controversial rumor that everyone is so upset about."

"It's not a rumor. It's true, but I just said it was a rumor to quell their fears. Well, hell, man, you're the writer. Haven't you read the book?"

Bob replied, a little sheepishly, "I only got it a couple of days before I came, and I haven't finished it yet, but I'm working on it."

This did not sound very reassuring—a writer who had not finished reading the book he has to write a script about. Les felt the project was headed for disaster. Everything was too quick, too-spur-of-the moment, not enough planning. Again Les remained silent, weighing his thoughts of doubt.

Mary continued. "O.K., I know everything is tight. The rumor goes...."Mary laughed, "Well, I don't mean rumor... The story goes, there was this illiterate sheriff, who incidentally happened to be a relative of Chief Lastraps. It was well known around town that Sheriff Larocque hated niggers, and one day he stopped a colored man for allegedly running a red light on Main Street. The sheriff then ordered the man to fill in his own traffic ticket according to the instructions that Larocque was giving him. The man did as he was commanded but he did not write what the sheriff was dictating. When the case came to trial, the man didn't show up and the sheriff presented the ticket to the judge with instructions to have the man arrested for not meeting the court date. The judge read the ticket and asked the sheriff if he knew what was written on the ticket. Sheriff Larocque said, 'Yeah, charges that he ran the red light.' The judge said All I see written here is, *Go to hell, you redneck son-of-a-bitch.*"

Bob fell out laughing. "That's funny. I see why they're so upset. Are you really going to put this in the movie?"

"Yes, but we'll have to film it away from here."

Les was getting more uneasy by the minute. He thought he should share with them his encounter with Police Chief Lastraps. He finished with, "And he thought that Cassius Clay was going to be in the movie."

Mary said, "He's right. I had a meeting with Don King, right after the "Rumble in the Jungle," where Ali knocked out George Foreman. Don agreed to invest some money, so I thought it would be a good publicity angle to put Ali in a scene that I have yet to write."

Les rode on in silence. The others chatted on about what a great idea this was, and how it would stimulate the box office and marketing.

Les did not like the sound of this. It was more dillydallying information that had not been revealed up front. And with this new information about Ali, the historical accuracy of her story *Accept Me Now*, just flew out of the window. He was glad he had not endorsed Bob's tribute of genius, because it was beginning to seem more and more like she was putting this project together as she went along.

Les wondered how the police chief knew about this. It seemed someone was leaking information and maybe, just maybe, this was another of the reasons why attempts were being made to run them off the road.

*   *   *

Day Four - Saturday

Early in the morning Les knocked on the door. It opened. Mary was dressed for the day with a cup of coffee in her hand.

Les said, "Mary, I apologize for troubling you so early, but I need some money."

"I know, hon. just put everything on the bill. Come on in."

She led him to the couch area of her suite. "Have a seat." She smiled that captivating smile and said, "Remember yesterday when I told you about Ali? Well, the money invested by Don King is supposed to pay for pre-production and I was counting on that to reimburse you and pay your salary, but that has not yet cleared my bank but I expect that it will any day now. You'll have more money than you can imagine to jingle in your jeans."

At about that time the door from the bathroom opened and a gum chewing, blond woman with a face the color of a steamed lobster, dressed in a red pants suit emerged, and said, "Hello."

Mary introduced Fran Gottcha, the publicist, who had arrived late last night.

"Fran has been working on a press conference to introduce our investors." Mary, continued, "We'll soon be headed to Nick's office to coordinate all of this."

With that, Les' early morning business with Mary came to an end, and he was no closer to getting his plane fare reimbursed than he was when he arrived. His hope for getting his money was fading fast, however his faith in the project was still alive.

Les saw Bob Peterson at breakfast and he revealed that he had been working on the shooting script. "Man, it's a breeze. Mary gave me the treatment and it's all there. All I've had to do was to put in the locations and times of day and I make a few changes here and there and now we have a shooting script."

A voice said, "I heard that and it makes me happy." Les turned and faced Harold. He had returned from Chicago and joined them for breakfast. The big three, writer, director and producer, discussed and planned how they would undertake getting the movie into production by August 18th, which was the projected first day of shooting. Today was August 9th and they had nine days left to get everything together. Les began to feel better about the possibilities.

Jim Rossini took Les on a tour of the production offices that he had set up in the hotel. There were four adjacent rooms fully equipped. The only missing items were telephones. Although the telephone company had been contacted they would not install until a deposit was made. Jim said, "I'll get a check from Mary and have the phones installed immediately."

With that done, Mary, Maggie, Harold, Bob, the recently arrived Fran Gottcha, and Les squeezed into the limo. On the way to the film commissioner's office, Mary dictated a memo concerning what was to be accomplished at this meeting. The one point five million dollar movie budget was being provided by Xerox, General Motors, and Max Factor, and the extra quarter million for pre-production was coming from Don King. It was expected that all of these donors would be present for the anticipated press conference.

Nick was waiting when they arrived. He had been alerted by Mary, and to Les' surprise Nick and Fran knew each other and had been in constant contact all along. Nick's opening question, directed to Fran, was, "What about the stars we discussed? Will they be here?"

The names of Loretta Long, Ruby Dee, and Ossie Davis, along with Quincy Jones, who would do the score, were mentioned by Fran, who said "I'll check and find out."

Les looked at Harold and they both shrugged in astonishment over the casting. This was the first time either of them had heard that any decisions had been made in regards to a cast. This was information that both the producer and the director should have known from the beginning. At least there should have been some discussion of casting between the director, producer and Mary, but there was never a mention of a cast until now. Les realized then that there was a lot going on behind the scenes that he was not privy to, and then a thought hit him like a ton of bricks. *What if Nick Powel was pulling the strings of decision making?*

Les thought back over the chain of events that he had become aware of in the short time of the four days he had been in Louisiana. First, the news article in the Estilette Chronicle, which no doubt had put the opposition forces on notice, which Nick could have easily influenced. Next, the truck incident, which Nick knew about but showed little interest in pursuing. Then, the story parroting Sheriff Laroque, which Nick surely had read in the book. Then, the second side swiping incident on the trip to New Orleans, of which there was no evidence that Nick knew about, but there was a possibility. And now this surprise revelation that Nick and Fran were old acquaintances. And finally the business of the casting and investors that no one on Mary's staff knew about except, Fran and Nick. With all of the behind the scenes maneuvering, Les concluded that something was rotten in Denmark.

Fran went to the phone to contact the investors, along with the celebrity actors mentioned, in order to determine their availability before setting a date and time for the press conference. However, the press conference had already been finalized by Jim Rossini with the people at the library. Les knew then that another screw-up in the making. Nick said, "I've arranged a meeting with some local casting people, equipment suppliers and the teamsters for tomorrow."

Mary concurred with a nod of the head.

The rest of the day was spent waiting for returned phone calls, which never came. Nothing could be decided until that happened, and nothing else was accomplished.

Les spent the rest of that Saturday at the bar of the Downtowner charging drinks to his room and trying not to allow himself to think negative thoughts.

*   *   *

Day Five - Sunday

All production facilities and equipment were ready to go except for the deposit to the phone company. Mary had not written the check for that to happen. Les had not gotten his plane fare reimbursed, nor had Harold or Bob. It was clear that money had not yet begun to flow.

In spite of the fact that the production center was established in Estilette, the group now headed back to Baton Rouge, sixty miles away, for the meeting that Nick had scheduled in a conference room at the Bell Monte Inn. They were now making daily trips to Baton Rouge.

Father Fisher, a Black Catholic priest who was a friend of Mary's and the pastor of the Newman Center at Southern University, opened the meeting with prayers and blessings for the success of the project.

Nick Powell, film commissioner for the State of Louisiana, then took over and introduced the people he had brought, who made their presentations and pledged support for the making of the movie.

First there was Henry Salazar, president of a film rental company in New Orleans. He was also a location manager and expressed his desire to "work with you people."

Then Roger Francoise spoke. He was a casting director from Baton Rouge who claimed to be in contact with all of the colored film actors in the state, "And others if you need 'em".

Then there was Kate Lovelace, also known as "Mother Goose." She represented the teamsters, and she assured the group that no travel on the Louisiana highways could take place without the cooperation of her union. She closed her presentation with, "Remember, you need Mother Goose looking over your shoulder." This brought laughter and lightness to what was, until this point, a dull and somber meeting.

The full staff of the production company was presented and each in turn gave an up-date on the movie's progress.

When they finished, Nick asked the question, "When can I expect to see a script?"

Bob Peterson immediately shot back, "I was not aware that you had script approval."

Nick replied, "Well, there are grave concerns about the contents of the book and some very important people are upset and want to make sure that there are no controversial issues in the script."

"Well, as far I'm concerned that amounts to censorship." Replied Bob.

"Censorship be damned, these people just want to be sure they will not be embarrassed by the movie, as they were by the book."

The heated exchange continued.

Bob replied, "Does this mean that your job as film commissioner is to cater to the script concerns of V-I-Ps?"

This question was like a stick up the ass. Nick stood and pointed a finger at Bob and said, "That question is out of order."

Mary stood and held up her hands in a gesture of surrender, "Brothers, peace. We did not come here to argue or debate. We've come in good faith and good will."

Then Harold leaned in over the table, turned toward Mary and said, "In addition to all of this good faith and good will, we need some money to pay the deposit, to get the phones so we can begin production, and Les tells me that he's not gotten reimbursed for his plane fare, and I haven't either, and neither has Bob"

At this point Les took the floor. "We want to thank all of you for your presentations and best wishes for the success of this project. So if you don't have any further information to present, we would like to thank you for coming. At the present time there are some other matters that we have to discuss in the privacy of our staff. We'll call you when we need you!"

That was when the proverbial, shit hit the fan.

Mother Goose rose immediately, and headed for the door, saying tersely, "Well, I've never been so insulted before in my life."

Mary intercepted her path to the door explaining, "He did not intend to insult you, he merely asked that we be left alone to take care of the rest of our production business."

"I heard what he said. Come on, Nick, let's get out of here and leave these people alone."

Nick knocked out his pipe leaving a trail of ashes as he headed for the door with the words, "Don't forget, folks, I need to see a copy of that shooting script before you begin anything."

With that the visitors left the production staff alone in the room.

Harold said, "Good work, Les. "You got rid of the crackers with, 'don't call us, we'll call you.'" He laughed then added, "My apologies to Maggie and Fran, I was not referring to you."

Mary responded with a firm look, "I would appreciate if you stopped throwing around that kind of offensive language."

Harold was silent.

Bob said, "Mary's right. We can do without that kind of jargon. And let's be careful how we throw around the word "Nigger." Make sure it's used only as a historical reference."

That statement brought the discussion back to financial and production matters. Mary announced that she planned to go to her mother's house in Baton Rouge after the meeting so that she could get to the bank early on Monday morning.

When the group left the conference room, the Belle Monte manager was waiting. He presented Mary with bills for four rooms for seven days, including the ongoing occupancy of the rooms, for the four days that they were not properly checked out of, the use of the conference room for the meeting, and all meals consumed by the group before they left to go to Estilette. The bill was substantial. Mary used her captivating smile to explain that the bill would be paid soon, which did not seem to soften the stern angry-looking face of the manager. He left with the comment, "The sooner the better."

Mary announced to the staff, "I'll have the money to pay him off tomorrow." Then, she said to Ron, "Take them back to Estilette and pick me up tomorrow at ten o'clock; I've got some banking business to take care of."

After everyone was let off at the Downtowner in Estilette, Les said to Ron, "Take me to the Black Eagle and I'll buy you a drink," convinced that his running account with Uncle Lightfoot was still open.

Ron took him up on the offer and while they were on their second round, Ron said, "This might be the last drink I'll have with you. I don't know how long I'm going to be around. My boss said if he doesn't get some money from Mary soon, he's going to pull the limo."

Les asked, "How long has it been since she paid anything?"

"So far nothing. I've been hauling her around for two

weeks before you got here, and the cost is mounting. My boss is getting pissed."

All Les could say was, "Wow. I haven't gotten any money either."

Ron finished his drink, shook good-bye and took off.

Lightfoot watched the events from the bar, then he came over to the table and took a seat. "What's the glum look about?"

Les told him about the events of the day and ended with the comment, "I'm having doubts about this project, Uncle Johnny."

"You know, I've been thinking about that too. Your mama let me read the book and there's some things in there that just ain't true."

Les looked his uncle directly in the eye. "Like what?"

"Well, for one thing she talks about some cousin getting murdered while doing some work with the NAACP. I knew her cousin. He was big, arrogant, trifling, drunk, called himself Black-Snake-Johnson. There was a warrant out on him for drunk driving and one night the deputy followed him to Tot's Tavern. When Deputy Miller tried to arrest him they had a fight. Black Snake kicked his ass, and then the coward little bastard went to his patrol car, got his shotgun and blasted Snake's head off. I know. I was there. But in the book she makes out that he was killed over some voter registration stuff."

Les was now curious about other things. "What about the story she tells about the ignorant sheriff in Washington?"

"Donno about that. 'Course everybody as far away as Estilette used to tell that story. Even your grandpop told it at hog killing time, but I never knew whether it was a rumor or the truth. It <u>was</u> funny though."

Then Lightfoot continued, "I don't know what she's up to, but she had eyes for your papa. She persuaded him to drop her off when she left here the other night."

"They left together?"

"Like I say." Lightfoot pointed his finger at his nephew and said, "You should take that woman with a grain of salt. She come from sharecroppers and she's trying to climb the ladder, and from what I know about those people, they'll do or say anything to get to where they feel they oughtta be. Why do you think she called her book, *Accept Me Now?*"

Lightfoot returned to the bar, and left his nephew to think on what he'd said.

Les called Dora to pick him up. "If you're free tonight I could spend the night."

She arrived at the Black Eagle a few minutes later. "Before we go to your place, I'd like to visit my Papa." Les explained.

"In Frillotville?"

"It won't take long."

"It's a half-hour's drive out there."

"It's important and I'll only be there a few minutes. And then we'll have the rest of the night together."

"You promise?"

He kissed her and they were off.

Lester opened the door. "What are you doing here this time of night?"

Les pushed past his father on his way into the kitchen. Lester looked out into the night at the lights of the car with the motor running. "Who's that waiting?"

"Dora."

"Invite her in."

"I don't plan to be here that long."

"What the hell is going on, son?"

"Papa, I came here for one reason. I have to ask you a question."

Lester slammed the door shut and took a seat at the table.

"Go ahead and ask. Your gal's out there waiting."

"The other night, did you take Mary to the hotel from the Black Eagle?"

Lester looked at his son with suspicion in his eyes and in his heart. "Yeah, why?"

"What did she want?"

"Boy, if you're implying what I thing you're saying, I'll kick your ass out of here."

Les was immediately put on the defensive and realized that he had approached his inquiry all wrong. "Papa, I'm sorry. I just want to know if she asked you for money."

"Yeah. How did you know?"

"Money is getting to be a problem with the project. And I thought she might have asked you to invest."

"No. She asked me to loan her five thousand for a few days."

"Did you?"

"Do I look like a fool?"

Les laughed, and embraced his papa in relief. "No. I know you're not a fool. But I had to know if she asked you for money."

"That's what you come all the way out here to find out? Why didn't you just pick up the phone?"

"I wanted to look you in the face. I gotta go. Dora's waiting."

Les was out of the door like a shot.

For several minutes Lester stood looking through the opened doorway watching the car lights fade into the darkness. He shook his head, muttered to himself, "That boy."Closed the door and went to bed.

Les, although not entirely happy with the answers to his questions, tried to put them out of his mind on the trip back to Estilette.

When they arrived at Dora's apartment, Les caught sight

of the late night's snack on the table. Dora went immediately over to the stereo and put on the music of Thelma Houston. Les got the message. He was in no frame of mind to resist or object. He went along with the program and Dora, who, by this time was getting impatient for his full attention. Les could not help but think of Caryn, and feelings of guilt surged through his consciousness. But here and now Les had a desire for sex and Dora helped him get it up, and he satisfied her every need for the rest of the night.

*   *   *

Day Six - Monday

Early the next morning there was not much else Les and Harold could do except explain to the constant flow of people who came looking to be in the movie, that it was too soon for anyone to be hired.

After lunch Les and Harold waited on the porch of the Downtowner for Mary's return.

Bob was up in his room typing away on the final draft of the shooting script.

Fran had just left, headed to the library to explain to the people who had made arrangements for the press conference, why it was necessary to postpone it.

Father Fisher drove up and stopped at the entrance. Les knew immediately that the limo had been pulled, for lack of payment, and Mary had talked Father Fisher into driving her back to Estilette from Baton Rouge.

Mary dragged herself out of the car with a heavy heart stamped on her face, dropped into an empty chair next to Les, and murmured, "It's not as bad as it seems."

Les looked at Harold. Harold looked at Les, then at Mary, "You got the money?"

"There's a slight delay, that's all."

Harold shot back with irritation in his voice, "What do you mean, slight delay? Either you got the fucking money or you didn't."

Mary took a deep breath and smiled. "I know you're upset. But trust me, the money's good. I've got letters of credit from the main investors in my lock box at the bank. The money I was expecting for preproduction hasn't been wired from Don King yet. In the meantime I'm planning to negotiate another advance on my book to tide us over and take care of the mounting bills."

Les and Harold exchanged looks, shrugged, and shook their heads.

Mary pushed herself up from the chair. "I need a cup of coffee. Y'all coming in?"

Les shook his head, "No." Harold didn't say a word and looked the other way.

The manager of the Downtowner held the door open as Mary entered. He let the door slowly swing shut and watched as Mary trudged toward the coffee shop, then he made his way to where Les and Harold were sitting.

"I hate to tell you guys this, but I just got a call from the Bell Monte Inn in Baton Rouge. They are holding you responsible for your unpaid bills over there, and if they are not paid today they are going to have you arrested for fraud and deception."

Harold said, "Fraud my ass. Mary is supposed to pay those bills."

The manager said. "I don't know any of those arrangements. All I know is what McDonald said. And he went on to tell me to be sure and get my money in advance from you people."

Les asked, "What do you suggest?"

"If I was you, I'd get things straightened out with the people in Baton Rouge. They can make trouble for you. Here in Estilette, you're homefolks and we'll give you the time you need."

Les and Harold thanked the manager for his understanding and consideration, and he left them to think on the new wrinkle in the rapidly growing complications of their situation.

"So what you think we oughta do," Harold asked.

"Let's go over there and straighten this thing out. Mary said she would pay our bills and that's the understanding that we have, and the understanding, she said, she gave to them."

Harold said, "Yeah, but before we go let's get a promissory note from her and take it to them."

Les thought for a moment then said, "Good idea."

Les called a lawyer friend of the family and had him draw up a document that they felt would get them off the hook with the people at the Bell Monte Inn. The lawyer came to the Downtowner and presented Mary with the draft. She read it silently,

I, Mary Thomas, being first sworn do declare that I am responsible for any and all hotel and other bills incurred by Les Martel and Harold Henderson with the Bell Monte Inn, in Baton Rouge, Louisiana between the dates of August 6, 1975 and August10, 1975.

She looked up from the document with a pained face, signed her name, and then the lawyer notarized the statement and gave it to Les.

Driving Lightfoot's Cadillac, Les and Harold arrived at the Belle Monte, went straight to McDonald's office and laid the document on his desk. McDonald picked it up, read it, and tossed it aside. "You boys still owe for your stay and you left without checking out, and the clock is still ticking, so I want my money now."

Harold spoke up. "Mr. Mac, be reasonable. You have a promissory note from Mary, which we brought all the way over here, so this should say something about our intention to do what's right."

"You boys are not leaving here until you pay what you owe."

At this point the door opened and a henchman, with a-no-nonsense look, entered and stood blocking the door. It was clear that McDonald had signaled his security and had no intention of letting them leave his office without paying the bill.

Les stood, looked back at the man standing between them and door, turned to McDonald and said, "You're making a big mistake. Now our business with you is over and we're leaving."

As Les and Harold approached the door the man, a muscular six-foot, two-hundred-fifty-pounder pushed them back. Les responded with a kick between his legs; the man doubled over in pain, and Les reached out, grabbed the man's belt from the back and sent him flying headfirst into the desk where the startled McDonald sat petrified. Les and Harold hurriedly walked out of the office, got into the car and high-tailed it back to Estilette.

Harold said, as he looked back in the direction of the Bell Monte fading in the distance, "Man you don't take no shit, do you."

"I just don't like people trying to take advantage. That's what I inherited from my kick-ass papa."

Back in Estilette, Les dropped Harold off at the Downtowner, returned the Cadillac to Uncle Lightfoot, and leisurely walked back to the hotel. He had had a long, disappointing event-filled day and wanted to be alone and have a quiet evening's rest.

A soft knock on the door brought an end to this wish,

and he opened the door to a smiling Mary holding a tray of boudin, boiled shrimp, sliced garlic bread and a chilled bottle of Champagne. She walked in, put the tray on the table and turned back toward Les who still remained standing in the opened doorway shocked, "Well close the door and have a treat."

Never in his wildest imagination did he expect this. He was so overcome he was speechless. Mary poured two glasses of Champagne and raised hers in a toast, "To Les. My right hand man, for his undying faith in our project." She drank the toast and Les followed, like a puppet.

She went on, "I'm sorry that you had to go to all the trouble of that promissory note. But I know that was Harold's idea. I had already told McDonald I would pay, so I guess you got everything settled once and for all."

Les decided that he would not even try to explain anything that had happened at the Bell Monte, so he nodded his head and sipped his Champagne.

Mary seemed different. She was calm, peaceful and intriguing and her captivating smile was radiant. It was like he was seeing another person, different from the one who had emerged earlier from the car with Father Fisher. She also seemed younger, prettier, and she had on glamour make up with the eye lash effect.

She said, "When I was growing up as a young girl I didn't have much time for romance. I was all about my mission to get an education and do some good for the cause of justice. There were not very many people who believed in what I was trying to do. When I got that letter from you after you read my book, I knew right then and there that you understood what I was about, and right then and there I fell in love. Now I know all of this might seem a bit forward, and I don't intend that it be so, but I want you to know how much your letter meant to me and how much you mean to me. And that's why I wanted you to be my producer because I know without a doubt that you believe in me and I believe in you. I owe you a lot and I appreciate your faith in this project."

Mary paused then smiled that magical hypnotic smile and continued, "Oh, I know I'm having a little setback right through here but everything is gonna be all right and you'll have the money I promised to jingle in your jeans. So I came here tonight to let you know how much I appreciate what you're doing,"

Then Mary began to cry.

Les did not know what to do or how to respond. So he did nothing. He just sat there looking at her. She went through her sobs then reached up and began unwrapping her tignon. For the first time Les saw her hair. It was processed and straightened and had been pushed up under the wrap. Mary shook it free and ran her fingers through and fluffed it out. She began to take on the look of a fashion queen. It was hard to believe that another person had been concealed under the wrappings, but there she was.

"Les, I know I'm much older than you but I want you to know, I need you in a way that a woman needs a man. Have me, Les, Have me now."

What could he say? What could he do? It was like his encounter with Shiela all over again, only this time there was no fragrance of jasmine, only the natural aphrodisiac of man and woman, which somehow he had to resist. But his manhood had begun to take over, and after he had nibbled away at the shrimp, boudin and garlic bread and drained the last of his glass, he realized that her lips were pressing against his and her tongue was rolling around in his mouth. One event followed rapidly after the other and before he realized what had happened she was sleeping peacefully in his arms.

His regret was immediate.

He knew he had allowed himself to do the wrong thing. He was not good at resisting sex.

He slipped his arm from under her head and went to the bathroom and got into the shower. The water did little to wash away that feeling of disgust, but it did bring an awareness of something that he had heard Uncle Johnny say, "Never lose your head over a piece of tail."

He got dressed, quietly slipped out of the room and walked home to spend the rest of the night.

*   *   *

Day Seven - Tuesday

Les was awakened by the perceived presence of someone else in the room. He turned over and Lala was standing in the doorway.

"I heard you come in late last night and I knew something was wrong."

Les could hardly believe his ears. How did his mama know about what had happened?

Maybe she was psychic? Maybe she was like Aunt Naomi and had second sight? He shook his head to clear his senses.

Lala went on, "Get dressed and come down, I'm fixing your breakfast and the newspaper's on the table." She closed the door and left.

Les got a whiff of the coffee, bacon and eggs as he descended the stairs. Lala had set his place at the head of the table, the same place that Phillip, his grandfather had occupied for all the years he was alive. The newspaper was spread out in the same place, right above the knife and fork, and Lala was pouring the coffee as Les arrived at the table. He picked up the paper when he saw the headline.

Lala continued, "I knew when I heard you come in that

things were not right. Now sit down and have your coffee, the biscuits will be done directly."

Les sank to the chair, holding the newspaper. The headline read: *Finance Problems Postpone Filming Here.* He went on to read.

Pre-production activities of the movie company have ceased and sources in Baton Rouge say the filming of a television series based on a book by the Estilette native Mary Thomas has been postponed indefinitely. Sources said that funds for the filming of the book Accept Me Now, *failed to materialize and the company that was to make the film had never been financed. Local sources said that the crew and the author were planning to check out of the Downtowner sometime today. Sources, including an official on the state level, said, "Because of the financial situation not previously anticipated, this film will be delayed, and perhaps it will be delayed indefinitely. The Estilette Chronicle could not contact the author or any member of the crew for comment.*

Lala put the plate of food and the hot biscuits in front of Les. "I know how much you were looking forward to this, and I know how disappointing it must be." Then she eased down into the chair next to him with her cup of coffee. "Are you all right?"

"I'm fine, Mama. Like you say, I'm disappointed. I just knew we could have made a good movie out of her book, but I guess it just wasn't meant to be."

At that moment Lightfoot burst into the kitchen. "Oh here you are. You had me worried."

"About what, Uncle Johnny?"

"Well, I read the paper and then went hightailing it over to your room at the Downtowner and Mary opens the door. At first I thought I had gone to the wrong room, but she checked the bathroom and said you had already left. Boy, did you sleep with that woman?"

Lala choked on a swallow of coffee, and showered it all over the table. She grabbed a napkin to cover her mouth but managed to get out, "Les, you didn't!"

"I'm sorry Mama, but I did."

"Les, that woman is twice your age."

"It's not like love or anything, Mama, it just happened, and I regretted the moment it happened."

Lightfoot asked, "Did she come on to you?"

"Something like that."

Lala, stood and threw the napkin on the table, "Now don't you go blaming that woman, Les should have known better." Then after a motherly look at a wayward son, she turned her face to Lightfoot and asked, "You want some breakfast?"

Lightfoot answered, "Yeah and a cup of coffee."

"Get your own coffee." On the way to the stove Lala's voice mellowed as she directed her inquiry to her son. "What happened? Did you invite that woman to your room?"

"I was just getting ready to go to bed and she knocked on the door with some snacks and bottle of Champagne."

Lightfoot interjected, "See there, just like I said. She came on to him."

Lala directed to Lightfoot, "You just hush. Go on Les."

"Well, she started telling me about the faith she had in me and how after that letter I wrote she began falling in love. . .

Lightfoot interrupted. "Fall in love my aunt fanny. That woman was using you."

Lala raised her voice, "Let the boy finish."

"Well after that, one thing led to another and before I knew it we were in bed together."

Lightfoot picked up. "Just like I said, she was using you. She got you as her producer because of your family name; she didn't have the money in the first place, or maybe she thought she did, but she figured she could count on your family connections to help her get what she needed to get started. She even went to Lester asking for money."

Lala turned so abruptly the grits, eggs, and bacon slid off the plate onto the floor. "Lester gave her money?"

Lightfoot explained, "She asked but he didn't give her any."

Les wondered how his uncle knew what had happed between his father and Mary, but then he remembered that Uncle Johnny had a way of knowing about everything that happened in Estilette. Les said, "That's right, Mom, she asked but Papa didn't give her any."

"Well that's a relief." Then with hands on her hips she stood next to Lightfoot, "Your breakfast is on the floor. I'll make you some more eggs."

Lightfoot laughed. "Just as long as you don't gimme the eggs from the floor." Then he went on, "The newspaper talks about some official at the state level who says the finances will be delayed indefinitely."

Les answered. "Yeah, I met him. I'm sure they're referring to Nick Powell the film commissioner. I think he was in cahoots with the mayor and the sheriff of Washington who were trying to stop us from making this movie."

"What would that matter if she had the money in the first place?" Lightfoot asked.

"I don't know, but she did have letters of credit from Xerox, General Motors, Max Factor and Don King for two million." Then Les paused, had second thoughts and continued, "At least that's what she said."

Lightfoot added, "All you know is what she told you. But you don't know who Mary Thomas is. She's a wanna-be and has always been. Why you think she wrote a book called *Accept Me Now*? She's just striving to be a somebody and has been striving all of her life. Now there ain't nothing wrong with trying to better yourself, but she wanted it by any hook or crook she could get. Maybe she did have access to the finances or maybe she just imagined she did, but the way I see it, this was all a flim-flam. A con game. She was jiving all of you film people to get involved to make her film, and at the same time conning the money people to pay for what she could show them when y'all put her book on the film. And when the dust settled, and all was said and done, she would be rich and famous. It sounds just like a scheme that Slick at the pool hall would cook up."

Lala crossed to the table with his breakfast. "You got one hellava imagination. Now eat your grits and eggs."

"You got this off the floor?"

Lala pushed his head in a playful manner, "Shut up and eat." Then she sat at the table, reached across and took her son's hand, held it tightly, brought it to her lips and kissed it. "What are you going to do now, son?"

"Go fishing."

Chapter 13
Flim-Flam

It had been a long time since Les sat under the pecan tree on the edge of the bayou where he and his grandfather had so often fished. There was a lot on his mind. Much had happened during the last seven days and many times he had wished that Grandpop was here to help him sort it all out. What he missed most was the way Phillip could put all of the events together and find a meaning. Like the time after the trial when the friends of Karl, angered because Les had told the truth in court, threatened to kill him, and he was forced to leave town to save his life. It was a time when he was lost for a meaning of it all, and he and his grandfather came here for one last outing before boarding the train to Chicago.

Les remembered like it was yesterday. Their fishing poles were propped in position by rocks and the lines floated lightly with the flow of the stream but they did not do much casting. Rather Phillip had brought his bible and he read a passage that seemed to answer the questions in Les' mind.

So justice is far from us,
and righteousness does not reach us.
We look for the light, but all is darkness;
for brightness, but we walk in deep shadows.
Like the blind we grope along the wall,
Feeling our way like men without eyes.
At midday we stumble as if it were twilight;
among the strong, we are like the dead.
We all growl like bears;
we moan mournfully like doves.
We look for justice, but find none;
for deliverance, but it is far away.

It was not the answer to all of his questions, but it did give solace and Les felt the comfort that his grandfather's reading from Isaiah brought, just the same as the Hebrews felt when the great prophet spoke to them seven hundred years before Christ was born. Phillip was like that. He always came up with an answer or an explanation to a situation that brought a challenge.

The one thing that troubled Les most was that he had slept with Mary. Why? He could not figure that out. She was twenty years older. Was it because she had made herself attractive? It could not have been because there was no physical or emotional attraction. Or was there? Maybe it was just as simple as the fact that she was a woman and he was a man and he couldn't resist the sex. Maybe getting a fuck was the nature of a man, like not being able to resist the temptation of taking a bite of the apple. Nevertheless, he felt ashamed and was still confused about why he had allowed himself to be lured in. He felt like a dog—an animal without the moral compass that points the difference between right and wrong, good or bad—an animal that responds to the base instincts and urges of nature. Is this who he really was? A dog? A creature of nature that would hump anyone in the heat of passion? Now at least he wanted to feel that the moral fiber that guided his choices was instinct. He did feel some solace, however because he had felt so full of shame afterwards.

It was not long before the peacefulness of the place and the distant chirping of the crickets and twittering of the birds brought heaviness to his eyelids.

The dream was a nightmare.

Mary entered his room with her two, well trained, well groomed, white poodles, hugging her legs, along with a procession of waiters carrying trays of food which were placed on a long table, in a setting at one end for him, and a setting at the other end for her. During the appetizer course of the meal, the poodle named Gottcha sat at Mary's end of the table and the poodle named Nick sat at Les' end of the table. As the main course was served, both poodles disappeared under the table. Les felt Nick unzip his pants and begin to lick his penis. He looked under the table and saw Gottcha's head between Mary's legs. Although embarrassed, he continued to enjoy his entree and pretended not to enjoy the sexual stimulation. Then, as often happens in dreams, the poodle Nick turned into the poodle Gottcha and jumped on the table and began to lick his face, and the poodle Nick ran along the top of the table to Mary, tore away her clothes and began to fuck her like a man. Then the poodle Nick transformed into his own image and Mary cried and kissed him passionately.

He was awakened from this nightmare by a soft kiss on the cheek and he opened his eyes to see Ann Marie kneeling next to him.

"Where did you come from?"

"Nashville. Mama told me where I could find you."

Les sat up and rested on his elbows, "Why are you home? Did something happen?"

"No. Everything's fine. I came to watch you make your movie."

Les fell back and clasped his hands beneath his head, "There's not going to be a movie."

"Mama told me. What happened?"

"I don't really know. It all happened so fast, I'm still trying to figure it out."

"Yeah, that was fast. It was only a little over a week ago that you called and said you were going to direct a film."

"And it was all downhill from there. I was supposed to have a prepaid ticket, but when I got to the airport there was no ticket, so I paid my own way, thinking I'd get reimbursed, but all I ever got were promises. Then I found out there was no script, and some of the stories in the book turned out to be made up, and that caused the white people to get mad, and there were two attempts to run our limo off the road. And Mary promised the colored people,
including BookTau, roles in the movie that they didn't get, so this left a lot of people pissed off, including me."

"Mama showed me the article in the paper saying that Mary never got the money."

Les shook his head in disappointment. "She said it was on the way, but it never got here." He went on to explain details of the events over the past seven days--the unfulfilled promises to have money jingle in the jeans of the staff--the trips to the bank to get the expected money that was never wired--the expectations of Muhammad Ali to be in the cast--the strange and unexplained involvement of Nick, the film commissioner, and his belief that it was Nick who had pulled the plug on the promised financing. He ended by saying, "Uncle Johnny thinks it was all a flim-flam."

"What's that?"

"A con game. And the way Uncle Johnny has it figured, maybe she did have some promises of money from investors, or maybe she just dreamed it up, but at the same time she got all of her film people committed to the project, and she kept dangling the carrot to keep us involved. And if, and when, we put anything on film she would take that, show it to the investors and receive the money they had promised."

"Well that was some plan."

"If that's what it was. Uncle Johnny calls it a flim-flam. I never heard of it before."

"Well, you know Uncle Johnny. He knows something about everything, or he makes it up."

Les shook his head in agreement. "Yeah, he's pretty wise. It all sounds like what I've been going through in Hollywood. There they call it blowing smoke up the ass. And to think, in only seven days that woman did it to her staff and a whole town without anyone being the wiser. Boy, she's good! But the thing that hurts most, is that she is one of us!"

Ann looked puzzled. "What do you mean?"

She's a Negro. And she lied and deceived, and shucked and jived just like they do in Hollywood, and it didn't seem to make any difference to her that she was flim-flamming her own people."

Ann said, "Why should it surprise you that she was colored? Colored people can lie, steal and cheat just like anyone else. Don't forget, it takes all kinds of assholes to make a shitty world."

They laughed and then went silent.

Les got up and inspected his line. He re-baited the hook and cast the line in another direction, propped up the pole, and came back to his place. He took a long look at his sister whom he had last seen on his way to Los Angeles in the spring of 1975. The sparkle had gone from her eyes; it seemed that her hair had not had the weekly grooming that was her style. She seemed tired and stressed out, which was not surprising because her studies in medicine were tough.

191

He wondered how she could just take off and come home like she had. His concerns now shifted to her.

"How'd you find the time to come home?"

"I just took it. I wanted to see you make your film, and I needed to get away. I told the dean that I had an emergency at home and I needed a few days. So here I am."

"Aren't you something. Thanks. Sorry it turned out to be a waste of time." Les hugged his sister again.

After a few moments, Ann said, "You are not the only one to have a flim-flam."

Then she began to tell her experience with her anatomy partner Todd. They shared a cadaver that was used to dissect and learn about the muscles and organs of the body, and because the student paring was alphabetical she and Todd Mitchell were thrown together. Once a week, according to their assignment, they would open the cadaver body to a different organ and reveal, study and become acquainted with that part of the body. Over a period of several weeks, the relationship between Todd and Ann grew close and intimate, and she fell in love. And because it was convenient, Todd spent more and more time in her apartment. And as time passed Todd shared his financial woes and decided to let his apartment go and move in with Ann. On top of that she began to loan him money for tuition and other things, which he promised to pay back from a trust fund that was due to begin within a few months. This went on for the entire semester of anatomy class. At the beginning of the next semester, Ann came home to discover that Todd's things were gone. She asked friends about his whereabouts and found out that Todd had left school and was getting a divorce. In addition, she discovered that he had borrowed thousands of dollars from other student friends, but the unkindest cut was, "And even though I had only loaned him a little over seven hundred, I had fallen in love, and didn't even know he was married."

"Wow! You fell for him." Les sat up and wrapped his arms around his knees and listened with interest.

Ann went on to say, "He was an attractive, likable guy, but he never said anything about being married or having a family. It seemed he was one of those people who talked a lot but never revealed anything, so I never knew where he came from or anything about his previous life. He was really liked by everybody, and he took advantage of that. Then I began to feel guilty. Papa kept sending the money I asked for but never asked why I needed it. I figured I'd get it back when Todd got out of his difficulties."

Les said. "I guess we're two peas of the same pod. We trust and believe in people and we get taken. Don't tell this to Uncle Johnny, he'll put you through the same lecture series that he gave me."

Ann said in a wistful moment, "Yeah, I know." Then she continued, "Like that other creep that I fell for. You remember Marvin Jefferson, the one you had to kick down the stairs?"

Les said, "Yeah, he didn't believe I was your brother."

"I'm through with men."

"Don't say that."

"No, really. They lie, take advantage, and say they love you just to get you in bed and then they vanish."

Les shook his head. "Don't let a couple of bad apples spoil the whole barrel of the good honest men, like me."

Ann playfully slapped his cheek. "Oh, yeah, you? Sir Galahad, no doubt."

For the remainder of the afternoon this brother and sister compared their life styles, coming of age experiences, and what had been learned from the crucible of life, all of which brought them closer in appreciation for each other.

Finally Les said, "Let's go visit Grandpop."

*   *   *

They stood in silence. Each with their own thought memories of the people encased in the white brick structures. In their two and a half decades of life these grandparents were the closest relatives they had known, loved and lost.

Martha was the most mysterious. Her headstone reported that she died in 1962. Ann was fifteen and Les seventeen. What they remembered most was that Martha had been confined as a mental patient for a number of years. So they were too young to remember very much of any meaningful interactions with their grandmother. What was foremost in their minds was Ann's statement at the time of a visit to Grandma during Christmas, "She smells like pee-pee." So, essentially this was their only image of Martha except what had been told to them by their mother, and grandfather. She was very beautiful and very religious—she loved the Catholic Church and went to Mass everyday—she was disappointed because the wealth that she was supposed to inherit was stolen from the family. But the questions that were still in the minds of both Ann and Les were--W*hy had she gone crazy*? *And how does this affect us?* No one had ever told them what had happened to drive their grandmother out of her mind, and therefore she remained a mystery.

Phillip was different. Both Ann and Les had had regular and complete contact with their grandfather, especially after the separation of their mother and father, when he became a surrogate father, in addition to mentor and hero. They remembered fondly his influence and the many times he told them about Negro history, the blues, rights and wrongs of the world, and the value of telling and living the truth.

Les broke the silence. "Remember how we used to fight?"

"I've never forgotten when you broke my tooth with that rock."

"And I've never forgotten the whipping I got because of it." Les reached over and put his hand on the headstone, then continued. "Grandpop made me promise never to hit a lady again and I've never forgotten that. He said, "'Don't get in the habit of hitting or pushing your sister, or any other woman for that matter. Women are special, and because of that they have a very special relationship with us men.' I've never forgotten that."

Ann kissed him on the cheek and then she went over and emptied out the dead flowers from the vase.

A voice from behind said, "Good. Now there's space for the fresh ones."

They turned to see Alexandrine standing there with a bunch of sunflowers in her arms. She was smiling. It was almost like she expected to find them there but this was not the case because she brought flowers to Phillips's grave frequently. After hugs and kisses, Alex arranged the fresh flowers and Les filled the vase with water. Then the three of them bowed their heads in private meditations.

"I'll always remember the day your grandfather passed on. I was reading my book to him and that was the day he told me that Ann was going to be a doctor."

Les asked softly, "Are you sure he wasn't talking about me?"

"I am positive. He said granddaughter. I wrote it down in my notes for the book."

Les continued. "Well, he was right. I would not have made a good doctor."

Alex added, "But what you are doing is important. I'm sorry that your film did not get the money it was supposed to have. Are you going back to Hollywood?"

"Yeah, in a few more days."

As the three of them walked towards the exit to the grave-yard, Alex put her arms around Ann's shoulder. "I probably should not say anything about this at this time but I think maybe you should know this before you make any other plans."

Ann asked, "What have you got up your sleeve, Alex?"

"Well, it's not only me. Dad and I have been thinking about bringing you back to take over Dr. Rossini's practice when you're finished."

Ann covered her mouth with both hands, gasped and said, "Oh my God!"

Alex quickly added, "That is if you would like to come back to Estilette."

"I'd love it. But I still have another year and then a residency."

"Whenever you're ready there will be a spot for you here."

Then Les had his say. "That would mean you'd be the first and only woman physician in Estilette. I like that."

Chapter 14
Birds of a Feather

In September 1975, Les returned to Hollywood.

He was depressed.

He was dejected.

He did little but drag from the bed to the coffee pot, to the TV, and then back to bed.

Caryn was worried about him. Whenever they talked, the subject was about what happened or didn't happen in Estilette and his disappointment over the film that was not made. It was a good thing that Caryn was getting called for extra work on a regular basis, so she was able to pay the expenses. But she was more concerned about Les's mental health.

He often talked about how his grandmother had gone crazy over obsessions that she had about what had not happened in her life, and Caryn was on pins and needles that this same thing might be happening to Les.

However, she believed that Les was at the beginning of his career and setbacks happen, and she gave counsel that this was to be expected, and he should pick himself up and keep on keeping on. She was satisfied that her message may be getting through to Les, because he would go silent after encouraging remarks of brighter tomorrows--sunshine after the rain--life being filled with challenges and keeping dreams alive. And then later he would pick up the *Prophet* and read for an hour or two. So for the next four weeks, she knew that he was trying to pick up the pieces and put them together into another perspective.

A man of his word, Al Buxton called in October and said there was an opening for an Associated Producer with the Tandem organization. Reuben Stein had a new series, *Mary Hartman, Mary Hartman* and they were moving the Associate Producer from *Good Times* to the new show, and he went on, "Would you consider being the Associate Producer for the sitcom *Good Times*?"

Les was shocked speechless. He had never been a producer, except for that brief fiasco in Louisiana, but otherwise he had no experience. By this time he had set his eyes on directing after giving up the notion of being an actor. But what the hell, after the flim-flam that he had gone through, this was a chance to get into the Reuben Stein organization, and maybe later there would be an opportunity to direct, so after a momentary paralysis, he said, "Yes."

Les had punched out his agent and had not gotten a replacement so he engaged a lawyer to negotiate his contract, which he was now convinced he should have done before going to Louisiana. Ultimately he found himself on the staff of Tandem Productions with a salary of seven hundred dollars a week.

After several orientation meetings with the outgoing Associate Producer, Vivian Dayton, and the business manager, Allen Shaw, Les set about learning his duties. It was his job to oversee the daily activities of *Good Times* –to schedule production time in the studio, rehearsal space, wardrobe and hair personnel--to arrange food deliveries for rehearsals and taping--to provide for script delivery to the actors--to fill office staff vacancies and attend weekly sweetening sessions.

Les had a real problem with sweetening. This was the process of adding music, sound effects and laugh tracks to the edited version of each episode. He thought of it a cheating, but it was his job to add canned laughter to joke lines and situations that the executive producer and the writers thought were funny, and always the biggest and longest laughs were given to the main character's yelling pronouncement of *dyn-o-mite*, which Les hated, but realized he was in no position to have an opinion about the process or the value of sweetening; it was simply one of the duties that he had to accept.

Soon after only a few weeks on the job Allen Shaw, the business manager, called all of the associate producers to a cost containment meeting and urged them to be mindful of spiraling production costs. He was especially concerned about wasteful costs incurred when schedules were not kept, and it was pointed out that one of the main offenders was Harry Finklestein, the director of *Good Times*. It was cited that he usually appeared one or two hours late for each of the weekly editing sessions and the company was being charged for the time that the facility was idle, and in addition was being charged the extended overage necessary to get the job of editing done. So now it fell on Les' shoulders to make sure that this director be on time for his scheduled director's cut.

Les was troubled. He had been on the job only a couple of months and now this very sensitive situation became his responsibility to correct. He thought long and hard about the proper action to take, and what he decided to do seemed like a benign approach, and it was, except for an unfortunate snag it the process.

Les wrote a memo to Harry Finklestein, reminding him

that he had a standing eight o'clock Friday morning appointment in editing, and he pointed out that this reminder was made in the spirit of his being new to the job and, "I'm simply reviewing schedules and procedures necessary to keep production on track." Les had instructed that the memo be placed in the director's box, as was the usual practice, and it would be picked at the end of the production day. But for some unexplained reason, an over zealous production assistant brought the memo to the director while he was in the control room blocking the show.

Harry Finklestein had a shit-fit. The memo got him so upset that he could not continue his rehearsal. He called in Les and wanted to know the meaning of the memo. Les tried his best to explain it was only routine and it did not change anything, but was simply a reminder that the editing session for the show being taped on Thursday night was scheduled for editing on Friday morning at eight o'clock. Nothing seemed to calm down the irate director. He was so upset he could not continue the rehearsal.

Reuben Stein was summoned when it was discovered by the Executive Producer that tape rehearsal had been suspended. Harry Finklestein complained that the associate producer was forcing him to make an early Friday morning editing session that was impossible because he had late night taping sessions on Thursday.

Reuben asked, "Why is it necessary to stay so late on tape nights?"

"To make pick-ups."

Reuben's response was, "Pick-ups should not take very long to accomplish after taping."

At this point Reuben gave a master class. He took Harry through a step-by-step process of marking the script for pickups during the taping. He explained how the production assistant should record the time code and shot number of each missed shots during the taping, and at the end of the taping session it would not take more that an hour to pick up all of the missed shots. So it was possible to get out of production at a reasonable hour on taping nights, and still make the early morning editing session.

As Les listened and learned from the master class given by Reuben Stein, a very capable and savvy executive producer, he wondered if any of this advice had gotten through to Harry. Even though he had been on the job a couple of months, Les had observed that Harry was not a very creative director. His blocking of actors usually had very little to do with motivated action or business. He lined up the actors on a horizontal plane to the camera position, and when it was time for one actor to respond to another actor who, inadvertently, happened to be at the far end of the line, he shuffled their positions as in musical chairs. Les had also perceived that Harry was, in effect, re-directing the show after taping. During this time he reviewed two half-hour taped shows, while the cast and crew sat around and waited. Then he made up new shots and restaged the pick-ups. This practice was time consuming and tedious and, unknown to Reuben Stein was the main reason for his pick-up sessions lasting so long.

At the very next taping session, Harry Finklestein was back to his old practice, because he was not accustomed to arranging shots any other way, so he totally ignored Reuben's suggestions. Consequently, the pick-up session ran very long into the early morning hours. Les could not ignore the extended overtime situation, especially in light of Allen Shaw's admonition concerning cost containment. Les wrote another memo addressed to Allen Shaw, the producers and other concerned staff, which was delivered Friday morning.

On Monday of the following week, soon after Les arrived at his office at eight, the phone rang. It was Reuben Stein. He wanted to see Les in his office.

Les was elated. As he walked down the corridor to Reuben's office his mind ran amuck. He was sure that his chance to direct had finally arrived. No doubt Reuben had seen his audition tape, and heeding the advice of Al Buxton, he was now being given a chance to direct. There was no other reason, in Les' mind, for Reuben to call him to his office this early in the morning.

It was too early for any of the office staff to be at work and Reuben's office door was open. Les looked in, knocked on the opened door and said, "Good Morning, Mr. Stein."

Reuben replied in a sharp voice, "Come in."

As Les approached the desk, Reuben slid a sheet of paper in his direction. "Did you write this?"

Les immediately recognized the memo that was put into Harry's box early Friday morning. He read it again for what seemed like the first time:

Date: Friday November 14, 1975
RE: Taping of #0314
From: Les Martel
THE SITUATION
1. *Last night we wrapped at 1:07am, after accomplishing approximately 6 pick-ups.*
2. *It took exactly 3 hours and 23 minutes to make decisions concerning the director's cut before 3 of the pick-ups could be decided upon.*
3. *Approximately 23 engineers and 9 production people were standing by during this period. Overtime overages came to approximately $4,166.25.*
4. *The head of makeup is threatening to quit because of what he terms, "the unreasonableness of this procedure."*

SUGGESTED SOLUTION:
1. *Immediately after the air taping all decisions relating*

202

*to pick-ups should be made by the director, with the
aid of his assistant, from the time code and shot sheet
marked by the assistant during the taping sessions.*

2. *Pick-ups involving all actors and crew should then
immediately take place.*

3. *After pick-ups all cast and crew should be dismissed;
with a skeletal crew necessary to accomplish
decisions relative to the director's wishes remaining.*

As Les retuned the memo to Reuben's desk He could see
fire in his eyes. He said softly, "Yes, I did."

"Les, you're a schmuck. Harry came to my house early
this morning. He was trembling. He said, 'feel my heart.'
The poor man was almost in cardiac arrest he was so upset
over this memo, and you did that to him. He's a good director and he's been with me a long time and I don't want him
upset. Do you understand?"

Les said, "Yes, sir."

"Now I want you to apologize to Harry and all of the
people to whom you sent this memo. Is that clear?"

"Yes, sir."

"That's all, you can go."

Les turned and headed out. He stopped in the doorway
and for a moment considered turning back and saying to
Reuben Stein, *That memo contained all of the suggestions
that you had made to Harry on Wednesday last week on how
to do pick-ups, and he ignored your suggestions and the result was a cost overages of over four thousand dollars. And
I wrote the memo because Allen Shaw had instructed the associate producers to report all overages of this nature. I was
simply doing my job.* But Les decided not to say anything
and he continued out of the door and made his way back to
his office. As he turned to go into the men's room he met
another associate producer, George Simon, coming out.

"George, what's a schmuck?"

Without hesitation the reply was, "A jerk, a creep, a fuck-up. Why? Did somebody call you a schmuck?" Then George laughed.

"No. I heard it on television last night. Just thought I'd ask."

George continued, "Well, the Hebrew meaning defies English translation because the connotation is much worse. To be called a schmuck is fighting time."

Les continued into the men's room. He wondered why he hadn't said anything to Reuben. Maybe he was intimidated by his celebrity and power in the industry; he didn't know, but he did know that it was not like him not to respond when he was taken advantage of. He thought of going back and facing Reuben and telling him what he thought of being called a schmuck, now that he knew what it meant. He thought of his grandfather and how much he needed him at this moment, how much he needed his advice. He wondered what he would have urged him to do.

His mind's eye traveled back to a time when he and his grandfather were sitting on the fishing bank watching a family of swans while they waited for the fish to bite. At that moment a flock of ducks flew in and landed on the water near the swans. In no time at all the swans were fighting off the new arrivals. Phillip said, "See that, birds of a feather flock together. Even though they are of the same species, the swans feel threatened by the duck's presence and try to protect their own. It's their instinct."

Les felt that this is what had happened with Reuben Stein. He was sure that Reuben had remembered the master class that he had given to Harry only a few days before, and he was sure the Reuben realized that Harry had seen the memo on Friday, but waited until Monday morning, three days later, to appear at Reuben's house in cardiac arrest. So it was clear that the memo was considered a threat. No doubt it was considered ample evidence of what an incompetent director Harry really was; and even though Reuben knew this he had to protect his own. And that's exactly who Harry was—his own. Les was sure this was the reason he was called a schmuck.

As all of these thoughts surged through his brain, Les was staring into the mirror and he didn't like what he saw. He punched the image. Glass shattered. Blood spewed from his fist. Les trembled. He grabbed the wrist of his injured fist with his left hand and tried to steady the shaking of his body. He took out his handkerchief and wrapped his hand, left the men's room, got into his car and headed home. He was sure of one thing--his grandfather would not have suggested that he strike out at this own image, no matter what amount of disappointment he felt because of his own failure to defend having done what he knew was right.

Les made the apologies that were suggested by Reuben Stein. To have not done so, would have been a defiance that he knew Reuben would not have tolerated. It was a hard lesson for Les but one that he would not soon forget. The next week as Les left the rehearsal hall, Reuben passed him in the hallway, put his arm around Les' shoulder and said, "Try and forget what happened. Put it behind and get on with your job."

Les did not believe he would ever forget—the metaphor of the birds of a feather told by his grandfather, or the lesson learned from Reuben Stein.

*   *   *

A few days later George met Les in the hallway and invited him to lunch. Les told George that he had planned to join his girlfriend at the Melting Pot for lunch and suggested that they meet for lunch together. George agreed that it was a good idea, "Now I'll be able meet the lady who takes up all of your time after work."

The three had a delightful time in the sunny autumn November weather, on the patio of the restaurant. They were seated next to an integrated couple who requested their check right after the three placed their order for salad Niocoise, gefilte fish, and fried catfish.

The conversation, of course was centered on the industry—Caryn's experiences as a working actress, struggling to survive in La-La Land, George's journey on the road to becoming a producer in the image of his hero, Rueben Stein, and Les' exploits as a disappointed actor turned associate producer.

And then it was clear; the reason that George had asked him to lunch. He said to Les, "I was just heart broken when I heard the news going around the studio that you were apologizing for that memo to Harry."

Les went silent. Caryn focused her eyes on Les' despondent face, and asked, "What happened?"

George was quick to reply. "Les wrote a memo, as was required by the business manager, about excessive overtime use by the director of *Good Times* and Reuben made him apologize."

Les had not said anything about this incident to Caryn and he had explained his cut hand as an accident resulting from the breaking of a glass cabinet in his office. He was not very proud of what had happened in Reuben's office and he did not want to relive the experience by explaining to someone he loved.

Now, here it was out in the open by a chance conversation with George. If he had known this was George's reason for requesting lunch he certainly would have tried his best to avoid it.

Caryn was visibly upset. Tears welled up in her eyes and

she said, "Oh, Les, I'm sorry. You didn't say anything."

Les was silent. Caryn reached across and held his hand.

George continued. "I was really pissed. He shouldn't have done that. Reuben is my hero but this time he was wrong. Allen Shaw had insisted only a couple of weeks earlier that we do just what Les did." Then he looked Les in the eye. "I just want you to know that I'm with you on this and I would have written a memo the same as you did. This apologizing thing is for the birds and I can't for the life of me figure out why Reuben made you do that."

After a short period of silence, Les figured it was time he said something. "Thanks, George I appreciate that, you're a good friend."

George continued, "I just wanted you to know how I felt about that. Anyway I'm sorta pissed with Reuben about something else."

Les was curious. "Oh, what's that?"

George replied, "When I started as associate producer they couldn't give me the salary that my agent was negotiating, so I was promised a second show, as soon as one was available to make up for the difference in salary. And so far nothing has happened."

Les asked, "So what are you going to do?"

George said calmly, "Wait them out and bide my time. Something's bound to happen soon."

Les caught the waiter's eye and called, "Check." Within two minutes the waiter brought the check.

The integrated couple at the next table saw how quickly Les had gotten his check. They had been requesting their check ever since Les and his friends had placed their orders, but had been ignored, so they decided to leave.

The waiter immediately called the manager and charged the couple with theft, saying loudly, "That Nigger is trying to leave without paying!"

Les was up like a shot. He pulled the waiter by the arm and pushed him against the wall next to where the manager was standing. Les brought his face within three inches of the nose of the trembling waiter and said firmly and softly through clinched teeth, "You bigoted bastard. Those people have been trying to pay their check ever since we ordered lunch and that was over an hour ago. You managed to ignore them all that time, and I watched you the whole while. And now you have the gall to yell out that, 'the Nigger is trying to leave without paying his check.' I don't like to hear that word. Now, I want you to go over there and apologize-- loud enough for me and everyone else to hear, and then you collect their money for lunch. And if you don't apologize for using a word I don't like, I promise I will kick your ass all over this patio." Then he looked at the manager and said, "And yours too if you try to interfere."

The waiter pulled his arm from Les' grasp and approached the couple standing at the exit confused, not knowing what was about to happen or what to do. The frightened waiter looked back at Les and said to the Negro man, "I apologize for using that word, and I'm sorry I was too busy to collect your check earlier."

The man, paid. The couple left. The waiter brought the money to the manager.

Les said, "Now, here is my check." Les counted out twenty-five dollars. Then he said, "And here is your tip." He gave the waiter a quarter. "I hope and pray you have learned a lesson for life."

As the three stood in the parking area waiting for the valet to bring around their cars, George said, "Man, you are something else. This must be the week for apologies. I couldn't hear what you told that waiter but whatever it was you scared the bejesus out of him."

"He used a word that I don't like to hear."

George said, "I could tell that. If I didn't know better, I would think that you were…" George hesitated.

Caryn looked at Les but didn't say a word.

George continued, "A Negro."

Les said, "That's right, I am."

George's face turned into an incredulous mask. He turned inquiringly toward Caryn then back to Les. "Surely, you joke."

"No, that's who I am. But I assure you, I am not a schmuck."

"But I don't understand. You don't look like a Negro. You don't sound like one either, so why…" Then he turned his face to Caryn, "Did you know this before?"

Caryn replied, "Like the man said, that's who he is." Then Caryn smiled and said, "Our car is here, let's go, Les."

George stood there, as the egg on his face began to dry in the hot sun.

*   *   *

The next week while sitting at his desk, Les received an intercom signal from his secretary in the outer office. "Mr. Martel, you have a visitor."

"I don't remember having any appointments. Who is it?"

"Just a moment."

No doubt his secretary was interrogating the visitor, which she had not done before calling him. She came back on line and said, "Mr. Dennis Thompson from NBC would like to have a few minutes of your time."

"Send him in."

A short, dark skinned, rather thin looking gentleman, dressed in an impeccable sports jacket with complimentary slacks, shirt and tie, extended a hand as he approached the desk behind which Les stood expectantly.

"Lester Martel, I bring you greetings, and congratulations. I am Dennis Thompson and I am associate producer of Short Form, whatever that means, over at NBC."

Les responded. "Thank you. Have a seat. May I inquire how I can help you?"

Dennis took a seat in a swivel chair in front of Les. His eyes traveled around the room as he turned round in his chair. "Well, it's just as simple as I said. I dropped by to offer my congratulations." After a pause he continued. "You have a very fine office. Most fitting for the first Negro associate producer of a major sitcom in Hollywood."

Les was dumbfounded. For a moment he didn't know what to say, or how to address the statement made by his visitor. Finally, he was able to put together a response and asked, "What does that mean?"

"It means that in this year of our Lord, one thousand nineteen hundred and seventy-five, you are the very first one of us who has made it to this position. And you are one of the few members of the Directors Guild of America, having been admitted only thirteen years after the very first, Wendell Franklin. And as a member of the DGA you have joined the likes of Ivan Dixon, William Crain, Charles Blackwell, Oscar Williams, Sid McCoy and a very few others as members of that holy white sanctum."

There was little doubt in Les' mind that Dennis sounded like he knew what he was talking about. He had shared with him historical information that he had no knowledge of, and as far as Les was concerned this made Dennis honorable. He was curious however, about his position at NBC. Les asked, "Tell me, what do you do at NBC?"

"That is one of the great mysteries of all times. I am an associate producer of short Form. And Short Form is anything that is under one hour, or anything that anyone wants it to be. I fiddle and faddle with something of everything. I am, in a word, *A Spook Who Sits by the Door*. And I am waiting and watching for that day when my time will come and I will rise gloriously from the ashes, like the phoenix, and take my rightful place in this crazy, but fascinating world of Hollywood."

There was no doubt that Les' admiration for this man named Dennis was growing. He had a true understanding of the business they were in, and he had a realistic perception of how they both fitted into the overall scheme of things.

Dennis held up his hand with one finger pointing upwards. "But, beware, you too can become *A Spook Who Sits by the Door*." There was a pause, and then he continued, "However, looking like you do, it will be difficult for them to consider you as they do me—A Spook." Dennis laughed. And it was a laugh that was so infectious that Les joined in to share the irony.

Les did not miss the chance to assure Dennis that he was a true color Negro, although the, "Color of my skin may disavow that fact."

Dennis stood and said, "Good for you. Now I've got to run. I've got to get back to my job at NBC, before I'm missed. But I want to leave one thought. In your position here, give as many of us as you can a hand up. With that I will take my leave. Let's have lunch. Here's my card."

Les took the card offered him and smiled.

With that, Dennis was gone as quickly as he had appeared. Les was impressed.

The very next week Les had another visitor. This was a young woman who was seeking a position as a makeup artist. Les inquired if she was a member of the union. She said, "No."

Les informed her that he could only hire union members to do makeup on *Good Times*.

She dropped her head and said, "That's the answer that

211

I've been getting everywhere I've applied. I can't get work until I get into the union. And I can't get into the union until I get work experience on a signatory show."

Les understood the catch 22 position she was in. He remembered the comment made by Dennis, and began searching his brain for a way he could help.

"I'll see what I can do…er..your name again?"

"Millie Jordan."

"Give me a few days Millie, and I'll give you a call if I come up with anything."

Les spoke to the man in charge of the makeup crew on the show. He understood the dilemma, and pledged support to help. It was arranged that Millie would come on as an apprentice, without pay, so that she could get experience. She was assigned to help with the makeup of the female lead on the show. Because of her dark skin, her makeup needs were the least complicated and required only a base to prevent the glistening of her skin under the lights. Both Les and the head of makeup felt they had found a way to help Millie get the work experience she needed to get into the union, without putting a burden on the makeup budget.

However, sometimes the best intentions go awry.

After a couple of makeup sessions, the female lead called Les to her dressing room. She was very upset, that an inexperienced, non-union makeup person was allowed to do her makeup."

Les did his best to explain that she was a capable makeup artist and had been approved by the makeup crew chief. And they were trying to help Millie get enough experience to qualify for union membership since it was so difficult for colored artist to get into membership otherwise.

The female lead would have none of it, and threatened to go to Reuben and report Les' violation if he did not get "*that woman*" off the set immediately.

Les had no choice but to apologize for the inconvenience, succumb to the demands of the lead actress and thereby dash Millie's hopes for getting into the union.

He could not really understand why a celebrity actress would not extend a helping hand to one of her own. This was a situation that defied the natural tendency of birds of a feather sticking together.

Chapter 15

History Revisited

In February, 1977, Les and Caryn curled up together on the bean bag couch and watched the most incredible television history of slavery ever compiled. Alex Haley had researched his genealogy for many years and traced his American family back to the coast of Gambia in West Africa. Then he put it into an historical novel entitled *Roots,* and that was finally made into a fantastic television mini-series that aired every night for a week.

One of Haley's ancestors, an African named Kunta Kinte had been captured and sold into slavery, brought to America in 1767, and the story of succeeding generations of his family was told in the saga.

It was incredible.

The stories had a profound effect on Les, and also on Caryn, but mostly on Les. They were both moved to tears as they watched the brutality of human ownership grind the dark-skinned creatures of God's creation into sub-human objects of labor. It was clear that the work, sweat and tears necessary to produce the crops grown, had been the source and substance of the wealth that had created the rapid rise of greatness for this young country.

And it was now crystal clear to Caryn that the perpetuators of slavery had so little moral integrity, although they pretended otherwise by religious hypocrisy, that they would engage in a bloody war to maintain their system.

The Roots series spoke volumes about the actions of their ancestors, and both Les and Caryn were saddened by hearing again the stories of abuse that chronicled the history of their country.

And it all started because Alex Haley was curious about his forefathers.

Now this same curiosity had been generated for Les. Although his racial origins were different than Haley's, he was curious to know about the Creoles from whence he came. He remembered the stories told by his grandfather but he wanted to know more.

Who? When? What?

He began his research, starting with his memories of stories heard from his grandfather, Phillip. He took these stories and began comparing them to census records, and soon he discovered that he was not that far from a valuable resource—the National Genealogy Archive in San Bruno, California. In addition to the Mormon Genealogy Archive in Salt Lake, Utah this was the most complete resource in existence.

He got into his mustang and drove to the Bay Area, where he spent four days with microfilm and magnifying glasses. The most compelling and unexpected aspect of his quest of the past, was how it stirred his emotions. When he had followed his ancestors back to his great, great grandfather, Placide Martel, he wiped away the tears that fell on the documents. There were more feelings here than he figured had existed in his being, when it became clear—that his father's father had been named for his grandfather—that Placide, the first, had married a Native American Indian from the Attakapa Tribe—that Placide's wife, Marie Ton Ton, was a practicing herbalist and mid-wife—that Placide's grandfather had come to the Louisiana Purchase Territory from Arcadia, where his ancestors had settled after leaving France in 1650.

It had caught Les off guard, and it was incredible; but now there was no doubt about who he was, or from where he had come. It was a gratifying feeling, and he put it all together into a simple format.

Caryn was amazed when she read what he had discovered.

Lester Martel, Junior from Estilette, Louisiana (me)
The son of;

Lester Martel, Senior from Frillotville, Louisiana, (b.1904) married Lillian Fergerson.

He was the son of;

Placide Martel, from Carencro, Louisiana, (b.1874) married Marie Broussard.

He was the son of;

Victor Martel, from Carencro, Louisiana, (b.1838) married Merida Broussard.

He was the son of;

Placide Martel, from Lafayette, Louisiana, (b.1797) married Catherine Marie Ton-Ton

He was the son of;

Louis Martel, from Lafayette, Louisiana, (b.1771) married Marguerite Thibaudeau

He was the son of;

Antoine Martel III, from Arcadia, Nova Scotia, (1704) married Marie Babin.

He was the son of;

Antoine Martel II, from Arcadia, Nova Scotia, (b.1682) married Anne Landry.

He was the son of;

Antoine Martel I, from Arcadia, Nova Scotia (b.1662) married Marie Bourgeois.

He was the son of;

Daniel Martel from Martaize, France (b.1626) married Francoise Gaudet.

He was the son of;

Rene Martel, from Martaize, France (b.1600) married Unknown.

He was the son of;

Alphonse Martel, from Martaize, France (b.1570) married Isabeau D'eatrade.

He was the son of;

Pierre Martel, from Martaize France (b.1550) married Unknown.

Les was proud of his research. He had traced his family name back to 1550 from France. And as far back as he could discover from his research, there were Broussards mixed in with the Martels, so the Creole influence in his family sprang from not one, but two fountainheads.

He knew that he had not done as complete a job as Alex Haley had done, but he was satisfied that now he knew more about who he was and from whence he came. The most disappointing aspect of his research was that he could only go back a couple of generations in his slave ancestry. Census records were not kept on the individual slave families, and those that were, reflected the name of the slave owner.

He remembered from the oral history he had heard from his grandfather that Phillip's grandmother's father, Valsin Savant, had been a slave and he died in 1921 at the age of one hundred and one. So the information that he got from the research supported his belief that he was indeed gumbo—a

descendent of the inter-mixed heritage from the colossal fornications of his forefathers.

*　　*　　*

By the spring of 1977, Les had successfully completed
his second season with *Good Times.*

Ann had successfully completed her medical studies and
residency, and arrangements were under way for the dedication of her office practice in Estilette. The date that Les
was given for the festivities in Estilette conflicted with his
obligations for the close out of the season of *Good Times.*
There was a memo from Reuben Stein's office stating that all
associate producers were responsible for cataloging and recording information for storage and safe keeping of all tapes
made during the season. The dates given for this to happen
were in direct conflict with the dates of the dedication of his
sister's new office. Les had a serious problem.

If the dates were on either side of either activity, Les
would have felt better. This was not the case. The dates
were smack dab in the middle of both affairs, and Les had
to make a decision about which to honor with his presence.
He thought of going to Reuben and presenting his dilemma
and asking to be relieved, or given permission to perform the
task at a later time. However, this option was not attractive,
in light of his previous conflict with Reuben over the issue
of the memo. He was reluctant to expose his vulnerability by
asking to be relieved of his duty to the show.

The other option was to get the work done under the
mandate issued, and not create any waves in the process. He
thought of getting it done prior to the dates that he had to be
in Estilette. He set about checking to see if that was possible.
None of the facilities or procedures would be in place to allow this to happen that far in advance of the date proposed.

So there was only one other option open to him if he wanted to be in Estilette for his sister's big day.

Les went to George Simon. He remembered that George had supported him in the memo apology situation and had pledged his friendship. Les had no reason to doubt that this was not George's true feeling, so he took the bull by the horns, realizing that he was flirting with disaster. Nevertheless, he sat in George's office as a friend, and laid out his entire situation and the dilemma that he faced.

"I've got to be at home for my sister's office dedication. Family is important to me. I love my sister dearly, so the thought of me not being there to celebrate her achievement is out of the question. So it would be greatly appreciated if you could do my archival duty while you do yours. I would be eternally grateful."

George listened carefully and smiled honestly. "You have nothing to worry about. I will take care of your records on *Good Times* as I do mine for *The Jeffersons.*"

Les gave him a hug. "Thanks, George, I knew I could count on you."

On his way out of the office, Les turned and said, "This is just between us. No one else should know anything about this. I'm sure the-powers-that-be would not take too kindly to me being away at this time."

George responded sincerely, "Don't worry about it. Everything will be fine. I'll take care of it."

With that commitment from George, Les made plans to be in Estilette on May first for the festivities. Caryn went with him.

*   *   *

The whole town turned out for the occasion.

A new doctor was moving into the office that had been

occupied by Dr. Rossini for fifty years. Not only was this new doctor a woman, she was a colored-Creole, which meant that she was an acceptable practitioner to all people, colored and white alike. This was the purpose that Alex and her father Stephen had in mind when they made the arrangements for this to happen.

The office complex had been remolded to a state of the art facility complete with office machinery and connecting laboratory facilities, all financed by the Estilette family, a contribution that Martha would have proclaimed as a part of the estate stolen from her family.

Ann Marie remembered the stories told her by her Mama, Lala—how her mother, Martha, had obsessed and grieved over the family fortune being lost to Judge Estilette, the progenitor of the Estilette family—how Martha had plotted and schemed for her son Bobby to marry Alex in order to reclaim some of the wealth. Now it seemed that a sense of fair play had taken over the passions of Stephen and Alex and prompted them to generously provide a stepping stone for an ancestor of the Broussard family to once again share the lost wealth. For this, Ann was grateful. However, no one else concerned thought of this event in these terms, or even remembered Martha's obsession with the idea.

The gala celebration spread over the entire municipal area. There were banners on light poles, flyers and posters in most businesses, and scheduled festivities in public and private facilities; of course the most obvious was the Black Eagle. A special concert featured Lightfoot himself along with Vitalee. They performed a collection of blues songs from Robert Johnson, to Son House to Leadbelly and Bessie Smith and included Lightfoot's compositions and arrangements from the *Train* to *The Sky is Crying,* to *Amazing Grace* from Martha's funeral. Needless to say, Ann was the honored guest at all of the festivities.

Caryn was dazed. She had never in her life witnessed anything the likes of this. Ann's acceptance as the new doctor in town was phenomenal, and far surpassed the reception her parents got when they established a practice in Bemidji. She indeed felt like an honored guest for the occasion, and she and Ann hit it off from the beginning. Lala accepted her graciously and put her in the room next to Les' bedroom, thereby subtlely indicating that they were not to sleep together in her house. Caryn's eyes were opened to the extreme devotion of the family to the Catholic religion and the practice of going to early morning Mass. This was her first attendance at a church other than Episcopal and she could not believe the range of skin colors exhibited by the parishioners. If she had not been told this was a segregated church she would have believed that it was integrated with dark and light skinned people who looked like Les. All of everything was a new and joyful experience for Caryn.

Alexandrine and her parents, Stephen and Victoria had a special dinner at their home honoring Ann and her family— Lala, Les, Lightfoot, Naomi, Elvina, Rosa and although she did not accept, Vel had also been invited. The only non-relative included in the gathering was Caryn and it became Les' job to explain to Caryn the family's life-long relationships to the Estilettes, a chore he took to like a duck takes to water.

The only question that he could not answer was, "And who is that?" as Caryn pointed to the huge painting adorning the wall of the library.

Alex chimed in to help. "That is Marie Laveau, the voodoo queen of New Orleans. It's a copy of the famous painting by George Catlin. No one really knows where the original is but my father lives with the hope that one day this will be declared the only remaining copy or possibly the original."

Naomi said, "She's my sister."

Caryn's eyes grew large and out came, "Oh, really! She does look like you."

There was explosive laughter throughout the room.

Les said, while looking at Caryn, "Aunt Naomi means that they are related by the sisterhood of the voodoo spirits."

Caryn was a little embarrassed and smiled blushingly and said, "There is a lot of history here that ties everybody together; it's incredible."

Alex saw the chance to say what was in her heart and on her mind for a long time. "Isn't that the truth? For example, the only man I ever loved was Rosa and Lala's brother, Robert."

This revelation caught everyone by surprise; even her parents, who had known about the growing tenderness between the two of them, for years. However, they understood the compelling power and specialness of the occasion, so they remained silent. Victoria reached over and held Stephen's hand in anticipation, as they listened attentively.

Alex continued, "Bobby was in collage at Fisk and I was at Vanderbilt and that is where our love fully blossomed. However it began here, when he lived with us, right up there," She pointed to the ceiling indicating the attic where Bobby was hidden away from the racist that wanted to kill him.

She continued, "He and I did not really date while we lived in Estilette. And although it was not that much different in Nashville, we were able to see each other more often and our love for each other grew. I've often wondered how different my life would have been had he lived and we had gotten married."

Lala said, "I remember, Mama used to say that you two would be married someday."

"Oh indeed. We had Martha's blessing." Was Alex's response.

Victoria felt that she had to intervene. "Alex, dear, do you really think you should continue with this story?"

With hearing this, Ann began to think back to the time when she and Alex had shared the intimate events of what it was she was about to reveal to everyone. This was only a few days before these events celebrating the occasion of her new office, and she and Alex were in her bedroom above the place where they were now gathered. In a flashback memory of what Alex said then, Ann remembered:

"I had just put Bobby's flowers in a vase and place them in center of the table and there was a jarring knock at the door, followed by a loud voice calling, 'Mary Ann.' I recognized the voice to be my roommate's ex-boyfriend. I thought it wise that Bobby hide in the space between the sofa and the wall, because I remembered that Chuck was a persistent, boorish, redneck, which was the reason that my roommate had cooled on their relationship. I opened the door only wide enough to speak to Chuck, but Bessie Smith was still singing in the background.

Hi Chuck, Mary Ann is not here."

'Where did she go?'

"Home."

'Home? She didn't tell me.'

"I thought you guys had broken up."

'Yea, well . . . this is Carson.' " *Chuck pointed to a friend standing nearby and said, referring to me,"* '*She's the one whose Daddy owns a newspaper in Louisiana.'*

"I could tell by that remark that I had been the subject of an earlier conversation and it did not sound complimentary, so I began to feel uneasy.

Look Chuck I'm expecting company. I'll tell Mary Ann you came by.

He asked instinctively,"'Who's that singing?'," *And he pushed past me into the room.*

I yelled, I didn't invite you in. But he went directly to the phonograph. He scraped the needle across the groves and yelled," 'Who the fuck is Bessie Smith?'

"*I yelled back, You're scratching my records, Get the hell out!*

He yelled back," 'Just like I thought, this is nigger music. You're a nigger-lover!'

"*Then Carson, who followed Chuck in, went into the kitchen and began wolfing down the food from the pot on the stove like a pig. I rushed furiously at Chuck and gave him a push toward the door yelling, yelling get out!*

He yelled back," 'You got a lot of nigger music here.'" *And then he began flinging my records against the wall. I ran at him, hitting, scratching and kicking. He held me off, and then Carson ran in to help him and together they were able to overpower me. They tore off my clothes, and forced me down to the floor, and each one held my arms while the other had his way with me. Finally, they left, taking our bottle of wine. Then, Bobby came out from behind the sofa, with tears in his eyes. I said, You'd better get out of here, or you'll get blamed. Bobby knew I was right, and he left, reluctantly."*

After a moment she said, "No, Mother. You're right and I won't. But I want all to know that we're all family here, because this is what I was taught to believe, and our history goes a long ways back."

Victoria put her fingers to her lips and threw a kiss.

Alex continued. "But the relationship between me and Bobby was not to be."

Alex took a deep breath and wiped away a tear. It was clear how deeply she felt.

There was a brief silence, then a spontaneous applause from the group. Stephen and Victoria embraced their daughter, and hugs and kisses came from all in the room.

Ann was especially moved, as she wiped away the tears, and said, "Oh, Alex, thank you for sharing. You don't realize how close this brings us. I will always love and cherish you. You are indeed my sister and a member of the family."

*   *   *

The next day Les took Caryn to his fishing spot on the bank of Bayou Coutableau. She look around in amazement at the huge oaks laced with the delicately hanging draperies of moss waving in the breeze, the cranes and herons flying out of the sky and slid onto the languid bayou waters. The two of them settled under Les' favorite pecan tree. It was pleasant. The sky was clear and a few clouds floated by and combined to make images that became prophets of the moment. Caryn said, "Look there's the ship that Almustafa was waiting for."

Then Les responded, "The one that brought him joy and sorrow."

And they languished in the peace of the place. Each in their own way relived the fleeting golden hours of the past few days, and enjoyed their time together.

Caryn had planned to go back to Los Angeles in a couple of days to fulfill audition commitments for acting possibilities. Les had planned to stay in Estilette for a couple of weeks longer to be with his sister and help set up her new office.

Abruptly, their peace and tranquility was broken when BookTau suddenly busted into their midst and collapsed, out of breath, at Les' feet. He was able to get out his urgency, in widely separated utterances... "I've been....looking all over ....for you. We've got a problem."

Les tried to comfort him. "Take it easy, BookTau. Take your time, get your breath."

Caryn's eyes were wide with inquiry. Who is this Goliath?

What does he want? I hope he's friendly. But what came out was a question to Les. "Is he a friend of yours?"

"Yes." Then Les turned his attention back to BookTau. "What's wrong?"

By this time BookTau had raised himself from the prone position on the ground to a sitting position with his legs crossed and his hands resting on his thighs looking directly into Les' eyes. "He's back, and he's at my house."

"Who's back?"

"That man that Miz Rosa married."

"Joshua? "

"That's the man."

Les was thoroughly confused and began to try to make some sense out of the report that he was getting from BookTau. "What's he doing at your house?"

"I donno. But he say Miz Rosa tolt him to come to my house 'cause he couldn't stay at hers and he didn't have money to stay in the hotel."

Les took a deep breath and asked, "Is he still at your house?"

"Das where I lef' him. Tolt him I had to get some food, 'cause he say he's hungry. Then I come looking for you."

Les loaded everyone in the car.

Caryn asked, "What's going on?"

Les told her the story, as far back as he felt she needed to know. "This guy that BookTau is talking about is married to my mama's sister and she was planning to divorce him. Evidently he just got out of prison and Aunt Rosa doesn't want him at the house so she sent him to BookTau's. I guess you could call him the black sheep of the family."

BookTau, added, "Das right he's a black sheep all right, and a no-good. 'Fessor didn't like him and was upset when Miz Rosa married him."

Caryn was trying hard to sort it all out. "Who's 'Fessor?"

"My grandfather."

Her eyes brightened as memory returned, "The one you're always talking about?"

BookTau chimed in. "The salt of the earth, as 'Fessor would say about any good Christian man."

Les laughed. "See, I told you, so there's little else for me to say."

They continued to the store and Les got the food stuffs that BookTau said he needed and they headed back to the house that Phillip had left to BookTau when he died.

When they drove up, Les saw a black 1969 Chevrolet parked in front. Joshua, dressed in a black suit, white shirt and gray tie, was sitting on the porch in the rocking chair that had been Mr. BoBo's throne for the many years he had lived there.

Les addressed him. "Well, Josh, I see you're out of prison."

"Yes. I am. You've grown up since I saw you last."

"Yeah, you can say I'm a man now. What you come back for?"

Les was direct and to the point. A man of few words.

Shivers ran through Caryn's body. She had witnessed the nature of the beast in Les' temperament before, and didn't want a repeat performance, so she reached out and took his hand as a signal to cool it.

Joshua turned on the charm. "Just wanted to see my wife, and visit with my relatives for a little while. Anything wrong with that?"

Les admitted, "Nothing's wrong with that. Well, we brought you some food. Have a good evening."

Les and Caryn left BookTau, Joshua and the food and headed back to the family home.

Rosa was a basket case. Lala, Lightfoot, and Elvina sat

around the kitchen table trying to calm her down. Ann had gone to bed. It was all too much for her, especially after the rejoicing festivities of the last few days.

Les and Caryn joined the jury that was assembled to decide what should be done.

Rosa said, "Lord God, I should have divorced that man when I came back from Chicago after Les graduated."

Lala said, "It's too late for that kind of thinking now."

Les added, "He seems like a changed man. Not as flashy as he used to be."

Rosa continued through her tears, "He's a Muslim and wants me to become one, and says if for some reason, I didn't want to live here anymore, we could move our business to Chicago."

Lightfoot added, "Now we've got to think about a way to get that bastard out of town."

Lala responded, "There's no need for that kind of talk."

Then Lightfoot retorted, "Lala, there's no need to pussy-foot around and handle this guy with kid gloves. He's a bastard and we need to get his ass out of town as soon as we can. I'll call Cat and have him arrested." After Lightfoot's comments there was silence.

Rosa broke the silence. "He said if I gave him his share of the money from the estate and the business he'd go back to Chicago."

Lightfoot retorted, "See? What did I tell you? He's a conniving bastard just looking for money."

Elvina had her say. "Well, no matter how you want to see it, he is married to Rosa and it is his right to have his share of the community property."

Lightfoot came back, "Who's side are you on?"

Lala said, "Look, Uncle Johnny, let's not get into this, my side or your side. We're all in this together. We're family and we have to stick together. Rosa, you've got to get a good lawyer and start divorce proceedings against this man immediately or he'll bleed you dry."

Lightfoot was a bit quieter now. "O.K., have it your way. Get a divorce but if that don't work out, me and Les will kick his ass out of town before you can say Jack Robinson."

Lala came back. "Now you leave Les out of this. He's sitting over there not saying a word, so don't get him riled up. You know he's hot headed like his daddy and I know that's what you're counting on."

Well that just about ended the conversation of the evening.

Elvina said, "I'm going to bed because I'll be headed back to New Orleans early in the morning."

Les saw an opening and asked, "Aunt Elvina, could you take Caryn back with you? She's got a plane reservation for Wednesday and it would certainly help me out a lot not to have to drive her to New Orleans with so much going on around here."

Elvina said, "I'd be happy to have her company, and we can have a nice dinner tomorrow night at the *Court of Two Sisters*."

With that, the evening ended and everyone went to bed; some to have a quiet night's sleep and others to have nightmares.

Chapter 16
Live and Learn

Ann was up bright and early. She went to her new office carrying a box of diplomas, license and other credentials that she began placing on the walls. When that was completed to her satisfaction she collapsed in the large leather chair that had been transported from Phillips den, along with his desk the day before. Lala had agreed that Ann's grandfather's desk and chair should be the centerpieces for her new office.

She was overwhelmed. Everything was perfect. The public acknowledgements, the parties, the receptions everything and the generosity of the Estilettes had made possible was gratefully appreciated, but there was one missing feature-- the presence of Grandpop. He was not here to complete her picture of fulfillment. She ran her hands along the well worn horse hair leather covered arms of his chair and tears welled up in her eyes. She surveyed the recently adorned walls containing her accomplishments and wished that he had lived long enough to make her joy complete. Memories of the precious moments they had spent together began to flow through her mind's eye, but this was short lived, because the image of a person materialized in the doorway.

Alex stood there holding two cups of coffee as her eyes surveyed the walls.

"Wow, you have been busy. I stopped by on the way from church to take you to breakfast but Lala said I would find you over here working, so I brought you a cup of coffee."

Ann walked over, gave her a hug and received the coffee, "Well, what do you think?"

"It's very impressive and looks great." Alex took a seat on the sofa opposite the desk and said, "But I would like to know why you've been crying."

"Oh, is it obvious?"

"Obvious enough to leave tracks in your makeup."

Ann laughed and wiped her cheeks. "Oh, that. I was just thinking of Grandpop, and missing that he is not here to see all of this. You know, when you walked in I was remembering one of the best times that he and I had ever had."

Alex took a sip from her cup, smiled and said, "Want to share?"

That was the only invitation necessary to coax Ann to stroll down memory lane. She took a seat beside Alex on the sofa. "I was seventeen and that was. . ." Ann paused a few moments to figure the date. . . ." in 1964, just a few months before that big trial that Les was involved in. Well, Grandpop's social club, *Les Bon Temps Homme,* had selected me as one of the debutants to be presented in New Orleans. That was the most exciting time of my life, and for me to be a part of their yearly *Fais Do Do*--the ball of all balls, during Mardi Gras, was more than I could ever imagine. Well, just before the time of the presentation waltz with our fathers, Mama came to me and said my Papa was passed out drunk in his room and would not be able to dance with me. I burst into tears right there in front of all the other girls and asked Mama, 'What am I going to do?' And just then a voice said, 'How about dancing with your grandpop?' And I did. That was the most beautiful dance of my life. Grandpop looked magnificent in his white tie and black tails, and he did not miss a beat, and led me around the floor like I was the princess of the ball. I have never forgotten the joy in my heart that night and the proud look on Grandpop's face as we danced to the music of Dave Bartholomew playing *The Blue Danube*."

By this time Alex was also crying and she said, "And I have not forgotten that occasion either."

"Were you there?"

"I was indeed, along with my mother and father we've always been part of the important events in the life of your family."

"Oh, thank you!" Ann leaned forward and hugged Alex, who then kissed her on the lips, a tender open-mouth kiss that was fleeting and brief but nevertheless caught Ann unexpectantly, and she smiled sweetly. She took Alex's hand and pressed it to her cheek.

"What's going on here?" Came a voice from the doorway. Ann turned to see Les. She ran to him like a little girl greeting the ice cream man and said, "Oh, Les, we're reliving memories of Grandpop!"

"And that's why you're crying?"

Alex said, "They were happy memories and joyful tears."

With that assurance Les said, "Good. Let's go have some lunch."

*   *   *

Joshua sat on the porch watching the dust cloud that signaled an approaching intruder to the quiet outback. He neatly folded the copy of *Muhammad Speaks*, that he was reading, tucked it away under his leg, then brushed off the front of his black coat and adjusted his tie in the manner of neatness that he was accustomed to.

Sheriff "Cat"Bobineau got out of the patrol car, and limped towards the house with the aid of his cane. He was now seventy years old and even though the city council had insisted that he resign at sixty-five, he had convinced them that he was still fit and able to carry out the duties of sheriff as he had done for the last forty-five years. Except for the arthritis in his left knee, which was helped along by the cane, that housed a stiletto steel activated by the push of a button in the grip, he got around just fine.

He stopped at the steps of what he remembered to be Mr. BoBo's house, and addressed Joshua. "Well, Joshua Cane, I see that you are out of prison and have returned to our fair city."

"That I have, Sheriff Cat. And I see that you are still on the job with that knife hidden in your cane."

Sheriff Cat was taken aback. *How in the world does this nigger know about the spring loaded knife in my stick?* After that brief moment of questioning Joshua's knowledge of concealed weapons, which he dismissed as a lucky guess, Cat continued. "I've got a subpoena here for you to appear for a divorce hearing."

Joshua reached out and accepted the document. "Thank you, Sheriff. I hope this wasn't too far out of your way."

"No it wasn't. And I hope that you do right by this good and upright family that you have brought so much pain and embarrassment to."

"Well, that's a matter of opinion, Sheriff but I do thank you for the advice. Good day."

Sheriff Cat looked at Joshua for a full minute before turning around and limping away. Confrontation was on his mind. He could just as well put him in jail on suspicion of breaking his probation, which he was sure that he had violated being so far away from Chicago so soon after his release, but he decided not to stir up any more trouble than he had to, so he got into his car and drove away.

Joshua studied the subpoena. A subtle smile crept onto his face. He decided that he needed a lawyer to be sure that he got all he figured was due. But he had no money to engage a good attorney, perhaps one from New Orleans. He knew that he would not be able to find someone local who would be willing to take on a divorce case against the well known and loved family of the Fergersons. This was going to be costly. He would have to have money, and the only way he could count on getting the sum that he needed was through poker. He knew that gambling was against his newly proclaimed religion but he had to chance it. No one in town, except his estranged wife, knew about his Muslim faith, so until his mission was accomplished he would return to being his former self.

He drove to the other side of town to a Salvation Army store to get fitted out in apparel more in keeping with his "Sugar Cane" image. He liked the look, although not the quality that he was accustomed to wearing, but it would suffice for the occasion. He had been away from Estilette for almost ten years and it was not likely that anyone that he had had insurance dealing with in the past would remember him anyway; however he knew that Slick would, so he dressed for the event.

The Sugar Shack Pool Hall hadn't changed. Slick sat on his favorite bar stool with that extra cigarette stuck behind his ear held in place by the skinny brimmed hat. His trade mark Bellefonte styled shirt opened down front revealed his golden chains, and brawny chest. Joshua's entrance did not cause any undue or different response from Slick, who tugged at the sleeve of his coat as he slowly shifted his head and rolled his eyes to follow Joshua's trek to the preferred pool table at the back of the room.

After Joshua selected his stick and turned around he became aware that there was a change that he hadn't noticed before. In the corner in the dark on the bench usually occupied by Sipzu, was the mammoth body of a dozing BookTau.

Slick sauntered over, kicked the foot of BookTau, and said, "Rack 'em up."

BookTau sat up with a start, saw Joshua standing there holding his pool cue and said, "Mr. Joshua, I didn't see you come in. I'll set up the table right away."

Joshua questioned, "What are you doing here?"

"I works for Slick, when I'm not working for Lightfoot."

Joshua turned toward Slick, "What happened to the other one?"

"You mean Sipzu? I don't know. He just disappeared. He was here one day and gone the next. No one has seen him in years. Want some one to shoot with?"

Joshua looked around at the three shooters at the adjacent table, and the half-drunk standing nearby and nodded his head to accept the challenge. He and Slick shot eight balls for the next half hour during which time Joshua made arrangement for a poker game.

Slick inquired the particulars. "How soon?"

"Saturday night."

"How many hands?"

"Four others. But they gotta have money to lose. I need some cash, and I feel like winning."

By the end of the game, the poker night was all arranged. However, Slick did have a problem because in four days he had to find three other big spenders to fill Joshua's request.

He had decided that he would count himself in. Then he thought about asking Lightfoot. It would be a good way to inform him about Joshua's plans, and he knew that Joshua knew that Lightfoot had the money that he was hoping to win; and he also knew that Lightfoot was not about to lose any amount to the likes of Joshua. He smiled as he considered the potential fireworks of the group that he was thinking of putting together. For the third hand he would get Cecil Peete, better know as the Cockeyed Man. He was born cross-eyed and there was no other cure except surgery but his parents never had the money, so he was raised with the stigma and the teasing of never looking in the right direction. He had made a small fortune as a brick layer and he loved to play cards. So he was in. The fourth hand was a problem and Slick figured he had to think on that for a bit, so he let the decision rest.

The next day, Les sat at the end of the bar sipping a Nehi, after revealing to his uncle the news that Aunt Rosa had just begun divorce proceedings, when Slick entered with a cigarette dangling from his lips and disclosed his proposition to Lightfoot.

Lightfoot said, "Lemme get this straight, you want me to play poker with you, Joshua and the Cockeyed Man?" Lightfoot closed his eyes and shook his head.

"That's right. This coming Saturday night."

Lightfoot ran his hand through his silky graying hair. "What's going on?"

Les left his drink at the end of the bar and joined the men. "I bet he's trying to win some money to hire a lawyer to fight the divorce."

Slick's eyes widened, "Ohhhh, so that's his game." He reached over and flicked his ash in the tray. "This is gonna be better than I thought. I need a fourth hand. Got any suggestions?"

Although Slick had addressed his question to Lightfoot, Les volunteered, "Yeah I want in."

Both men turned toward Les. Lightfoot laughed, "You

don't know shit about poker, at least not enough to play with him." Then he turned to Slick, "What you need is a tough, bull-shit-talking, devil-may-care, lying, sunuvabitch."

"Know anybody like you describing?" Then Slick chuckled and added, "Except me?"

"Yeah, Vitalee."

"The blues singer? You're shittin.'"

"Naw. She's a cold mutherfucker, can't be rattled under any conditions and will look you straight in the eye and tell a lie."

Slick laughed, "Wasn't counting on a woman but come to think on it, along with Cecil Peete that's just who I need. But does she have the money to get in the game?"

"No, but I'll stake her. I don't want to see the Candy Man walk away with any money in his pocket."

"Then it's a done deal. See you Saturday." With that Slick headed toward the door.

Les followed a ways and said in a loud voice, "I want to be there to see this."

Slick stopped, turned and said, "You can serve drinks and clean up with BookTau, if you want to. But keep your mouth shut and stay out of the way."

"I can do that." Les said with a smile.

After Slick slammed the door shut, Lightfoot said, "Boy you don't have no sense a' tall. You don't know what you're getting into; we could be playing all night and way into the morning." Lightfoot limped away towards his office.

Les yelled out as he picked up his drink, "I can do it."

Lightfoot yelled back, "Yeah, that's what troubles me."

*   *   *

Everything was set and ready. Several decks of cards were stacked in the center of the army blanket covered table.

Glasses, bottles of booze, coke, beer and ice were on a small bar in the far corner behind which Les and BookTau stood and waited. Slick, Lightfoot and Vitalee laughed and told jokes as they smoked and drank.

Slick took a long drag from his cigarette during the laughter and said to Vitalee, as he bobbed his head and jived-walked in her direction, "Baby can you top that?"

Vitalee, dressed in her tight fitting pink dress suit with gold jewelry dangling over her delectable cleavage, said, "Oh my man, you stand there in all your funky glory thinkin' you betta den me? Well, put this on for size." She tucked up her breasts revealing their lushness through her too small blouse, reached over and put her hand on Slick's shoulder, and asked, "You ever hear how Tarzan got his yell?"

BookTau began to get excited and did his circle dance, "I nebber heared it neither."

Slick said, "Shut up, man, fill ma glass and shut yo ears, dis is for me only. Tell it mama."

"As Tar-zann was swingin' thru da trees he saw that Jane was in trouble. A 'gator was chasin', her ass, and she was runnin' and yellin', and runnin' and yellin', and the gator was gaining. So Tar-zann swings over her on his vine and he yells down to Jane, 'grab the vine, grab the vine!' And Jane reaches up without looking …and she grabs what she thinks is a hanging vine, and holds on for dear life and Tar-zann yells oooooh…..ahhhhh….oooooh." She mimics the traditional Tarzan yell.

Slick banged his fist on the bar and doubled over in laughter. Lightfoot, blurted out, "She's gotta there brother." Les gave approval with yells, and repeated slaps of his hands over his head. BookTau did his circle dance again.

As the fun and laughter of enjoyment begins to die down, Vitalee puts her hands on her hips, wiggles sexually and says, "Ebber' since then they call me Jane."

The joie de vivre starts over and grows again.

Vitalee said to Les, "Dat made me thirsty, rack me up again, baby."

The door opened and Cecil Peete entered. He was a short, balding, middle aged, cigar smoking man with a beer belly overhanging his beltline. He was good natured and laughed at most things that were not funny, a peculiar trait cultivated from the many years of taunts about his eyes. He shook hands with Slick and was greeted around the room; then he looked over at BookTau and said, "Jax beer is my drink, and keep it coming."

When Joshua entered, dressed in the apparel that he was seen in the last time he was seen in Estilette, there was a pause in the conversation and Slick approached and said, "My Man, Sugar Cane. Meet Cecil Peete, and I know you know Lightfoot and Vitalee."

Joshua said, "Yes, but I didn't know we were going to be entertained by a songbird."

Vitalee came back, "But this songbird is not singing tonight, just playing a winning hand of poker. Hope you brought money to lose."

Joshua was caught a little off base but he did not show any signs of discomfort. He looked around the room at Les and BookTau and then at Lightfoot, laughed and said, "Well it seems the cards in the deck of the Fergerson family are well represented and stacked against me."

That was very funny to Cecil who put his arm around Joshua's shoulder, blew a puff of cigar smoke and said, "So you're the Candy Man. I just love your sweet stuff and can't eat enough. For a long time I've wanted to meet up with you, and now here you are in the flesh."

Word of the man who started *Sweet Rosa's Fudge* had spread like wild fire. And when he disappeared, rumor had it that he had been run out of town because the sheriff didn't like the pink Cadillac he drove, and his uppity father-in-law didn't like him. But everyone figured that someday he would return to his local wife after the old man had passed on. Whatever the truth, the candy that Joshua was responsible for bringing to the public was a good treat, and this story and others about the Candy Man had made him a legend.

Then Slick chimed in, "Well all right then, let's play some cards."

The game had been going on for about an hour during which Les observed the mannerisms, hand gestures and body movements of the players.

After a hand was dealt, Vitalee would look in Lightfoot's direction and either smile or pick her teeth with the fingernail of her little finger. This was done so frequently that Les began to believe that they had signals going.

When Joshua got a new hand he raked in the cards and neatly stacked them by running his thumb and middle fingers around the edges keeping them face down on the table. He slowly picked up his hand and brought it up close to his face, gradually fanning out the cards one by one.

Cecil usually had his eye focused in Joshua's direction and this began to irritate the Candy Man. Finally, he could not stand it any longer and Joshua blurted out, "You trying to see in my hand?"

Cecil laughed, "I hadn't thought about that, but if you'd rather me look in the other direction, I will."

Les thought that his Uncle Lightfoot would bust a gut he laughed so hard.

Joshua was visibly upset over the interruption of the outburst from Lightfoot, which from that time on was disguised as a broad smile every time Cecil's cockeye was focused straight ahead. Lightfoot knew that Cecil was now looking directly into Joshua's hand, and Cecil's stacks of chips began to grow; and it seemed for a time that Slick's strategy was working.

The one mannerism that confused Les was Slick's use of his red plaid handkerchief. He would wipe away the sweat and either throw it over his shoulder or pile it on the table. From time to time it fell on the floor, and it just happened that Les was refreshing the drinks on one occasion when the handkerchief fell. He bent down to pick it up, saw the small pistol that was taped under the table; he picked up the handkerchief and put it back on the table. Now he knew the reason for what appeared as Slick's tricky behavior with the handkerchief.

As hard as they tried, they could not keep Joshua from winning, especially when the deal was passed to him.

During a break, while the players were at the bar, Les overheard Slick whisper to Cecil, "Is he dealing from the bottom?"

"If he is, he's faster than I can see."

That was as close as they could get to catching Joshua cheating.

When the break was over, Joshua said to Slick, "Why don't you and I switch seats. Sitting next to a beautiful lady always changes my luck."

Les was curious about how Slick was going to handle the situation, but he was cool and made no objections. It was clear to Les that Slick had figured out if the need came up he could always duck under the table and retrieve his weapon.

After the seats were switched, Les arrived at the conclusion that, for some reason Joshua suspected that the Cockeyed Man was reading his cards, and wanted to move away from his gaze. There was little doubt that Sugar Cane was a master gambler. However, Les did observe that the other players would from time to time win a pot, but he figured that was part of Joshua's strategy to lure them in.

Vitalee was a trip. Now that Sugar Cane was sitting next to her she did everything to distract—opened her blouse and fanned her titties to cool off, crossed her leg in his direction and pulled her skirt up, thigh high, and made sexy vocal sounds whenever she picked up a good card or got one she didn't like. She did everything she could think of to take Candy Man's mind off his game, as was her plan, but nothing fazed him. Nothing distracted him. He was focused on one thing—winning. As close as Les could figure, Joshua had nearly a thousand dollars in stacked chips in front of him, which was far more than anyone else.

The mixture of cigar and cigarette smoke continued to hang like a cloud and the booze continued to flow, and so did the cards.

It was early Sunday morning when Cecil crushed his cigar under his foot, stood up, stretched and said, "I've had enough, and lost enough. Now I bid y'all good morning. I'm going to Mass."

That ended the game.

Joshua cashed in his chips and folded over two thousand dollars into a rubber band, and left with a smile on his face.

The other players, especially Lightfoot, were not too happy that they were not able to keep him from winning, but rather had aided his effort to get a stake to fight the divorce. Lightfoot had lost about one half of the amount that Joshua won, considering the money that he had put up to stake Vitalee. He left in a huff, followed by Les, who wanted to get a ride home.

In less time than one could say Jack Robinson, the place was deserted, except for BookTau who was left to clean up and lock down the Sugar Shack. He made a quick job of his chores and began walking the long way home to the outback. He decided to take a short cut through the cemetery, and when he saw Joshua's Chevrolet parked on the roadway, he decided to find him and get a ride home.

After walking around the cemetery on a search for

Joshua, he finally saw him, but he was not alone. Joshua was headed towards Rosa who was kneeling in front of the family tomb. BookTau decided that it may not be a good time to make his presence known, so he hid behind a large crypt where he could watch, but was too far away to hear the goings-on between the two.

When Rosa heard someone approach, she turned. Completely shocked she said, "Joshua! What are you doing here?"

"I came to talk. You wouldn't talk to me when I came by the house the other day, so I thought we could talk here."

"How did you know I'd be here?"

"Now, Rosa, I know you. You come by here after every Mass."

Rosa had forgotten how clever and resourceful he was, and for a brief moment she was flattered, but then she remembered all that had passed between them, took a deep breath, pursed her lips, and said "I guess you got served with the papers."

Joshua was persistent and he spoke softly. "It don't have to be this way. Look, . . ." He pulled out the roll of money. "I got all of this money. . ."

Rosa interrupted. "Don't try to buy me. You're a Black Muslim and I'm Catholic and will be until the day I die, so there's nothing left for us but divorce."

"I was going to say I got this money to get a lawyer for the divorce, but I'd rather keep it for us if we could go away from here."

"No, Joshua. I've made up my mind. There is nothing left between us. You killed everything that we had when you joined that other church." Rosa started to walk away.

Joshua followed. "If we could just talk. Just hear me out. We had some good times together."

Joshua was now walking beside Rosa and they were

headed in the direction of where BookTau was hiding. Rosa kept walking and Joshua kept talking. "I just joined the Muslims to save my life while I was in jail."

Rosa stopped. She looked deep into Joshua's eyes. "You are some piece of work. I should have listened to my Papa, and not have had anything to do with you in the beginning."

Joshua put his arms around her. "Rosa, do you remember the first time we kissed. It was not too far from where we are now. Let's go back to that time and start all over."

He tried to kiss her. She wrenched herself out of his arms, slapped him, and backed away.

Joshua advanced.

Rosa kept backing away until she was trapped with her back against a tomb.

Joshua embraced her once more and tried to kiss her. She struggled and yelled out, "Stop! . .stop . . .leave me alone. . .I don't want to be with you!"

At this point BookTau ran from his hiding place, grabbed Joshua around the neck from behind, and began choking him, "Leave Miz Rosa alone. She don't want to be with you. Now you just leave her be!" Not realizing his own strength he kept putting pressure on Joshua's throat. All the while he was choking the life out of him. For a brief time Joshua struggled but soon his body went limp. Rosa stepped to the side and moved a slight distance away. BookTau continued to squeeze his throat. Rosa ran to BookTau and tried to pull his hands away. "BookTau, that's enough, leave him alone."

BookTau turned and looked at her, "He was trying to hurt you. I won't let him hurt you."

Rosa continued to insist and continued pulling at his arms. "It's all right. Let him go."

BookTau released his hold on his neck and Joshua's body crumbled to the ground.

Rosa screamed.

This seemed to bring BookTau to reality. He looked at the lifeless body lying on the ground next to the grave and he knelt down next to Joshua. "Mr. Joshua. Mr. Joshua . . ." He shook the body. "Wake up. I didn't mean to hurt you, just wanted you to leave Miz Rosa alone."

Rosa was a basket case. She didn't know what to do. She ran one way than the next. She told BookTau to stay there until she came back. She ran out of the cemetery and down to a corner telephone booth. She called Lightfoot and told him what had happened. Lightfoot instructed her to go back to the graveyard and wait. "Don't leave; I'll take care of everything from here." When she returned, BookTau was sitting on the tomb next to Joshua looking down at his lifeless body with tears in his eyes.

Sheriff Cat looked down at the body and shook his head. "I had the notion to run him out of town last week. Wish I had. When you play with dogs you get fleas."

Then he turned to BookTau. "Big guy, I'm gonna have to take you with me."

Then he turned to Rosa. "Tell Lightfoot to come by my office."

Cat limped away on his cane and BookTau followed as the coroner picked up the body and rolled it away.

Chapter 17
Rare Breeds

When Lightfoot returned from the Sheriff's office Les was waiting at the Black Eagle.

He was full of questions and Lightfoot answered most, and then laid the roll of money, bound with the rubber band, on the table and said, "This is for Rosa. Sheriff Cat say since she the surviving wife, it belongs to her. That and the car is all he had, so she gets it all."

Rosa didn't want to have anything to do with the money or with the car either. She told Lightfoot to do what he wanted with both. Lightfoot used the money to pay BookTau's bail so he could get out of jail, and he sold the car and planned to use that and the remainder of the money for a defense lawyer.

Les was very upset about the charge of murder but there was little he could do but hope and pray that BookTau would get off with a light sentence. Most people around knew he had no intention to kill the Candy Man; he was just protecting Rosa whom he thought was in danger.

Les tried to be upbeat, and did what he thought his Grandfather would do—so during his weekly visits outback, he kept BookTau thinking that everything was going to be all right. He would talk about the old times and the fun they had catching 'gators, but no matter how much he tried to keep his mind off the murder, BookTau would constantly ask, "What's gonna happen in the trial?" And then he wondered, "Am I gonna die in jail like Mr. BoBo?"

Les spent the rest of the summer in Estilette, trying to assure BookTau that everything was going to turn out just fine, and his main reason for staying was to be a friend to BookTau, who had no other.

It was during this month that word of Elvis Presley's death hit the news. Lightfoot planned a special evening dedicated to the music of this popular star who had boldly built a bridge between blues and rock and roll. It was well known that he listened to and was influenced by many early blues people especially Robert Johnson.

Lightfoot took the stage to a packed house, and made a special dedication to lift the spirits of, "My friend BookTau, who's been having a few troubles in the last few weeks. But no one can feel down long with Vitalee singing the songs of Elvis. We wuz real sad to hear about the death of the king. And we wanted to do something to honor his memory, so tonight every song we do is gonna be a song that was sung by the king. And I want y'all to understand that summa the songs he made famous was first sung by our own blues men and women. Now y'all just sit back and enjoy the singing of Vitalee doing the songs of Elvis Presley. And if y'all wanna dance, you can do the crazy legs like the king did. Our first song is Hound Dog."

With that, Lightfoot hit the opening chord on his guitar that turned Vitalee on with a high pitched vocally sustained attack on "Yoooooooooooooou ain't nothin' but a hound dog." And it also turned on BookTau. He was up and out of his seat on the first note. Les smiled to see that he was having a good time and seemed to have put all of his troubles behind him.

*   *   *

Les had stayed in Estilette a lot longer that he had planned, but he kept in touch with Caryn through frequent phone calls. It was well into August when he got back to Los Angeles. He figured that it was about time to get back to work, and planned to check with Al Buxton to get the startup date for the production of *Good Times*. Caryn had gotten a reoccurring role on *The Young and The Restless* that paid the expenses and kept her challenged as an actress.

For the first few weeks back they caught up on missed lovemaking time. They went to concerts, movies and sight-seeings whenever Caryn's character was not in the script storyline. They even visited the Los Angeles Zoo and had fun doing the trivial things that make memorable moments. Their relationship was settling in to be satisfying to both, and after the ten years they had known each other, and after the trauma of events they had been through together, and after the ideals of life that had been tested in each, they were convinced that they were now a significant couple. The only matter not engaged was the attitude of acceptance by Caryn's parents. They knew very little about Les and were told only that he was a good man with whom she was living. So it was time they paid a visit to Bemidji.

Les and Caryn were met by doctors Helga and Dana Ericksen at the same train station where Les had arrived years earlier. He was coached by Caryn, to remember that he was not to recognize any structure or feature of Bemidji; and he had to keep reminding himself about this.

They were taken to the family home which was a beautiful, half-timbered-stuccoed, high pitched tiled roof home,
in the style of Danish architecture. At dinner, which consisted primarily of the venison and pheasants shot by Dana,
the conversation centered on the background of Les; from
which they learned--his ancestors were Creole, descendants
of the French Arcadians, Indians and Freed Africans-- he
lived in the small Louisiana town of Estilette-- his religion
was Catholic-- his grandfather was founder and principal of
a high school--his father was a sugar cane plantation owner-
-his mother was a school teacher, and he was an aspiring
television director. All of which brought smiles and wonder
to the faces of the elder Ericksens. They turned and looked
at each other and both agreed with the statement uttered by
Dana, "You are a rare man." Then came a question from
Helga, "How did you and Caryn meet?" After a lengthy ti-
rade by first Caryn and then Les, and then back and forth
explanations, with each adding colorful details, the delightful
and full disclosure dinner of three hours had finally ended.

After a tour of the premises in which Les recognized the
same style objects d' art that he had seen in the cabin, which
he was not supposed to recognize, they settled in the living
room and listened to the music of Dvorak and Grieg, followed by a question from Helga, "Les, what kind of music
do you prefer?" This was a question that she secretly wished
she had not asked, because it launched the history of the
Blues along with the many stories that Les had heard told
by Mr. BoBo, and so the evening wore on and on and finally
came to an end two hours later.

Helga showed them to their room. They were being bed-
ded together which was a surprise to Les, who had fully
expected to be sleeping in a room separated from Caryn.
This was to him a full admission of his acceptance by her
parents.

The next day was spent on Lake Bemidji in the family house boat. It was a comfortable forty footer which slept four with a kitchen and toilet. Dana was a skillful skipper and he navigated them into a quiet cove and then anchored for fishing. After giving a preliminary lesson in casting, Dana recognized immediately that Les was an experienced fisherman, and it was not long before he had bagged the limit in Bluegill and Rock Bass that were cleaned and prepared for dinner.

After tying up at the boat dock, where Les and Caryn had previously watched geese fly into the sunset, they walked the short distance to the recently rebuilt cabin. Les remembered the flames that had so rapidly consumed the place over ten years before and he took Caryn's hand and tenderly squeezed it. She looked into his eyes briefly and the two of them followed her parents to the cabin that was built on the same footprint as the one before. Upon entering Les realized it was exactly the same, and it became important that he not know his way around. Caryn made sure that the first thing she did was to take him on a tour of the place to acquaint him with the location of everything, and when that was done they both felt comfortable and relaxed.

After a delicious dinner of fish, Danish potato salad and string beans, the family settled on the dock and watched the sunset fade into twilight and then into one of the most thrilling moonlit nights that Les had ever seen. It was the perfect ending to a delightful day.

Out of the darkness came a voice calling, "Doctor Ericksen."

Dana turned and looked into the shadows. He stood and took a couple of steps toward the source of the voice, and then asked, "Buster?"

Caryn turned and looked in the direction of the man standing there and breathed out softly, "Oh my God." Then she whispered to Les. "Don't look back. Keep your face turned away." Les could feel his heart beating in his throat and Caryn grasped his hand and held it tight.

Dana now approached and Buster said, "Doc don't come any closer. I don't want you to see my face."

"Where have you been? It's been over ten years."

At this point Helga joined Dana and they stood listening to Buster's explanation.

"I've been in Canada. My face got burned in the fire and my leg too. I don't walk so good now and I don't look too good either so I don't want you to look on my face, you wouldn't recognize it was me. I just come back to tell you I'm sorry about that fire. I was drunk and don't remember too much of what happened that night, but when I came out of the wine cellar the next morning, the place was burnt down and I was hurting something awful. So I took off and headed north. I knew you would be angry with me and that's been weighing heavy on my mind all of these years, so I come back to tell you I'm sorry about everything."

Dana extended his hand. Buster backed further away. Dana, realizing that he did not want his face seen said, "Thank you, Buster. Is there anything I can do for you?"

"No sir, doc. Just being here to hear me out is enough."

Buster turned and hobbled off, dragging his left leg, which he could not bend at the knee. When he got some distance away he stopped, turned and yelled back, "Tell Miss Caryn I didn't mean what I said." Then he disappeared into the darkness.

Caryn bit her bottom lip and tears slid down her cheeks. She laid her head on Les' shoulder and squeezed his hand tighter. Les breathed a sigh of relief and he was thankful that it was too dark for Buster to recognize that he was the one who had punched him in the face.

Dana and Helga came back to the dock and sat in silence.

Finally Dana said to Caryn, "There was no need for him to know that you were sitting here."

Then Helga said, "Oh, Caryn I am so sorry for putting you through everything we put you through by not believing what you told us about the fire. Now we know that everything was just like you said."

Dana continued, "Yes." And he went on. "Every now and then when the breeze blew the leaves and the moonlight streaked across his face, I could see the scar tissue that had now replaced his face, and he stood there stiff-necked and stigmatized. It took a rare breed to come back and tell me what happened."

A shiver went through Caryn's body and it continued like a chilly wind blowing into Les' memory.

Although they knew it meant missing the Dragon Boat Festival and the plays at the Paul Bunyan Playhouse, Caryn and Les announced they had to leave to get back to work in Los Angeles. That was a fact but also there was the desire to put as much distance between them and Buster's appearance as they could.

Chapter 18
Revenge is not Always Sweet

Les went to see Al Buxton the day after he got back. Buxton was surprised to see him. He had been informed that Les had decided to return to Louisiana because of family problems, and the job of Associate Producer of *Good times* had been reassigned.

Les was stunned, and for several moments he couldn't speak. He just looked at Buxton. Finally he said, "I did go to Louisiana to take care of a family matter but that was during hiatus. I'm back now and I had no intention of giving up my job. We do have a contract."

"Yes, I know. But there is a stipulation in your contract that makes it renewable only if we call you back to work."

"But I never got a call about anything." Les was getting more steamed by the moment and he struggled to control his emotions.

Buxton was visibly sympathetic and he said, "The information that we got from a reliable source was that you had left town, so we did not call you back, but went into production with someone else."

And out of Les' mouth came an impulsive question that sounded like a demand. "Who?"

"We assigned the position to George Simon."

"But he's the associate on *The Jeffersons*. Does this mean that he now has two shows?"

Buxton struggled to make his response understandable, "Well, he did have an agreement with the company to get an upgrade in salary, and when the position on *Good Times* opened, the staff used that vacancy to fulfill his agreement."

Les saw the handwriting on the wall, and he was furious, but struggled to conceal his anger. It was clear. George had stabbed him in the back. He was the only one who knew about his trip to Louisiana. He was sure George had seen the opportunity to get a second show, and spread the news that, Les was not coming back. There was no doubt in his mind that the decision makers had gotten that message from none other than George. Les tried hard not to show his rage. Finally, after a few seconds, he extended his hand and said, "Thanks, Al, for all you have done for me. I really appreciate it."

"I'm sorry that things turned out the way they have. If anything changes, I will give you a call."

Les headed out of the office but when he got to the door, he turned and asked, "Is George working today?"

"He's over at the studio meeting with the technical staff about facilities and equipment needed for production startup in two weeks."

He thanked Buxton again and left.

Les had revenge on his mind. When he got to his car he drove to George's address and parked across the street where he could see the comings and goings into the garage. As he waited for George to come home, he visualized how he would punch him out. He was not decided whether he should first try to find out why he had done what he had, or just begin punching when he opened the door. At any rate he planned to give him a good comeuppance.

His mind's eye went back to the time when he had taken out his anger on the boys who had disrespected Dora. He was seventeen then, but the words of his grandfather were just as clear today as if uttered yesterday: *You should not be so quick to fight.* And that admonition was about defending the honor of a woman, which his grandfather had always encouraged him to do. Now he wondered what his grandfather would say about him kicking George's ass because he took his job. He imagined it would be something like: *There is something meaningless that occurs on earth, righteous men who get what the wicked deserve and the wicked men who get what the righteous deserve, and this too is meaningless.* He didn't know why that verse was still in his mind. It was from Ecclesiastes and had been recited to him by his grandfather twelve years ago, and he was now twenty-nine, so it must have had some profound meaning to still be in his memory.

Being the ingenious person that he was, Les said to himself, *I know, since Grandpop would not approve of me kicking his ass, I'll give him a taste of his own medicine.*

At that moment Les saw George drive into the building's garage, but rather than follow him in, he started up his car and headed to the Shangri-La.

He found Shiela sprawled on her usual lounge at the pool. He sat in the chair next to her and said, "Hi, remember me?"

"I sure do." And she followed with, "Did you come back for more?"

Then Les asked, "No more of what you have to offer. Tell me, are you still doing research for that acting role in *The Scarlet Hooker?*"

Shiela took off her sunshades and looked him in the eye. "Yes, why do you ask?"

"I've got a role for you. It'll be the biggest acting challenge that you'll ever have. And you'll get paid for it."

Shiela sat up, put her shades back on and said, "Keep talking."

Les explained that he wanted her to come on as a girl-fiend, to a producer who worked for Reuben Stein, and get him fired. He gave her all of the particulars. Her initial meeting was to take place at the Melting Pot on Monday of next week. She was to casually appear for lunch, see Les and pretend that she was a former acting acquaintance, at which time she would be introduced to the subject of her affections. She would then be on her own. She would get two hundred fifty dollars up front and another two fifty when the producer was fired.

"Sounds like a piece of cake," was Shiela's response.

That evening at home he revealed to Caryn that he had lost his job and had to look for another, but he did not give any other details of the circumstances. Caryn was very supportive and suggested that he might give a call to Wes Hendricks, executive producer of the *Young and the Restless.* "They are looking for new directors." Les thought he might give it a try, but in the meantime he planned to wait for the report from Shiela.

On the appointed day, Les had a scheduled lunch with George. He was on time, as all good producers are, and he approached the table where Les waited. "Hi.Good to see you. When did you get back in town?"

"A few days ago. How is everything at the studio?"
George seemed a little nervous. He took out a handkerchief and whipped his face. "Ohhhhh, all right I guess." He tried to change the subject, "Where is your lady?"

"We're not together anymore."

George smiled, thinking he was on to something. "Was she upset to find out that you were a Negro?"

"I don't know why that would upset her or anyone for that matter."

George leaned in closer to gain Les' confidence, and said in a whisper, "You know, if I were Negro and looked like you do, I'd never admit it."

Les realized then that George was a hypocrite and decided to twist the knife. "Are you back at work?"

"Well, yes, sort of."

Les was beginning to enjoy this. "What does sort of mean?"

"Ohhh, just that there are lots of meeting and shit, you know how that is."

"Yeah, I do remember." Les decided to let him twist in the wind. "So I decided that I had had it with all of that shit, as you call it, and I enrolled in the director's program at AFI. So I called in and told them I was not coming back."

Just then the waiter came to take the order, and interrupted what Les was beginning to enjoy. After giving their orders, George picked up the conversation. "Hey, that's great. That's the way to go. You know being an AP is just like being a gofer. You should be pleased as punch you're out of this rat race."

"Yeah, It was some kind of rat-race. By the way, I hear from the grapevine that you got my old job."

Now George <u>was clearly</u> uncomfortable. He laughed nervously, ran his hand through his hair and said, "Yeah well, they called me and told me you said you were not coming back and the job was mine if I wanted it. Well at first . . . I didn't know what to say, you know, you being a friend and all. But I didn't have your number to call, and check out things with you, and they kept pressing me for an answer, so I finally said yes, let's go with it."

Les knew then that he was lying, and he felt that anything that he had planned for George's comeuppance was justified.

The food came and they began eating.

Shiela appeared on cue and became quite the actress. "Les, darling it's so good to see you." She gave a Hollywood kiss on the cheek, and took a seat. "I haven't seen or heard from you since we auditioned for that awful movie. You should thank your lucky stars that you were not cast because it was dreadful, but I made lots of money, well you know how that is…" She reached over and gave a quick flick of her fingertip to his arm. "The producer liked my style, and I stayed on because the money was golden." Then a little giggle rushed from her lips and she continued. "But I've missed seeing you…what, pray tell, have you been up to?"

Les began to reply. "Haven't been up to nothing much, look, I'd like for you to…."

And Shiela played it to the hilt and cut him off…."Ohhhh, you don't have to tell me. I know you have sooooo many young starlets standing in line, you don't have much time to do or think of anything or anyone else, not to mention poor lil' ol me." Then her timing kicked in and she looked admiringly at George, fluttered her extended length eyelashes and said, "Aren't you going to introduce me to your handsome friend, or were you saving him to introduce to one of your many wannabees?"

Then Les said, "Shiela meet George Simon, George, Shiela Longstarr."

That was all he had to do. Shiela was off and running her game, and she executed it so well that in no time at all, George was talking about himself, and impressing her with his position as a producer for Reuben Stein on the sitcoms *The Jefferson and Good Times*.

Shiela was delightfully impressed.

Then without them paying much attention, Les paid the check, including drinks and food ordered for Shiela, then cunningly excused himself, leaving them to discover each other.

Over the next few weeks, George fell head over heels in love with Shiela. And according to her reports to Les, "He said I was the best pussy that he had ever had. And that was my signal to make him constantly late for meetings and tapings."

Word soon circulated around the office grapevine that since the new girl had come into George's life he was having a hard time keeping up with his two shows.

Shiela continued her periodic reports to Les. "It was easy. The man was starved for sex. We got it on in his apartment for five days straight. Then I started dropping by his office during the day. We fucked on his desk, under the desk and on the floor in front of the desk; and one day his secretary came in while we were getting it on. I knew then that the word that he was fucking on company time would be getting around. Then there was this big company dinner celebrating the opening of the season. Everybody was there, all of the bigwigs from the networks, celebrity actors and everybody who was anybody. George took me as his date, and I thought, it's time to have my field day. And I did. I was dressed, no I mean costumed, in the most seductive apparel of my wardrobe—a sheer, see-through, off-the-shoulder, tight-fitting, ass-hugging, red and white outfit that was sure to get attention. And we danced every time the music played. I kept my body glued to his—like fucking him on the dance floor. Everybody was watching us and we even got some scattered applause. I checked out the table where his bosses were sitting and they didn't seem too happy. And then on that Monday after the weekend, when I went to his office he was talking on the phone, and from what I could hear it sounded like an important conversation, so I got on my knees under his desk, unzipped his pants and started sucking him off. He didn't know what to do, get off the phone or get it off. He got it off. Then almost on cue the door opened and his secretary came in. She was horrified. She slammed the door and ran out. I knew it would not be long then."

Hearing this report brought a smile to Les' face and he waited expectantly to hear the fait accompli.

A couple of weeks later, after being told repeatedly not to be late for another taping, George left Shiela's bed in a hurry. It was a fifteen minute drive to the studio and he had left five minutes late. In an effort to make up the difference in early morning traffic, he ran a red light then swerved to avoid hitting a lady in the crosswalk, and ran into a sidewalk fire hydrant. Water shot into the air, drenching pedestrians, bringing traffic to a standstill, bringing out the police and the fire department, and creating such confusion that George did not get to work at all. When he did call in to explain his delay he was fired on the spot.

Shiela called Les the day after George was fired. They were sitting on lounge chairs around the pool as she gave the final report. Les fell out laughing when he heard. He laughed so long and so hard that Shiela looked at him like she thought him crazy. He finally noticed her non-smiling gaze, and his enjoyment slowly faded into silence. He asked, "What?"

"You owe me two hundred fifty dollars."

Les paid her the money. "Thanks. Now you're really ready to do *The Scarlet Hooker*."

Shiela stuffed the money in her bra and said, "And you're a sick sonnavabitch." Shiela got up from the lounge and left.

"Yeah" Les replied, as she walked away, "that may be, but you don't know what he did to me."

Shiela was headed to her room, then stopped, turned and said, "That bastard could have died or killed that woman in the crosswalk, and you think it's funny." Then she disappeared into her room, slamming the door.

For many minutes, Les sat looking at the people splashing in the pool, thinking about what had just happened. The people in the pool were having fun and laughing, just as he had been laughing when he heard the report about George. But it was not the same. There was joy and pleasure about what the swimmers were sharing. Shiela was right. There was no joy or pleasure about what had happened to George.

Then he felt the powerful blow of a fist on the right side of his face. He tumbled off the chair onto the concrete surface of the pool area. Les rolled onto his back and looked up into the angry eyes of a man holding a gun. Freddy, Shiela's pimp was back. No doubt he had been stalking Les during his entire dealing with Shiela. Les quickly rolled over and away from where Freddy was taking aim; he stumbled to his feet and began running. He heard a pop, then he felt what he thought was a hot arrow piercing his back. He fell into the pool.

It was a plunge into a white swirling mist, which continued for what seemed like an endless journey. As the whiteness began fading into blackness, two, long, arm-like tentacles enveloped his body and pulled him back into the light. He recognized his grandfather and then didn't see anything more.

*　　*　　*

Les opened his eyes. Caryn said, "Thank God you're alive."

He mumbled, "What happened?"

"You were shot two days ago. I thought you were dead

but you pulled through." Tears from Caryn's eyes fell on Les' hand as she brought it to her lips.

He whispered, "I remember Freddy aiming a pistol at me. But that's all I remember, except that Grandpop was there."

Caryn remembered hearing Les talk about his grandfather who had died years ago and felt for certain that he was delirious. "Look, why don't you get some rest. I'll be right here."

Les closed his eyes.

Lala and Lightfoot looked through the mirage of tangled tubes leading from banks of machines into the many punctures in Les's body. Lala's tear covered hands were clamped over her mouth. Lightfoot just shook his head in disbelief as his arm caressed Lala's shoulder.

Caryn whispered, "Let's go to the waiting room. They'll call us when he wakes up."

When Lala was able to speak she said, "When I got that call from the Los Angeles police, saying that they had a driver's license of a Lester Martel, Junior who had been shot, I couldn't believe it. But that's all they would tell me. So I called you. Were you able to find out what happened?"

Caryn said, "After I talked to you, I came here to the hospital and he was in surgery and would be for the next six hours. There was nothing I could do here, so I talked with the police officer on duty and found out where this happened and I went over there. The Shangri-La is a resident hotel in a questionable tourist section near Hollywood Boulevard. That's where Les stayed for a short time when he first got here. Then he moved in with me because of some unpleasant dealings he had with a wannabe actress named Shiela and a pimp called Freddy. Well, for some reason, he owed Shiela money. That's what he told me. He had come by to give her the money. Freddy saw him, beat him up, and shot him. He fell in the pool and one of the swimmers pulled him out and called the ambulance. They came, and the police came, and the fire department came to put out the flames. Shiela said that Freddy set fire to Les' car. She told me Freddy's was still pissed off because Les had beaten him up several weeks earlier.'"

"Lord have mercy. That boy is turning out to be just like his father." Lala whispered softly to herself, as though she didn't intend for anyone else to hear.

Lightfoot said, "Yeah, I'd like to meet up with this Freddy man and set his butt on fire."

The nurse appeared in the doorway and said, "He's awake."

Lala and Lightfoot had taken up residence for the week in a hotel not far from where Caryn and Les lived. Les had been out of the hospital for two days now, and since Thanksgiving was coming soon, Lala talked them into the idea of coming to Estilette for a few days of rest. The idea was attractive to both, and they said, "We'll *think about it.*"

Now that Les was up and about and healing, Lala could not resist the urge to give some motherly advice. She began as gently as she could. "Now son, from what I've heard Caryn say about the circumstances of the event that almost took your life, I want to say something. Now, I know you're a man, but you're still my son and I love you, and if something happens that would take you away from me, I would just die. I don't expect to bury my children, they should bury me. I thank God that bullet in the back went right through and out the front just nipping your lungs, and no permanent damage was done, but you were lucky. Now. . ."

There was a pause as Lala took a sip of coffee which gave her the chance to think about how delicately she should approach her next statement. During this pause Les was itching to make a comment, and he cleared his throat, a gesture before speaking, that he had learned from being around his grandfather all those years. But before he could utter a word, Caryn said, "I told Lala as much as I knew about that man, who shot you, and right now they're trying to find him and charge him with attempted murder, but beyond that I don't know much else."

Les didn't say what he had planned to say. He sat silently listening.

His mother continued. "Now from what I hear, this Freddy fellow does not sound like the kind of person you usually associate with. And I don't know how you happened to get involved with him, and I don't want to know. But I do know if you continue to have dealings with people like this you are headed for more trouble. Now, I know you have a hot temper, and like your papa, you will kick butt in a minute. That's why I was against you joining the Civil Rights Movement. You're a good boy, er, I mean man, and you have a good heart and I suspect that all of this came about because you were trying to help somebody else get out of some kind of trouble that they were already in."

Les could not help but notice the wisdom in his mama's words that sounded like the advice he had so often heard from his grandfather.

Lala continued, "So I just want you to promise your mama that you will stay away from people like this Freddy fellow. I know you're a man and you will do what you have to do, but please don't do it with those kind of people."

After several seconds of silence it was clear that Lala had finished saying what she wanted to say. She looked over at Lightfoot, giving him unspoken permission to speak his piece, but he didn't say a word. Les shifted his eyes toward his uncle as Lightfoot ran his hand over his mouth and slowly bowed his head up and down affirming what Lala had already said.

Les cleared his throat again, got up from his stretched out position on the sofa, embraced his mother and said softly, "I love you, Mama."

The next day Lala and Lightfoot said goodbye and boarded the plane back to Louisiana.

Les continued to improve and regain his strength.

Chapter 19

Handwriting on the Wall

The phone rang on October 16, 1977. Les Answered.

"Les Martel here, may I help you?"

"This is the office of the vice president of Tandem Productions."

"Al Buxton's office?"

"Sir, Mr. Buxton is no longer with the company. This is the office of Jennifer Fox, Al Buxton's replacement. We are calling to set up an appointment with you to talk about a position that has recently been opened."

Les could see the handwriting on the wall, but he wanted to be sure. "Is this about a position as associate producer?"

"Yes, sir. Are you interested in making an appointment to talk with Ms. Fox?"

"How about this coming Monday?"

"That's fine. Do you know where our office is?"

"If it's the same place as Al Buxton's was, I do."

"Then we'll see you on Monday ten o'clock. Thank you, sir."

Les hung up the phone and dropped his head. Caryn came over and began rubbing his neck. "What was that all about?"

Les shook his head unbelievingly. "They want me back as associate producer."

"But I thought they had given that position to someone else."

"They had. But I didn't tell you everything that happened."

Les went on to explain what had transpired with George and Shiela six weeks earlier, and ended with, "I had no intention of it turning out the way that it did." Then he said, "I'm not sure I want to take that job."

Caryn was on her way to the kitchen to fix lunch. She looked out over the counter that separated the kitchen area from the living room. And said, "Are you out of your mind? After all you just told me you went through with George taking your job, now you're saying you're not sure you want it back? What are you thinking about?"

"I'm thinking about Grandpop."

"Your grandfather's dead!"

Les closed his eyes and took several deep breaths.

Caryn laid out lunch on the low table in front of where Les sat with his hands resting, palms up, on his thighs. He opened his eyes as she settled on a pillow across from him. "I know he was there."

"Who?"

"Grandpop."

"Eat your lunch."

"I could feel him. I remember running from Freddy. And I felt the sting of the bullet, and then I musta blacked out. All I remember was floating down into a white bubbly mist. The further down I went the brighter it got. Then I felt Grandpop's hands holding on to stop me from going into the

267

blackness that was coming up fast."

Caryn took a sip from her teacup. "Those were the hands of that swimmer who saved you."

"No. It was Grandpop. I remember his voice. He said, "This is my grandson. He needs a new life." I would recognize his voice anywhere. I'm sure it was him. His spirit was with me. I'm sure about that."

Les dipped into his soup and took a bite of his sandwich.

Caryn asked, "And what does this have to do with your decision about this job?" She was beginning to feel that maybe Les was getting a little obsessed. But yet there was something about the look in his eyes that told her that he had had a manifestation of something more.

"Grandpop never wanted me to be in this business. So it wasn't only about what happened with Freddy, it's about everything that has happened since I've been here. He's been talking to me the whole time."

Caryn now paid more attention. He was serious. Slowly she began to understand. The old man had done such a complete job of instilling his value system into Les' sub consciousness that it was finally becoming real. Yes, he had had a near death experience and yes, she had heard it said that when people do, they sometimes imagine things that did not really happen. Whether or not this was a correct analysis of what was going on, she did not know. However she did feel, as she listened to him describing his feelings that something had happened to bring a new awareness that was now inducing Les to consider changing the direction of his life.

She listened more carefully as Les told how he felt about all of these experiences. First, with his agent, his deception, his cunning, his practice of blowing smoke up people's asses and then creating the illusion that everything would be fine— his experiences with Shiela who wanted to be an actress so badly she would sell her soul to the devil to play glamorous roles— his attraction to a film project that seemed to have meaning and purpose but which rapidly turned into a flim-flam of deceit---his ordeal with George who put no value on sincerity, honesty or friendship, and who believed that the road to success was in back stabbing, deception and lies.

And he continued. "To think I was also on that road. I played the game. I joined the process. I wanted the glamour and the spotlight so much that I was willing to do to George what he had done to me. And then all of everything that Grandpop had taught me came rushing back with the sting of that hot arrow in the back. That was my awareness, my wakeup call from my grandfather. So I'm getting out of this cesspool. When I go to the meeting on Monday I'm going to tell that lady, 'Thank you, but no thanks.'"

Caryn blurted out. "Then what will you do?"

After the flourish of emotion that had just come forth, Les felt hopeless and lost as he whispered, "I don't know."

Caryn reached over, rested her hand on his knee and said, "You don't have to be like everyone else in order to work in this business. Ever since I've known you this has been your dream. You were a refreshing breath of air for me when we used to rehearse our scenes and act them out. You were my inspiration. You believed that you could make a difference in people's lives by showing in performance how people should live to get the most out of life--how they could find the true meaning of things. And you are not always going to be an associate. I'm sure you will one day be a great direc-tor, or you could be a fantastic actor if that is what you want to be. But please don't throw it all away because a few bad apples seem to stink up the pile."

Caryn thought for a few seconds, and came to the con-clusion that this was the time to say some things that she had not said before.

"You just can't continue throwing away opportunities because of your precious principles. Your agent had gotten you that leading role of Jordan that you auditioned for. You had made an impression on the producers. They realized that you had found the spine of their story, because they changed the title to Sins of the Father. That was your suggestion. And then you threw all of that away because that immoral man tried to get into your pants. You've got to stop kicking the asses of the people who violate your sense of values. And now you have a chance to get back to work at Tandem and you're having second thoughts because you feel you are becoming one of them. Well, I've got news for you mister-above-it-all, there are a lot of fucked up people, in this fucked up but fantastic business. And there are also some honest and talented people, like you, who sometimes turn out brilliant productions in spite of the odds. Is your memory so short you've forgotten Roots? I'm sure that Alex Haley ran into some of the same people like A.B., and George or even a producer like the one on the Rhoda Show who overlooked your qualifications and gave the job of director to a Jewish person."

Caryn was on a roll. She felt that he was confused as he tried to get it all together--to realize his potential--to reach out and grab his coming of age in his own image, and she hoped that because of the things she said he would somehow come to an epiphany.

Les reached over and took her hand and gently pulled her body towards his lap. He kissed her long and tenderly.

Then she changed the subject. "I have to work tomorrow."

"Have you had time to learn your script?"

"Yeah. Remember I was telling you about Wes Hendricks?"

"The producer on your show?"

"Ever since I've been on the Young and the Restless, I've been hearing good things about this man. I think he's your kind of person." Caryn turned over and readjusted her position so that now she was laying on his left shoulder looking up into the vaulted ceiling. "There's a black guy who comes in to direct every so often, and a few weeks back we sat at the same table in the cafeteria for lunch. He told me some admirable things about his friendship with Wes that went back to a small college in Ohio where he was the designer of a Shakespearean production that Wes directed. Many years passed and Wes had just finished the pilot for *The Jeffersons* television series and this black guy, his name is Marcel Lenoir, had just arrived in Hollywood and was looking for work as a director. So he and Wes were united again after all of those years. Well, Marcel said that Wes was not able to direct the series of the *The Jeffersons* because he had just gotten promoted to Executive Producer on *Y&R*, so he recommended him for the job. Marcel didn't get the job, but Wes now uses him as one of his rotating directors. Wes is a good man."

Caryn turned over and looked Les in the eye. Then she continued, "Wes returns phone calls and he does everything he says that he's going to do. He's not like the other phonies in the business. He's honest and sincere and he helps people."

Les said, "I'll give him a call."

On Monday Les met with Jennifer Fox. He told her that he had decided not to take the job.

Her response was, "I'm sorry to hear that. I understood from Reuben Stein that you had done a remarkable job before it was passed on to George Simon, and now that he not coming back, it's yours to have again. As a matter of fact, we have both positions open, *Good Times* and *The Jeffersons*."

Les said with some regret, "I appreciate that, but I've

decided to get out of the business altogether."

Oh, really? May I ask why? I've never heard that anyone had so decided after being offered positions like this."

Les felt uncomfortable. He realized that he just could not share with this lady all of the reasons that he had discussed with Caryn. None of it would make any sense to her, especially his guilt over causing George to get fired, which he surely could not reveal. He was embarrassed to try and explain that his grandfather did not want him to be in the business in the first place. He was trapped. He smiled graciously and said, "I'm thinking of leaving Los Angeles, and going back to…" He hesitated and then continued, "I know this does not make too much sense, But I'm thinking of going back to school."

"Oh, that's always a good choice. You can't go wrong going back to school."

Les thanked Jennifer for the offer, shook her hand goodbye, and headed out of the office.

Jennifer's voice stopped him at the door, "What will you be studying?"

"Oh, I'll be working on my master's degree."

"Good luck with your studies."

Les felt that he had fucked up all around. He had lied. And he could not tell the lady that he felt guilty about taking the position after what he had done to George.

He was a mess.

He was disturbed. Upset.

*   *   *

A few days later, near the end of October, 1977, the phone rang. The delightful and charming voice on the end of the line announced herself as Dorothy Cross of the Creative Artist agency. Les was congenial and answered in an inquiring voice, "Yes this is Les Martel, may I help you?"

"I'm calling because our agency has been engaged by the producers of a film production company to offer you a starring role in the movie "*Sins of the Father.*""

Les was dumbfounded. He could not believe what he had heard. Several months earlier he had kicked A.B.'s, ass and he thought this project was a dead duck. However, he gathered his wits and asked, "Can you give me more information about the project?"

"Sometimes back you did an audition for the role of Jordan that the producers have not forgotten."

Les pretended. "Oh, yes, I had forgotten about that."

"Well, they have just been able to get the financing and are ready to go into production, and would like very much to have you come in for an interview."

Les took a deep breath and asked, "When and where?"

He was given all of the particulars.

He hung up the phone as Caryn came out of the bathroom and asked, "Who was on the phone?"

Les replied, "You will not believe this. A lady from the Creative Artist Agency wants me to come in to interview for the role of Jordan in *Sins of the Father.*"

"You're shitting me."

"No, I kid you not. She was serious, at least she sounded like she was. She wants me to come in for an interview this coming Monday."

"Did you accept?"

Les said, "You're damn right I did."

"Are you out of your mind? That asshole you beat up, said you'd never work in this town. And now he's calling you back?"

"This was a call from another agency."

"What do you think this is all about?"

"I don't know but I'm gonna find out." Les became

serious and put his arms around Caryn. "Baby, this is a crazy-ass town. They do things that don't make any sense at all."

"And so do you. Just a few days ago you were determined to get out of this cesspool, as you call it. You even gave up an offer to go back to work for Tandem and fill two positions, not one, but two. And now you're setting yourself up for smoke in the ass again."

"That'll never happen, but I am curious about what makes these people tick."

"Yeah, I know," Caryn said despairingly.

In an effort to perk her up Les responded, "Baby, I felt bad about taking that job after what I did to George; I just couldn't, in good conscience, take that offer. And after you said, I should not continue to throw away opportunities because of my principles, I thought I might try this."

Caryn shook her head in disbelief and ran upstairs and fell on the bed. A thousand thoughts raced through her mind. Only a few days ago, in spite of her arguments against him giving up because his precious principles were violated, she was now worried that he was in reality just like everyone else-- attracted to the glitz and glamor. Now he was giving second thoughts to star in a movie that he had closed the door on, and just when she had begun to admire him for standing up against the amoral, vicious, and unprincipled practices of the business. She was beginning to feel that he was like everyone else, all sound and fury signifying nothing. She finally fell asleep with conflicting feeling flowing pro and con about his coming of age as his own man.

Sure enough, on the following Monday Les sat in the reception office of the Creative Artist Agency, sipping a Dr. Pepper, that he was given when asked, "What would you like to drink?" Soon afterwards, a pleasant looking, short, lady, attractively dressed in a Sachs Fifth Avenue knit, appeared and greeted him graciously. She ushered Les into a large windowed office, where he was introduced to the executive producer, whom he remembered seeing at the audition, the director, and a fast talking publicity woman, who immediately stood and gave him a hug.

Dorothy, the agent, began by saying, "Ever since your audition, many months back, the producer and the director were impressed by your insight into the nature of the character Jordan."

Then Stan Levin, the director, added, "Not only were you able to perceive the through line of the entire story from the brief descriptions that you were given, but you also had a thorough and accurate grasp of the character's subtext and motivation. I was impressed."

The producer, Alan Leach, said, "Ever since you walked out of the audition with the words, '*Sins of the Father*', I've thought of nothing else more appropriate for the title of this movie, and you are the exact image of the character that the writer has created."

The hugging lady publicist, Eve Michaels, said, "And your marquee name, El Tigre is a dead ringer for the character of Jordan.

Les sat silently listening to all of the accolades and homage that were being heaped upon his one brief down and dirty audition, and he wondered what was going on. Finally he decided to take the bull by the horns and asked the question, "I was wondering, what if anything does my former agent, Andy Blinkey, have to do with all of this?"

Dorothy responded immediately, "He's given up all rights to whatever agreement you had with his agency."

Then the fast talking Eve took over, "You're a natural for this movie. You're a kick-ass kind of guy anyway, and I can see the hook for publicity now." Eve fanned her hand in the air as if tracing the line on a movie marquee, "El Tigre,

Kicks Ass in the 'Sins of the Father. Its a million dollar advance that very few actors can bring. Young man, consider you're fortunate to be standing on the brink of a fantastic career. Some take years"

From that point on the publicist, producer and the director had a field day anticipating and projecting the marketing potential of the money this movie could/would make with this kind of support casting, coupled with the possibility of the lead actor, Robert Redford, who was being considered and negotiated with.

After what seemed like hours of promises, projections and dreams of success, along with comments like,— "You gave that turd of an agent what he deserved, he's an egotistic bastard anyway,"— but in reality was only about thirty minutes, Les was triumphantly chaperoned to the exit. In his hands were agency and acting contracts, along with the understanding that they should be returned in the next few days after signing. On his way out, the girl at the reception desk said, "I brought this with me when I heard that you were scheduled to be here. I thought you might like to have it, if you don't already." She put a copy of **Variety** in his hands. Les looked at the headline. *"Young Tiger Actor Puts the Bite on Aggressive Agent."* He thanked the young wannabe and headed home.

He read the article to Caryn.

'Last evening there was a fantastic and luscious end of the season party at the estate of Andy Brinkley. It was complete with miles of tables of good eats and barrels of the bubbly. All of Andy's, aka A.B's, usual cortege of staff and hangers-on were dressed in attractive roman togas and made certain that everyone's wishes and desires were satisfied. The evening wore on graced by the jazzy sounds of The Heshee Wonders. Then all of sudden everything came to a screeching halt, when A.B., was assaulted by one of his clients. Word

has it that some newcomer, named El Tigre, planted a left and right cross on A.B's jaw. One of our sources claims that this guy, El Tigre, was insulted by A.B. Another of our sources said the A.B., called his assailant a Nigger. Still another said the guy, El Tigre, was high on coke. No one knows exactly what happened. But it was clear to most of our sources, that the El Tigre whirlwind did not look to be colored. Rumors are circulating far and wide about exactly what happened, including the speculation that A.B.'s genitals were kicked into his upper abdomen. He was rushed to the hospital on a stretcher for attention. And this is what Andy Brinkley got plenty of on the evening of his lavish party, along with, a big bite from the Tiger.'

Caryn fell out laughing. "I don't believe it. How could anyone make up this bullshit out of what happened?"

Les chimed in. "Maybe he was rushed to the hospital, we don't know."

If all of what is printed here is so true, why didn't he sue you for assault?"

Les said with a smile on his face, "I guess he figured he could not prove he didn't assault me first, so he let it go."

Caryn mused, "I wondered why we didn't see this article when it came out?"

"You know we don't read this crap." With that Les put the article on the table and picked up the documents that he brought from the meeting. "This is the crap that I have to read."

"What's that?"

Les replied as he flipped through the pages, "An agency contract and the agreement to do the film."

Caryn looked at him with amazement. "Are you serious?"

"Why not?"

"Just a few days ago you were through with this town.

You didn't want to have anything to do with this…. this…. cesspool as you called it. You turned down a good gig with Tandem. You had had it. Now you've turned around one hundred and eighty degrees… are you seriously thinking about accepting this?"

"I've got to have some work."

"I told you to call Wes Hendricks."

"I'm gonna do that too."

"Caryn exploded. "You don't know what you want to do. You're full of shit."

Caryn turned with fury and took off in a huff—headed to the stairs that led to the bedroom on the mezzanine. She threw herself across the bed. Les followed her path to the bottom of the stairs. He stopped. He was confused. This was their first and most serious disagreement and argument over anything. He thought he was doing what she had said he should do. Only a few days earlier she had made the point, "you can't continue throwing away opportunities because of your precious principles." He decided not to follow but rather turned and took off through the door.

He headed the car towards West Hollywood, why he didn't know. Perhaps because it was some distance away and he wanted to put space between them. He ended his exodus at a sidewalk café on Melrose Avenue. He watched the flood of people flowing by; pierced and tattooed, strangely dressed with multicolored hair and alien makeup, all wanting to be noticed. All wanting to be different---to be their own person—to be a star—to be in the movies, which was why they were here. Just like Sheila, they had arrived in Shangri-La. And so had he. He took a bite from the cheese snack plate that the waitress had placed on the table, and then sipped from the glass of wine. His mind's eye traveled back to his argument with, Caryn, the woman he loved. They were at odds over who he was or wanted to be, and the actions he had taken to get there. He remembered her asking, *"Why did you hit him?"* He was convinced that her attitude had started from this. There was no mistaking his motivation over this action. He was not a sissy; and did not want anyone to believe that he was. Perhaps he was more like his papa than he thought—a real kick-ass kind of guy. And he knew that his Grandpop didn't want him to be thought of as a homosexual either, so he was comfortable with his response to that come-on, even though it mean losing the agent and killing the deal. That's why he hit him, and he was quite comfortable in losing the deal because of this. But now he has a second chance at playing the role and realizing his dream, and he did not have to lose integrity by doing it. He would not become one of them. Caryn had said, *"You don't have to be like everyone else to work in the business."* And now it seems that she was upset because he had decided to do just this. He was confused. She was getting him all twisted up.

He saw a homeless man, passing on the street in front of the café, pushing his entire life's possessions in his cart. He didn't want to end like that. He wanted more out of life. He wanted a family, and a job and a career. That was what he had come to Hollywood for. He wondered about the man, who was he?—a former actor?—a director?—a stock broker?—a former teacher?—a drug addict?—whomever, he didn't want to be like him, so he had to get some work. He had to be successful. He had to make his dream a reality. He really felt that the answer to his dilemma was the movie, in spite of Caryn's feelings. His eyes followed the man down the street. Then his eyes were drawn to another man sitting in a café on the other side of the street talking to a beautiful woman. Les did not believe his eyes. It was Freddy. Hollywood was getting too small. He paid his check, left the café and turned the corner in the opposite direction. He left West Hollywood.

On the way home he stopped and bought a dozen roses

and planned to take Caryn out to dinner. Perhaps he would be able to explain what had run through his mind at the café.

A few minutes after they returned from dinner the phone rang. It was Ann Marie.

"Les, Papa had a stroke."

"A stroke? What does that mean? Where is he? Is he going to die?

"Les, Les slow down, not so fast. He's in the ICU. He's stable, but he is paralyzed on the right side and he's in a coma. We won't know how severe it is for a few hours. In the meantime, I think it's important for you come home as soon as you can. Mama told me that you were recovering from that gunshot. How are you feeling?"

"I'm getting better."

"Are you breathing like before?"

Les laughed weakly, then he said, "I don't get out of breath when I have sex."

Ann responded. "Then I guess you are in shape to get your butt down here to see Papa. How is Caryn?"

"She's fine."

"Give her my best. I'm really sorry to have to call with this terrible news. I'll keep you up to date. Hope to see you soon. I love you."

"I love you too."

Les hung up the phone and crumpled onto the sofa in tears. Caryn cried with him.

Chapter 20
New Intentions Revealed

The next day Les stood next to his Papa's bed with Ann Marie by his side. He had never seen so many tubes and machines before in his life. However, he did remember that he too had been connected by tubes to machines only ten weeks before but this was so overwhelming it did not look encouraging. Ann inspected the chart hanging on the foot of the bed and when the nurse entered she and Ann went into the hall for consultation. Les continued to look at his father who breathed in time with the rhythm of the machine. His eyes were closed, so Les assumed that he was still in a coma. When Ann came back into the room she motioned to Les to follow her. They went to the waiting room, and she revealed the status of their father.

"Papa is not responding to the medication as we had hoped. The stroke left him paralyzed and whether or not he will be able to speak is still uncertain. It looks like he's going to be hospitalized or in special care for the long haul."

Les was visibly upset. He dropped his head into his hands and dropped his elbows to his knees. Ann said nothing and indulged his silence for several minutes. When Les felt his pain subside he lifted his head and embraced Ann. "I am so sorry. I wish that Papa and I had not had all of the ups and downs that we did."

"That could not be helped. He is who he is, and you are who you are, and the two of you were just being yourselves. It does not mean you do not love each other."

Les looked at Ann for a brief moment, then said, "Thank you. What do we do now?"

There's not much point in staying here all night. They'll call me if there's a change. Let's go home."

Les stood to leave as he said, "I'd like to stay in Frillotville."

"That's a good idea. I'll stay with you."

When they arrived they found the house spick and span, just the way their papa liked it.

Les said, "I see Miz Noonie is still around."

"She'll be here as long as Papa needs her."

Les looked in the refrigerator. "You hungry?"

"Anything edible in there?"

"Some crawfish bisque, corn muffins," and he continued as he lifted lids, "boudin, pork chops and rice."

"Bring it out. I'll heat it up."

Les found a bottle of wine that he had left in the liquor cabinet and he and his sister enjoyed the banquet of leftovers.

Ann said while cutting into her pork chop, "You know Les, Papa was just getting ready to do the fall planting when he got sick."

"Looks like he won't be able to make it this year."

Ann said wistfully, "That is, unless you do it for him."

Neither was aware that this was a turning point in their

lives; as so often happens in the lives of people overwhelmed by unexpected crises that bring them to a crossroad.

A thought was planted and Les said impulsively, "That's not a bad idea." He took a sip of Bordeaux and a light in his eyes brightened. All of a sudden a new avenue of escape from the trap of Hollywood had presented itself, or rather Ann had unknowingly presented it; but either way it could be the answer to the dilemma he was having about what to do next. At least he would not have to put up with the phoniness, back stabbing, lies and deceit. Even though he would have to plant and cultivate nearly seventy-five acres of seedcane and then harvest it next summer, it was not a bad choice between the hypocritical life of Hollywood and one as a farmer in Frillotville.

Maybe it was the spirits, as Naomi would say, giving him a chance to make up to his Papa for fighting him all the time. He discussed the idea with Ann as they continued to eat.

"You know it's strange the way things happen. When you called about Papa, I was ready to take a role in a film. But now I'm not too sure."

"You have your life to live. Things like this happen all of the time. Believe me I know."

Les continued to try and make her understand what was on his mind. "It's like an outside force, maybe God, I don't know, is trying to tell me something. Months back I beat up my agent who came on to me like I was a sissy, and I lost the chance to be in a movie he had gotten me a part in. This was the same movie that a few days ago I got a second chance to play the same role. Now these people are interested in me because as they said, 'You're a natural for this movie. You're a kick-ass kind of guy.'"

Ann had stopped eating and hung on his every word. "Were they referring to the conflict with the agent?"

"Yes in a way. But more than that, they gave me the feeling that they were using me to sell the movie."

"Isn't that what people in that business do?" Ann said, as she filled her fork with crawfish bisque.

"Yeah, I know that. But I feel different about this. They are really making a big thing about my bad-boy behavior."

Ann laughed. "Do you deny that you are a bad-boy?"

"Oh, come on. I just take a stand against injustice or abuse, and you know that. But what I'm really talking about is those people in Hollywood will take any wayward behavior and make it into something that should be admired, like being in prison, or being a druggy, or beating up on your woman. Understand what I'm trying to say?"

I think I'm beginning to."

"It's hard to explain but I got a strange feeling when the publicist described the marquee, 'El Tigre, kicks ass in the Sins of the Father.'"

"Who's El Tigre?"

Les breathed out heavily, "That's my Hollywood name. It means the tiger."

Ann smiled and a slight giggle escaped her lips, "Man you have created a reputation in Hollywood in a very short time."

"That's what I'm talking about. They're giving me a reputation I don't want to have."

Ann raised her glass, "It'll be good box office."

Les bit into a cut of boudin and chewed for a few seconds, "Yeah, that's why I think someone is trying to tell me something, Grandpop or God, I don't know who."

"You're really having growing pains, aren't you?"

"If that's what you call it."

Ann began clearing the dishes from the table. Les sat silent. In the stillness he tried to connect with the prophet in order to surrender an acceptance of what must be. By the time she reentered from the kitchen he said, "I've got to think on this for a bit."

Ann added another incentive, "I'm sure Papa would appreciate if you decided to plant his cane." Then she went to the phone and dialed.

Les wandered into the living room. He began looking through a stack of magazines and various papers, which caught his eye. In the meantime Ann completed her call and entered the room, with the bottle of wine and glasses.

"Was that Mama?" asked Les inquisitively.

"No. It was Alex. I called to say I wasn't coming home tonight. I planned to stay over here."

"Why does she have to know that?"

"That's where I live."

"That's where you what?"

Ann could tell by the tone of his voice that Les had been left out of the loop of information about the change in her life. There was a lot that he needed to be updated on. She began. "I guess you didn't know that Mr. Estilette had died."

"No, I didn't and I'm sorry to hear that. He and Grandpop were such good friends."

Ann went on. "And two months after he died Miz Victoria had a heart attack and needed around-the-clock care. Alex was having a hard time balancing everything, the newspaper business, the commercial properties and taking care of her mother, so I offered to move in and help."

"Why would you do that? You have your own problems--your practice and looking after Mama and Aunt Rosa."

"Mama and Aunt Rosa are not infirm. After all, I am a grown woman and can live with whom I choose."

The tone of Ann's voice let Les know that there was something else implied. He and Ann had never before been at odds over anything, but he suspected that there was something unspoken. His mind flashed back six months earlier when he dropped by Ann's office unexpectedly, and found her and Alex in an embrace. He didn't think much of it at the time but in retrospect they reacted as a couple of deer caught in the headlights. Plus her tone of her voice and the words she had just spoken was a reason to question.

Les repeated slowly and emphasized each word. "I–can–live–with—whom—I—choose? What the hell does that mean?"

Ann rushed into his arms with tears flowing down her cheeks. "Oh, Les. I wanted to tell you and didn't know how, but I figured the day would come when you would know."

"Well it's a good thing that Papa has already had his stroke because this would surely give him one. When did you become a dyke?"

"Please, don't use that word. I don't think of my love for Alex in those terms."

"She's over fifty years old, Uncle Bobby's age, and you're just thirty. What in the hell are you thinking?"

Ann poured two glasses of wine, gave one to Les then crossed to sit in the wing chair facing the fireplace. Les sank down on the sofa facing Ann next to the stack of magazines.

Les said, "I'm sorry if I sounded like Papa, and from all those years of him believing that I was queer and I wasn't, I know how this must make you feel. Now, I guess the chickens are coming home to roost."

He chuckled at the thought and then he told her about his encounter with A.B., his agent.

In conclusion he added, "I know it's going to be hard for me to stop kicking ass at the drop of a hat, but I'm going to try. So I've arrived at this new attitude of, *to each his own.* As long as somebody's lifestyle does not affect what I do, and that makes them happy, then so be it."

Ann lifted her glass in a salute. They drank a toast.

As the wine trickled off her tongue and down her throat, Ann felt the need to give her brother more explanation. "I know Alex is a lot older. But we have a lot of common threads that tie us together. She lost the love of her life in Uncle Bobby and, I, too was disappointed in love. And so it follows that we bring a lot of reconcilement to each other; not in the way of sexual love that you guys feel is the be-all and end-all of a relationship, but in so many other ways. Plus the fact I feel a family kinship with the Estilettes that goes back a long way, so I really see her as an older sister."

Les said, "You know I'm trying hard to accept this relationship as you describe it, but I keep going back to things that Grandpop said. One time he read something to me from the bible. I think it was from Leviticus, and if I remember correctly it was, 'Do not lie with a man as one lies with a woman.' At that time he was telling me about homosexuality, and he said that meant homosexuality for both a man and a woman. I've never forgotten that. A few minutes ago when I said what I said, I didn't want you to feel that I was against the relationship that you're having with Alex. I was trying hard to accept it because I love you, but I think that Grandpop would have a problem with y'all living together."

Ann Marie responded, "Just keep on working on your new attitude, 'to each his, or her own.' And I'll accept that because I love you."

Les lifted his glass in a salute to his sister and they drank another toast. Les felt it was time to change the subject and he reached into the stack of magazines and pulled out some papers. "Look what I found." He held up a copy of several pages held together with a paper clip. "You ever hear of a man named Norbert Rillieux?"

"Oh, yeah, Grandpop used to tell us about him when we were growing up. Don't you remember? He was a Creole who invented the heating and evaporation methods of processing sugar."

"Yeah. That's what this copy is all about. I recognized Grandpop's handwriting on this note he sent to Papa, suggesting that he make sugar rather than syrup. It was attached to this article about Rillieux."

Les had not remembered hearing about Rillieux before. It had escaped his attention. But apparently it had not left the memory of his sister. He was embarrassed that he had not placed any importance on it at the time. But Ann remembered, no doubt an indication of the intellect that prompted her to study medicine.

So much had overwhelmed his mind in the last few days that he needed time to figure it all out. And one of the prominent thoughts was maybe he should take over his Papa's cane production for sugar and not syrup. It was something else he had to sort out, but for now, he only wanted to close his eyes. He suggested to his sister that they turn in and get some sleep.

*   *   *

No calls from the hospital came during the night.

Ann and Les were up at daybreak, had breakfast and went to the hospital. When they entered they found that Lester had come out of the coma. His eyes were open. They approached the bed and each kissed their Papa. There was a frightened look in his eyes, as they traveled back and forth from one to the other of his children looking for answers. He tried to speak but only unintelligible noises came out of his twisted mouth that moved involuntarily in grotesque configurations towards the left side of his face.

A voice from the doorway said, "He's paralyzed on the right side and he's lost his speech. His hearing is unaffected but he's alarmed and doesn't know what has happened."

Ann turned and approached the man. "I'm Doctor Martel and this is my father. Are you his doctor?"

"Yes. I'm Doctor Prejean." He extended his hand. "Sorry to meet you under these circumstances. I heard that you had joined our staff a few months back. Welcome."

They shook hands and Ann looked towards, Les. "This is my brother, Lester Martel Junior.

"Nice to meet you." Then Doctor Prejean gave them an update of what happened. "For some reason that we do not know, the blood circulating in your father's brain was blocked, causing hemiplegia," he smiled and then nodded toward Les, "paralysis on his right side and his speech has been affected. He will need lots of therapy. And whether he will walk and talk again, we do not know."

Guttural sounds came from Lester and the three turned to look in his direction. Dr.Prejean said, "Apparently his hearing was not affected and he's trying to say something." Then Doctor Prejean took a pad out of his coat pocket and brought a pencil to Lester. He held the pad while Lester scribbled his message. Since his dominant hand was paralyzed he took the pencil in his left and wrote, '*what happened*?'

Dr. Prejean showed Lester's message to his children. The scribbles looked, at best, like those of a first grader just learning to write in broad, wiggly, capital letters. Les looked at the scrawled chicken scratch and walked away crying.

Doctor Prejean wrote to Lester that he had had a stroke and with constant care there was hope that he would someday be able to walk and talk again. Ann added at the end, *"We love you and will be here to help you through."*

Ann wasn't sure, but it did seem like she saw a smile somewhere in the twisted mouth contortions as she watched him react to her statement. She thanked Doctor Prejean for his help, and found Les sitting quietly in the waiting room.

When they got home they found Lala and Rosa in the living room saying the rosary. Ann brought them up to date on the condition of Lester, which brought additional tears to both of their faces. Les sat quietly looking from face to face at their reactions to this family tragedy. He didn't know what, but he felt that he had to do something to make things right again.

Les called Caryn. The answer machine was on. No doubt she was still on the set taping her episode.

The next day Les flew back to Los Angeles. Caryn was surprised and confused to see him. He explained that because of his father's stroke his life had changed and there were things that they had to work through and discuss.

Caryn said, "I'm scheduled to work tomorrow, so let's talk when I get back."

After Caryn left early in the morning, Les spent the rest of the day cleaning the apartment, washing clothes and preparing dinner. He cooked Caryn's favorite shrimp creole, and by the time she got home the table was set, candles were lit and the wine decanted. She stood in the middle of the living room speechless, with her hand covering her mouth. When she recovered she said, "I can't imagine what it is we have to discuss, but I can tell it must be serious for you to go to all of this trouble.

"I was trying to keep busy, so I wouldn't just sit around and think too much."

Caryn remarked as she sat at the table, "Apparently there's a lot on your mind."

When they began eating Les said, "I'm thinking about taking over and running the cane plantation, for Papa."

Caryn dropped her head, took a fork full of shrimp, chewed and swallowed, then asked, "What about us?"

"I'm counting on you being there with me."

"Counting on me? What does that mean?"

Les was caught off guard. "Well, what I meant is, I am hoping that we get married and be there together."

"What about my career? I have a contract with Y&R, and I can't just take off on a passing fancy."

Les rested his chin on his folded hands, with his elbows propped on the table, "I know. That's why we have to talk and plan things out."

For the next few moments both silently picking at their food with many unspoken thoughts and questions flying through their minds. Finally Caryn blurted out, "Why?"

"Why what?"

"Why are you giving up your life-long dream of being an actor to become a farmer?"

Les drained his glass of wine and poured another and also filled Caryn glass. "That is a question I've asked myself, and it's not an easy one to answer. All I know is, the answer comes from the person I am and who I want to be. I believe that the answer has been forming in the back of my mind for a long time. Yes, I've always wanted to be an actor, because I still believe it's important to examine the whys and where-fores of life through drama stories, but after really finding out what that means, I think I wanted to be an actor for the wrong reasons. At first, I thought it would be fun. Then I found out it was hard and uncertain work. It's not that I'm against working hard at anything, but I found out that I didn't like the people that I had to work hard with. And on top of that are all of the events that have happened. They were like lights turned on in dark rooms that showed me what I had not seen before, like—getting shot—the flim-flam—losing my job by deceptions—the person I became to get back at George—smoke up the ass—the fiasco with A.B.—and now papa's stroke. It's like all of these things were trying to tell me something."

"Like handwriting on a wall?"

Les enthusiastically responded. "Yeah, something like that. Only...now don't laugh and think I've lost it...but, as Naomi would say, it's like the spirits were talking to me."

"What do you mean, by spirits?"

"That force inside of us that controls what we do. Grandpop called it God."

Caryn questioned, "Are you becoming a psychic?"

"I don't know. All I know is I'm not as driven to be an actor as I was before. I'm more concerned with the peace and happiness that we bring to each other."

Caryn asked, "So what you're saying is, you want me to marry a farmer and move to Louisiana?" She phrased it as a question then laughed.

At first Les did not understand what was funny, but when he thought back over the irony of everything he was trying to say,—*I still believe that there is virtue in being able to examine the whys and wherefores of life through the visual forms of drama, but it is the business of show-biz that is not my cup of tea, and I feel more at home with nature, watching things grow and die, the seasons come and go, and the birds flying over the fishing bayous.* Then, he joined Caryn's laughter. He continued, "Well what do you say, will you marry me?"

She responded immediately, "A Creole and a Dane joined together seems like gumbo enough. Of course I will, you silly." Then she added, "When, is another question."

"We'll let that work itself out."

They finished off their dinner and spent the rest of the evening in the quiet and peacefulness of love.

The first thing that Les did the next morning was to place a call to Dorothy at Creative Artist. He told her that he was sorry but he had to turn down the offer to play Jordan in the movie, "Because my father had a stroke two days ago and I'm going back to Louisiana to care for him."

Dorothy, of course extended her best wishes for a speedy

recovery and gave assurances that since production was not scheduled to begin for several months, there was no need for him to be hasty about a making a decision at this point.

Les said, "I thank you for this consideration, but I think it best that you continue this project without me. Give my thanks to Alan and Stan for the faith they placed in me, and my best wishes for a fantastic movie."

They boarded a plane headed to Estilette for the Thanksgiving holiday.

When they arrived in Estilette, Les learned that his father had been discharged from the hospital and moved to a therapy unit where he would remain for six weeks. He and Caryn went to visit. He looked much better than when Les had last seen him. With all of the tubes and machines gone, he seemed almost the same as Les had remembered before the stroke, except that he was now in a wheel chair and his movements were involuntary and shaky. His face was contorted and slightly twisted to one side.

They communicated with pad and pencil and Lester wrote that he was happy to see Caryn and hoped that one day she would give him grandchildren. When she read this she smiled and passed the pad to Les. Les wrote that he was planning to make the fall planting and do the harvest in the summer, *so don't worry about a thing*. He was delighted to see his father's eyes light up as if charged by electricity, and a smile curved distortedly upwards from his lips. Les knew without a doubt that he had brought happiness to his father.

On Thanksgiving Day the family was assembled, as usual, in the Phillip Fergerson family homestead, which Lala and Rosa now occupied. The sumptuous dinner was prepared by Lala, Rosa and Naomi, and consisted of all the favorite dishes passed on and handed down through the generations from Martha Broussard's father and his father's father. Lightfoot was appointed to give the blessings and he gave a moving and memorable recounting of the year's trials and tribulations but especially the blessings for which all were grateful, notably the hopeful recovery of Lester.

Most of the prepared vittles were consumed and now it was time for dessert, at which point Les clinked his glass with his knife for attention. "I want the family to know that I have decided to move back to Frillotville and take over the sugar cane plantation and Caryn and I are thinking seriously about getting married."

The announcement was received with mixed response. Basically there was a round of applause and verbal approval, especially from Ann, Lightfoot and Rosa. Lala and Naomi were reserved and tentative in their reaction.

Ann turned to Lala and said, "Mama, isn't this thrilling?"

To which Lala replied, "Well, yes in a way."

"Mama?" Then she whispered, "Mama, what's going on?"

"We'll talk later."

The dessert and good wishes continued, with lots of questions from all, except Naomi. It was clear from the phony smile on her face that she was not too approving. All of which was noted by Lightfoot.

That evening when they got home Lightfoot asked, "What's going on in your mind, Naomi?"

"What you talking, man?"

"I'm talking about what I saw on your face when Les said he was thinking about marrying that girl."

"We just don't need another golden haired Martha-like bitch in this family."

Lightfoot was visibly upset. "I knew when I looked in your eyes you were up to that skin color shit again."

"Why can't he marry up with that nice girl like Dora?"

"Cause that's not who he wants to marry up with. Now leave it be."

Lightfoot didn't say another word. But he knew from past experiences that Naomi would not leave it be. This disappointed him terribly, because he knew that as often as skin color prejudice went from white to black it also went from black to white. He wondered when, if ever, all this prejudice shit would be laid to rest. He knew he would have to be on the lookout for any contrivance that Naomi was likely to make in this direction.

The kitchen was spick and span, everything was put away. Les and Caryn had just taken off to Frillotville and Rosa had gone to her room. Ann folded the table cloth and put it in place to be washed, then she turned to Lala and asked, "All right Mama, what's wrong?"

"Wrong? What do you mean?"

"Mama. When Les made his announcement you didn't look too happy. You said, we'd talk later."

"Oh, that. Well, I was not overjoyed to hear that he's going to leave his dream of Hollywood."

Ann knew her mother well, and suspected that there was more to her opposition than what she admitted. She wanted to get at the truth. "Les and I talked about that in depth."

"Ohhhh, you knew?"

"I knew that he was not happy with what he found in Hollywood. And he told me about all of the deception and backbiting that went on, and especially after he was shot he didn't like the environment he had to live in. You should have known this, you were there."

Lala found herself in a difficult position. She moved pointlessly around the kitchen picked up the table cloth and refolded it. "I just don't see any reason why he has to come back here."

"And plant Papa's cane? That's it. Isn't it?"

Lala didn't say anything. Ann continued. "You are still angry with Papa, and don't want Les to help him out. Isn't that it?"

"All those years of boozing and running around, that's what did it. That's what caused his stroke."

"Mama, that's not true. The stroke was caused by a blockage of a blood vessel in his brain. There is simply no evidence that drinking had anything to do with this. Of course it didn't help, but you're still angry because you had to get a divorce, and that's the real reason you don't want Les to help."

Ann had hit a nerve and Lala knew it. She began crying, so Ann backed off and lowered the intensity of her voice. She put her arms around her mother and said softly. "Everything will be O.K. Don't worry about Les taking over the plantation and leaving Hollywood, that's what he wants to do. And don't be angry with Papa because he didn't turn out to be the man you wanted him to be. Just let it go."

After a few moments, Lala wiped away her tears, gently pushed away from Ann's arms and headed out of the kitchen. At the door she turned and said softly, "You're right. I'll just let it go, just like I let go that situation with you and Alex. Good night."

Ann watched her mother fade into the darkness of the hallway, with tear filled eyes. Then she turned off the lights in the kitchen and headed home to Alex.

Three days later Caryn headed back to Los Angeles.

Les began making plans for the fall planting.

Ann made arrangements for her father's therapy to be moved to his home in Frillotville.

Chapter 21
Thru A Glass Darkly

By the end of November, 1977, Les had completed the fall planting.

Ann had completed the arrangements for a physical therapy facility to be constructed next to the master bedroom of their papa's house. The complete package of parallel bars, weight lifting equipment and a stationary bicycle had been installed. Enlarged toilet facilities to accommodate the wheel chair, along with widened doorways, and ramps into and out of the house had also been provided.

A physical therapist was employed to take care of Lester's daily exercise program, and to put him to bed at night. Once a week he was taken to the Therapy Center at the hospital for a workout in the pool. No expense was spared to provide the best in care for Papa. Even Miz Noonie, the long time housekeeper, had her own private room so she would be on hand in case Lester needed anything at night.

Les took advantage of the construction in progress and converted two rooms on the second floor into a master suite with a sitting room and library; preparing, of course, for the time when he and Caryn would be married. It was a grand remodeling of the family home in Frillotville, on which Lightfoot was the general contractor. Although he had not done any construction work since opening the Black Eagle, he was eager and willing to help Les with the renovations.

When Lala saw the improvements that had taken place in her former residence, she smiled graciously but in her heart felt pangs of resentment. She wondered if her children would do as much for her, if she, rather than Lester was in need of care. Deep down inside she still blamed her ex-husband for the whys-and-wherefores of their divorce. She still remembered the long pilgrimage in the middle of the night fog, trudging with her two young children, away from Lester's drunken abuse to her father's house. This was a repeat of the pangs of resentment that she still carried in her heart for her mother. After all of those years, from the time Martha had slapped her face in front of all those people in that tavern for playing the blues, until the time she died, Lala still felt the sting of embarrassment like it had happened only yesterday. There was nothing that anyone, outside of herself, could do or say about the wisdom of carrying pain so long, but nevertheless these feelings were real and still alive in her heart.

It was fortunate that Lester's yearly cane crop had provided enough revenue to have built up a healthy bankroll. Les however knew that this would not last very long unless he continued to build the income, which he had plans to do by redirecting the yearly cane crop to sugar rather than syrup. He had already made contact with sugar refineries in Thibodeaux and New Orleans, setting the stage to continue building wealth.

Christmas was approaching and so was mischief.

Lala and Rosa decided that they would have a traditional Christmas dinner. They laid out the family guest list, Ann,

Les, Elvina, Lester, Lightfoot, and Naomi all members of the family and then Rosa suggested Alexandrine, who was in fact regarded as a member of the family. So when the guest list was finalized, they set about arranging the menu. Because Naomi was the only one who was able to prepare a seasoned deep fried turkey, they called her to reveal their plans. Naomi graciously accepted her part of the preparations, and saw the opportunity, without revealing her intentions to Lala and Rosa, to add another guest to the list. She called Dora and casually mentioned that Les was back from Hollywood and would be having Christmas at home, and "It might be nice if you can find the time to drop in around dinnertime."

Caryn arrived from Los Angeles a few days before Christmas, and had time to ooooh and ahhhh, and bring female touches to the new space that was being prepared as her new home. She was overwhelmed and grateful that Les was so dedicated to the commitment of their marriage. However, she was still undecided about how long to pursue a career in acting. The work on the soap opera Y&R was satisfying and challenging, although limited. Now more than ever before, she realized that she could stay on the series playing her character as long as she wanted. It was secure. But if she had any desire to do anything else, like a movie or a different type of role, she would have to leave The *Young and the Restless,* and join the hundreds of other actors pounding the pavement and competing for the choice roles. Although these thoughts flowed around in her head, more and more frequently, she had not shared them with Les. She decided to let the status quo remain undisturbed until a compelling event made a decision necessary.

On Christmas morning, Les and Caryn helped Lester into the quarter ton truck used on the farm. His wheel chair was loaded in the bed. When they arrived at the homestead they discovered that Alex had also brought her mother,

Victoria, to Christmas dinner. This was the first time that Lala and Rosa had to prepare places at the table for disabled persons.

As usual every inch of the table, which had now been stretched with extra panels to make it twelve feet long, was covered with delicious and attractive things to eat. There were all of the traditional dishes, of the Fergerson/Broussard family, along with a touch of Danish cuisine prepared by Caryn-- rice pudding and roasted goose with potatoes, gravy and red cabbage. These traditional dishes from Caryn's family fitted right in with the traditional dishes of Les' family. It was sufficient enough to qualify as an approved *family of man* dinner.

When all were comfortably seated, especially Lester and Victoria, Rosa asked Les to say the blessing.

He began, "Bless us, O Lord, for these thy gifts, which we are about to receive from thy bounty through Christ Our Lord…." Normally this was the end of the Catholic table blessing and Rosa had picked up her fork, ready to eat, but Les continued, "And especially are we grateful on this birthday of Jesus, for the healing and recovery of our Papa and Miz Victoria. May they live to celebrate many more birthdays. And may the perpetual light continue to shine on our dearly departed Grandpop Phillip, and Grandma Martha, and most recently Uncle Luther and Mr.Estilette, all of whom are missing from our table this year. And bless this family, Aunt Elvina, and Aunt Rosa, and Uncle Johnny and Aunt Naomi and Ann and Alex and Caryn who is about to join this family, and thanks for all the hands that prepared the food that we are about to eat. All of these things we ask in the name of the one you sent. Amen!"

Lightfoot was the first to speak. "Damn boy, I thought you wuz gonna pray forever. Your Aunt Rosa had already started to eat long before you said Amen."

This brought laughter from the group and smiles from Lester and Victoria.

Ann fixed a plate for Lester, and Alex fixed a plate for Victoria and then food was passed around for what seemed like the next ten minutes, and finally all were served and all got down to the business of eating.

The door bell rang and Les was up to answer before Naomi could completely push back her chair. When Les opened the door, Dora rushed in, threw her arms around his neck and kissed him on the mouth. "Oh, Les it's good to see you. I heard you were back. Here is your Christmas present." She handed him a beautifully wrapped box. All of this happened before Les had a chance to say a word.

Finally he was able to say, "Merry Christmas, Dora." Then he turned and directed his voice to Lala, "Mama, set another place for Dora." Then to Dora, "Come, let me introduce you around..."Let's see I think you know everyone except maybe, Alex Estilette and my fiancée Caryn Ericksen. I want y'all to meet my long time friend and High School classmate Dora Johnson."

Cordial responses were made in return from both Alex and Caryn.

Lala was busy pushing place settings around to make room for another plate.

Dora's spirit seemed to collapse after she heard the word fiancée, and she said, "Oh Mrs. Martel please don't go to all this trouble. I don't think I will stay for dinner. I just dropped by to give Les a present."

Naomi responded, "Oh girl, don't be silly. Just sit down and make yourself a part of this family."

As soon as Lightfoot heard this he knew Naomi had set up Dora's arrival. His face showed the displeasure and Les noticed that his uncle was upset.

Lala had finally arranged the space that was needed, and

she got willing help from Naomi who brought in another chair and placed it next to where Les was sitting at the head of the table. Then she said loud enough for all to hear, "Here's a good spot for you, right next to your old boyfriend."

Dora laughed nervously and said softly, "I'm not gonna eat much, and I don't plan to stay long."

To which Naomi said, "Hush, girl, you can stay as long as you have to."

Lightfoot was listening, and when Naomi headed back to her seat across from him, he said as graciously as he could, "Naomi could you help me with something in the kitchen?"

Les had been observing the body language and comments from both ever since he had noticed the displeasure on his uncle's face.

Naomi and Lightfoot left the table and headed toward the kitchen.

When Les felt they had arrived at their destination, he excused himself to go to the bathroom, but he stopped just before crossing the doorway to the kitchen. He listened.

Lightfoot said, "What the hell you think you're doing?"

Naomi crossed her arms and pretended innocence. "I don't know what you're talking 'bout."

"You know damn well what I'm talking about. You invited that gal here."

Naomi responded with the same intensity as her accuser. "So what if I did?"

"I know you. You're trying to fuck up the marriage between Les and Caryn."

"He got no business marrying up with a white woman."

Lightfoot was getting madder and madder. "That is not your business."

"It's my business to keep peace in this family. And when your sister, that so called white woman, was alive there was no peace."

302

"This is not the same thing, and you got no business meddling in that boy's life."

"I jus don't want another white woman in this family keeping skin color prejudice alive."

Lightfoot was furious. "It seems to me that you're the only one who's keeping skin color prejudice alive. And I know you're not speaking in the tongues of angels."

"What are you taking about, man?"

Lightfoot said with emphasis, "I'm talking about love, which you say all the time does not delight in evil."

Naomi was getting more pissed by the minute, "Love don't have nothing' to do with this."

"You're damned right. "Cause you're getting the wrong reflection of that girl. All you seeing is your own evil thoughts. Now I don't wanna see or hear no more of your conniving shit." With that Lightfoot walked out of the kitchen, right past Les on his way to the bathroom.

Naomi walked outside through the back door in a huff.

Les thought long and hard about the wisdom of facing down Naomi over what he had overheard. Before, in his kickass days, there would have been no hesitation, but now he decided it was best to leave it alone, however, he could not forget what was really going on, and now he understood why Dora had mysteriously appeared.

During the remainder of the dinner feast, the conversation was focused primarily around everyone's curiosity about Caryn. How did she like being an actress?—What was Hollywood like?—What church did she attend?--What did her parents do for a living?--et cetera, et cetera. The more she answered the barrage of questions thrown in her direction, the more pride Les felt and the more comfortable he was about bringing her into the family.

Dora wanted to know, "Did you and Les meet in Hollywood?"

"No, in college, long before Hollywood," was the immediate response from Caryn.

"Now tell about his knight in shining armor rescue," Ann inquired.

Caryn blushed, and said, "Oh that. How did you know?"

"Les told me. Now you can tell everybody. I think it's a great story."

Caryn went on to tell about the attempt of sexual abuse by the son one of her professors and how Les stopped him and then had him arrested.

And after that story, Ann added one of her own, which ended with her declaring, "I think of Les as my Sir Galahad."

Dora, not to be outdone, thought about telling of the time that Les had defended her honor by demanding an apology from two ruffians in high school. But then she thought better of it, rationalizing that it might seem as if she was competing with his sister and his fiancée, for attention. So immediately after dinner, Dora left. Perhaps she had sensed that her furtive quest was of no purpose and felt that discretion was the better part of valor.

Lightfoot looked around for Naomi but she was nowhere to be found. Later, she quietly reappeared with lifted spirits of love and cooperation.

The rest of the evening was filled with a Glogg of Caryn's creation—a hot red wine with brandy, and flavored with cinnamon and raisins-- a Danish favorite. Everyone, including Naomi, and especially Lester, enjoyed its intoxicating potency which stimulated wild imaginations. Anytime anyone called for a refill Naomi volunteered, and when she took Caryn's glass into the kitchen, along with others to be filled from the pitcher, she was careful that she dispensed the proper portion from the vial of *Stop Love Elixir* into the proper glass.

Early the next morning Caryn was awakened by sharp

pains in her stomach. She ran to the bathroom. She was taken with an acute case of diarrhea, which lasted for the rest of the week. Caryn was so sick and weakened she was not able to return to Los Angeles to meet her scheduled time for work on the series.

There was no question about a case of diarrhea stopping love, but this was not how Naomi had planned for the hex to work. Apparently the cinnamon in the wine had altered the affect of the ingredients in the elixir, and produced a different outcome. Nevertheless it did have a negative result. Caryn was too sick to get back to Los Angeles to play her recurring role on the series, so someone else was hired to do her role.

When Naomi heard what had happen, she became furious. All she could say was, "Shit that's not how that hex was supposed to work"

Chapter 22
Truth Stranger Than Fiction

Shortly after the beginning of the year, January, 1978, the trial of BookTau for the murder of the Joshua Cane was the talk of the town. Les and Lightfoot had agreed to engage Kenneth Malveau as his defense attorney. He was the same attorney who had cleared Mr. BoBo's name of the charge of murder thirteen years before. He was now a well known attorney sought after as a trial defender of those who were falsely accused of wrong doings. Although his docket of cases was filled for years in advance, he agreed to take up this cause because he remembered Les and knew the family.

Malveau would be facing his old nemesis, Mario Lazzaro who was still the city prosecutor. Lazzaro was convinced that BookTau had motive to kill the man who had married the woman he was secretly in love with, and he wanted to see that he serve years in jail for this premeditated murder.

The trial judge was none other than judge Perrodin who was now on his last legs. He looked to be at least one hundred years old, but in reality was only eighty five, which meant that he was in his early seventies when he presided over the BoBo trial. It was not unusual for judges in this parish to serve until they were incompetent or dead. Judge Perrodin was neither. He was still feisty, and as wise as Solomon with his long white hair and bushy eyebrows. Many felt that he was too old to be the sitting judge of the city, but there was no one on the horizon to take his place or who would dare to oppose him. Many thought it best that he just die being the judge of record. And so it was.

The trial was set to begin in a week and BookTau was a basket case. It was all that Les could do to keep him calm and cool. BookTau was convinced that he was going to die in jail the same as Mr. BoBo.

Les said, in an effort to give him hope, "Look if that was the case you would still be in jail. You are out. And you're still breathing. If you'd like we can put you back in jail so you can die. Is that what you want?"

Les looked BookTau in the eye for an answer after his soul searching question.

Then after turning around in circles several times, BookTau said, "No, I don't wanna die. I'll do what you say."

Les considered this a step forward, then said, "Now, I want you to go home, take a bath, and put on your dressy clothes, and be ready at nine o'clock tomorrow. I'll pick you up and take you to see your lawyer. He's gonna talk to you and I want you to do everything that he tells you to do. O.K.?"

BookTau said, "O.K."

At the appointed hour Les picked up BookTau who had dressed up in his new overalls and red plaid shirt and blue tie, and they went to Malveau's office. BookTau was instructed about everything that was going to happen. He was not to answer any questions but to be calm and quiet. He was not going to have to testify about anything, except say, "Not Guilty," when the judge asked, "How do you plead?" So far everything was fine with BookTau, and he added, "As long as Les is next to me, I'll be fine." Malveau explained that that was not possible because Les was a witness and had to wait outside. BookTau seemed deflated but nodded his head in acceptance.

Judge Perrodin banged his gavel for the trial to begin. "This is a trial of the city of Estilette, versus Booker T. Washington for the murder of Joshua S. Cane. How do you plead?"

Malveau pushed his elbow into BookTau's side as a signal it was time for him to speak. He said, in a quiet voice, "Not guilty."

The judge asked, "What was that? I didn't hear you."

BookTau said louder, "Not guilty, sir."

The judge banged his gavel again, as he liked to do as a reminder to all that he was in charge. "All right Mr. Lazzaro make your opening."

Mario Lazzaro stood, pulled up his pants and then pulled down his vest making sure there were no wrinkles. Then he walked to the jury box. He was still the same ambitious, self-aggrandizing prosecutor who had tried the dead man, Mr. BoBo, for murder.

"Good morning. Ladies and Gentlemen of the jury, we are going to prove beyond a shadow of a doubt that, this man," He turned and pointed his finger at BookTau, "Booker T. Washington, did on Sunday, July 15, 1977 murder Joshua S. Cane. And he killed him in the Holy Ghost Cemetery after stalking his victim from an all-night poker game. Mr. Washington had motive and opportunity to do this dirty deed. His motive was the money that he had seen Mr. Cane win in the poker game. And he had another motive, Mr. Canes' estranged wife. Mr. Cane had just returned to Estilette to be reunited with his wife, the well known Rosa Fergerson Cane, the daughter of one of our city's highly respected families. Mr. Washington did not like the fact that Mr. Cane had returned to make peace with his wife. He wanted Rosa Fergerson Cane for himself and he saw the opportunity, under the guise of protecting her from her husband, to do away with his rival."

At this point BookTau could not be still. He blurted out, "That's not..." And that was all he could get out. Malveau clamped his hand over BookTau's mouth and whispered into his ear. "Be quiet."

Perrodin cast a warning eye in the direction of the defense table.

Lazzaro continued without missing a beat. "And he had the opportunity. Mr. Washington provided a place for Mr. Cane to stay while he was in town seeking reunion with his wife. He invited him to stay at his house. And he created the opportunity of a poker game to lure Mr. Cane in because he knew he was short of funds. He arranged this poker game so he could keep an eye on his whereabouts. And after the game was over, early on the Sunday morning of July 15th, he followed Mr. Cane to the cemetery where Mr. Cane had arranged to meet his wife and give her the money he had won. When Mr. Washington witnessed this meeting, it was more than he could stand and he choked Mr. Cane to death, right in front of his wife. All of this we will prove beyond a shadow of a doubt. Thank you, ladies and gentlemen of the jury."

Perrodin banged his gavel and as customary, pointed the handle in the direction of the defense table. "Mr. Malveau."

"Thank you your honor. Ladies and gentlemen of the jury you have just witnessed one of the greatest stories of misrepresentation in the entire career of our illustrious city attorney. The only thing he got right was the names of the participants in this tragic event. It is tragic because it was an unintentional accident. I say accident because Mr. Washington did not wish, plan or intend to kill Mr. Cane. True, Mr. Cane is dead. True, Mr. Cane was killed by Mr. Washington's actions. True, Mr. Washington pleaded not guilty. But there are mitigating circumstances that make Mr. Cane's death an accident. And we intend to show beyond a shadow of a doubt all of the circumstances that led to the unfortunate death of Mr. Cane. It was an unfortunate death because Mr. Washington did not have any intention of taking the life of Mr. Cane; he only intended to restrain the man from forcing himself on his estranged wife. And as you listen to the testimony, I ask that each and every one of you imagine yourselves in Mr. Washington's place, as you decide his guilt or innocence. Thank you."

Perrodin banged and said, "We'll have a brief recess and then Mr. Lazzaro, you will call your first witness."

Outside in the hall, Les, Lightfoot and Lala sat next to Rosa who was fingering her rosary. She said, "I wonder how long it'll be before they call me."

Lala answered, "Attorney Malveau said he couldn't tell. It depended on when the prosecution witnesses were finished." Then she nodded her head toward the other side of the hallway where they sat.

Rosa asked, "Who are those men?"

Les said, "Cecil Peete and Slick. I don't know the other man."

The other man was Percy Tucker who, like BookTau, had also taken a short cut through the cemetery that morning.

Rosa responded, "It's not too many so maybe I'll be called next."

The door opened and the clerk called out, "Cecil Peete."

Cecil was sworn in and he took a seat in the witness chair. Lazzaro began.

"Mr. Peete, how did you know Mr. Cane?"

"He's the Candy Man." A few people snickered. The judge banged. Then there was silence.

Mr. Lazzaro asked, "Mr. Peete, would you be kind enough to look at me when you answer?"

Mr. Peete said, "I am looking at you sir." The people in the court laughed. The judge banged again. The clerk got up and whispered something in Lazzaros' ear. He responded. "Oh, I see…errrr…I understand."

He continued. "Sorry for the interruption. What do you mean by candy man?"

"He's the one who sells Miz Rosa's fudge. And I buy a lot of it."

"Did you see Mr. Cane on Saturday night July 14th?"

"Yes sir."

"Please tell the jury about that."

Lazzaro was still uncomfortable with the direction in which Cecil was focusing his eyes and when Cecil adjusted his gaze towards the jury box, Lazzaro moved to get out of his line of sight, but in actuality he now stood between the witness and the jury. The clerk got up and gently moved him out of the way.

Cecil continued. "It was like this. Slick, the owner of the pool hall, called and told me there was to be a big game on Saturday night, and if I wanted to win some money I should be there. So I went. That's the first time I ever met Mr. Cane. I calls him the Candy Man. Well, I figured like this, he musta had some money to be in this game in the first place, and I was aiming to win as much as I could."

"Did you win anything?"

"No, sir. Well, at first I won a few hands, then we changed

seats and the Candy Man won just about every hand after that."

"Did you see that man at the game?" Lazzaro pointed to BookTau.

"Yes, sir. He was there, fixing drinks."

"Did he join the game?"

"No, sir."

"Was there any time when you noticed any bad feelings between Mr. Cane and Mr. Washington?"

"Who is Mr. Washington?"

"That man." Lazzaro pointed to BookTau again.

"Oh, BookTau? No sir. He don't have bad feelings towards nobody."

With that Lazzaro felt he had gotten all he could from the witness and he looked over at Malveau and said, "Your witness."

Malveau replied, "No questions."

Judge Perrodin was as confused as Malveau was. The likely question on both of their minds was, *What was that all about?*

The gavel was banged and the judge said, "Next witness."

Percy Tucker was called to the stand.

"Mr. Tucker, do you know that man over there?"

"Yes, sir. That's BookTau."

"You mean Mr. Washington?"

"I means BookTau. I don't know what you call him but that's BookTau over yonder."

Lazzaro decide to leave the identification alone. It was clear to the members of the jury that they were referring to the same person.

So Lazzaro asked, "How do you know him?"

Percy scratched his head. "Let's see." Then he repeated the question. "How do I know him? Been knowing him a

312

long time. We usta pick cotton together and then we usta do odd jobs together, and we had some drinks together."

"Did you see him early Sunday morning on July 15th?"

"Don't 'member what date it was but I did see him one early Sunday morning. I 'members that 'cause I was headin' home from a saddy night out."

"Where were you when you saw him?"

"I was cuttin' through the graveyard and dare he wuz."

"Was he alone?"

"No, sir. Dey wuz two other peoples with him."

"Tell us sir, what happened?"

"Well, its like dis. Dare I wuz taking a short cut through the graveyard and I heard a woman yelling, and she say, 'stop, stop, I don't wanna be with you. Leave me alone.' Well, dat made me stop and look over in dat direction. And soon as I did, I seen BookTau jump out from behind a tomb and grab the man around the throat. Well then, I jumps behind the Abdalla's tomb, 'cause I didn't want nobody to see me seeing what I was seeing. And I knowed the Abdalla's tomb was big enough to hide me 'cause I passes it every time I cuts through the grave yard….and."

Lazzaro wanted Percy to stay on the subject, and he interrupted and asked. "Who was the lady that you saw yelling?"

"Oh, dat was Miz Rosa, everybody know Miz Rosa. She's a teacher and a nice lady."

"What happened next?"

"Well, I saw BookTau holding the man around the neck shaking him. And Miz Rosa started yelling again, "That's enough leave him alone." And pretty soon BookTau released his holt on the man and he fell to the ground. When I seen that I hightailed it outta there."

Lazzaro was finished. He felt he had made his point. He looked over at Malveau. "Your witness."

Malveau knew that he had to take what the eyewitness

had seen and use it to BookTau's advantage.

"Now Mr. Tucker you said that you and, errrr....Mr. Washington or BookTau had known each other for a long time, is that right?"

"Yes, sir. A long time."

"Have you ever known of him hurting anyone?"

"No, sir."

"Have you ever known of him being in a fight?"

"Oh, yes, sir."

"Could you tell us about that?"

"Well, it wasn't like he wuz in a fight. He would stop a fight. I 'rembers this one time we wuz on this job cutting trees for Mr.Bill Blue and these two boys got to arguing. At first it was 'bout much of nothing, but this one boy starting lowratin' the other boy's mama, you know playin' the dozens. And that made the first boy so mad he picked up the ax and wuz swingin'to cut that second boy in two. Well BookTau jumps up and caught that ax in mid air, ripped it outta dat boy's hands and hit him wid his fist, so hard in the chest, dat the boy slamped up against a tree five feet away, and knocked himself out cold. BookTau he strong. We all thought dat boy was dead. Nobody said nothing and then BookTau, he went over, poured some water on dat boys head and then sat down next to him and held him like he was a little baby 'till he woke up and say, "Where am I." Then BookTau called the other boy over and made 'em shake hands and be friends again."

"Have you ever seen BookTau hit a man for no reason?"

"No, sir, you gotta make him real mad for him to do somethin' like that."

"Did you know the other man you saw in the graveyard?"

"Never saw him before in my life."

"Did you see the man do anything to Miz Rosa?"

"Oh, yes sir. He had her backed up against a tomb, like

he was tryin' to get some, then she slapped him, and started yelling, 'leave me alone,' and beating on his shoulder all the while.

"From what you saw and heard, did you think she was in danger of being hurt?"

"I wasn't close enough to hear regular talkin'. All I could hear was the yelling, and she wuz yelling real loud, like she knowed this man was 'bout to do somethin' real bad to her."

"Now tell me Tucker, If BookTau had not been there and you were the only one around, would you have gone to help the lady?"

Lazzaro was on his feet. "Your honor I object. This calls for a supposition."

Perrodin was beginning to like the direction in which this case was now unfolding. He had wondered why Lazzaro had called the first witness who had not added to his case of motive or opportunity. Now the cross examination from Malveau was moving in the direction of truth and justice, and he was interested in hearing what an eye witness would have done under the circumstances he had observed.

"He said, "Denied. Answer the question."

"Oh, yes sir I woulda done jes what BookTau done, help Miz Rosa. But he was there, so there was nothing for me to do but hightail it on home."

Malveau said. "Thank you. No more questions."

Lazzaro stood for cross examination of his own witness.

"Mr. Tucker, do you want all of these fine people on this jury to believe that you would have committed murder?"

"No, sir. I didn't say dat. The man ask me if I woulda done what BookTau done and help out Miz Rosa, and I say yes. And I'll say it again, if you wanna know."

Lazzaro felt he should leave well enough alone and dismiss the witness. "No further questions." When he got back to his table he looked over his list of witnesses. The only one left was Walter Waters, and he doubted if he would be able to add anything more. So he decided to hold him as a rebuttal witness if need be.

"The prosecution rests your honor."

Perrodin was taken aback, especially after the elaborate opening from Lazzaro. He looked at his watch and said, "I was prepared to give a break after the prosecution witness, but since we still have daylight left we'll take a recess and hear from the defense after lunch."

Les took BookTau to lunch at the Black Eagle along with Lightfoot, Rosa, and Lala. Lightfoot had called ahead and Naomi had everything on the table by the time they arrived. She asked as she dished up the plates, "How are things going uptown for y'all?"

Rosa answered, "All right I guess. We haven't been in yet, that's going to happen when we go back."

After Rosa's report, Les added, "I spoke with Mr. Malveau and he says everything gonna be fine."

Then Naomi asked, "How you think it's going, BookTau?"

"Them people lying on me. That lawyer man say I killed Joshua on purpose, and nobody else said it wuz a accident."

Les extended his hand to BookTau's shoulder, "I told you not to let what the prosecutor says get you upset. That's his job to make it look like you're guilty."

"Well I ain't guilty, and I told that to the judge, and I think he believed me."

"Now you just listen to what Les says. And don't you be worrying about what that prosecuting man says; he ain't got good sense anyway." Then Naomi continued. "Here's an extra chicken leg for you." She patted him on the head and kept on serving.

Les thought back to Christmas and what he had overheard.

It was difficult for him to reconcile how Naomi could be so compassionate now, and so narrow-minded then. But that was not something that he wanted to spend time thinking about. He said, "Y'all hurry and finish. We gotta be back by two o'clock."

When court reconvened, Malveau called Rosa as his first witness. She rose to enter keeping her hand tightly enclosed around her rosary, as she did when she placed her hand on the bible to be sworn in.

Malveau hesitated before asking the first question. He was playing for time to give her a chance to compose herself and feel comfortable on the stand. She looked around at the people in the jury box looking at her.

Judge Perrodin leaned over his desk, "Mr. Malveau?"

Then he knew it was time to begin. "Mrs. Rosa Cane, is that how you feel comfortable in being addressed?"

"No, sir. I haven't been comfortable with that name since Joshua was in prison and became a Muslim."

Malveau saw, out of the corner of his eye, several people in the jury look from one to the other. He continued down this path. "What was Joshua in prison for?"

Lazzaro was on his feet instantly. "Objection."

"I withdraw the question." Then Malveau continued. What name then would you like to be addressed by?"

"Rosa Fergerson."

"All right then, Miss Fergerson, where were you on Sunday morning, July 15th?"

"I was in the cemetery near Holy Ghost Church. I had gone to visit the graves of my father and mother."

"Please tell us what happened while you were in the graveyard."

"I was saying my prayers and I heard footsteps behind me. I turned and it was Joshua. I asked why was he here, and he said he had come to talk. I figured he had just received the divorce papers that I had filed and I said there was nothing left to talk about. He showed me a roll of money and said he would like to keep it for us, rather than spend it on a divorce lawyer. I told him that he could not buy me back, that my mind was made up, and it was all over between us. Then I started to leave. He followed me and kept talking about things--about the first time he kissed me--and when we danced to Nat King Cole--and all the money we could make with the candy. He was a good talker and then he started making excuses about why he had joined the Muslim faith and said it was only to save his life while he was in prison. Well that made me mad because I knew then, that he was a liar and I told him right then and there that I should have listened to my Papa and not had anything to do with him in the first place."

Then Rosa remembered the scene between she and Phillip when she announced that she had gotten married. Her Papa had said, "You have just thrown your life away on some law-breaking hustler who schemed to marry the finest woman from the best family in Estilette."

And all she could do was cry.

The Judge handed down a box of tissue and Malveau passed it over to Rosa. After a few minutes she took a deep breath and looked up at Malveau.

She continued. "I just kept walking away and he kept walking with me, talking and saying we could still make it together. Finally, he reached out and stopped me and tried to kiss me. I slapped him, then I struggled out of his arms and began backing away. He came after me and I backed into a tomb and he grabbed me and kept trying to kiss me. I slapped him again, and tried to get out of his grip but he held on to me, and I got frightened and started yelling as loud as I could, 'stop….stop leave me alone…I don't want to be with you,' and he kept trying to kiss me, and I kept struggling to get out of his arms and kept yelling as loud as I could. Then BookTau ran up from behind and grabbed Joshua around the neck, and I broke free. I remember exactly what he said, 'Leave Miz Rosa alone. She don't want to be with you. Now you leave her be.' And all the while he had his hands around Joshua's neck. And BookTau is so strong he had picked him up off the ground and Joshua was kicking and struggling. Then, when I realized what was happening, I ran back and started pulling at BookTau's arms, and pleading for him to let go. I told him I was all right, so he could let him go now. And finally he did, and Joshua just dropped to the ground. He was dead."

The silence in the courtroom could be felt. A couple of the ladies on the jury covered their eyes and bowed their heads. Several sniffles were heard from people in the courtroom.

After a few moments, Rosa continued. "Then BookTau knelt down next to Joshua and started shaking his body and saying, 'Mr. Joshua…. Mr. Joshua, wake up…I didn't mean to hurt you, I just wanted you to leave Miz Rosa alone.'"

Rosa reached for another tissue. Malveau said, "If you would like, we can stop." Rosa held up her hand and shook her head.

"My Papa always said…"

Lazzaro was on his feet…"Your honor…."Before he could get out his completed statement, Perrodin held up his hand for him to stop.

Rosa looked up at the Judge and he nodded his head. She continued, "Papa always said BookTau was just like a ten-year-old child, who never realized he had the strength of Goliath."

Then Judge Perrodin looked at Lazzaro and asked, "Did you have a question, sir?"

Lazzaro said, "No, thank you, Judge."

Malveau looked thoughtfully at Rosa and decided that she had been through enough so he turned and said, "Your witness, counselor."

Lazzaro rose and approached the witness. "Now tell me, Miss Fergerson, when Mr. Washington knelt down to shake Mr. Cane did you see him take any money out of his pocket?"

"No, sir."

"Were you in a position to see him the whole time he was kneeling next to Mr. Cane?"

"Sir, he didn't take any money. The money was still in Mr. Cane's pocket and the sheriff took it and sent it to me later on."

Lazzaro felt he had to pursue his theory. He persisted. He wet his lips and crossed his arms. "Were you and Mr. Washington lovers?"

This question threw Rosa into silence. *Why would this man ask such a question? I am a teacher and BookTau has the IQ of a ten year old, and is from a completely different social background. What would cause him to ask such a question?* She was confused. Her first inclination of a response was, *'What a ridiculous question.'* Then she thought better of answering in such a manner. It was simply not in her nature to do such a thing. So she finally said, "No, sir. Mr. Washington is a good friend of the family's and of mine, that's all."

"Miss Fergerson, do you know of any reason why Mr. Washington would allow Mr. Cane to stay at his house?"

"Because he's a kindhearted man, sir, and Mr. Cane didn't have any other place to stay."

With that, Mr. Lazzaro decided that there was no reason to continue, he said "No further questions, your honor."

Malveau thought carefully about who should be called next, and then he asked, "Sidebar, your honor?"

Judge Perrodin motioned for them to approach and when they were standing in front of the bench the Judge asked, "What's the problem?"

Malveau said, "Your honor, I would like to call a witness from Mr. Lazzaro's list. One that he did not call."

Lazzaro looked from one to the other, and all he could say was, "Your honor, this is very irregular."

"But not illegal. However, Mr. Malveau you realize that you may be calling a hostile witness."

"I know your honor, so if I may I'd like to do that."

Mr. Lazzaro, do you have any objections?"

Lazzaro hesitated and then asked, "Who is the witness?"

"Walter Waters."

He thought for a few moments and could not imagine anything that Waters could say that would harm his case. So he said, "No objections."

Slick was called as a witness for the defense.

Malveau began. "Mr. Waters, how did it happen that Mr. Joshua Cane was involved in a poker game at your place of business?"

"Sugar came in and asked me to set it up."

"I'm sorry, who is Sugar?"

"Joshua Cane. That's what he called himself. Said he was Sugar to the ladies. Most people knew him as 'Sugar Cane.'"

It was beginning to sound better and better to Malveau, and he decided to get as much mileage as he could out of this newly immerging image of Joshua. "Oh, I see. So it was Sugar Cane who came in and asked you to set up a poker game. Is that right?"

"That's right, sir."

"Tell us about that."

"Well, first off he and I set about shooting a game of pool. Then midway in the game he asked if I could set up a game of poker for the next Saturday night with four people who had money to lose because he needed some cash and felt like winning. So I said, 'yes', and set about setting up the game."

"Had he ever played poker at your place before?"

"Oh, yes sir. Many times. He was a pro. I don't ever remember a time when he lost at poker. He was so good, I always suspected he was cheating, but I could never catch him at it."

"So why would you arrange another game?"

"Well I figured like this, everybody's gotta lose sometimes, and I called in some players that I thought were good enough to call his bluff and that's how it went."

"And what happened?"

"He cleaned everybody out, and early Sunday morning one of the players just up and said he had lost enough and was going to church, so that broke up the game."

"How much did you figure that Mr. Cane had won?"

"Don't know exactly, but I figured it was over two thousand."

Malveau could see, out of the corner of his eye, the effect that this testimony had on the faces of some of the jurors. He had hit a gold mine and he decided to dig deeper."Do you know anything else about Mr. Cane, like where he was from, or what he did for a living, in addition to poker?"

"Yes, sir. He came from Chicago and sold insurance. Then after he was in town for a while he started selling Miz Rosa's candy. She was a good candy maker, and Sugar saw the chance to make additional money."

Lazzaro shouted, "Objection. Side bar."

When they arrived at the bench Lazzaro said, "Your honor this line of questioning doesn't have anything at all to do with this case."

"Mr. Lazzaro, I remind you that when you agreed to

allow Mr. Malveau to question your witness as hostile, it was assumed that you knew what evidence your witness could, or could not provide. So I'd say you opened the door for whatever testimony that you knew your witness could provide. Now, do you, or do you not concur?"

"Well your honor, if you put it that way…"

Perrodin said, "Over-ruled. Step back."

Both counselors headed back to their tables. Halfway there Lazzaro turned and headed back to the bench. Perrodin waved him back.

Malveau continued. "Mr. Waters do you have any other knowledge about Mr. Cane's activities in this candy business with Miz Rosa?"

"Oh, yes, sir. The candy was doing real good. He had put on a nice looking wrapper, and it was selling like hot cakes all around, and in my café and pool hall too, and Miz Rosa was working real hard to keep up with the demands."

"What happened after the successful marketing of the candy?"

"Well sir, next thing I knew he was arrested by the sheriff and sent back to Chicago. And I heard tell…."

Lazzaro, yelled out, "Objection."

"Sustained. Hearsay is not admitted."

Malveau had reached what he thought was the end of the testimony from this witness and Waters had given him an idea. Why he had not thought of calling the sheriff before was a mystery. So he thought it was worth a try. He asked, "Sidebar your honor?"

Perrodin looked down at the two attorneys standing below his bench, and Malveau said, "In the interest of justice, your honor, I think we should have some testimony from the sheriff."

"Now, that's an idea. I was wondering why he wasn't called in the first place. Which one of you would like to call him as a witness?"

Before Lazzaro could ponder the pros and cons of the sheriff appearing as his witness, Malveau said, "I will."

"Make the arrangements and have the sheriff here day after tomorrow and we'll continue then."

With that the trial was recessed.

Malveau now had to make a decision whether all of the witnesses he had scheduled would be needed. He figured that the testimony from the Sheriff would be sufficient to establish his case in favor of BookTau, so it was not likely that he would need testimony from Les or Lightfoot.

*   *   *

Two days later when the trial was reconvened, Lightfoot and Les were sitting in the courtroom right behind BookTau who was smiling for the first time. He was filled with hope, now that his friends were nearby, and he figured that now those people sitting in the box across the room would understand that he did not kill Joshua on purpose.

Sheriff Bobineaux limped in with the aid of his cane and was sworn in.

Malveau wasted no time in getting to the matter at hand. "Sheriff what were the charges on which you arrested Mr. Joshua Cane?"

"Fraud and extortion of insurance money, on a warrant from the police department in Chicago."

"And when was this?"

"1965."

Malveau repeated the date. "1965. Thirteen years ago. And what happened as a result of that arrest?"

"I sent him on back to Chicago and he was tried and convicted and sent to prison for ten years. Then in June of 1977, I found out he was back in town, staying out back at

BookTau's place."

Malveau interrupted. "For the record, do you mean Mr. Washington's place?"

"Yeah that's right. He was staying there and I went out there to find out why he come back. I figured he was trouble."

Lazzaro was up like lightning. "Objection."

"Overruled. The sheriff is considered an expert and as such is allowed to express his professional opinion."

Sheriff Bobineaux continued. "I was tempted to arrest Joshua Cane on suspicion of breaking his parole, but naw I didn't. Now I wish I had. Three weeks later I had to go to the cemetery and arrest BookTau, I mean Mr. Washington for choking Cane to death to keep him from harming Miz Rosa. BookTau just didn't know his own strength."

"When he was arrested, did Mr. Washington give any resistance?"

"Naw. He come along like a little boy. I didn't even have to handcuff him."

"When you examined the body of Mr. Cane did you find any money?"

"Yeah. He had two thousand five hundred dollars held together by a rubber band, and I gave that to Miz Rosa, since she was still legally his wife."

"Is there anything else you would like to add?"

Cat Bobineaux thought for an instant and realized that any opinion that he might express may have the effect of being prejudicial and could lead to a mistrial. Then he thought a second time and figured, *what the hell.* He said with conviction, "There sure is. BookTau did this town, and Miz Rosa, a service and a good deed by getting rid of that pile of garbage."

Lazzaro jumped up. "Objection! Objection, your Honor. That should be stricken from the record!"

"Accepted."

Cat Bobineaux hobbled away from the stand with a slight smile on his face, understanding very well that in spite of his words being stricken from the record, they would not be stricken from the minds of the jurors.

Judge asked, "Next witness?"

Malveau responded, "Your honor, the defense rests." There was a slight smile on his face as he returned to his seat.

"Mr. Lazzaro are you ready to make your closing?"

Mario Lazzaro seemed a bit hesitant as he rose; he was not sure that he should be closing. Maybe, he thought, as he gazed around the courtroom, there was something or someone he had left out that could make his case. It was too late to have doubts, so he took a beep breath, summoned up his resolve and began. "Ladies and gentlemen of the jury, this was a short but clearly decisive case. You have heard the same thing from all of the witnesses, first, Miss Fergerson, then Mr. Tucker and Sheriff Bobineaux himself. All of these witnesses said that Mr. Washington strangled Mr. Cane to death. And two of these witnesses saw him do it. Even the person, whom the defense claims he was protecting, admits that he killed Mr. Cane. The defense has tried very hard to produce evidence that justifies this killing. But we know murder is murder and it cannot be lessened by any mitigating justification like, saying, he was a bad person, or a gambling man, or a lying husband. But not one of these excuses makes the killing of another person justifiable. Even the Commandment, which most of you in this court believe, says, thou shalt not kill. And this is the issue here. This is the only issue here. A man is dead and the weapon used for his death is sitting right over there." Lazzaro stretched out his arm and swung his body around pointing his finger at BookTau. "And you should bring in a verdict of guilty. Thank you, ladies and gentlemen."

BookTau dropped his head to the table and Les reached

over and pulled him back into a sitting position.

Judge Perrodin called out, "Mr. Malveau."

Malveau stood and walked to the center of the jury box and leaned over, and for the next several seconds he looked at the jurors, and his eyes traveled from one set of eyes to another.

"Ladies and gentlemen, we all believe in the fifth Commandment and have hoped for the retribution that it brings on those who violate it. And we also believe in the Commandment that says *Love Thy Neighbor as Thyself.* I ask you to remember this Commandment as I tell you a story. Once upon a time there was a giant of a man who was described by his friend, George, as thinking like a child but being as strong as a bull. Now let's call this giant of a man, Lennie. Lennie depended on George for everything, and George told Lennie what to do, what to think, and what to hope for, and George loved Lennie and gave him the faith to believe that as soon as they had worked hard enough and saved enough money they would buy a little farm across the river where Lennie could raise rabbits. George knew that Lennie had a passion to feel the smooth, delicate, silkiness of the fur and hair of animals. But in his tender heartedness Lennie did not know his own strength, and as they walked to their next job Lennie accidentally smothered to death, the mouse that he carried in his pocket. When George found out about the dead mouse, he made Lennie throw the mouse into the river. This made Lennie very sad because he loved the mouse, and liked to pet him. So George promised that as soon as they got to the farm where they were to work, he would catch another mouse for him to pet. And when they arrived at the farm, George discovered that the owner's dog had just delivered a new litter of pups. So he got a pup for Lennie to feel. And the same thing happened. Lennie petted the pup with such strong tenderness that he accidentally smothered the pup to death. Lennie did not understand why it seemed that everything he loved to touch kept dying. Then he went into the barn to bury his pup in the hay. Well, the wife of the farmer came in and questioned what he was doing. Lennie told her he liked to feel the softness of his dead pup. The lady felt compassion and said that her hair was as soft as the dead pup's hair, and invited Lennie to caress her hair rather than that of the dead animal. Again because Lennie did not know his own strength, he was hurting her with his caress, and the woman yelled out. Lennie became frightened, and to keep anyone from hearing, Lennie put his hand over her mouth and accidentally smothered her to death. When his friend George found out what had happened, he helped Lennie escape the lynch mob that had gathered to avenge the death of the farmer's wife. And when they got to the river, George made Lennie believe they had arrived at the place where the rabbits were, and he convinced Lennie to look across the river to see where he would spend the rest of his days caressing the rabbits. This story was written in 1937 by John Steinbeck, and it is titled *Of Mice and Men.*"

When Malveau finished his story there was no movement by anyone. The silence of the courtroom could be felt, and Kenneth remained motionless, still holding on to the rail of the jury box. Finally he walked away and then turned back and faced the jurors.

"Before I started this story, I asked that you remember the Commandment, *Love Thy Neighbor as Thyself.* And you also remember, the honorable prosecutor said in his opening statement, that he intended to prove that Mr. Washington had motive and opportunity to kill, and that you should remember the Commandment, *Thou Shalt Not Kill.* Well, as you are now aware, the prosecutor did not prove a motive because there was none. Mr. Washington did not have any plans or reasons to kill Mr. Cane. It was an accident. And Mr.

Lazzaro did not prove opportunity because Mr. Washington was not guilty of creating one. He simply took a short cut through the cemetery on the way home early Sunday morning, saw Mr. Cane assaulting Miss Fergerson, and ran to her rescue."

Les reached over and put a reassuring hand on BookTau's shoulder. He turned around and Looked at Les and smiled.

Malveau continued. "And it is now time for you to decide which is the more compelling of the two Commandments, *Thou Shalt Not Kill, or Love Thy Neighbor as Thyself?* To punish Lennie for the accidental murder of a woman he had no intention of killing, or to save Lennie with the love of a neighbor as George did. Like George, this is a decision that you must now make. So I ask you to search your hearts and minds and souls to arrive at your decision." Malveau leaned on the rail toward the jurors and slowly perused the faces of each.

"How will <u>you</u> judge the actions of this man before you? You have one of two decisions to make—guilty, who like the prosecution claims has committed a premeditated murder— or not guilty, who, like Lennie, has love and compassion, and killed accidentally, because he does not know his own strength. Thank you Ladies and Gentlemen of the jury. The defense rests"

Judge Perrodin banged his gavel and said, "The jury will retire to consider the verdict."

Four hours later the court was back in session. The Judge called out, "Mr. Foreman have you reached a verdict?"

The foreman stood and shook his head. "Judge, we are deadlocked and have a hung jury."

When BookTau heard this he went berserk. He rose up, turned over the defense table and yelled, "I ain't gonna be hung." And before anyone could recover, he was headed for the doors, burst into the hallway and out of the courthouse.

The judge was furious. After banging his gavel longer than any one could remember, he said after the silence, "I'm issuing a warrant for Mr. Washington to be held in contempt for wrecking my court room. Jurors you will be secluded until you come up with a verdict. This court is in recess until Monday morning. Dismissed."

Les and Lightfoot sat in stunned silence along with Kenneth Malveau. Then Malveau turned to Les and asked, "Think you can find him before Cat does?"

"We'll try."

*   *   *

Later that day, Les and Lightfoot went out back to BookTau's house. They did not suspect that he would be there but they went anyway. Les noticed that the mule that BookTau had received from Phillip was not in the pasture. Lightfoot said, "I have a good idea where he is. I'll go but you stay with Rosa. She's going out of her mind."

Lightfoot dropped Les off at the house and he took off to the thicket. He figured that's where BookTau would go to hide away, plus the fact he suspected that Tante might know a thing or two about his whereabouts.

On the way there the clouds turned black and the daylight faded into a Louisiana summer thunder storm. Quicker than Lightfoot could say Jack Robinson he found himself in a downpour. Raindrops were hitting his truck like small rocks. Thunder and lightning surrounded his travel and seemed to follow his path down the narrow road into the swamp. Between the rain and the darkness, Lightfoot could hardly see where he was going. He could not turn around and go back; there was no place where he could do that safely. He had to keep on going. The bushes and small trees were slamming back and forth across the windshield, so he turned on the head lights to be able to see. When the lightning flashed it was so bright he had to shade his eyes. The thunder vibrations actually shook the truck, but he kept inching along.

Night had set in by the time he had reached the clearing, and the rain was still pouring down and the thunder and lightning was still raging. He had never seen a storm like this. He honked his horn until he saw a small orange glow from a hurricane lamp emerge from the doorway. He turned off the headlights, and ran in the direction of the glowing light. There was a blinding flash of lightning and Lightfoot was sure that he saw the silhouette of someone running away from the house.

When he got to the porch, a crackly voice asked, "Who dat?"

"Lightfoot."

"What you doing out here in all this storm?"

"Looking for BookTau."

"Well, he ain't here. Com'on in outta the rain."

Lightfoot had not seen Tante in years. From what he could make out in the dim light from the lamp, she seemed to be over a hundred, but he knew she was only in her eighties. Her wrinkled face resembled a muddy path of wagon tracks, and a corncob pipe dangled from her mouth. He knew this was where Naomi came to do her wangas, and this was where the gals with unwanted burdens came to get relief. Tante's was a place of refuge for those in trouble, and the old woman had been helping out for as long as he could remember.

It was not a place one could stumble on by accident; you had to know how to make the twists and turns through the saw palmetto and the bushes and brambles to get there. Tante and her husband had put this place together from odds and ends of construction material over many years, and the smoke smudged, news papered walls reeked with the commingled odors from tobacco, bacon and the stale aroma of time.

He looked around in the dim light to see what or whom he might see. It wasn't much. The storm still raged and surprisingly the trees that surrounded the place acted like a windbreak and protected it from the full force and power of the elements, so it was relatively peaceful except for the constant whistling of wind through the cracks.

Tante pointed to a ragged sofa bed against a distant wall and said, "You can hunker down over dare, til morning. It'll all be over den." With that she disappeared behind a crooked door held together by a large "Z".

Lightfoot was awakened by the smell of coffee and the sizzle of cooking bacon. He joined Tante and the old man for a breakfast of grits, eggs, bacon and biscuits. And when he had eaten his fill, he opened the door and looked out. It was bright and sunny. And except for the litter of broken branches scattered around, one would never suspect that such a storm had raged only a few hours before.

The old man squeezed past Lightfoot and began picking up the broken limbs. Lightfoot had never heard him say a word. It was like he was a mute and he seemed to be about the same age as Tante.

Lightfoot had an idea and he walked to the edge of the porch and sat down. He took out his harmonica and started playing, *I'm the Hoochie Coochie Man.* He knew that if BookTau was within earshot he would know it was him. The old man stopped what he was doing, went into the house and got his guitar, and joined Lightfoot on the porch. They played together. Pretty soon, just as Lightfoot figured, BookTau appeared from the chicken coop a little ways from the house. His clothes were still drenched and he looked awful and tired. He came up to where the music was playing and said, "I thought it might be you."

Lightfoot stopped playing but the old man continued.

"I've come to take you back."

"I don't wanna die."

"You ain't gonna die."

"I heard them people on the jury said I was gonna be hung."

Lightfoot got up and put his arm around BookTau's shoulder and said, "They were talking about a hung jury, not you. That means they couldn't make up their minds about whether you was guilty or innocent. Chances are they'll say you're innocent."

BookTau's face lit up like a young boy's on Christmas. "Really?"

"But you gotta come back. The trial ain't finished."

Tante was standing in the doorway listening to everything, and she said, "Comon in here boy, I got your food on the table. And you, old man, stop that playing and pick up them limbs scattered all over."

*   *   *

On Monday BookTau was back in court wearing the new outfit that Les had bought early that morning.

Judge Perrodin looked down at BookTau through irritated eyes. Then he focused his attention on the jury box. "Has the jury reached a verdict?"

The foreman stood and said, "Your honor, we are still hung by a vote of seven to five." Realizing that it seemed impossible to get a unanimous vote of guilty or not guilty Judge Perrodin gave instructions, "Clerk, let's take a poll of the jury."

This the clerk did and said, "Five guilty, seven not guilty.

A hung jury."

Malveau turned to BookTau and patted him on the arm. "You're a free man."

BookTau smiled.

The judge banged his gavel. "The jury is discharged with thanks. The accused is freed of the charges. However Mr. Washington is being charged with contempt of the court and is sentenced to spend six months in the parish jail. Bailiff, take custody of the prisoner. Court is dismissed."

Before BookTau had time to react, he was surrounded by four policemen who immediately handcuffed him. Les went to him immediately and said, "It's all right. You'll be out before you know it. This is about you breaking up the court's table, not about Mr. Cane. Just go along. Please."

BookTau nodded his head in agreement, and was led away to jail.

A few days later Malveau dropped by Lazzaro's office. "Just for the record, I thought I'd ask if you have any plans for a retrial."

"Do chicken have teeth?" Was Mario's reply.

Then they each had a shot of bourbon and that was the end of that.

Chapter 23
Paradise Found

In July, 1978, BookTau was released from jail and Les was there to pick him up and take him directly to the Black Eagle where a welcome home Blues Feast was in progress. There was a large banner stretched across the front of the stage, announcing it's For You BookTau. As he walked through the door, Lightfoot started playing his favorite, *I'm the Hoochie Coochie Man,* and BookTau was so overwhelmed with shock that all he could do was hide his eyes with his hands and turn around in circles. And when he uncovered his face, the ladies, beginning with Rosa, then Ann, then Lala, and a lady that no one was familiar with, planted kisses on his face. Vitalee took up after Lightfoot finished the introduction and began performing all of his blues favorites. BookTau wanted to dance but instead was lead by Naomi to a special table set up with all of the foods that he liked--red beans and rice, hot sausage, pig's feet, collard greens, boudin and cornbread, and he ate like he hadn't eaten for the entire six months in jail. Everybody else ordered and paid for what they wanted and joined the feast.

After eating his fill, BookTau started dancing. A strange lady in a sparkling golden pants suit, a curled blond wig, red, white, and blue fingernails and finely sculpted scarlet lipstick, that no one had seen before got up and danced with him. She did not seem to be a stranger to BookTau, and Les went over to Lightfoot and asked, "Who is that woman?"

Lightfoot said, "I seen her around before, I don't know her name, but I know who does."

Lightfoot crossed to the bar where Slick sat nursing his drink and nibbling on pickled pigsfeet. Les followed close behind.

Lightfoot tapped him on the shoulder and asked, "Say, man, who is that woman dancing with BookTau?"

Slick twisted his head around and said, "Oh, that's Sally MoDaddy."

Les responded, "I've never seen her before."

Slick said, "Well, you wouldn't. She's a whore from The Bottom."

The Bottom was that section of Estilette where the whores, pimps, hustlers, welfare takers, and petty criminals lived. It was the gathering place of the down—and--outers of society—a place that the keepers of the peace only went when there was a killing—a place of ill repute-- the ghetto---a place that had earned the distinction of the term "bottom" just as it had in most other urban communities throughout the country.

Lightfoot asked, "What she doing up here?"

Slick swung around on his stool to face Lightfoot on one side and Les on the other. "Y'all don't know? That's BookTau's pussy."

Lightfoot said, "What you talking, Slick?"

Les said, "I thought BookTau was a virgin."

Slick fell out laughing. "Y'all don't get around the Bottom much."

Lightfoot agreed, "Well, you got that right."

Les looked back to the dance floor at BookTau and the woman getting down, and shook his head. He realized no matter how well one thought they knew somebody, it was possible that they really didn't know them at all. Then he asked, "How long's this been going on?"

Slick turned up his beer bottle and drained the remainder, wiped his hand across his mouth and started his story. "Well, it's like this. Along 'bout the time that BookTau was catching gators for Bill Blue, he rode passed Sally's house on that mule your granddaddy let him ride, on his way back from the store. He'd go to the store about once a month to get his foodstuffs. And he'd put 'em in a gunny sack and tie it across his mule. Well, this day he was passing by, and Sally run out of the house wid a man chasing her and she almost run right into that mule. And that man caught up to her and started beating her black and blue, yelling and claiming she stole his money. BookTau jumped off the mule and gave that man a licking he was not likely to ever forget. That man ran off, yelling and cursing back at BookTau who didn't pay him no mind, cause by then he was busy helping Sally to her feet. She was all swole and bruised up and was crying up a storm. And BookTau told her that everything was gonna be all right and if that man ever came back to give him a call, and right then and there he give that woman all the food stuffs he had in his sack. And the next month when he passed by with his groceries, Sally was sitting on the steps and she invited him in. She told him she was much obliged for the kindness he had shown her but all she could do to thank him, was see that he got a good time at no charge. And every month from then on, when BookTau would get his food stuffs he'd stop by and have a good time with Sally."

Lightfoot said, "That's some story you tell, 'bout Sally MoDaddy. Is that her real last name?"

No, it's Moore. Sally Moore. But she got that nickname 'cause when the men she's been with got it off, she'd ask, 'Would you like some mo', Daddy?' And when the word got around the name stuck, Sally MoDaddy."

The music and the dancing went on most of the evening, and Les and Ann watched from the special table that had been reserved for their Grandfather Phillip. Ann reached over and took a sip from her wine glass and asked, "So, what are you going to do now, Sir Galahad?"

"What do you mean, now?"

"Now that your campaign to save BookTau is over."

Les looked back over his shoulder then back at his sister. "Look at him out there. He's as happy as can be. He's had lots to eat, and the music that he loves is playing, and he's dancing with his woman."

Ann asked with surprise, "What do you mean, his woman?"

"That woman he's dancing with means a lot to him. He doesn't ask for much and he doesn't need much to make him happy. His love is simple, he is kind, he is not boastful or arrogant or rude. He's like a child accepting and believing in all things. I wish that my life could be like that."

"What are you talking about? You have so much more that he does. So much more to look forward to."

"Do I? I've been thinking. Here I am, thirty-three years old and I've just given up the dream that I've been running after all of my life." Les took a deep breath, and a sip from his glass, then looked his sister in the eye. "You remember in the trial, Kenneth Malveau used that story from the play *Of Mice and Men?*"

Ann nodded her head in agreement.

338

Les continued. "That's what I've always wanted to do. Use the theatre, or the movies, to give people an understanding of the values in their lives. To take meaning, and substance, and compress it into a shorter time span, and then give it relevance to those who are seeing, and hearing, and needing that focus to help them make decisions about the direction their life should take, is what I've always wanted to do. Kenneth did that for those jurors. That's why I wanted to be an actor to start with, and that's why I wanted to be a director. But it's all gone now."

"Why? Why do you think it's gone?"

"I've given it up. With Papa's condition being what it is, there is no way I can do that now."

"I hope I'm not hearing that deep down inside you're blaming Papa's condition for changing the direction of your dream."

"Well, I donno. But that's a part of it."

Naomi appeared with a bowl full of boiled shrimp. "I just finished cooking these and thought you might like some."

Ann said, "Thanks Aunt Naomi." Then she turned her attention back to Les. "And the other part?"

"Grandpop."

"Oh really?"

"Yeah. You remember how I used to be a kick ass?" He reached over and started shelling shrimp.

"Used to be? When did you change?"

"That bullet in the back was the beginning of the change." He flipped a couple of shrimp into his mouth. "Grandpop used to say to me, 'You're too quick to fight. Don't be so hotheaded'. Well, after all of what happened in Los Angeles, I realized that a lot of that I brought on myself because I wasn't patient and I was moving too fast. I didn't give myself time to think and be kind, like BookTau. And I was vengeful. If someone did something to me I'd get them back, and that was the same thing that made Freddy shoot me. He was getting back at me because I had kicked his ass."

Les paused a bit, filled both glasses with wine, put a shrimp into his mouth and said, "I don't know if you'll believe this or not, but it was Grandpop who saved me from dying. Oh, I know that he didn't really reach out from the grave and pull me back, but there was something there, like his spirit that kept me from dying. And when Papa had his stroke it was a sign that I had to do something different. It's all connected."

"You really are coming of age, aren't you?"

"Yeah. Just struggling to be what Grandpop wanted me to be."

"He wanted you to be a doctor."

"In one sense yes. But more than that, he just wanted me to help make a difference in somebody's life."

"Are we now talking about Caryn?"

"Possibly. I don't really know." She has some decisions of her own to make. But if we're able to put our lives together on the same track maybe that will turn out to be the right direction."

And they talked on, like a brother and sister should talk.

And Les continued. "Yeah, I wanted to be like my grandfather more that I wanted to be like my own father. I sometimes wish that I could have been the doctor like he wanted, but I just didn't have it in me. So I am happy that you did. I'm sure he would be right proud of you, even though you've taken up with Alex. Mr. Estilette was his best friend."

Ann was shocked that it now seemed that he had a change of heart. "Les, that is not what you felt when we talked about this at Papa's house."

In the interval of time since then, Les had tried hard to open his mind to acceptance of the relationship that his sister had with Alex. He knew that if it was in the cards that he would grow in the direction of acceptance, and he had to close his eyes to his perceptions of love between the same sexes.

He said, "You know I always go back to what Grandpop said, and on the subject of love he always said, 'Love *your neighbor as yourself,*' and he talked about agape, or what he described as Christian love. And I'm sure he would want me to feel the same way he did about that."

"Oh, my brother." Ann began crying.

"I'm sorry. I didn't say that to get you upset."

"I'm not crying because I'm upset. I'm crying because I realize how much you've grown as a loving person."

He reached over and caressed her hand, then leaned in and kissed her head. After several moments she raised her head from the table and said softly, "Thank you."

"You wanna dance?"

"Yeah."

And they joined the others on the dance floor. And Les and his sister partied to the rhythm of the blues for the rest of the night.

*   *   *

It was 1980 and a lot had happened over the last two years.

Rosa had put the events of Joshua Cane behind her but she continued making and selling her fudge and pecan pralines, and Lala had now decided to join her in the production. So the two sisters changed the name from Rosa's Fudge to Two Sisters' Pralines and they were happy doing this as a side line to teaching the young people of Estilette as they had always done. So their lives were full.

And Lightfoot and Naomi continued running the Black

Eagle as it became more and more popular as the center of the Blues music for the area.

Caryn was not getting the weekly calls on Y&R as regularly as she had been before that Christmas in Louisiana, when she had not returned in time, because of Naomi's hex. So it became necessary to rewrite her recurring role for a look-alike sister to keep the story line as close to the script as possible. Now she was being called in for half as many scripts as before. This unexpected free time gave her the opportunity to attend cattle-calls for roles in "B" movies. Although this gave an opportunity to seek fame and fortune outside of the soap opera genre, it was not as satisfying as she hoped it would be. On several occasions she entertained the thought of calling Les and saying, "Let's get married." However, she did not want it to seem as if marriage was a fallback position because she could not achieve stardom in Hollywood. So she continued pounding the pavement.

Les also had his problems. Loneliness. However he was very busy, looking after his Papa, and the crop, and his Mama, and BookTau. It was a full time occupation but he missed being with Caryn, so once a month he'd jump on a plane and fly to Los Angeles. Not only was this putting a crimp in his wallet but it took time away from matters in Estilette, so it seemed that they were both ready for a change.

Dora was still in the picture, at least as far as Naomi was concerned. One aspect of Naomi's success as a voodoo practioner was persistence. She had been accustomed to long waits between the effects of hexes to show themselves. It was a matter of faith and the steadfast belief in the outcome of the thing wished for. To some extent the use of fetishes, talismen and good luck charms came from rituals in the Catholic Church's practice of adoration for the statues of the saints and especially that of the Virgin Mary. So there was much similarity between the belief system in Catholism and that of Voodoo.

It was in this manner that Dora was a prime subject for suggestion from Naomi. "Girl, if you want that man you got to put your spell on him. Now you take this paper and do everything that I outlined here for you to do. And when you're ready, two week after your menses, get yourself over to his house and make him lie with you."

Les was in the cane field at daybreak. Today was the day his new Combine harvester was scheduled for delivery and he had assembled his crew to be instructed on its operation and function. It was a very costly piece of machinery, and would make a big change in his entire operation of cane farming; it would now be possible to harvest two crops a year.

His father, Lester, was also present, in his wheelchair with his caretaker, to witness this event. They watched as the combine cut, cleaned and loaded the stalks onto the transporter in one operation. He smiled, and wrote on his pad, "Son, this is the way to go. I like it." It was an exhausting day for Lester, and his caretaker decided that he had had enough activity and took him back to the house.

Les completed the day and headed home at sunset. He was ready for a shower, and a good meal. When he walked through the door of the kitchen he heard soft music playing and got the unmistakable aroma of an inviting meal. Then he saw Dora standing in archway to the dining room, with candlelight flickering in the background. She met him with a kiss, and "Welcome home from work, fella."

Les was too shocked to move. He reached up and took off his straw hat, sailed it across the room where it came to rest on the top pole of a ladder-back chair. Circles of sweat had stained the arm pits of his torn cut-off cotton shirt. He tucked his thumbs into the straps of his dirt encrusted coveralls, and a slight smile played at the corner of his lips.

"Well, this is a surprise. What brings you here?"

Exuding the aroma Yves Saint Laurent's Opium, Dora, still holding her body close to his, reached up and lovingly wiped away the sweat from his brow, her fingers slowly tracing the contour of his face. "I had you on my mind and thought you might be due for some loving attention."

His immediate reaction was one of appreciation because he didn't feel like being alone after another hard day's work in the fields. He was getting tired of the loneliness and wanted company. He said, "That was very thoughtful of you. Look, I'd like to get out of these work clothes and take a shower. I'll be right down."

Dora watched as he eagerly took the steps two at a time, and for a brief moment entertained the thought of joining him in the shower. But she had second thoughts and decided to stay close to the plan that had been mapped out by Naomi.

After the delicious steak, potatoes and green beans, a-stick-to-the-ribs meal, for a hard working man, Dora said, "And now for your entertainment and dessert." She went to the stereo unit, took off the soft music, and put on an album of Olatungi's Drums. It was an exotic, pulsating, rhythm that stirred up the emotions. Dora approached Les with a slow, seductive, sexual movement as her hands kept time with the music and followed the outline of her body. And at that moment the sound of a cow bell was heard along with the exotic music.

Les got up immediately. "Excuse me, that's Papa calling." He went to his Papa's room.

Lester seemed agitated and wrote on his pad, "What's going on?"

Les wrote back, "I'm playing some drum music."

"Sounded like Naomi's voodoo out there."

That statement brought it all home to Les. Yes. That was it. The conversation he had overheard between Lightfoot and

Naomi. He left his Papa's room and went directly to the stereo unit and took off the album.

Dora turned and asked, "Why did you do that?"

"It disturbs Papa."

"Ohhhh, I'm sorry. I didn't realize that he was back here."

"Yes. He had been in a care unit but we fixed up a therapy facility and brought him home."

"Well, in that case, would you like to come over to my place so we can finish off the evening?"

Les went on. "Look, Dora, that was a good meal and I'm very grateful, but I've had a long day and I'm getting a little tired. Can we make it another time?"

Again Dora's spirits were deflated. She smiled sweetly and said, "I understand." She kissed him lightly on the cheek, picked up her record albums and was out of the door.

Les watched her drive off.

At the end of the month Les went to Los Angeles.

He and Caryn decided to get married.

Caryn had come around to realizing that it was too agonizing to keep hoping for a lucky break for a career in acting. Plus she was missing Les as much as he was missing her.

They made plans for a wedding in Bemidji.

Caryn's parents were delighted to make the arrangements, and they were delighted to have Les as a son-in-law. They planned a modest event to be attended by friends and professional associates of the family and a few high school classmates of Caryn's who were still in the city. The pastor of the Episcopal Church performed the ceremony and afterwards there was a reception at the best known hotel in the city.

After spending a few days at the family home in Bemidji, and a brief honeymoon at the cabin in the woods, Les and Caryn went to Estilette and revealed the news.

They had made a faux pas. It was unforgivable that they would get married and not inform or invite the family to the wedding. Lala was hysterical. Rosa was livid with rage. Uncle Johnny said that Les had forgotten that he was Creole. Naomi didn't give a shit because she did not approve of the marriage in the first place, and was delighted that it had created so much turmoil in the family. Elvina and Ann thought that there might be a solution, and this was the salvation for the happy couple.

Lala would plan and execute an announcement ceremony, with the blessing from the Catholic Church. A tent would be set up on the proposed site of their intended homestead on the Bayou Coutableau, where a second wedding ceremony would take place, attended by all of everyone who was anyone in Estilette.

Les listened to the proposal then turned to Caryn for an approval. She dropped her head into her hands and thought, *what have I gotten myself into?*

Les understood the traditional social and family customs which made this request necessary, and he tried his best to explain to Caryn, and ask forgiveness for not thinking of their inclusion before. Finally after much thought and compromise Caryn agreed that this proposal from her mother-in-law should be allowed to take place.

For several days afterwards Les experienced the fate of all new husbands; the distress of a new wife. He felt sure that she was having second thoughts about their marriage, when in fact she was simply humiliated over that fact that she had not thought to include his family in the first place. Les felt that he should do something to make Caryn feel loved.

It was a late August summer downpour. They had just gotten into bed and Les looked out into the night; the slight breeze was swishing the cane fronds back and forth. Les said, "Come on." And he and Caryn ran, hand in hand, out into the rain as naked as they were the day they were born. They ran through the gate of the horse pasture, causing the Tennessee Walkers to gallop off in various directions, and they jumped into the antique wagon which now served as a hay feeder.

They laid there quietly looking up into the sky as the rain cloud sailed across the full moon momentarily shadowing the light. Les looked into Caryn's eyes which reflected the shafts of light that had escaped the clouds, and explained that this was the same wagon of hay that he used to jump into from the roof tops. Now it served as a soft wet bed, and they were serenaded by the gentle wind-music rustling through the leaves of the cane, as so many strings on a harp. It was a music made for lovemaking.

Les then acknowledged his previous lack of awareness for the concerns of the family, and apologized for putting her through all of the distress of a second marriage ceremony, and revealed his complete happiness and pleasure at having her as his wife.

As they lay on their backs, feeling the warm rain falling on their naked bodies as soft aphrodisiac needles of pleasure, Les turned over onto Caryn and they kissed passionately. She wrapped her legs around his body and pounded her heels into his buttocks in the same rhythm as his thrusts into her body. The tracks of the scratch marks on his back were a testimony of the pleasure of the pain that was only perceived as enjoyable. It was the most memorable moment of lovemaking they had ever enjoyed. Les rolled over and the two of them lay face up, looking into the shimmering moonlight.

Then they felt the warm nuzzles of the horses as they settled around the wagon nibbling at the hay. Les reached out and slid his hand over the nose of one, and felt the warm tongue of the leader of the herd. The constant stream of the warm exhales of breath from the horses served as approval of their natural instincts.

Then they turned over and went for seconds.

They lay exhausted on the hay as the downpour dwindled to a drizzle.

It was daybreak when they awoke and walked hand in hand back to the house.

The second wedding ceremony went off as planned, and Caryn's parents came for the occasion and stayed several weeks getting to know every part of Louisiana life from New Orleans to the sugar cane farms of Estilette.

As a wedding present Les presented Caryn with the keys to the old Delta Theatre, which had long been the only movie house of the town, complete with its traditional balcony for the colored people. When the owners decided to build a new multiplex in a different part of town, they decided to sell, and Les decided to buy, and turn the historic landmark into a community theatre. This was going to be Caryn's project. She would be the person to select and produce plays. Now all of her passion and training would be directed to Theatre U, as Les decided it would be called. It would be a place that would challenge the talents of the town's people to act out, on stage, the roles they had often dreamed they could play. Caryn had never imagined that it would be possible for her to have her cake and eat it too. It was the best gift that Les could have ever given.

Because of the approaching harvest Les and Caryn decided to postpone a honeymoon until Christmas when they planned to take a cruise.

And things were looking up for Les with cane farming. The last several harvests were very successful because the cane cutting combine made it possible to plant more acreage. And although it also reduced the number of laborers necessary, Les was able to focus on a select few hands like BookTau and Mose and pay them a lot more. This made Lester Senior smile more often than before. He was now walking with the aid of crutches and spent more and more time outside watching as his cane empire grew under his son's guidance.

In 1985, a parade of architects began coming and going from the Martel home, as they planned the new estate to be built on the land that Phillip had left to Les, which looked out onto their fishing site on the Bayou Coutableau. Lala had a lot of influence on what the new estate should ultimately look like. She invited Caryn to spend hours upon hours of looking through picture albums of the family history. All of these albums contained photogravure pictures of Antoine Broussard's family as far back as 1865, along with his plantation home and furnishings. It was an inspiration to Caryn, and along with well placed suggestions from Lala, it was also a temptation to recapture the image of the past. And so it was.

Gradually the design took on the look of the plantation home that Les remembered hearing his grandmother, Martha, talk about.

After entering the main door from the columned portico, which extended the entire width of the house, one entered into the foyer. Herein was the majestic splendor of a grand staircase, beginning on the right and the left of the entrance and ascending in a spiral up to the second floor ballroom. At the back of the ballroom was a single staircase that led up to five bedrooms on the third floor. And right underneath the center of the landing to the mezzanine, which surrounded and overlooked the foyer, was a corridor to the back of the house where the family room and the kitchen were located, along with a recreational /pool room. On the first floor, and to the left, before ascending the spiral stair, was a large archway into the parlor, which flowed into the dining room that could easily accommodate twenty guests. On the right of the ascending spiral stair, was another archway leading to a music room and library. And this formed the basis of the design that Caryn and Les worked out with the architects. All was furnished with antiques acquired from shops in New Orleans and everything was beautiful.

It was the best of times.

Now it was time to fill the rooms of this mansion with children, which they began working on as they cruised to Hawaii.